MARSHSONG

By Nato Thompson

Marshsong
©2017 by Nato Thompson
ISBN: 978-0-578-45998-1
Published by Nato Thompson

Cover image by Theresa Rose

This book is a work of fiction. Names, characters, places and incidents are the product of the author's imagination or used fictitiously. Any resemblance to actual events, locales, or persons, living or dead, is coincidental.

Dedicated as strange as it sounds, to Occupy Wall Street, my mother, father, bird-winged brother, my child who holds his namesake, and to my life-affirming love Theresa.

May our dreams find their way back into the world.

Chapter 1

Isabella woke up. She was small. Her brain was big. Sometimes it felt like a melon stapled to a leaf. But she couldn't help it. She was just ahead of everything. It didn't matter. She woke up the same as anyone— some strange drumming in her head, some peculiar space between fantasy and reality and then *vaboom*, life in the most peculiar iteration. Yes, the curtain opens. There begins the story. She wakes from a slumber without dreams.

Just as the sun kisses goodbye the passing plane of the earth, Isabella's very black eyes blinked open and stared across the riverbed where the glittering dance of fireflies played amidst the mangroves and salt grass. The air hummed electric with mosquitos, dragonflies, and wetland toads, burping and whizzing their saturated symphony. Isabella rose up straight off her mattress and just as she so often did, stomped out knee-high into the Aliber River letting her feet squish heavily in the mud. The silt rose up through her toes and the sensation of soil on flesh pleased her immensely. Isabella felt free for one of the first times in her life. He wasn't around. That was that.

She was in one of those odd moments where time stood still. For so long, she had possessed a tangible fear (a veritable backpack that she carried around), but that weight no longer existed. It was gone. Gone like the sun that had just tipped its hat to the moon. What was once was no longer. It felt good, she told herself.

The staccato buzz of the marsh hummed on without care. The world, it seemed, cared not whether she was free or in a cage and she loved it nonetheless. It would go on and on until the moon and the earth collided again together to make a clumsy orb. She stared into the night and the night stared back with envy. Her eyes were much blacker and darker than anything it could provide.

Fennel was back in the cave already, scrubbing away in the tub. She could hear him humming to himself a curious narcissistic melody. A strange bird he was. He worked feverishly on his fingernails and then moved with great determination to every inch of his pale frail frame. His top hat, cane, and coattails hung on a peg and Isabella shook her head at what an odd dandy he seemed to be.

She headed back to the cave. They were twins, it was true, tied by some biological bond that made one wonder about nature versus nurture. It mattered not between them. He was a song and she was a lyric. She didn't care. She just needed space.

The twins prepared for their evening ventures locked in their thoughts with Fennel crooning and Isabella wondering. A ritualistic choreography, they exited the cave and entered their boat at the same time. They pushed themselves off the sand shore and slid like duck feathers into the black wet. Their small oak boat carried inside its diminutive hull two pieces of technology whose cranks and gears spoke of a time before the world had gone digital. A brand new record player sat in the corner near Fennel where they played records of gypsy songs—the jangling of bells, the strumming of mandolins and the melodic howling of women whose lives were full of magical sorrow. Isabella would crank the film projector, which projected black and white grainy images of birds hovering in the air over cities full of train cars and the bustle of people going to work, their day-to-day grind becoming a strange sad opera on the back of the Aliber River flickering in front of them.

This was their land, a hovering aroma slightly on the air and less on the water. The air was thick with wet and the night beckoned them on. They were comfortable here. They laughed in regal appreciation knowing that as routine as it all was, the unexpected, the tragedy of it all, was all that could make them smile.

Their boat slid wet as oil across the water where the marshes beckoned them. Alive with the frenetic buzz of insects and the humid sweat of ragweed and Manzanita, the swamps cradled them as they moved gently downstream. Fennel paddled soft as gentle night, the wood on the oars barely skimming the water making the slightest ripple along the river's arched back. They glided toward the city that time forgot—past the drunkards and harlots, past the neon signs and the compost bins, past the patisseries and eggplant bushels. The gleaming of the gas lamps gradually peeked their way through the southern Cypress groves. The sound of carriage wheels and the occasional guffaw of a person having too good a time entered their extraordinarily acute ears. And most of all the smell, the combination of fetid dissolving vegetable matter, poorly mixed colognes and the not so faint hint of upturned sewage told them that their bodies would soon be again haunting Barrenwood.

They docked their boat at Le Chevalier Noir. Fennel was dressed to perfection in his finest black suit. Everything he ever wore was black. His overly emphasized cravat billowed out below his small tucked chin. His tailored pants pressed perfectly against his thin frame. His short black hair was slightly greased and combed tight against his boyish head. His face was pale and resolute. A look of contempt shown on his lips, but faded as they pulled into port. Isabella stood slightly shorter than Fennel and her visage was just the faintest bit scrappier. Her face equaled his in its pale qualities and her hair was short underneath her silk cloak. At present, her mind was swimming in a pond with petal-winged gnats and wispy legged skimmers. Heinrich grabbed the rope Fennel threw and pulled them against the dock.

"Good evening, monsieur and mademoiselle," said Heinrich, making a customary bow.

"Good evening, Heinrich. Expecting us?" said Fennel as he assisted his sister onto the dock.

"It is your customary time, sir. I see you have a new phonograph."

"Isabella was getting very irritated with the last one. It tended to fade in and out."

"Well, it looks absolutely charming in your boat. I would have you know, Mr. Fennel, that the Barrenwood Festival Auxiliary Planning Meeting is coming up soon."

Fennel smiled and leapt on the dock. His feet landed solid and he twirled upon landing. "Now that is the kind of information I want to hear, my good man. You are ever worth your keep, dear Heinrich."

"Very well, sir. Shall we go?" said Heinrich, motioning toward the restaurant.

"Yes."

Isabella headed toward the restaurant first and Fennel looked upon her. Her cape dragged behind her—her fragile figure like chalk in between the giant dark folds of her robe, her steps so articulated, her little boots so sure. Fennel smirked at the sight of his sister's steps.

"With such class," he thought, "even being as little as she is she makes innocent Heinrich nervous."

Heinrich pulled at the ends of his moustache. His Turkish eyes were small grains of pepper below wiry, bushy eyebrows. Fennel patted Heinrich on the back and handed him an envelope. Heinrich smiled graciously and led them to their table.

Le Chevalier Noir was their favorite establishment. Besides the fact that it was in convenient proximity to the Aliber River, the clientele was generally visiting from abroad. The local elite tended to frequent establishments in the Calliope District. It was equally understood by both that in order to eat in peace they would need a comfortable anonymity (with the customary sybaritic amenities, of course). Their corner table sat next to the roaring fire, gargoyle fountain and the pungent odor of meals yet to be consumed. Out the window, they could watch the crocodiles peek their yellow dead eyes out of the rippled river and the meat traders make their rounds in their ragtag ferries.

"So, what shall it be, my dear brother?" asked Isabella.

"Spinach ravioli," said Fennel, having trouble focusing on the menu. "Tonight is a night for the ravioli. Wandering tasty delicacies floating about

3

wishing to be contained. I sense out there in that hot, smarmy night small decadent spinach people."

"What if tonight is the night of the light bitter green salad with vinegar and oil? Something more slight and less obvious."

"Yuck, Isabella! Don't be so vulgar. I can't stand bitter greens, and plus, I want something overbearing. Someone wild with life. Not some sophomoric riddle. I want a little package full of zest. Little dolmas, grape leaves and surprises."

She laughed, her small white teeth glistening over her grape juice. "I like that as well. There is definitely something appealing in those dolmas. They are like tapas but like a burrito. Are you feeling Arab?"

"Sort of. I think I am always sort of feeling that way. I always wished you and I were Arab."

"Me, too. I could see you as a bratty Arab boy. All full of tricks and silent laughter."

"Yes, I'm afraid this flat white existence is not nearly as aesthetic as I had hoped. You would make a terrific Arab girl. Like Rana. She's very much like you."

"Yes, well, her problem is she is far too wild. And well, she is Turkish and not Arab."

"Well, of course, Isabella. I mean I would only take it so far. She obviously isn't the illustrious you."

"Thank you. Comparisons don't seem to work well with us."

"They simply require a modicum of impossibility. Heinrich, I would like the spinach ravioli and Isabella will have . . . dolmas?"

"No, I will have the minestrone soup and more grape juice."

"As you wish," said Heinrich as he took the menus and made his way back to the kitchen.

They were in good spirits that evening. It was not in full measure due to the acquisition of the phonograph, though Fennel was very pleased with its snug fit in the corner of the boat. There was more. Marty McGuinn had not been at home for some time now. His business trip to the Muddy Carnival had apparently been extended. Not having to stop by his shack was a welcome weight off their minds to say the least. His absence left the twins with far more money than usual and an opportunity to get to know each other, and themselves, without much interference with all his to-do items. He always had them off doing something or other for some peculiar investment or misaligned plot that never truly made sense to them. They were his cogs in a machine that made no sense. At least that was how they saw it.

With Marty gone they were able to sort of prance about. The world was a weekend and the world remained vast. Possibilities were available in

4

every side street, every window, and every door. And like all sudden freedoms, its reception for each remained a strange new emotion. For Fennel, this gap in time lurched forward like a hunting call—a great bellowing horn that resounded across the coal smoked skies of Barrenwood. For Isabella, however, the sudden freedom had hit her in the face. The taste of time fell on her lips bittersweet. She was startled and confused by the feelings it stirred in her. Yes, there was pleasure for sure, but in her freedom, she found she knew very little of what she wanted. Her lack of clarity left her a bit beside herself.

Marty's absence obviously allowed more freedom to experiment. Fennel had already managed to drive the Laughing Bowler's to drink, he had reworked the art commissioner's plans in his favor, spent some time in the Pedigree District (which was a place that had always fascinated him) and was all the while slowly developing a new toxin with the help of mad Derrilous. Under ordinary circumstances, he couldn't have achieved so much in a year's time.

It was a time when their limbs were allowed to grow. The rain of spring was nurturing their chittering roots. It was as though the gardener had left the Bonsai tree to its own frantic devices. For Fennel, such freedom meant a proverbial license to ill while Isabella allowed for proper distillation. She was courting her own pores, letting them open like lichen and spread across the husk of Barrenwood. Slower, measured, precise, her assault would be an adroit vanishing act. Poof! She looked at Fennel wiping his plum lips. What a caustic cherub he was. His cowlick slightly sticking up, resisting the hair grease lathered on his head.

He gave her a wink and whispered, "Shacker." He laughed. "Shacker! Yes, of that I am convinced. Down by the rail station there is that anarchist shacker. I saw him collecting bottles and cans the other day with his ragtag shopping cart. You can hear him for miles really. He is a loud so-and-so. He's the kind of guy that is always in a fight with himself. Out loud, no less!"

"He sounds like you if you ask me," smirked Isabella and she meant it. In her opinion, Fennel was a hair's breath away from a homeless lunatic.

"I don't collect neither bottle nor can, my dear," said Fennel correcting her. "Listen, no need to be smarmy here. This shacker is our guy. Tonight is a night for a shacker. I'm sure of it. See, I was thinking, Izzy, I was ruminating on the qualities of hermits and then I couldn't get the thought out of my mind. Shackers are brilliant! Are you with me?"

"Slow down. You are doing it again," snapped Isabella. She was used to her brother interrupting her thoughts with incoherent blubbering.

"So, so sorry. I just get carried away," he laughed and scooted his chair closer to hers. "Anyway, I am now coming to see the connection between beavers and shackers. They both have this kind of burrowing and biting and hiding thing going for them. As you know, I have always believed that on a few occasions the animal world slips over to the human world and we find ourselves with odd hybrids. Thus, introduce the shacker. The man who, unbeknown to even himself, is a relative of sorts with that gnawing creature called the beaver. You do follow me."

"Let me think on that," Isabella paused and swallowed. Most of what Fennel talked about was a prolonged rhetorical question, but she enjoyed playing the game. "I follow you in that you believe that homeless people and beavers have a commonality. But I would simply say that you are talking about a reclusive tendency that could be found all across the animal kingdom. I mean it isn't as though this particular shacker actually gnaws on wood. The comparison falls apart rather quickly."

"Well, they sort of gnaw. I mean they can often have a sort of nervous tick that has their mouths moving this way and that. A constant chewing kind of thing. It is most probably muscular. Some kind of ancient memory of past beaver lives evincing itself in their peculiar behavior. And I also really do believe that there is much more to a beaver than just their biting and chewing. It is a mistake to reduce them to their most unfortunate front teeth. I mean they are also nature's architects. You have to give them that. A dam? A beaver makes a dam. That is amazing if you ask me. Yes, clever little bastards." He gave his fork a tap on her plate.

"But would you really call a shacker an architect. I mean, yes, this particular shacker did build an extremely unsafe house of discarded wood out along the tracks, but the human corollary of the beaver would be an actual architect wouldn't it?" asked Isabella. She really needed to stop this soon.

Fennel stared at her—his eyes, like hers, pools of squid ink, unfathomable. "Ha! You're right. But you know, there is nevertheless something special about this ol' bloke and I gotta feeling he will give us our fill of water for the eve. I now declare that I will withhold judgment until this evening's chips are down!"

Isabella squinted at Fennel. He was either too clever or too loose with his psyche's bungee cords, but in the chaos that was his head he did have a sixth sense for the water. He was a bloodhound for enticing undercurrents. He knew the kind of person that would crack under their mutual pressure and unleash a flow of delicious liquids.

"So it is to the rail station, I suppose?" she said, tossing one of Fennel's ravioli into her mouth.

"Most astute, Iz the Wiz. To the rail station where we can hear the engines churn and smell the coal wind blow! I'm excited. I love hopping aboard. That is just too much. Please, let me handle the directorial

6

requirements. Just follow my lead tonight. I am feeling o' so at one with my twittering wits!"

They finished their meal and were out on the street. The campanile struck midnight as they hit the road. They smiled. They enjoyed the clanging of the bell. It startled people in their sleep and shook them as they walked. The city's clumsy inhabitants were not yet allowed to get the proper rest they so desirously needed.

The streets of Barrenwood were wet. It was the rainy season. Fennel immediately opened his umbrella and wiped the smoke hazed raindrops off his Chesterfield lapel. Isabella kicked the puddles as she walked alongside him. She gazed at the littered road. What a grumbling dump this town could be. Sidewalk salesmen, corner deputies, and red-socked laundry girls all scurried in the hubbub of night. The oyster salesman was hard at work squirting lemon onto the alien innards of the mollusks—their shells a stormy sea blue—his coarse dirty scarred hands against smooth lift off lemon and the lugubrious beckoning of oyster meat.

The Pig and Onion bar across the way was boisterous with the sound of eye-patched men lifting mugs, *clink, clank* and *slurp* as the beer hit the hardwood sawdust floors, throaty, raspy laughter, the *ping pong clong* of the Kalahari pinball game in the corner and the flipper catapulting steel balls into resilient flamingo bumpers. The evening clouds radiated a dull orange that reflected the city's recent gas lamp industrial victory. Bourgeois bearded men in bow ties were toasting the bubbly somewhere out there in recognition of the invisible hand. Above the twins a billboard shouted, *Raise your glass, the world is watching!*

The night was their trampoline and they were more than ready to bounce. They would skip and glide from the Calliope District to the District of Jed to the Pedigree, from the crotchety grottos of six-toothed maidens to the well-stretched high kicks of the Coriander Monks. Barrenwood was a smorgasbord of pleasures for them. Constantly they foraged the back alley cat calls for yet another clue into the elusive joys of this convoluted delirium. They shared a sweet tooth for manipulation and a soft spot for forensics. It was a natural inclination to dabble in the hackneyed trials and tribulations of the citizenry. What the twins saw as a poorly scripted comedy, the citizens took as true grit. The utter seriousness of such grim fantasies simply provided an irresistible backdrop on which the twins cast their wicked charms.

Heading toward the rail station meant hopping a freight. It would be hopeless to argue the flaws of the rail because the twins were sold on its corrosive decor. As they waited for their train to come in, they arranged a row of soda bottles on the tracks and chucked rocks at them. *Crash! Smash!* Shards flew. Their aim was exact. Their prowess at flinging small rocks was well honed by countless years along the banks of the Aliber River. These urban Robin Hood hijinks tended to be a little too easy and as such the bottles were set up at a distance of two hundred yards; the bottles now small gleaming flecks in the distance. Even at such range, the twins were breaking the glass with veritable ease. In no time, they could hear the high-pitched whistle along the tracks. The train was coming. The sound of the engine built up as the train curved along the west bend.

"Can't get enough of that sound!" shouted Fennel.

He ran toward the train along the center of the rails. Isabella waited. She watched as Fennel dexterously bounded out of the train's path at the last second, caught the side ladder with one hand and was within the first boxcar. The train quickly approached. Fennel reached out his hand to help Isabella aboard. She grabbed it with a mean grin, launched Fennel off the train with one hand and hauled herself on board with the other. He went tumbling into the sage below. Dust and rubble. She was correct in assuming that Fennel deserved such treatment. His cocky shenanigans surely invited retribution and who but his lovely sister would be capable of dishing it out?

Sure enough, within seconds he was back on his feet and bounding back into Boxcar 673. Even from a respectable distance, Isabella could see the formidable crease in his brow. She folded her robes about her and escaped into the darkness of the corner, her body thinning out like ink in water. He was soon springing inside her car, his hair dusty, his tailcoat a bit torn.

"Oh, sweet Isabella!" he called out. "Oh, sweet sissy? Where are you?" Fennel carried a crooked stick with which he began to poke into the corners. *Tap tap.* Isabella lunged out from her hiding place and sprang upon him. They wrestled and tangled like cats in a shower. Cackling and growling they dug in their nails and attempted to pin each other to the metal floor. Sure enough, their combative escapade had them so enthralled that they scarcely noticed their joined bodies slipping out of the boxcar altogether.

They went head over heels into the dirt. *Thump a lump dump bump a rump skid*—they finally halted. Panting and heaving, they took stock of their situation.

"A fine mess!" Fennel said, dusting himself off and looking a little annoyed. A small cut on his forehead was bleeding. Isabella was relatively unscathed, her lip a little swollen where Fennel had given her an adoring sock.

"Might as well throw this outfit away. Thank you so much. My allowance only allows for so many . . . oh my, oh my. Fortuitous for sure.

Looks like we are in luck. If I am not mistaken, that is the home of our beleaguered shacker."

Isabella turned to see a ramshackle shack with a hovering lantern on a hunk of wood peg outside. The dozing Rottweiler with its saturated jowls lay ineffectively by the umber door. Yes, it was the home of the anarchist shacker. A small sign was hammered into the ground, which read: *Not only are you not invited, you are abhorred!*

"Love that," thought Isabella. Just by the anguished bend in the sign's prop, she could sense his feverish existence. Rash and out of whack, this man was in hot pursuit of a paranoid *joie de vivre*. He spent his life alone in these bedraggled confines without a pal, without family, without witty conversation.

"Dusty books, manuscripts and surrealist algebra," she said to Fennel.

"Huh?" Fennel was dusting himself off.

"Nothing," she said, wiping the blood off his forehead with her handkerchief.

"Ow! That smarts! I swear you play too rough. I could have been knocked unconscious."

"I doubt that. Now, what's the plan?" She combed his cowlick down. Her brother just was not himself if his appearance was left unattended.

"Right. The plan, the plan."

They huddled close and in a cloaked whispered play-by-play, the evening's antics were given a score.

Isabella pounded her fist onto the peeling wooden door—its raw exterior crackling even under just the slightest pressure of her tiny little mitt. The Rottweiler outside kept snoring. Inside, they heard the shacker start with a tumble of books. Guests most assuredly came as a surprise.

"What? What is it you want?" came a lonely, surly growl from behind the desiccated door. While Isabella knocked, Fennel petted the lazy canine and even lifted its lips to poke at its incisors.

"What is wrong with this creature? Some sort of external hibernation? What purpose could this lumpen canine serve?" he laughed.

"Please, sir," said Isabella through the door in a wimpy British urchin accent. "Me and me brother, we need ya help. We could only think of ya. Only you would help us."

"I'm not a charity service," the shacker yelled from inside. "What are ya, ten years old? Get! Get or I'll sic my dog on you!"

"A fine threat that is," Fennel whispered as he continued to pet the snoring pet.

"Please, sir! You must hurry! We stole some bread to eat and now the police are crawling all over Barrenwood to get us. We'll go to jail for

9

sure. Please, please, help us!" Isabella continued to pound and pound on the door until, in a whoosh of stinkiness, the door finally opened.

In his hands the shacker held a small musket and his eyes were bloodshot. He was a bald man in an ancient green double-breasted suit. His fingers were yellow from too many nervous cigarettes and from the room one could smell the musty odor of solitude. He shook the barrel in the twins' face.

"Hey, you! Get away from my dog. He'll tear your head off without even waking. And you, get away from my door. I've used this gun before and I'll use it again! I'm not against violence. Ya hear me? I'm no pacifist. I've sent them straight to the grave for less." His arm was shaking and his legs were buckling. He was scared, almost coming out of a dream. His lips twitched, his bleary eyes blinked and Isabella could feel the pain in his shoulder from some long ago wound. Behind him lay a sprawling pile of books and the cluttered desk where he must scribble his resistance. A faded poster read: *Never Forget the Haymarket Martyrs*.

"But, sir, I thought you were an anarchist. Surely an anarchist would have some sympathy for our situation? We're just two orphans trying to get by. Surely, surely, sir, you can take pity on us." Isabella pouted her lip and pulled the hood from her head.

"You're a girl? A girl and her brother on the run? From the pigs? Hey, I said get away from my dog." Fennel stood up and pulled his finger out from the dog's limp lips. He shrugged and saddled up next to Isabella. "So, you two are on the run, huh?"

"That is correct, sir. On the run since we was born. Came all the way from Odessa when the high boots of the infantry were making their raids. But tonight, see, the police have got our number. If you don't help us, we'll be sent to one of those correctional children's camps where they chain you to your bed at night and beat you for saying what ya be thinkin'," Fennel said. He loved playing the part of the tawdry waif. He had even added some dirt to his cheeks and spoke with an affected low caste slang.

"Ah, come on in. But don't touch nothin'! Berkman will scare off the pigs no problem."

He led them into his home. Fennel shut the door behind him. The shack was just a pile of dingy books with cigarette butts everywhere. There were several gaping holes in the ceiling and Fennel could see some of the books in the room were sopping from last night's rain. His bed was a pile of moth-nibbled wool blankets on the floor. He pulled some books off them and offered the twins a seat. They sat down graciously.

The shacker sat down on a wooden stool in the corner, lit a smoke and put his rusted musket on the dirt floor. He wrote in there day and night. Fennel could feel his trepidations from the piles of writing littering

10

the room—the handwriting frantic, exclamation marks slap dashed madly throughout.

"He he, so I'm an anarchist, am I?" the shacker inhaled. "What makes you say that?"

"Oh, you're known in the circles of the vagabonds," said Isabella. "There are older ones who say you are very wise, some sort of man with vision who was attacked for his views."

"And isn't that the truth?" the shacker stammered. "But what do they know? And what do you know? An anarchist. Ha! What does it mean anymore anyway? I'm just a man in a shack. That's what I am. Does that make me an anarchist? Huh, girlie? Huh?" He stood up and pulled on his vest, sat back down and dragged on his smoke.

"I don't rightly know, sir. I just know that you let us in your home when we were on the run. I know you gave us a place to hide and for that I am thankful. I have heard you described as the last anarchist. And from the little I know an anarchist is an enemy of the state and a friend of the vagabonds." Isabella smiled her pretty smile while noticing his yellowish, rotting teeth. The shacker squinted skeptically then began to cough.

"(*Cough cough*) Whatever you might believe, let me tell you right now (*cough*), I am no friend of vagabonds. Those slouching buffoons that just sit on their asses and piss their lives away. Who would be proud to be associated with them? Not I!" He stood up. "See, kiddos. Hey, stop pokin' around!" Fennel placed a book back. "See, I'm my own creature. I live on an antiquated attribute known as integrity. I'm self-sufficient. I'm my own master. What has that to do with vagabonds?"

"I don't know," said Isabella.

"Of course, you don't. Why would you? You two, look at you, you're growing up in a world of parasites."

"Don't I know it," said Fennel.

"What?" said the shacker.

"I said amen, brother, preach it!" shouted Fennel.

"Parasites, baby, parasites. People are weak with need just squirming around for a handout. My god, and it isn't just the pitiful vagabonds. It's those businessmen and those governmental pinheads! Livin' off the slave labor of the masses. Up in their perfumed roosts pretendin' their shit don't stink! They work ya into the ground and speak of bootstraps! Pull yourself up, they say. Well, the only thing I need a bootstrap for is a noose for their loose goosenecks! Of course, lowest, lowest on the evolutionary totem pole are the sick ass pigs! Hey, of course, I took you in if you're running from them. Think I don't know about what it is to be on the run? Sheeoot!

11

"Back when I was editor for *Dare To Tread*, I used to also run speed through Barrenwood in my suitcase. I lived a double life of narco-journalism. Muckraker and racketeer extraordinaire! I had it good for awhile! I gave those politicians ulcers with my editorials. The truth, baby, the truth! Not like they tell it anymore. Nope. Back when the truth was told and it sent waves out into the people 'cause they listened and they would get pissed and they would get drunk and blammo! Riots, baby, riots! People used to believe it so bad it hurt 'em. It hurt 'em and they had to get it out. They had to. They had to tear it down before they exploded. Self-preservation, baby. Pre-ser-va-tion! Yes!"

"Amen, my brother, amen!" cheered Fennel. He could hear the sarcasm in his voice. His eyes glowed in duplicity. He would encourage every word.

"In the beginning there was the word and the word was Liar! Cheat! Villain and thief! Without these words, a people just sit by and let their hard work go to not. And, and, and, become parasites. Just fighten for the scraps like a bunch of rats."

"Fighten for the scraps!" yelled Fennel, smiling gleefully.

"Boy, don't you get funny with me. I got a funny bone myself, ya know. Yes, I do. And my jokes are pretty damn hard to laugh at. But I'll laugh. Oh, will I laugh. Back when I was editor of *Dare To Tread*, I used to make jokes so funny I'd get sent to the big house. Right on into the big house. I'd laugh so hard the constable would go crazy. Pound his gavel as he might, I'd laugh at 'em and tell 'em, what I'm tellin' ya—liars, cheaters, villains and thieves. But they just don't have it in their hearts to laugh, so they locked me up. And they'll try it again."

"They'll do it again!" screeched Fennel.

"I said, they'll *try* it again! They're not going to *do* it this time. Now boy, if you're going to cheer me on, you better get the words straight," he said, giving Fennel a wink.

"Getting straighter!" Fennel barked with a smile.

"You were sent to jail for writing what you thought?" asked Isabella. She wanted to get in his niche. In that part of his brain where the web tangled and the shutters were drawn. Where the synapses met like a superconductor and the thoughts wound about in a circular vertigo. Yes, though his heart was young, she felt that familiar knot in his brain—the knot that brought so many humans to their elder's knees.

The shacker stood up again and moved to the door. He opened it and looked out over the sleeping Berkman into the dusty shrubs across the tracks.

"Yes, yes they did. Those weren't the charges, of course, but that was the reason. To silence me. To shut me down. To put the children back to sleep." He turned around.

"What were the charges?" Fennel asked.

"Huh?" he asked.

"I said what were the charges? You said those weren't the charges, so what were they?"

"Oh, right. Well, it was on account of my drug running. They busted me for narco-trafficking and threw the book at me!"

"But you *were* running drugs. You said so yourself!"

"Sure, I was and what of it? So, what? What are you supposed to do? You telling me you don't know someone who sells? You telling me you didn't steal that bread? I mean what are you supposed to do if you don't want to work forty hours a week for some half-ass slacker, middle management loser? It's called the informal economy, you little eggheads! I had to get my own and it wasn't going to be through the charity of *the man*!"

Fennel stood up and laughed his high squealing laugh. It was his bluff-calling screech that would never sit well with Isabella—the arc of its wailing sending shudders down her spine as it sounded like the squealing of a merciless pig.

"Shacker, shacker, aren't you just the most precious peach? I suppose you really believe that to be the story, don't you? Oh, you're such a martyr, aren't you? I suppose some sort of Haymarket Martyr, is that it? Well, I wonder, I really wonder if those Haymarket Martyrs had dabbled in the goods you did?"

Fennel was moving in for the kill. He had sensed the shacker's weakness—the way his eyes had lit up, his forehead perspired at the mention of this narco business. A fiend. It had ruined him. The shacker stood there in dumb silence.

"I wonder, Mr. Shackerific, if *the man* was really that concerned with your poorly distributed propaganda rag or if he was more concerned with your deteriorating life? Thought you were stronger than that white magic, didn't ya?" Fennel gave him a wink. "Tut tut. Look, I think we both know who the real parasite was, don't we, Mr. Shackadoodledoo?"

The shacker yelled inarticulately and reached for his musket. It was gone. Isabella stood pointing it straight at his quivering brow. The shacker just froze there. He looked so lost. Resigned. Poor thing. He probably didn't care if Isabella pulled the trigger or not.

"Don't be afraid, my good anarchist. My brother and I have no interest in your past crimes. We just thought we would remind you of any inconsistencies. That is fair, isn't it?" She pushed the muzzle to touch his

13

forehead. It stayed there and shook. "Fennel, please grab his manuscripts. I believe we must give them a copious analysis."

Fennel began to collect them under his arm. The shacker began to protest.

"Please, no! I have been working on these for so long!"

"Hey, shut shut. You need to let it go, bro. Fennel, ready? Okay, I wish you well and right. Do remember to muckrake your own life as well?"

Isabella hurled the musket onto the bed and exited. Fennel gave the crumpled over shacker a quick kick to the head. It landed hard and the poor man lay prostrate on his moldy bed. The two little miscreants whisked out the door, past Berkman, over the rails and into the beyond. Behind them, they could hear the shacker sobbing in the shack.

Tears ran, flowed out the door and into the night and entered their bodies with a taste divine. It was the sound they enjoyed leaving with—like grass peeking through concrete or bottle glass breaking on the tracks. It felt good to hear it, to feel it, to taste it. Fresh. Revitalized. It was the taste of the water. That liquid that let them know that people finally understood that life itself was a tragic unrelenting joke. The twins lapped up the tasty pain of that infinite wisdom, for it was their irresistible fuel. They left his home feeling accomplished.

"It's not right, you know," said Isabella, making her way back toward the cave,

Fennel smiled, staring wildly back at her. "Hitting a broke, weak old man when he's down? I know. Isn't it the best?" he laughed out loud and Isabella did as well.

They made their way back to the cave and hoped for more nights like this one to land in their laps.

Chapter 2

He was never far away. She could feel his nasty breath heavy on her neck with its familiar scent of bourbon, tobacco and trout spit that ever lingered in his ratty clothes and greasy hair.

He was a haunting figure. Bent, crooked, wiry and wild-eyed, Marty McGuinn had leered over her and Fennel for as long as her peculiar imagination could recollect. He had his moments to be sure. Lessons of life came in drunken fits replete with manic stories late into the night that as sure as steam would rise from the river and end up with him crazy angry about something or other. His violent spurts erupted out of his ranting monologues as he pranced about the cave, smashing his cane against the granite walls—his words, already incomprehensible, slipping into a series of spurts and slobber. He would make a point to some God not listening above, and then laugh in condescension to himself, and then turn angrily toward the twins. His knobby liver spotted hands would grab firm onto her hair and toss her or Fennel headfirst into the mud or dunk them down into the freezing Aliber River. In his sliver of remorse, after they were freezing or bruised or both, he would concoct some twisted lesson of life that was the supposed rationale for his brazen ferocity.

To call him demented would be too kind a term for a hateful intentionality shadowed his every slur and gesture. He was terrifyingly aware of his heartfelt commitment to that familiar element of cruelty. This sensibility that squished the saccharine and sentimental from the world in a hard clasped hand might be his defining character. Running alongside his blood cells, cruelty was the iron in his mosquito-sucked blood. And in that nefarious Pavlovian response to the universe, the twins could certainly relate. They sympathized with his desire to laugh in the face of agony and despair. They chuckled on the sweaty brow of heartache. But it wasn't this element of Marty's egregious personality that Isabella resented so deeply. She was too self-aware to hate the part of Marty that was most definitely in herself.

Isabella knew that hiding behind his bravado, Marty was obscuring dark, beautiful secrets. Whatever lingered in the cobblestone streets and baroque mansions of Barrenwood, Marty McGuinn did not want them finding it out. The twins' actions had been circumscribed in every which way. No visiting the school. No random visits to the government. No newspapers. No public displays of their powers. No making themselves known. No, no, no! All was *verboten* and with that, Barrenwood—that melancholic city that time forgot—had blossomed magically.

For, of course, the sway of Marty's stubborn resistance had produced its equal counter resistance. Side by side with their peculiar antics, these strange siblings were crafting a longer-term strategy. And while they both told themselves their distractions were harmless curiosities, Isabella, in particular, was hell-bent on doing just what Marty would have her not. With each delicate mission into the city that Marty sent them on, they were able to carve out just another piece of their niche of insubordination. They were as savvy, conniving and out for tragic fun.

Their entire enterprise had never set right with Isabella. They slept in a cave during the day and went out at night in a city chock-full of inhabitants who seemed oblivious to the charms of this life. Even Marty's strict limitations couldn't prevent their wandering eyes from noticing that the twins were steadfastly different in every way.

These urban denizens seemed to not notice what the twins could so plainly see. It was their gift. Tears that dripped from the somber eye made manifest in actual flows of water, running through gutters and dripping off rooftops: the sobbing of a mother for a child born stillborn brought forth an orchestra of sound that reverberated in their ears. They called it the water and it was the tragedy that lent life its luster. It was a hypnotic sort of drug—this water—that lured them ever so carefully into the lives of these simple but fascinating people of the city of Barrenwood.

Perhaps Marty knew this. Perhaps he sensed that she was crafting either escape or more simply becoming seduced by the lure of something that only humans could offer—poetic sadness. Either way, it infuriated him. His sixth sense took hold of him like a plague and he would warn them both to not fall prey to their predilections.

"Ya don wanna folla da call but ya best not. Dat watta be wet, but it also gone get ya a lickin' from ma belt. I will wallop ya 'til ya sick and a sore and I put ya pretty heads in da sick pit."

He was a frightful beast.

Not too long before his sudden departure to the Muddy Carnival, he had truly been on a tear. His greasy mane sticking out of an old tattered Fedora he had found, Marty had debarked a midnight skipper to come prancing up on her and Fennel as they studiously sat by the fire in the cave. Isabella had been reading the biography of Ella Fitzgerald and Fennel had been collaging architectural blueprints—the fine lines of potential construction transforming a home into a series of portals and gangways. They each had a workstation in the cave with Isabella's a pile of books, glue and spilled grape juice and Fennel's a closed manila folder and a mechanical pencil.

16

Their quiet activities were disrupted by gleaming yellow boat lights as the skipper came trolling up the river. The twins knew what would come. They had by this point developed acumen for that "something on the wind" when Marty would arrive belligerent. The howl off the boat merely made the future crystal clear. They heard his raspy gargle cut into the night as he belched out his cacophonous coyote howl baying at a moon obscured by the marsh-laden haze. The sound sunk into the cloud-like puffs of the cotton grass and set the hair of the twins on end. Here came the wretched madness of their keeper.

"Get in dat cannoo! D'ya hear me? I said get on in dat cannoo!"

Marty was waving his gangly arms madly. The fourteen white hairs on his chinny chin chin breezing in the still air. Marty tossed his grubby leather briefcase against the side of the cave. It landed in a muddy mess and gold coins and napkins with doodles burst out in a gust. The skipper boat had barely stopped but continued on its way further down the river. Isabella could sense without even looking the relief of those on the boat to have Marty no longer aboard.

Fennel hopped to it and ran out of the cave. "You're back! Welcome home, captain." Fennel saluted in his peculiar humor. Marty ignored him with a harumph and scurried to the back of the cave toward that dark alcove where only he ever would go. He came back out with a backpack, some Ziploc plastic bags, and a thermos.

"A campin' time. Let's get on out before da moon chews da vines," he said. "Da cannooo, I said!"

Isabella quickly put her stuff away and gathered some clothes and a granola bar she had under her bed into her knapsack. Fennel scurried to do the same and, in no time at all, were all piled into the canoe. Fennel had the oar in his hand and Marty was already pouring some sauce from his thermos into his cup.

"Where are we going, may I ask?"

"Ya may, Scratch. Ya may. Just hed yerself out and beyond da willa grove. We gone donna make our way out towad da back alleys of da marsh here."

Isabella lit the lantern and stayed quiet. As warm as the marsh could be, this night wasn't. She had a chill in her and a sudden trip to the back regions of the marsh wasn't exactly appealing. She remained quiet for she sensed what was a hair's breath away from occurring—the tangled emotions in Marty's every move told her that his frantic mood swing might easily erupt. In the canoe, it would be a nightmare, a wet mess.

As Fennel paddled, Marty hummed to himself and smoked his corncob pipe. His long fingers like talons, he rapped on the side of the boat with a drumming sound of nails. Fennel warmed to the journey quite early.

He smiled his crazy smile and was ever so cautious to not get a drop of Aliber onto his pressed attire.

"Marty," Fennel said, his eyes on the distant crescent moon, "what happens in this part of the marsh?"

Marty reached his long arm across the boat and grabbed Fennel by the shoulder. "Ma boy, dat be a damn good query. Dat be da kinna thing a man otta ask in every which way day can. Dis part of da wetland, is home to some a squirmin' howler. Der be a lady so skinny and hungry, she don scared all da peoples away. She special but special in da way gunpowder be special. Just a box a fire sittin' pretty in da fog. Drink up, Scratch. I'm a gonna see da bitch but pray to ya dead granny dat yous twos don don't."

Marty handed Fennel his thermos lid and Fennel made a disgusted look and sipped the smallest amount he possibly could. Fennel began to cough violently and Marty slapped him on the back far too hard.

"Ha, ha, ha, boy! Ya gone be ready for dis camp trip afteralls."

They rode on through the fog as Marty pointed out each turn in the maze of the swamp to make. Twisting to and fro, they rode toward some backwoods of the marsh that neither of the twins had set eyes on. The buzz of bugs grew louder and louder with every push of Fennel's oar. Isabella fantasized that it would be here, on the sopping banks, that Marty would at long last end their special lives—his rage taking on a finality she sensed he longed for.

But as it happened, the night would lead them to a small inlet with a boat dock. Marty motioned for Fennel to tie up and Fennel did so with precision and grace. His hands could move quick in a whirl and the large ship rope tied fast to the chiseled mooring. "Land ho! I see seagulls and the smell of saltwater on rocks, o' *capitan*!" shouted Fennel with a smile broad and bright. Marty took a backhand to the side of Fennel's head.

"Keep it down, ya dum. Dis be da bed of dat she-beast. Ya best keep ya yipper on low if ya wanna see da cave night nex."

Marty flung himself out of the boat and skipped rapidly along a barely visible trail. Isabella grabbed her bag, the lantern and followed. Fennel picked his top hat off the wetland floor and followed suit. They tread only about fifty yards along the path before they reached a small clearing where signs of an old fire still remained. Beer cans littered the site with small candy wrappers—all tell tale signs of Marty.

"Dis be home tonights, ya varmints. Get ya rucksacks out and let's say night to da night. Iz, ya gets da wood and Scratch, clear da rubbish."

Isabella was more than happy to take a break from his presence. She headed further into the marsh, wondering who this she-beast was. Who was it that haunted the dark recesses of her tropical homeland? Another mystery for her to lay on the pile. Sticks were hard to find, as the

18

ground was a mess of moist vines and leaves. As she searched the ground, her furtive eyes quickly lost the point.

She couldn't help but wonder if she would enjoy being a witch of the wet. Living alone in a hut of her making, she could invent languages to chat with the fireflies and commune with the aurora borealis on the odd night when it graced the evening. She could have a large oak library lounging out here with tomes and science fiction paperbacks stolen from Barrenwood; and children that were lost in the world could put on their galoshes and stomp their way through the muck to find her and have a good read. It would be a library for the geniuses, lost and ever so looney tune. She could hold private dances out here and invite only the most wicked to celebrate with her in revelry most mad. Costumes of fish and fowl would be all the rage and they would enter through the mouth of a frog with eyes gone psychedelic.

Her mind wandered as did her feet and she became aware quite quickly that she had gotten herself lost. She would never be lost for long and as she stared up to the sky to get her bearings (the North Star would never let her down), she heard the faint hint of something most hair-raising—the slight wheezy snore of what could only be an old woman. It was heavy and full of congestion—air trying to make its way through a cavernous nasal passage full of crusty obstacles and viscous moisture.

Isabella lowered herself to the ground to get herself a look and sure enough, not but twenty feet away, she could make out the silhouette of a spindly body supine on the wetland floor. Its hair a tangle with sticks and whatnot stuck in it, the she-beast snored away face first in the gunk. Before she could even gasp, she felt the strong arm of Marty McGuinn rough on her neck and they were racing with a speed most rapid back to the camp. She found herself hurtling through the air to land in a tangle in the marsh briars. The thorns cut into her, but she didn't feel a thing. She could make out, glinting in the fire already started, the mad mad eyes of Marty, nearly spinning in their shells with rage.

He shook his head violently and took his cane and slapped it against the mud. He then lurched toward Isabella and the cane came crashing down—down and down again it came—blow by blow, driving her deeper into the mess of thorns, ripping her skin apart on her hands and forehead. She felt the blood come as it sometimes did. He didn't say a word (perhaps his rage too big for words at this point). He reached down and catapulted her out from her landing. His crooked teeth and alcohol stained breath came right up close to her face.

"Curiosity killed da cat. Hear dat? Didn't hurt da cat but kill it ded on da spot. Ya don a dum and ya gona get yas. Shoulda neva brought yas heres. Shoulda neva let ya see dis. Sendin' ya home, if ya can make it."

Marty hobbled his way toward the riverbank. Isabella stayed quiet. She didn't want to aggravate him any further. She couldn't feel any of the tears on her body, and her face and mind were numb in the face of his immense hostility. She truly didn't want to die but just tucked deep inside herself for safety as she always did. One day this would end.

Marty grabbed an old log from the side of the bank and proceeded to literally stuff Isabella into it. The smell of moss, mold and snake eggs filled her nose as she found herself folding like origami into the emptied shell. Her knees bent up toward her mouth and her body squished tightly into the woodish orifice. She felt the splash and kick as Marty sent the log sailing out onto the Aliber to go floating back toward the cave. Isabella could faintly make out the image of her brother, quietly hiding behind Marty, making a small wave, his eyes fearful of the monster that was their master.

This all happened before Marty had left in a rush toward the Muddy Carnival. His departure was perhaps the greatest gift the twins had ever received. They took the news with great solemnity so as to not betray their excitement. But Marty was not so drunk as to not know the truth of it. But it mattered not. He had to go and go he did. And as such, that curiosity that killed the cat was out of the bag.

That was some time ago now and things had, well, loosened up. They had shaken the fear, the cuts had scabbed, and the world of Barrenwood had opened up, a flower in bloom. Within a few weeks time, they had already begun to make a claim on numerous adventures in the city. Not that they didn't have their own machinations while Marty was around. Even when Marty haunted them from his ramshackle abode, they could occasionally carve out some time to do this and that. Isabella had her nightclub and Fennel had his alchemy. Isabella still bought books by the dozen and Fennel continued his fine Velonton shoe collection. At times, they could sneak off to sit outside an active funeral, the air filled with the guttural groans of a family beside itself with sadness. They would crouch in the dark and cackle in abusive laughter at a family's laments—a cheap shot indeed but sometimes the water flowed all the finer when the cruelty was mixed with a gesture more crass than elegant.

On this particular eve, after having robbed the shacker of the last thing in the world he had in his possession, the twins headed into Barrenwood with little to no plan. They dined at Le Chevalier Noir, eating boiled eggs, pheasant and pears and more than their fair share of grape juice. Isabella listened only obliquely as her brother rambled endlessly about the fine smell of chimney smoke. It was like silver, he said. He had plans to place a chimney in the cave, but Isabella doubted this particular endeavor would come to fruition.

Isabella, on the other hand, turned a growing sentiment over and over in her mind. She looked at the people in the restaurant—gussied up for their big nights out on the town. They smiled and laughed with such peculiar emotion. As insipid as they tended to see the residents of Barrenwood, Isabella often felt a brief pang of envy. They were stupid, yes, but at times happy nonetheless—their dumb qualities almost gentle. The whole notion made her frown and all the more moody.

They wiped their lips and scooted out into the night. The streets of Barrenwood were wet. It was the rainy season. Fennel immediately opened his umbrella and wiped the smoke hazed raindrops off his Chesterfield lapel. Isabella kicked the puddles as she walked alongside him. She gazed down the littered road.

Barrenwood was awfully wet this time of year. People ran past with magazines over their heads in attempts to protect their top hats and ribbons. In the night, pipes were being smoked and hermits were huddled. There was the ongoing sound of creaking that slipped out of the many cracks in the bumpy roads, cobbled walls, slipshod mansions and huts, even out of the lines in the women's faces. Everyone was a stranger here. Their eyes carried a frenetic expanse that cast long shadows between them and the other. Cowering and recoiling were frequent mannerisms. Every dog shook in its sleep, the many streams under bridges ran silent, every dream turned belly up. With each step, Isabella's mind turned over. She was lost in thought in the maze that was the city. She naturally walked in darkness avoiding all attention. All eyes. The lanterns on the street still flickered fire and the glow from the video arcades cast electric zig-zags into the puddles.

Fennel skipped and jibbed to his ritualized evening fancies.

"I love the dribble. The drabble. The rain makes me dreamy. I am the Raven. The raven guarding lore. I glide over the cobblestone sloppiness and caw out a rickety tune. I have these giant talons made of obsidian and my eyes glow yellow! Yes!! Yellow is good—an off yellow the color of old bananas. There will be music following me. Just a bassoon and a tambourine. Oh, I wish I could just swoop down onto people. Swoop down from heights most terrifying! Barroooumph!! What about those two? They look like little rodents scurrying about. Trying to get home? Trying to get to work? I'm sure they scurry like that wherever they go. They just nibble and burrow and scurry. Just little mice. Mice. And I am the cawing, clawing Cretan!"

Fennel laughed out loud, ran back along the street and tripped one of two old men—his glossy boot catching a colonel dead on in the shin. The colonel went crashing down into the wet street, his cane sliding across the road, his head thudding on the ground. His companion stared in consternation, his mouth shaped like an O.

Fennel ran off laughing, "I warn you little mouse! Don't tempt the Raven!"

He slipped around the corner, jumped through a hole in a stone wall and ran up toward Scarlet Square. He panted and panted and laughed. Isabella walked up behind him completely composed.

"Having fun now?" her eyes showed a glimmer of joy.

Fennel looked up, his hands on his knees. "Yes. Yes, my dear lady. I should say so. Now that was, in fact, (*pant*) that was, in all truth, my display for you. Yes, I wanted you to witness the sweet articulation of gravity."

"You demonstrated the forces of nature for little me? Well then, I thank you, Fennel. You're much too kind."

"Well, kind is not absolutely correct. I am not kind. I am an educator. I was concerned not only for you but for those two men. They seemed far too unaware, oblivious, that they were in the presence of the Raven! Caw, caw!" He flapped his arms around and swooped at Isabella. " It was a lesson and now," Fennel threw his jacket to rest on the wall. "I must teach you a lesson in Battle Ball."

Isabella took off her cloak, laying it on the edge of a brick wall and turned around with a small red rubber ball. The twins proceeded to play Battle Ball. They bounced the ball off the concrete and attempted to get it into the other's square. Above them, the Cathedral Ogre loomed ominously—the minarets lined with the faces of laughing children and the sound of their ball played off the cold stone walls. Games were a necessity for them. They played them ritualistically without reproach or being patronizing. It was more akin to a bath than entertainment—just a simple pleasure that washed away the debris.

They played it with only laughs and smiles, a simple pleasure so important to their world. The wetness of Barrenwood splashed in luminous spray in the gaslights that hung on the gateway above. With each bounce, Isabella's mind kept wandering off. Currently, she was thinking of Mao—the road to revolution starting with the first footstep and then heading, with so many compatriots, out along the winding trail toward victory. She could faintly here Fennel rambling on about something or other.

"Wasps, Iz. Wasps. You see, you have to keep your eyes out for things like this. They are peculiar aviators. They have those dangling front limbs. See, they are at the height of bourgeois fanaticism. Just like concubines with bound feet or behemoth dictators too fat to raise a finger, the wasps' legs are an auspicious declaration of superiority. Yes, and you can see how they flaunt them. They just dangle their limbs with a snobbish pretension. Just a never-ending fashion show for these aviary aristocrats."

"Wasps?" asked Isabella bouncing the ball absentmindedly.

"Duh, yes, wasps. Pay attention. What I'm saying is just so basic. There are hints in the apiary. The honeycomb must be combed and the hierarchies that nestle themselves away inside their labyrinths say much about the way much of humanity hangs its hog. Think about House Revan with their limp wristed majesty. It is as though one must blend a barrel chested masculinity with the sign that one need not lift a finger. Have you seen those pictures in the *Guinness Book of World Records* of that crazy Asian guy with the super long fingernails? It is like that!"

He was such a yapper and Isabella usually found herself divided between enjoying it and tolerating it. It was at that moment, while the twins were bouncing their little red ball back and forth, that their lives were suddenly turned topsoil. Their minds were given access to secrets long buried in the inner heart of a city most surreptitious.

It came in the form of a howl, or more appropriately, a chorus of howls. It hung on the wind and entered the twins' ears simultaneously. Their hair stood up on end and sweat bubbled up on their pale flesh. The sounds that they heard came out of a deep place in the soul—some kind of emotion most rare, most precious, most divine. They sensed these kinds of things at times but this sound was elegantly specific. The twins stopped Battle Ball and stared at each other hypnotically. A smallish growl let loose off the lips of Fennel.

"What was that?" asked Isabella, holding the ball in her small paws.

"*Is* that, you mean," Fennel said, still sensing, his head suddenly taking on a wolf's mannerism. He sniffed the air, nostrils twitching, and tilted his slicked head back and forth. He smelled for it at the edge of the wind. He listened for its ghoulish harmony at the horizon of his acute auditory spectrum. There! There it was—a rising chorus of madness in terror out there in the night. Whatever it was, it was many—many mouths howling out against the sky.

They were wild and crazed and operating on the kind of psychic level that most assuredly got the attention of these two peculiar creatures.

"Something," said Fennel slowly, "is greatly amiss in Barrenwood this eve."

A smile grew on his lips, his teeth sparkling in the gaslight. His smile, always menacing and ironic, was never more so than now.

The twins dashed out to hunt down the source of the sound. They were up on rooftops, bounding about with leaps and twists—their motions a blur unable to be seen by the denizens below. They flew over Barrenwood with unrelenting speed. Their small feet catching the roof tiles with assured grip, sending them up far into the coal-stained haze above to land again on the next. They both enjoyed the thrill of the hunt—that adrenaline surge that moved in their veins as they gave their minds over to overwhelming instincts.

The sound grew all the more, filling their ears, and with it came other sounds—men yelling, the crack of a whip, wood crates loading, a symphony of the disaster that was to greet them. As they launched onto the final roof top that allowed them a view of the waterfront, they were greeted by a most fascinating sight.

The gas lamps blinked and shuddered in the evening mist, making a strobe effect on the docks below. Lining up along the dock, covered in the muslin robes that they were known for, were none other than the mad— the literal lunatics of the Barrenwood asylums, prisons, dripping alleys and backwoods villages—lined up, with a man keeping them at attention with the flailing of his leather black whip. They were being hauled onto a large frigate—their bodies teeming in the hundreds. As the hoard of the mad clumsily made their way up the gangplank, their faces howled in resistance—each face a map of a million kinds of raw desires where their emotional states were able to carry them.

"Get up there, ya rabble!" yelled the whipping man, his arm a mechanism of cruelty and order.

The lunatics stumbled their way onto the ship and huddled together at its stern. Some hugged each other in a pile of wet cloth. Some tried to fling themselves overboard. Some crumpled into a ball and wept uncontrollably. Some laughed hysterically, pointing at some phantom beyond the eyes of all. Surrounding them were the mangy brutal sailors whose lives had always been one of herding those whose lives were a hair's breath away from their own. The eye patches, tobacco stuffed in lips, the scars along the necks, and the rum stained breath were the calling card of this mercenary class. Travelling from shore to shore, dock to dock, dollar to dollar, they used the wetlands of the world to put hand to mouth. The flag above waved wildly in the evening wind. A ship riding amidst high-bloodied waves was emblazed on it with the simple tag: Le Bateau Ivre.

For Isabella and Fennel, the sight brought up in them the best kind of emotions, ones unfamiliar, strange, bordering on nausea. Their entire petite frames were made for the consumption of this kind of fanfare. They were compelled to the source of this great cacophony by the overwhelming presence of passionate emotional heft. They could literally see it—a river of water that they could lap upon. Spraying out of the mouths and bodies of this flailing chorus, the water splashed into the air surrounding the frigate. If the shacker had given them a teacup's worth, this ensemble provided a lake. It called to them. Made them salivate. Their bodies were ever craving the tragedy and vibrant resistance that suffused the human soul and all the more so in the souls of the mad—their undisciplined lunacy stirring a raw life full of uninhibited perversity and embarrassing magic.

"So much water," whispered Isabella. She licked her lips as the water cascaded into her and Fennel. Filling their bodies, the sight and the energy fueled them. Gave them life. Made them feel alive.

For perhaps once in his life, Fennel was speechless. He stared down wide-eyed. His heart stirred as it always did—through his whole frame. He curled his lips in distaste. As wondrous as the sight, it only confirmed an emotion in him he need hardly reinforce. Antipathy.

"People are so stupid," whispered Fennel. "Torturing their greatest citizens. We are looking at a perfectly painted picture of the end of humanity."

The docks were crowded with crates of oranges, pomegranates, bananas and kiwis. Along the western piers were the Korean plastics with their fire engine red and milk white robot toys needing batteries, children and flat linoleum surfaces. There were glistening automotive parts sticking out of plastic wrapped large boxes being hauled by the hydraulic dolly. Somewhere in the myriad of boxes was contraband of glocks, pills and who knew what else being smuggled. The smell of herring and sea salt was infused with the rotting dregs of seaside refuse. The hustle and bustle along the docks were ever renowned as the later the hour, the more the bustle. Men and women from distant isles worked madly around the clock to get the boats of spices, silks, limestone and foreign seeds, into the growing economy of this town folded up origami-style in time.

And in the midst of this, in the bosom of this mad scene, they spotted yet another sight of peculiarity.

A woman screamed her head off in the dark shadows near Le Bateau Ivre. She was beautiful and strained. Her features were tortured and nearly as crazy as the people on this boat. She yelled as though the world were at its end. Her hair and clothes were soaked to the bone as though she had been out there for hours. One of the sailors was holding her at bay as she tried desperately to get herself onto the ship. The smile on the sailor's lips added extra cruelty to the crying angry eyes of this distraught chiseled beauty.

"You don't know what you're doing!" she cried. "You can't do this! Look at 'em. They are not clear on what is going on. You can't just steal them out of here. Stop this! Stop this! Such insufferable morons, all of you. You think you know what you're doing, but you don't. Obeying orders. Everyone always obeying orders. No one is in charge they say. But someone is—some stupid bureaucrat high above recklessly making the world boring. You don't see it. You don't care. Because you gave up. You gave up. You all gave up ages ago and now you wash away the world of the world's songs. You make me want to throw up. You make me want to vomit."

The woman bent her head down and bit into the sailor's arm. He winced and let go and she ran with all her might toward the ship. Another sailor tackled her on the dock and her body landed with a thud. They wrestled in a wild pile as the other sailors on the ship whistled, laughed and continued to crack their whips. She continued to yell, but her words became muffled in the hubbub of the event. Her body writhed under the surly grip of the sailor. Her arms were strong with veins showing and the sinuous taut qualities in her muscle showing them as she resisted.

"She screams our thoughts," said Isabella, turning to Fennel.

Fennel's eyes were wet. Tears. They slipped down his cheeks in small dribbles—little snails making their way down a porcelain short cut. He was angry beyond reproach. He wiped them with a tissue he pulled from his pocket. He was dainty. A sad priss. His heart a soft plum in the mouth of a gorilla.

"She is speaking a strange wisdom. That is true but look at her, she is so carried away. She really needs to keep it together. Insights don't mean everything," Fennel said, as he placed his paisley olive handkerchief back in his pocket. He didn't like messes and this woman was certainly that. The scene was both frantic and calm. In the midst of the screams of the woman and the howling of the lunatics, the other boats and their merchants and loaders continued their work unabated. The night wind blew across their efforts without a care. The flags on all ships blowing most serene.

"That man," said Isabella pointing down. "He knows."

Her finger pointed down to a solicitor dressed in fine raiment, his tapered fingers and grey silk suit speaking of a kind of class that could only be making money off these efforts. He was no sailor and yet he stood with what could only be the ship's captain with a small notebook in his hand. He scribbled something and his eyes looking upon the scene were rather calm, if not altogether bored.

"The bridge," said Fennel, eager to find someone to blame. "Whoever is robbing the city of its water is going through that fragile fledgling down there. Good work, sleuth sis. It occurs to me that Barrenwood is the riddle. The city, that is. It is a place of making and unmaking. It is a conjurer much in the same way that we are. If I were to hop down there and push that annoying man in the river, the city would just spawn another. Someone would inevitably replace him and the boat would continue to be loaded with our true friends. But if we were to untangle the knot that is Barrenwood, perhaps, yes, perhaps, I could beat with my cane the true insufferable nimrod that brought this stupidity into being. I could tease it out like a flea on a dog. Burn it off. And then rearrange this riffraff town more to my liking. That is what is at stake. I must cut the head from the snake!"

Fennel stood proudly. He considered his insight a sudden burst of vision. He had carved a plan out for himself in a flash of disdain. It washed over him in a bath of purpose.

"You can't beat the sense into a city, my brother. People are bumps in the flow. To move a river, one must adjust the riverbed. The city isn't a problem to be solved; it is a riddle without an answer. Do you really think you can just find the solution to this city's war on the mad? Is that what you think?"

She found her brother to be ever so reductive. Such a male—always thinking he could solve something with his puny might. She knew quite well, looking at this tragedy that played out in front of her, that there wasn't a single person one could blame for this. Fennel on the other hand saw her comments as further evidence of her ongoing reluctance toward action. He read sympathy as fear and fear, he often told himself, was the defining characteristic of humanity.

"I couldn't disagree with you more. In fact, my sweet ricket, I am going to demonstrate the first phase of my now long-standing mission to cut the head off the snake. I am the Raven after all."

Fennel made a motion to jump, but Isabella stopped him. Her small hand held him rock still at the roof's edge. He was very bad indeed.

"There are a lot of people around my over-zealous companion. A little prudence might go a long way. As much fun as we are having, our master will not take kindly to us making our presence known."

Fennel acquiesced, his shoulders slumping back from their tense desire to attack. "Don't I know it," he said. "I can't promise I will be good, but I do promise that my efforts will go unnoticed. And, by the way, the city isn't a riddle. It is a joke and I am its punch line."

With that, Fennel leapt down onto the street below, his feet landing with the slightest touch. Isabella let him jump and waited to follow. She knew she couldn't stop him and felt little desire to do so. He wasn't wrong. The city was a joke and this latest display of expelling the mad provided only further evidence of its operatic idiocy. She turned back to the woman now being dragged across the docks by two sailors. She was kicking her legs and Isabella feared for the woman's safety. The woman had shifted from anger to slight hints of fear. She was realizing that her protest had placed her in the paws of creatures who should not be allowed to touch a frantic, attractive woman late in the night.

Isabella leapt down and joined her brother who had already begun his skipping walk along the docks. Even at his most casual, he remained a peculiar sight—a little boy with a top hat making his way across the city as though he owned it. He clicked his heels across the dock whistling a little song. Grabbing some kiwis out of one of the crates, he began to juggle for a few of the sailors. He was extremely adept at most circus tricks. He had the kiwis roll across his top hat and bounce down back into his hand then fly back up to land behind his back and then back up into the air. The sailors were laughing and smoking and enjoying his show. He continued to make goofy faces, all the while sticking out his tongue and looking overall like a sort of village idiot. Isabella stayed to the back of the road hiding in the shadows making her way ever so gently toward the woman being dragged away. The sounds of her screams merely blended into the cacophony of the lunatics' moans.

She didn't have much time to watch her brother's antics as the time to save the woman was nearly running out. They had disappeared into a back wooden shack and Isabella rushed after them with blinding speed. She slipped in the doorway, not seconds after she saw the leg of the woman still kicking fall back into the shack.

Fennel continued his pantomime. His sister would be fine he was sure. He wouldn't miss her watching eyes anyway. Let them feel the wrath of the Raven, these soiled sods. The men laughed and pointed at him as he continued his juggling idiocy. He pulled off a leap onto a railing and continued juggling. He then slid down and landed on the docks with a summersault all the while keeping the kiwis circling in the air. He, at last, bowed down low to the solicitor and tipped his hat.

"A few coins for your dockside entertainment, good sir?" said Fennel with a look of great supplication playing on his lips.

The man rolled his eyes and searched his pockets. He hadn't liked the performance and knew this would arrive. "I knew I would end up paying for this. I really don't have time. Don't hold it against me if I can't find a ha'penny. I'm really busy and you're slowing down the pace of work here."

The man found some change and motioned to put the change in the top hat. Fennel pulled it back ever so rapidly and the change went careening onto the dock.

"Dear god, boy, now look at what you have done."

Fennel stared down at the change as it found its way gently into the salt worn cracks. He didn't search for it at all but instead just stared after it in wonder. "You don't mind picking it up for me, do you, sir?" he asked, looking up. The solicitor's face was aghast.

"You're worse than I thought," the man said, moving to walk past Fennel and back to the work at hand. "Be off with you!"

28

Fennel's small hand grabbed him by the leg, his little fingers gripping into the silks that comprised the man's fine suit. Below the silks he felt the meat of the leg and below that the humble bones of a mortal man, too mortal to handle him.

The solicitor looked down with a shred of fear on his lips and a shred of disgust. "Let go of me, you little wharf rat!"

Fennel stared up, still on one knee, not having moved one iota. "I'm afraid, dear sir, you only make matters worse. Your hostility only encourages me. It's like momma's fine cooking. Makes you just want to take a bite."

And with that, Fennel did just that. He bit into the man's leg making him howl in pain. The meat went into Fennel's tiny teeth splitting under the pressure of a mythical jaw. Silk, bones, blood, tendons, veins, and pain. Blood spurted from his mouth and Fennel pulled back in victory. The man fell to the wooden dock below madly screaming and gripping his leg. Fennel brushed himself off and tipped his hat at the sailors who were laughing hysterically at the shenanigans below.

"It's true. That was great fun. But don't think any of you is excused from this. You're all next. Every one of you!" And with that, Fennel headed into a most poorly planned battle.

Meanwhile, the woman was yelling as the two men tried desperately to pin her down on the ground. The room smelled of termite victory and the lanterns that hung on the wall barely illuminated. It was nearly dark in the shack.

"Shut 'er up, Jangles. This one's a real screamer. She just won't shut the hell up. Listen, lady, we ain't gonna harm ya, we just gotta get ya outta the way. You're messing up the work we gotta do. Cap says tie ya up and that's what we going to do. Don't worry, your ladiness won't be harmed by the likes of us. You can stay the virgin ya clearly are."

The other sailor laughed as he returned to the two with a long pile of rope. They were going to tie her up.

The woman's eyes were fire. She was filled with hate. "You call that a joke?" she snarled. "Hey, Jangles, tell this one, he is about as stupid as his mommy always said he was. You boys don't know what you're doing. You would tie your own self up if the cap'n told you to. Do you ever wonder about life or the next day or what makes you actually tick? No, you're just like my last husband. Robots. Men. Idiots. Robots walking the planet. Beware the zombies. Here they come. Do you see those people you are loading on the ship? Who do you think that is for? Why is that? What is that? Do you think? Hey, Jangles, do either of you think?"

"Ya gotta shut 'er up," said the one named Jangles. The other one reached down, pulled off his shoe, then his sock and then proceeded to

29

stuff the foul cotton attire in the woman's mouth. Isabella waited. She didn't want to interfere unless she had to, but her heart went out to this wild beast of a lady. She was like Isabella but different. She was, in a sense, in the world. She was fighting it. Pushing on it. Resisting it. Crying in it. She was the water and her tremendous tragedy filled Isabella's heart with a fever. And then, quick as lightning, something even more remarkable transpired.

Without warning or smell, the entire shack literally exploded. Shards of wood crashed and exploded everywhere. Isabella briefly saw both sailors flying through the sky as though launched from a catapult— their bodies bent in exasperated pain. A massive shrouded figure grabbed the screaming lady. It was huge. If it was a man, it was hard to say—more like a beast. It had exploded through the front door, grabbed the woman and then with a launch of its enormous legs, headed straight up into the sky. It hovered briefly above and Isabella could tell, whatever it was, took a brief second to feed on the water. The water that filled the air from the howls of the mad and the howls of the woman all moved through the air and entered into the body of that creature hovering high up in the night.

Isabella wanted to shout out, to say hello, to call on it for answers, but nothing came out. She was prone, surprised and off guard and with one smooth motion, the creature disappeared into the sky—the brief spectral figure of their silhouettes barely visible in the black Barrenwood night. They were gone without much of a trace. All that was left, sitting heavy on the air of sawdust and sea salt, was the pungent odor of gasoline.

Chapter 3

She woke in a flash. The cave was still dripping and the Aliber River was still flowing. The mosquitos were out, their long noses filled with the blood of deer and vermin. She flew off her sleeping mat and went straight out toward the water. When she needed to think, she had to have her frail feet in mud, had to feel it squishing between her toes. She really needed to ruminate. Her mind was a beehive, buzzing with ideas ever elusive. Something most peculiar had happened last night and it wasn't her brother throwing seven sailors overboard.

Her feet sank into the river bottom and algae and moss pushed up around her legs. She paced back and forth as the pull of the river played on the edge of her skin. She could smell the last vestiges of twilight and feel the humidity gradually diminishing with the farewell of the invidious sun. Thinking is a rhythm, a movement. She had to have it to get the gears moving. She paced to and fro and felt the waking of her brother back on his mat. She couldn't stop thinking about that creature that had rescued the screaming woman. That figure, whatever it was, she knew for certain, had flown. It had disappeared in the hair's-breath-of-a-second up into the sky, blasting that cabin into smithereens. It had been for all intents and purposes supernatural—and that kind of behavior had always been, for as long as she had ever known, the sole territory of herself, her brother and that wretched drunk Marty. What that meant, in the short, she knew, was that she and her dear brother were not alone.

But it wasn't just that it could fly. While that was most curious indeed, there was something much more engrossing. That creature had come for that woman—that woman that spoke in harmony with Isabella's thoughts, that woman that screamed against the world and pushed up hard against it. That massive creature hadn't rescued one of the many sailors that Fennel had most inexcusably tossed off Le Bateau Ivre. It hadn't flown down in heroic anguish over the biting of the solicitor's silk leg. No. It had rescued her. It had come to her calling. It knew, as Isabella did, that this woman was special beyond measure. It knew, with divine inspiration, that this woman saw the ghosts that walked this somnambulist plane. This creature—that moved with such blinding speed she had only sensed the one thing it left behind: the smell of gasoline—had been attracted by the water.

"Disgusting as ever. As ever," said Fennel as he brushed his teeth and walked up to her in his flip-flops. He would never deign to put his feet in this mud. "Let me guess, you want to go find that woman. Don't tell me, I know. You're a sucker for a singer, my dear."

He was in good spirits. He felt he had made some strange victory over the world with his exploits, although the boat itself had nevertheless sailed away. He couldn't stop that. He merely inconvenienced it. But Fennel wasn't much of a big picture thinker in that regard. He had given it a good fight and enjoyed the encounter.

"Fennel, I dare say, we might have had a brief encounter with one of our own last night—that mysterious crash on the building—it was something like us."

"Tut tut, dear sis. I know you. I know what you want. You want company and I take it to heart. I'm just not good enough for you. Make it up, if you will. It matters not. I admit something strange this way came, but it never can claim to be us all the same. That's my humble opinion. I do appreciate your poetry, however. It's eloquent and sincere. And frankly it goes well with the gruesome lack of hygiene. That being said, I want to get the day going."

With that, Fennel went back into the cave. He took much more time to get going than she as he had a lot of prepping to do. Isabella wasn't surprised at his reaction. He wasn't curious like that. He had his own version, but the desire for camaraderie generally stopped at Isabella and Marty. Three was a crowd, but it was *his* crowd. Four was beyond the pale. In that, he was an awful pain. He just couldn't let things flow. Isabella was too excited at the current prospect and she had to talk to someone.

She made her way back to her desk in the cave. Pencils, notes, drawings, and ink stains abounded. She got out some parchment and wrote out a letter to the Persembe Sisters. She needed information. They had to find it for her. That would at least be a start.

"Fennel, I think that creature came for that woman's water."

Fennel was picking lint off his overcoat, consistently looking at the mirror to see how he looked. "Let me think on that," he said. "Perhaps. Perhaps. But don't get all spun out thinking about it. I know you better than you do. Stay with me and my vengeful pursuit. It will be more comforting and perhaps more adventurous."

"Congratulations but you aren't working with me in the slightest. Oh, never mind!"

Isabella stopped this train of thought. She knew it was a non-starter with her brother and, at times, he scared her. He could be cruel when he was uncomfortable.

Fennel looked up from his jacket. Something about her giving up on that particular subject irked him. "You aren't alone, sis. You have me. And if you don't start recognizing that, I'm going to throw you in the river too!"

Fennel smacked his sister upside the head and danced in front of the mirror. He then clapped his hands together and jumped over to Isabella.

"You are such a romantic, my sis. I almost think you invent these games to make life more interesting for yourself. Myself, I am a pragmatist. I know all we have is this lame town. I am just going to un-lame it by acting as sheriff and clown. Once that statue goes up, people are going to simply see themselves differently."

Isabella shook her head in frustration. She really shouldn't have started this conversation with him in the first place. She knew his worldview quite well.

"Very well, but it isn't boredom I am worried about. We do not have much time before Marty comes laughing himself through the door and I for one have no interest in being shoved back into a log."

Fennel shook his head. The thread of this conversation was slowly bringing down his usually chipper mood.

"Thinking like this will surely get you back in the log."

Isabella stood up and dunked her feet in the footbath. She was excited now. She was talking herself into a new adventure.

"Oh Fennel, as fierce as the Raven is, he is a rather timid beast, wouldn't you say? Let's not let Marty's wrath prevent us from following our inner calling. You can solve the city and I will find its fire exit. And furthermore, whether you admit it or not, that creature that came flying down from on high, told me one thing that I always suspected: we are not alone. There are others like us out there."

"Wait, did you hear that?" asked Fennel as he finished lacing his shoes and raced out the door. He held his hand to his ear and stared into he glistening night.

"What?" asked Isabella, following.

"It's the night. It is speaking to me. It is saying . . . wait, what is it? Yes. That's it. The night tells me that you are losing it. Amazing! I think it might be right! You are losing it! The cat is out of the bag at last!"

He gave his sister a shove and ran to the boat. Isabella regained her balance, shook her head, stowed the letters in her pocket, and met her brother in the boat. He had already put the needle on the record and out came a low song of Berlioz's *Le Damnation de Faust*. They let the record play and sailed down the river without a word. As chatty as they were, they also appreciated the music serenading the marsh. It tempered them like a finger on a lizard's belly.

Pulling into port, they saw the silhouette of Heinrich. Ever dutiful, he had met them for many moons, to tie up the boat and await their needs. He caught the rope as Fennel tossed it and helped the twins disembark.

33

"Heinrich, I have these letters for the Persembes. Can you please get them delivered at once? They are of the most utmost of importance."

"Very well, Lady Isabella. I am sure they will be most pleased to hear from you," he said, twisting his moustache, as was his custom.

"Heinrich," said Fennel, playing with something in his pocket. "Can you have these delivered to the Persembe sisters as well?"

Heinrich put out his hand and Fennel delivered a fresh bluefish that wiggled in his paw. Heinrich recoiled immediately and Fennel laughed hysterically. "I'm sorry ol' chap. I shouldn't do that to you, but I couldn't resist. Please forgive me. I am still suffering from the malady of appreciating my sister's company."

Heinrich squished up his nose. Isabella, for the hundredth time that evening it seemed, shook her head in bewilderment.

"I should mention you have a guest this evening. Mr. Barrister Bruno has stopped by the restaurant and was inquiring as to whether you two would be making an appearance."

Isabella's eyes perked up. Just as I had hoped, she thought. "What do you say, brother, a little time with our war vet?"

Fennel shook his head. He had no intention of meeting the Barrister. He felt he was too chatty. The way Isabella talked about him, he could imagine being bored to tears as the old man waxed nostalgic over his glory years. Fennel wasn't one for sitting around and hashing out old tales. He was perhaps more kinetic than Isabella in that way.

The Barrister was one of Isabella's many pet human projects. That's at least how Fennel thought of them. Little projects that she would at some point put back on the shelf where they would gather dust. She got bored easily though she would never admit it. She liked to think of herself as sympathetic. Fennel, on the other hand, just couldn't be bothered with this kind of deep interest mercurialness. He had to keep it moving. Had to have parts of the world in motion. There was his longstanding plan with the toxin that was going to help him do exactly what Isabella had been rambling about—solve the riddle of the city. (Well, by solve, he meant destroy.)

Barrister Bruno was waiting at the bar. Unbeknownst to Fennel, he had been summoned clandestinely by Isabella the night previous. She had already figured that she would need to speak to him about matters as soon as she saw the lunatics being loaded on the ship. This business about the riddle of the city was not going to slip away. She was dead set on it and when she got her mind onto something that was it.

The Barrister was in his late fifties, a man of many wars with a trimmed white beard, his brain a receptacle of knowledge, wise and prosaic. A man of constant dinner parties, constant jokes, constant drinks, constant gossip, constant love affairs, he strode about town with knowledge of every nook. He had traveled to Crail as a journalist for a five and dime newspaper to monitor the last anarchist revolution and was so overcome with its romance that he had, now famously, joined in—famously because he had written about it in several books that had made him a Barrenwood celebrity; his times throwing dynamite to stop the trains of the fascist government; his falling out with the anarcho-syndicalists about nationalism. He now spent his time like an ex-patriot of who knows where going from dive bar to House Imbetta, spinning his charming tales of battle, tortured love and metaphysical heroism.

Isabella had encountered him in an editorial she had read titled *If they could only remember*. It was a story about how the Mayor and City Council had forgotten the glorious claims on which Barrenwood had been founded. That amnesia wasn't just a sign of old age but a sign of old government. The Barrister had seen firsthand what happens to a place that forgets the torment that spawned it. Out in Cairn, the earth was soaked in the blood of benign tyrants, not unlike the United States of America, a revolutionary culture that had forgotten its roots. Isabella had read it, slammed the newspaper down in the cave and had said to Fennel, "We will find this man!"

He wasn't hard to find, of course. Isabella merely inquired with Heinrich who had directed her to Catfish Saturday where the Barrister held court. She had introduced herself and the Barrister had been intrigued, he had scooted her off to a private room to continue their conversation. He said he had heard rumors that she existed and that he was overwhelmed that it may, in fact, be true. He had stared at her most intently and said, "From the dust of stars comes a child of ever." From there, their friendship had grown quite close.

Fennel knew the time had come to bid *adieu*.

"Don't try to dupe a duper, my sis. I know you summoned that ol' coot here and you also know I have no intention of being bored to tears while he talks about the greatest toreador or something. So have it your way. I will head off on my own. It doesn't bother me, you know."

Isabella smiled at her brother. His words made her sad. He was smart and she wished he just would let these things go. But he would probably resent her for the rest of the night for breaking their unsaid bond of cohabitation.

She patted his hand. "You're too smart for your own good, o' Raven. Let's think of tonight as a homework night, a chance to get some things done before you know who returns."

She winked at Fennel and Fennel demurred. He turned back at her and punched her in the shoulder. "You've lost it. I think I mentioned that."

With that, Fennel sprinted out of the building and out toward the city, leaving Isabella to meet with the Barrister. She made her way toward the bar where the room was half full of people visiting from far outside the Barrenwood gates.

"Isabella, so glad to have your company this evening," the Barrister said as she made her appearance at the bar. He sat fat in a white cotton shirt. The numerous large rings on his fingers glinted as they turned the bourbon on ice in his hand.

"Grab a seat, Isabella. So much to discuss. You know, as I have heard it, they are tearing up the Onion's Den on Rue de Kaiser," he said as he pulled out a chair for the small lady to sit upon. The barkeep handed her a glass of grape juice and she laid out her query. Isabella sat down and provided the Barrister with the thing he loved most, attention.

"Yes, it's beat up. It's old. I will give you that. Do you know the building I speak of?"

Isabella shook her head.

"It doesn't matter. Here is the deal. It's an old building but not all that long ago, it was the spot to catch great opera. They would bring plays in from Brilliance and James, from Castleton to Bellspa. In a way, going to the Onion's Den, was a way to get in touch with the rest of the world, which, let's face it, this city could certainly use. Sure, they fell on hard times but hasn't the whole city in general? So now these bureaucrats are just in the out with the old and in with the new mode. Listen, I may be old, but I am not into old for old's sake. You know that, Isabella. But the Onion's Den. I heard they are clearing the ground for some mattress manufacturer or something. It's enough to make you sick."

Isabella shook her head. These kinds of things bothered her as well. "It really does. I've never understood why certain decisions like this happen. They seem to be such clearly bad ideas."

The Barrister stared at her and smiled. He was lost in his thought. He laughed. "You know, I don't think I get it either, except that most systems are the result of small opportunists that add up to bad big decisions. That much I know. But when you tear down the Onion's Den— dear god—barkeep, another bourbon for me please! You know, maybe that will be a chapter in my next book. It's on Barrenwood you realize. Well, kind of. It's actually on all cities in a sense. All of them mixed in together. I have this sense there is a genre waiting for me. It is a chronicling of the rise and fall of this great city, but that rise and fall is of many cities when you think of it. I want to become an urban geography pulp writer. That is my dream."

The Barrister took a large sip of his newly iced bourbon and stared into the lights lost in thought over his future genre.

Isabella took the opportunity to jump in. If she didn't she might find herself bulldozed, like the Onion's Den.

"I must change the subject, dear Barrister; although, come to think of it, they are related. Last night, the reason I wrote you with such urgency, is that I witnessed a very coordinated loading of the lunatics of this fine city onto a frigate."

"Oh, " said the Barrister, raising his eyebrows. "The Drunken Boat, you mean? Yes, you know what, they are related."

"I believe it is called Le Bateau Ivre. That is it."

The Barrister shifted in his seat. He had spent the last few weeks on the subject and wasn't surprised to hear about it again.

"There has been a lot of discussion around that in every circle. It is not a dull subject but what is your particular interest?" Bruno asked. He didn't presume to know what she wanted.

"I guess my most basic question is why or more specifically why now? Who would do this?" Isabella tried her best to not sound too emphatic, but her voice betrayed her.

The Barrister chuckled and stared into Isabella's eyes. He wanted to know what lay in there, but those two sockets were impenetrable black pools. Inside resided a nothingness that sank deep. She remained opaque in the extreme. He had heard just the slightest hints about the existence of her kind (the rumors actually spoke of a pair of twins but he kept that to himself). One could always discount the gossip of ghosts and trolls, of gnomes and ghouls, but some rumors were specific and consistent. The ones about creatures who danced between worlds and fed on cruelty came up every now and again—minions who haunted the nights of Barrenwood bringing with them strange messages from beyond.

"I really shouldn't try to guess the direction that you are coming at this from. If I were to answer any layman on the street the question you have asked, I could say that it was an order executed by the Department of Psychological Services, newly established by the Mayor. But I suspect this isn't what you are asking, is it?"

"No, no," said Isabella, thinking how strange she must sound. "I don't mean that. I'm interested in something a little more broad. Although, come to think of it, the small answer is the beginning of an actual answer to which I might find use. This Department of Psychological Services, how long has it been active? "

"The department is particularly new. They built it out at the edge of the Mortestrate where property is cheap. Just a bulldozer and some cranes and the building went up. It is part of the entire new vision for the role of the city that the Mayor has desperately reached out to. Same mindset that is bulldozing the Onion's Den, I'm afraid. An army of opportunists, Isabella!

Frankly, Big Boy Charlie probably doesn't believe a shred of it but he is a politician after all. He bends in the breeze. I am going to assume, dare as I may, that you find the carting off of the mad the most recent example of a stupid city's hubris and I couldn't agree more. There are so many more examples: talk of making the roadways larger, streamlining prisons, more ordinances on health and safety. Ugh. Makes your head hurt and your stomach turn. They are very caught up in the new plans of which this is just one.

"Funny enough, when the Department of Nutjobs opened up, you would be amazed how many people all over the city woke up convinced that they were, in fact, crazy. Madness became *en vogue*. It's comical when you think about it. People in this city, particularly the bored, are ever eager to be diagnosed. They want to have a name for themselves. I know for a fact that the facility just around the corner has a waiting list of people voluntarily asking to be interned. I also know that at the new building out by the Mortestrate—I think it is called Wellington Manor—they have admitted Chelsea Revan for analysis. She was always a strange bird anyway, but as soon as these facilities opened up even the royal families were eager to get their foot in the door. I believe it was her parents that asked to have her under supervision.

"I feel for her though. As strange as she is, I don't think this kind of remedy is going to help. She is just a timid little thing—small and overwhelmed at the world. Anyway, her being admitted, only made it all the more fashionable to send your kids off to the shrink. Those facilities are now a strange hybrid of homeless and the well-to-do.

"It's a racket, don't you think? Running those things can't be cheap. And now they are carting the mad off onto the boats. I am not as far removed from that affair as I would like, I am afraid. You might catch me in your net of fishing if you pull it up. I know, I am a hypocritical creature, it is true. But romance often trumps politics for me these days. I happen to have a recent acquaintance that makes a good chunk of change doing the city's dirty work by facilitating the carting off the lunatics. I don't agree with it. Don't get me wrong. He is a pawn in someone's game but a handsome pawn at that. I can't find it in my heart to hold it against him." The Barrister smiled a bewitching smile indeed.

"I think I might have seen your little friend, oh, just last night," Isabella said. "You are a very bad man, Bruno, I must say. I am going to be honest with you because, well, I don't really have anyone I can turn to."

"Fair enough."

"I am clearly different."

"Yes, you clearly are."

"I don't think or feel the way others do."

"I can relate, but sure, I get that."

"I had a hint recently there might be something like me out there in the world. I smelled it briefly last night. So there is that. This lingering suspicion that I'm not alone."

"We're all alone, my dear," said the Barrister

"Now you sound like a friend of mine, reminding me that wanting the company of others is some sort of weakness."

The Barrister laughed. He found the idea amusing. He couldn't imagine the last time he truly sat alone with his thoughts. "Putting it that way, really makes me seem like the pot calling the kettle black. I can't stop being around people. I wonder at times if I experienced some trauma that haunts me such that I desperately need the company of people."

"Age is a kind of trauma," said Isabella.

"So it is. But do you know anything of it, really?" The Barrister asked and he realized he had no idea how old this young or old lady was. Who was Isabella again?

Isabella just shook the question off. "I can see it play out in people. Wisdom is a form of sadness really. It is an awareness of the tragedy blowing through the world—most succumb to its imperative, a few, find it beautifully ironic. I put you somewhere in between."

The Barrister gave her a hard look and then turned away. "Oh, don't psychoanalyze me. I really don't want my personality interpreted. I work very hard to obscure it from myself."

"Many do," Isabella mumbled. She meant it. She didn't find that part of humanity actually troubling. She imagined if she was like them, she might do the same. Her brother, on the other hand, considered this aspect of people most unforgivable.

The Barrister recoiled at her words. He was a bit of a town celebrity and rarely did he find himself in the company of those that didn't enjoy his every word. He reminded himself that his bristling was healthy. That is why he liked Isabella.

He took a drink and then chuckled. "You might be right. No, you are right but enough about me. You are on the hunt for others of your ilk, is that right?"

"In a manner of speaking. I must admit, I don't exactly know what I mean. It is all just a hunch."

The Barrister looked Isabella over. He had never encountered anything remotely like her. It was no wonder that she felt alone. She was unique in a most profound way.

"I really don't know. In my opinion you are very much alone. I have been a guest to many a city across our lands and nary an iota of your personality have I encountered. Unless you would like me to point you toward a Montessori school. That is about the closest I could think of."

"Actually, children terrify me. I'll pass." She smiled. (It was true. They scared the socks off her.) So, no progress on this topic with the Barrister. One last try:

"Okay, so you know nothing. Who might?"

"Might know about others that are like you?" The Barrister smiled at such a question. "Now, I'm having fun. It is a kind of mind game you are playing here. It is like asking who in the city knows the way to heaven."

"Do you really think I come from heaven, Bruno?"

"Heh heh, let's hope not or heaven is a most peculiarly cruel place."

Isabella laughed at that thought. The joke brought a vision of her in the clouds with drooping black wings. She liked it.

The Barrister continued, "All I can guess is that you are asking for who knows the old secrets in this town. I can always tell you the obvious answers but I think they are the reasonable places to start as well—the oldest family and the oldest religion, that being House Revan and the School of the Divine Line. If anyone knows anything of this sort, it's them, darlin'."

The Barrister gave her a wink. He had told her the most obvious thing but for Isabella it seemed to be of assistance. She stewed the idea over in her mind as though thinking about it for the first time.

"Maybe I am from an old world after all," she said.

It occurred to the Barrister that perhaps this beautiful young woman didn't know how old she was. She seemed amazingly unaware, in a sense, of who she was.

She stared off in a daze and the silence lasted for a good while. Her mind wandered into a space that was cloudy and grey. She couldn't quite rectify what or who she was. It bothered her but only in a vague way. In a sense, she thought, the present has always been the ultimate past and future for me. She snapped her head and came back to the world.

"Right, wow, that really got me thinking. Thanks for that, Bruno."

The Barrister tried to hide his amazement of his little friend. "You are most welcome."

"Now, let's get to the matter that I think you could be much more helpful."

"Where to get the best veal?"

"Yes, do tell. No, don't. I have had this sense of late that something is changing in the city. Something is shaping it—not just the buildings, not just the waterways, not just the streetlights and sidewalks but the entire mentality of the city. I have this lingering suspicion that there is something amiss in Barrenwood. That the city is falling victim to an overarching assault and it, in some capacity, threatens everything I believe in."

"You might want some alcohol in that grape juice of yours, Isabella," said the Barrister. He continued,"Your concerns sound very much like many of the poets I have been spending late hours with. The nostalgia for the city is heavy upon us. New winds are coming and they are blowing romance out the door, but in so doing, also making the romance all the more fleeting and present. Yes, everyone feels it changing. The growing tide of bureaucratization and ordinances mixed with this incessant demand for maximization. Words of life that stink of math. Yes, you sense it. I sense it. Anyone with any sense senses it. And yes, it *is* at war with us. But it is the city. One can't resist such a thing, at least not one of my sensibilities. That might be the calling for those younger than I. Myself, I try not to hold on too tight in this life. You don't know which direction the wind is blowing."

Isabella relented. She at least had some clues and this had been what she wanted. "I have summoned the Persembe sisters. They might know a thing or two."

The Barrister laughed. The sisters were even more renowned than he. "Oh, they will know something for sure. If you had more of an interest in sordid gossip, you would perhaps be taking greater advantage of their company. But they are from the Houses to be sure, so maybe, they know something."

"Okay, enough about me, Bruno. What is new in your life?" Isabella said, pretending to take an interest in the life of her friend. She hated that she was so self-absorbed. It didn't reflect well on her in her extremely rare social situations.

"Me? I'm a tired old drunk. Nothing is new with me. I scribble my crankiness to the paper every now and then and wait for my royalty checks to come in the mail so I can continue to have dinner and drinks. It is a really simple and perhaps even at war with that thing called the new. But don't be bothered by inquiring about me. I am simply happy to be your humble servant, even if perhaps, I haven't helped all that much."

Isabella hopped off her seat and curtsied. "It is always a pleasure to meet with you, my good sir. I am afraid you have been of enough use to me that I must follow up on something you said. In the meantime, have some dinner and drinks on the house. I will see you again I am sure."

The Barrister got off his seat and bowed low to Isabella. "It is my honor to serve," he said, and Isabella whisked herself out the door. Time was ticking, she knew. And what lay in front of her was the inevitable Wellington Manor.

Chapter 4

Fennel flew out into the world—a bat swooshing out of a cave. He skipped and leapt across the cobblestones trying to shake his annoyance at his sister's surreptitious behavior. The city greeted him as a black milk trash can. Every corner an opportunity to disappear into obscurity. The neon signs of pink and electric greens, advertising dim sum, and snapdragon carrousels, cast bolts of color into the absorbent shadows that dominated the cracks and creases. The air was thick as usual with the corrosive blend of coal stoves and marsh sweat. The sky was a beat up wrestler from the badlands dripping down on the town. An occasional old cart pusher would creak its way down the roadways with bushels of grey pears or golden sweet-toothed pomegranates—their eyes set back into a realm of can-do with their aged arms sinuous and strong from a lifetime of pushing. Urchins occasionally sat on squat chairs at intersections hoping to fetch a fancy shoe set to shine—their missing teeth an oracle of the brute they were to become.

Fennel kicked his feet and sped along, occasionally kicking himself off the side of a brick building or leaping off a small wall. He was pure calorie exhaustion and this little trickery of his sister's had gotten under his refined skin.

She could have just told him about the Barrister's visit. Did she really think him that dumb or sensitive? Always plotting. As nefarious as he imagined himself, he wasn't much of a conniver in that way. Not for the kind of socialite comings and goings and especially not behind the back of his sister. His plots were much more grand. Operatic. She was often lost in the moribund qualities of the lay people while his eyes were focused on the grand musical called life as we know it. His own plots held a different flavor, a different texture. If Isabella sought the comfort of those like themselves (a plan naïve in the extreme), Fennel sought a plot more diabolical.

Last night's events had only cemented what had already been a hint of a notion before. He couldn't stand Barrenwood and its people. Even if he had, in fact, felt wonderful tossing those sailors into the mire below, he still overall felt sickened by the antics of the city itself. Carting away the mad. It was a crime against dreaming. What a profound testament to the arrogance of humanity that they would treat their shamans with no shame.

"And that," said Fennel, standing on a brick wall shouting at the Cathedral Ogre looming overhead, "is that! Reap what you sow, oh Barrenwood. I merely exact justice, not fault."

He leapt up into the air and set out for a place he simply would not be allowed to visit if Isabella had been with him. He figured he would make lemonade with his lemons. As much as Fennel told himself that Isabella didn't know what she was doing, he also found that without her, he didn't know much of what he was doing either. She was his weathervane, his compass. She would lead him by the hand and he could then complain how stupid the plan was. This time she wasn't around, and he was left to his own devices. He could visit Derrilous, but he knew that the Blue Goo wasn't prepared yet. It was still much too early. No, he would have to kill time, and he thought to himself, so rarely do people take as seriously as I do, the notion of killing time. Let it bleed.

Fennel wandered the streets with his head spinning. He proceeded to the Miser's Quarters first hoping to find a rich man to rob but the streets were already dying down: the urchins putting their pennies back in their pockets. the rich men asleep with visions of usury setting their heart to a beat; the windows of the shopkeepers already going dim; and the sounds that did sound out in the night were those of too many drunks, guffawing all too loud. The Miser's Quarter was dead as a doornail—nothing but the glinting of jewelry in the windows and the faint smell of perfumes clogging nasal passages, pheromones, deer piss and lilacs.

He smelled a pack of wet dogs down an alleyway and scooted his way toward them—their fur a haven of fleas, sweat, trashcan effluvia and canine saliva. He loved that dogs traveled in packs. Mobs of camaraderie. It made him smile. The ragtag lot—the Basset Hound and the Pikingese, the Doberman and the Boston Terrier. As a group they were the definition of motley and the sight of them made him laugh out loud. They were clustered around some garbage cans, snarling, yapping, grabbing a late night snack of pizza crust and fish heads and snarling with their teeth to get even a smidgen of a bite.

Fennel got on all fours and scampered toward them. He hated what the streets would do to his little hands, but he couldn't resist becoming one with the dogs. He sniffed some butts and raised a leg or two. He banged his head against the leader of the pack; a mean eyed English Bulldog and let his presence be known. He gained acceptance fast—his smell, more than anything else, suddenly sending off a secret call meant for a world that humans had long past noticed. He joined in the pack making the motley gaggle all the more motley.

They took him in without even a blink. A Daschund gave him a sniff or two and Fennel seemed to check out. Fennel got into the mix and tried his best to get a bite of pizza crust with his teeth, but he could only fit in so much. The dogs were far more skilled at that than he. They then bounded out and he traveled with them. Let the dogs lead where they may. Fennel howled at the night and the Boston Terrier joined him. Awoooo!

They scooted out of the Miser's Quarters and followed a side road where the cobblestones gradually became dirt, the streetlights becoming fewer and fewer until only the light of the roadside campfires and porch lanterns illuminated the way. They were in the District of Jed, a part of town familiar to Fennel only in that he had not so long ago engaged in one of his more fond escapades. He had actually titled it, *The Episode of the Sedulous Doctor.*

It was only a few weeks back when he and sis had embarked on this tragic venture. The doctor, a resident of this broke part of town, had broken the cardinal rule of doctoring—a fate typical of many a doctor in Barrenwood. He continued to get high on his own supply. Though he was one of the more prominent physicians in town, rumors had begun to circulate regarding his medical practice. He had begun to suffer from paranoid hysterics. Word had reached the twins by way of the Persembe sisters, and the twins couldn't resist the temptation to interfere. Fennel found particular pleasure in anyone else's paranoia. He had taken it upon himself to exacerbate the situation for the mere pleasure of being a terrible person.

Heading out toward the District of Jed so late in the night, one could call it morn, he had begun to appear in the doctor's room clad in white sheets. White, of all things! He would saunter about in ghostly fashion trying out his ghost voice, whispering faint suggestions into the room. The words would hover somnolently into the doctor's ears.

"You have betrayed us, Doctor Seppy. You have sent us deep, deep into the grave. We have not forgotten. The dirt has not forgotten! Go now and dig us up. Release us from our premature burial!"

Much to the pleasure of the twins, the doctor reacted with little surprise. At the sound of Fennel's screechy ghost voice, the doctor merely looked up into the tin roof above his bed as though finally receiving confirmation of things long suspected. The twins watched in bewilderment as he calmly began to carry out Fennel's whispered demands. Doctor Seppy wasn't quite sure who specifically this ghost had been referring to so he simply began to dig up the patients he held the most guilt about. This turned out to be a long list. Strangely enough, they were all old women.

The doctor's strict adherence to Fennel's orders was most pleasing and so, at Isabella's request, Fennel began to take another direction.

"I take it as a great affront the manner in which you conduct our liberation! You have not only failed to free us, but you have released the

44

spirits of ghosts who are consumed with thoughts of your demise! Go put them back, quickly! We are the bodies to the north of those."

This began to panic the doctor. What at first began as a surprisingly carefree routine became a frantic damnation. He could not for the life of him understand what "to the north" could mean. With no small effort, he placed the old women's bodies back in their graves. His tired muscles ached after the tenth body had been dragged back to its bucolic residence. Tired as he may be, the doctor persevered with tired, tired eyes and strained limp arms. Fennel found the doctor's sedulousness so inspiring he even one evening crawled out from behind a tombstone and assisted in the digging for at this point nothing surprised the flawed doctor.

Finally, these demons had been silenced and now he was able to begin digging everybody up on the north side of the cemetery. (He wanted to be sure he carried out the order!) He had calculated that within six months, he would be able to excavate and release 427 bodies. He was beginning to have small blackouts in the cemetery from exhaustion. Fennel would visit him at night in the cemetery and issue soothing words of encouragement. It was not long before he awoke one day in a grave for the body of Darian Pith with the groundskeeper staring down at him. Within a few days, the magistrate raided his home under suspicion of "improper theft of the dead". To the dismay of every gentleman on the search, the home was chock-full of corpses, an inordinate supply of morphine, and a multitude of letters he had written to "the ghost boy."(Letters of which the twins retained in their tragi-comic scrapbook,) The good doctor was then committed to the Pea Green Correctional Facility and the twins were pleased as grape punch.

Such was Fennel's last visit to this area, and now here he was on all fours, romping around with canine brethren. The pack worked its ways along the dirt roads, knocking over trash and finding fish tails hocked out by the increasingly gruff denizens. The pack entered the center of the district with each corner home to a different ale house. As asleep as the city had been, this particular area was in full swing. People suddenly appeared, some lounging on benches, others holding their hands over barrels full of fire. There was the smell of infatuation and desperation in the air—old stories of the wars gone by and new tales of children who had lost their way. Boasts and regrets mixed in the hazy steam of suds and rain. A crazed child ran after the pack with a stick and Fennel decided to make himself scarce for fear someone might notice a small boy on all fours at one with this mangy pack. He dusted himself off and bid *adieu* to his temporary canine community. He looked at his hands. He would need to find a basin.

He walked through the center of the square to see a preacher man standing on a stool. The bald bespectacled man flailed with his arms and sermonized to a largely uninterested crowd. Propped up behind him, scrawled upon pieces of cardboard, were reminders of the wrath of god that was to come. Repent. Fire awaits. You shall burn in hell if you don't accept his love. The writing was desperate, adding all the more madness and urgency to the preacher's call. The sign's writing was done in a scrawled quality as though the devil himself had etched the words with a long callous fingernail. Fennel stopped and stared. He couldn't get enough.

"There isn't much time! It's running out! You can feel it slipping through your fingers, people! You while away the time, hoping that it won't come, but you can hear it in your hearts, in your fear. You know, as the lord wants you to that the end is nigh. You know that all this shall fade and you shall stand on the great bridge begging for forgiveness. But it will be too late. Because you ignored what was so obvious all your life. That you are nothing in the face of the great lord! That your obedience to his will is not an option but a necessity. You there, drinking yourself to death. Yes, you! I see you and the lord does all the more. He knows why you drink. He knows why you suffer. He only asks that you travel that golden roadway toward his abundant love. Drop the glass and come a walking! Bask in his glory!"

Not a person paid attention—not an eye was batted—only Fennel and his dirty hands who stood a mere three feet from the self-appointed man of the cloth. The preacher took no notice of Fennel but instead continued his loud abrasive oratory on and on as though the only audience he truly desired was the lord mighty above.

"Excuse me, dear sir," said Fennel in his trained proper cockney.

The preacher barely heard him. He was lost in the magic of his own voice—a sermon on the mount for one. He continued preaching and Fennel thought to himself, this man is a piece of work.

"Excuse me!" said Fennel, jumping up and down, finally getting the preacher's attention. The preacher looked down from his position on top of the stool. His eyes seemed to strain to get back into the world, his face clearly frustrated by having to stop what he considered perhaps one of his greatest oratories to date.

"I didn't know if I would ever get your attention. You get much too carried away, you know. Anyway, being the good holy man that you are, can you offer me a cloth to wipe my hands? I'm afraid I have sullied them," said Fennel.

The preacher screwed up his face. He had but one read for most of those who came his way; they were lost sheep, he was the shepherd. The preacher reached into his jacket and handed Fennel a handkerchief. Fennel wiped his small hands off and bowed to the preacher.

"Thank you, my good man."

The preacher took the handkerchief back and placed his hand on Fennel's head. Fennel wanted to not let this happen. He hated when anyone laid a hand on him, let alone on his head. It would take a while to fix his hair now. But he couldn't resist as he enjoyed the prospect of being blessed by this man of an extremely cranky god.

"Come to the light, my child. Repent your sins and walk toward the lord and his glory."

Fennel felt the preacher's grip getting stronger on his head. He was really feeling the magic of the moment. He went with it and began to tremble. He let his own spirit move through him and began to wiggle and waggle and began to speak in a gibberish that shocked the preacher. He stared up at the preacher with eyes gone wild.

"Gleh, gleh, muah gone pocknall. Zull frick nillben, chiz fish willykins. Zurgen crill naighshock!" Fennel let the spirit of strange words come out of his mouth, enjoying the increasing freakish look on the preacher man's face. Fennel did a flip in the air and raised his hands high in the air.

"Preacher man! Hear me, preacher man! For I am the wrath of that god you so badly wanted to meet. I have come home with the chickens to roost, preacher man! Your words have become poison in a god's ear, an incessant pounding, pounding, on the door of my slumber room. Have you no capacity for silence? You preach my words but you know not their meaning. You are a mouth without a brain, a mouth without a heart. Your capacity to speak outstrips your capacity to learn. You are a maw unfeedable. I am your lord, Preacher Man!"

Fennel pointed his finger at the man and the man recoiled, stepping off his chair. He got on his knees and placed his hands together to pray. Fennel pointed his finger down on the man hoping to get him to lay prostrate on the ground, but the preacher man had resilience. He suddenly gained strength and stared back with fire in his eyes. He climbed back onto the stool and the two found themselves pointing at each other.

"Devil be gone!" said the preacher man. "You haunt me this day and try to waver my mission. You tempt me, but I will not bite your apple!"

"I have never offered you my apple to bite!" laughed Fennel. "You, my preacher man, are the devil's playground. A loathsome child lost in the wilderness of a dream of grandiosity. I cast you out, o' Devil!"

"No! I cast you out!" The preacher countered, his finger shaking as though it were a wand of great power.

"Preacher man, don't be so naïve! God is a villainous beast and he plays not with the games you toy at. Your morality is a bent up tawdry outfit to cover up your puniness. Your fears are your blanket, your god your fears. You don't know god. You only know bewilderment under a fog of certainty. God, the true god that haunts this world and the beyond, is a god of great displeasure. On that, you are certain. But it is also a god of great magic and wonder. It is a god of spirited motion that loves a good drink and a good hard hoedown. It's a God of fear and loathing but also a god of grand irony. You know nothing of this. You speak on behalf of a hell, but you live in that already. Your mind shrunk to a fig of nothing. Your imagination a twig in a turd."

The preacher looked upon Fennel furious. Now it was Fennel's turn to be caught up in his words. He was hypnotized by his own eloquence, he didn't notice the preacher literally leaping at him and taking them both in a pile onto the ground. The preacher intended to beat the devil out of him. Fennel wrestled with the preacher, overwhelmed by the mad smell of urine and mold that seemed to have sunk into the preacher's attire. Fennel could have cast him off much easier, but the smell really got to him thus making their wrestling match last a lot longer than he had ever wished.

At long last he kicked the preacher off him who continued to rant over and over, "Devil be gone!" Fennel looked at the mad man and then took account of himself sprawled out in the town square. Fennel began to laugh hysterically—this whole event catching him as rather amusing. He laughed and laughed. The preacher was ridiculous, but so too was Fennel. Fennel laughed, hoping to see the preacher join in, but the man of god merely sat up and stared into the beyond with eyes of victory. What a stupid, enjoyable encounter this has been.

Fennel found to his dismay that his laughter had an echo—a resonance in the air that sang along with it in harmony. It was joyful, free, with a strong hint of the water in it—something that reverberated in the pure joy and absurdity that he felt right then and there. He looked up from his position on the ground to see across the plaza standing in the doorway of a whacked-out bar on the corner, equipped with a glass of red wine in her hand, the laughing face of none other than the screaming woman from the night past.

Fennel stood up and dusted himself off. The woman threw back her drink and headed back into the bar. He looked over at the preacher and reached out his hand to help the ol' boy up. The preacher waved him off and Fennel decided their game had come to an end. The preacher stood up and got back on top of his stool and began to preach as though nothing had even happened. Besides the screaming woman, it seemed no one had even noticed their peculiar duel. They were wrestling Cain and Abel in the epoch lonely drama in front of the eyes of god.

Fennel again giggled to himself at how stupid the whole affair had been. He thought about investigating the woman but figured he should wait for his sister. She had demonstrated such a profound interest in this frail creature. His sister would be most pleased with his discovery—but that thought made him most hostile inside, his good mood quickly evaporating as he was reminded of her two-faced plotting. She was up to no good and not in the way that Fennel approved.

It was time to head back to the cave—the faint hint of glow in the sky above was making the black turn into the slightest shade of grease. He made his way toward the alley where he scampered up to the rooftops climbing a drainpipe like a rat. He then bounded toward home, letting his feet find the solid footing of the roofs and then launching further out. He let the air fly through his hair and he sang into the night, a cruel raven heading back to the bony nest.

He was first back to the boat and he decided, whatever his sister was up to, she could find a different way back. He played the projector and unmoored from the dock. The black and white grainy images of a chef spilling pastries wobbling down a flight of stairs made him laugh as he wound his way up the labyrinthine channels. The mangrove roots sent their spindly limbs into the water, sucking up sea salt and making a chalk web around the edge of the water.

Fennel landed the boat on the sand and started up a fire on the beach. The fire crackled in the humid air and he went back to the cave to find a small pouch hiding under his mattress. He tossed into the fire a possum tail, a wren tooth, cinnamon, and dried plantains. The fire sparked with each toss of his hand and Fennel sat before it increasingly in a daze—the fire hypnotizing in its brilliance.

He reached out, placed his hands straight into the fire and said, "Hear me, as I call upon you, Marty McGuinn. I'm afraid my sister is behaving as you predicted. She is acting very, very bad."

Chapter 5

Isabella bid *adieu* to the Barrister. He would probably walk into the dining room, spy some friends, and ask to join them at the table. She couldn't imagine him sitting alone for long. He would drink their wine and eat their food and they would still leave thinking him the most charming of men. Such was his gift.

Her feet pushed her out into the wetness of the Barrenwood night. She pointed her internal compass toward that delicate region where the Mortestrate touches the hem of the Miser's Quarters. The wealthiest and poorest neighborhoods of Barrenwood, of course, were geographic neighbors. The two economic opposites were literally separated by the railroad tracks that headed out of town connecting Barrenwood to the high end shopping districts of Danderill then out toward the remote villas in Valencia, and then further out, if one ever wanted to really go that far, to the belching black smoke of Eskisehir. Beyond that, Isabella really had no idea. Barrenwood was plenty.

Her lack of interest was a force of habit. She wasn't allowed to go that far. Not only by word but by biology. Marty had forbidden many areas of the world she and her brother traveled near. They called it the sickness and this phenomenon of territorial delimitation simply made them painfully nauseous when they were somewhere or near someone they shouldn't be. It was a rumble in the belly that stirred up their guts; a vomitus gurgling that churned inside them making their brows sweat and their pale faces all the more pale. She had seen children walking the streets tethered by a leash to their parents, but Marty had them tethered by an invisible rope of barf. They were captives even when he was off making bets in mud strewn slot machines. It did, of course, make Isabella more interested in those parts of the city that were off limits, but then again, she couldn't do much about it.

The Wellington Manor Department of Psychological Services emerged just where she had imagined it. It was right where days past she had spied a large vacant tract of mud and the brick shard rubble of buildings around. The bulldozers had made mincemeat of the old row houses that once cradled together on the corner. Just weeks ago she had remarked at the hints of home belongings, a football t-shirt, a golden trophy for basketball, and the faint remnants of a teddy bear, all crammed with earthquake determination under the cracked wood of the bulldozer's might.

Now standing in that empty lot stood the correctional facility in its modernist glass and cheap construction—a bureaucratic erasure of any past on this corner. The teddy bear now lost in some landfill to be buried away from time. Memory is a spatial issue, she thought.

She didn't have much of a plan when she got there. It was night, but she knew the building itself did not slumber. Locked up inside she was sure were more of the newly defined lunatics of Barrenwood. Newly defined because even the term itself was rather new, let alone the buildings to support the definition. She had heard hints of it only in the language of those she met—utterances by those sophisticated enough to believe in the new stupidities of the age; strange ideas about sicknesses in the mind and healings of the heart; strange corollaries between broken limbs and thoughts with rashes; therapies and shock treatments to cure the mismanaged dreams of people off the reservation.

Somewhere in that building of reflective new glass control was the jailer, the warden who had to protect those inside by keeping them caged like beasts. They weren't all that unlike her, she thought. Marty was her jailer, keeping her at bay from the knowledge that he was wrong and so, too, was the jailer in this insipid prison.

Isabella decided to enter the front door, but of course it was locked. She pulled on the handle only to have it clearly refuse her. Next to the door was a white intercom that she pressed with her finger.

"Visitor," she said with as little enthusiasm as she could muster. No one replied. She tried again but to no response.

She had to pick the lock, which required very little effort on her part. She wasn't Isabella for nothing. The lock went click and she opened the large door to find herself in the caged welcome area that was the waiting room. The lights were out and she could only make out the distracted flickering of the fluorescents somewhere further into the building. Like all recent developments obsessed with security, the front room was a cage in and of itself. The room acted as a sort of purgatory—for keeping in and for keeping out. As much as the inmates of the mad weren't allowed into the soiled streets of Barrenwood, neither were the mentally intact allowed access to the inner workings of this brain prison.

The waiting room had to be about the saddest place in the world— a cracked, brown vinyl couch with a tear in it, some magazines on a side table from years' past (the entire building was new and already everything was out of date), and the overall mood was one of endless submission; a cruel world of forces too complicated to ever push against. Isabella unlocked the next massive caged door to gain access to the main hall of the asylum. It opened with a large creak that rang out against the vastly overly fortified metal interior.

She saw a shadow move with great rapacity and then a flashlight coming quite rapidly toward her down the hall.

"Stop, stop!" the voice said. "This place is off limits and you are trespassing. Stop at once!"

Isabella had no intention of running anywhere. She stood in the black pool of herself and greeted the lights with the same somber childlike look that worked everywhere she went. The guard came running up. He was overweight with keys jingling. a Santa Claus of security. His eyes were tired and who knew what kind of dream Isabella had woke him from.

"Little girl, how did you get in here?" he asked, coming out of a daze. Sweat built up on his brow. A man ever in a state of heavy breathing and sweat.

Isabella stared at him without a word. She wanted to understand the world. Why did this man do this? He wasn't cruel. He was a boring dullard sympathetic as the rest. Just doing his job. A guy caught up in forces he had no interest in understanding. He wasn't a sadistic man, but this job might make him that way over time—a lump of clay to be shaped by the steel, glass and cracked vinyl couches of the world around him.

"I'm from your dreams, dear William," she said, finally staring into his already greying eyes.

The man screwed up his eyes to get a better look. He even rubbed them. "Little miss, ya can't be in here. How did you get in here?" he asked, vacillating between a threatening tone and a paternalistic tone.

"William," Isabella said with as much kindness as she could muster. "I am here to rescue you. You have to leave this job. It is going to ruin your life. No one should be in charge of guarding another person. It destroys their soul. It will most surely destroy your soul."

William was as dumb as a doornail. He hadn't thought about his soul in a long time and Isabella's words bounced off him like hail. He grunted at her words and made a move to wrap his arms around her. She evaded him quite easily and gave a little karate chop to the back of his head. He landed on the floor with a bounce, his head knocking straight into the linoleum-checkered floor.

Isabella reached down and rubbed his head. "I tried, William. You're a lost little sheep, my sad boy." She stood back up. The world was endlessly painful. She made her way down the hall skipping at the thought of no more guards; just she and the newly produced loons.

The place was at no vacancy, each room occupied, and Isabella moved with the quiet qualities of a cat. Fortunately, her dialogue with William hadn't awakened the inhabitants and through the small glass windows in the grey-green doors, she could see huddled figures on mattresses quivering in the shakes of their tortured slumber.

First stop, the office. She really enjoyed being a sleuth. With one guard and easily picked locks, Wellington Manor turned out to be a candy store for her taking. She had full access and she had a specific plan in mind. The office door opened with a pop and she found herself in no time at all with full access to the office. Pencils, sticky notes, sad calendars with sunsets, photographs of children smiling in piles stuck with pins to corkboard, decaying yellow daffodils; the entire room had the weight of a place resisting its own nature. A downward drag of doldrums that was the tedium of the workday being fought off with snapshots and pollen. Across the far wall, Isabella saw what she had come for—a wall chock-full of files.

She opened up a file at random to find rows upon rows of paper loaded into manila folders—names scrawled across the top with analysis and reports under each: hysteria, schizophrenic episodes, chilling of the ear, Chelzmere's nodal, confine syndrome, bipolar disorder, aching heart, the list of maladies went on and on. Each person had become a list of observations to be recorded. It truly was an amazing industry. With a malady, one now gained a reason to observe and record, something to focus on and to describe and pontificate about. Forget lightning or gravity, now they could study the shift in moods and laughter. Isabella marveled at just how much writing had been produced in Wellington Manor's relatively short lifespan. She scanned the files alphabetically making her way to R—R for Revan. Ta da, there it was: Chelsea Revan. Room 21A.

"Now that that work is done, let's move to the next phase of this mid-eve jaunt."

Before she left the room, she took a peek back at a photograph taped to the side of a cubicle wall. It was of a large woman in a red holiday sweater standing by a Christmas tree with her tiny blonde child. The mother was beaming and the child was looking dazed. Isabella felt the odd nostalgia combined with the madness of childhood, the look on the daughter's face terrifying Isabella in that special way that children did. A dangerous combination this thing called parenting. Isabella licked her finger and smeared the girl's face. The nitrate smudging made the girl's face a blob of brownish yellow.

"There, that's more fitting." Isabella licked her finger again and tasted the chemical residue: salt, motor oil, and sesame seed. Not bad. She headed out toward 21A.

Chelsea Revan clearly had special treatment. Room 21A was in the far back corner of Wellington, tucked down its own special hallway. It appeared that this area had been constructed for the very real necessity of housing what might be considered celebrity cases. She was most definitely one of those. As the daughter of Blount and Cudress Revan, she was in the inner circle of the most powerful family in Barrenwood. She had five siblings each of whom was more terrifying than the last. She nevertheless suffered at the bottom of the ladder, as the youngest at the tender age of sixteen. Her family was a startling blend of loathsome boredom and sadistic mendacity. They gossiped constantly and possessed a philosophy that centered on cuisine, fashion, soirees and society. Chelsea often stared in wild dismay at their gardener because he at least possessed a reason to wake up every morning. As young as she was, she already felt as though she had lived a hundred years. Her heart gained weight with every day, dragging her further and further into a sinking pool of nothing. Sleep and exhaustion were her constant bedfellows. She had stopped washing her long stringy black hair.

By the time she had been interned, she had moved from a participator of gossip to its sole subject. Everyone in all the families, and most particularly her very own, were eager to have placed outside the spotlight. Now that her embarrassing mutterings and odd odor were no longer ruining dinners, Chelsea had become a delightful source of chatter. Having her fixed had become a *cause celebre,* with her mother now spending much of her time telling her friends what wonders the scientific community were working on these days. Any subject at all gained fascination in her tiny rich world and the thought of it made Chelsea all the sicker.

Not only was Chelsea of the royal line, but she also happened to be of the oldest one. The Revan's were Barrenwood's most esteemed family and her Uncle Gerald, the Duke of Revan, was considered by all to be the king. Gerald's sister, Chelsea's aunt, was her true hero, however. The witch of the family, Minasha Darkglass, was a brooding, terrifying figure with bone necklaces and black lipstick. Renowned for her fealty to the occult, Minasha existed as a tolerated novelty. Chelsea's tangled hair might have scared the bored sacks of meat that were her siblings, but they all could tell that it was a sign of her allegiance to her black sheep aunt.

The royal families lived a life outside of the rabble's drab existence, which consisted of 98% of the population. The 2% were nevertheless a large part of civic life as they meddled in everything from city governance to the announcing of festivals. Barrenwood still held fast to an era where royalty acted as the patron saints of their hamlet. The town had the day off and a parade for the King's birthday and the fashion houses still took their cues from the gowns of the ladies.

As intriguing as the royal houses were, they had never been a source of interest for Isabella. Sure, she still spent time with the Persembes, but that was about the extent of it. The rich tended to lose the water rather quickly and thus they never called to her. Isabella and Fennel were drawn toward vast tragedy and not ones thin with little imagination.

She did have a vague memory of some fine dining moment a long time ago when Marty had brought the twins, like little pets, to some event in a big room. They had played in a corner while Marty talked with what must have been a king. The memory was vague, shrouded in cobwebs, as those days were long since passed. In the present era, not only did the twins not rub shoulders with House Revan but, in fact, were strictly forbidden to interact with them. The sickness welled up inside them when they even remotely got near the gates at the bottom of the Elegiac Hills.

Isabella stared inside the small plexiglass window where she could see a small black bundle that must be Chelsea Revan. She lay fast asleep in the corner of the cot in the corner of the room covered by a small lily pad green blanket with pink polka-dot flowers. Isabella slipped the lock and creaked open the whiny door. The sound rang out in the cells and before Isabella could even close the door behind her, Chelsea Revan's eyes had become very open. She sat up on the bed with her knees folded under her arms. It was as though this small girl with wiry black hair had become the smallest creature possible. Her eyes appeared to bulge out of her head and she just stared at Isabella, rocking back and forth. She looked extremely scared.

Isabella sat on the far edge of her bed and spoke in her flat unemotional style. "I don't work here. I am sure you could guess that, but I thought I would tell you so."

Chelsea just rocked back and forth, the slight awareness fading as Isabella spoke. She was slipping again into another realm in her mind. Isabella reached out to touch her and Chelsea inched away.

"Don't touch me," the small girl hissed. Her face contorted into a revolting sneer and Isabella wondered if this visit had been at all advisable.

"I don't need to touch you, but I do need your attention. Will you answer some questions for me, Chelsea?" Isabella asked, standing up and beginning to pace the room. She really didn't feel the need to play therapist. She just wanted to know if the Revans did, in fact, know something about her kind. Looking the traumatized girl over, she wondered if anything of any value was clunking around in that snarled head. Chelsea continued to rock back and forth.

"Have you heard anything about mythical creatures walking around Barrenwood? A pair of twins that haunt the city? Anything like that?" Isabella felt a little pathetic as the grand inquisitor of a sixteen-year-old. She really had to step up her game.

Chelsea suddenly looked at Isabella with fierce eyes. She stared and stared. Isabella enjoyed it. Go ahead, I could never lose a staring contest. Time went by, but Isabella did not care. She had the patience of a fat stone.

Chelsea stared into those black pools of oblivion and found herself swimming around in there. It was dark. Brooding. Wild. Uncaring. Frantic. It was many things, none of which gelled with her orderly world. She found herself dazed by Isabella's intensity. She felt something that she couldn't distinguish, whether it was kindness or ferocity. Whatever it was, it made Chelsea all the more vulnerable. She blinked.

"I knew you would blink," said Isabella in bland fashion. "So now answer the question."

"You snuck in here? That's funny. Billy will hate that," said Chelsea with a strange smile on her lips. She wrapped the blanket around her body and wiggled in it nervously. "This place is easy to get in, though. It is just hard to get out. I don't want out, though. I'm crazy." Chelsea stuck her tongue out at Isabella and made the face of a lunatic. Isabella recoiled. She didn't like this girl's energy.

"There is no crazy." Isabella responded flatly. "You can't be crazy, you silly girl. There is only fear and hunger. Which are you?"

Chelsea turned away and looked at the wall. She then spun back around. "I hate eating."

"I didn't exactly ask that," responded Isabella.

"You don't like eating either. We're the same size," said the not-crazy girl, sizing up Isabella.

"I try to graze. It is a better way of supplementing a diet."

"I'm royalty. You should have curtsied when you came in."

"I don't really do that."

"Yes, you do! Bow before me!" said the girl, standing up on the bed and pointing over at Isabella. Chelsea then fell back on the bed laughing. "I'm kidding. I mean, I am royalty but you don't need to curtsy. You can continue being boring! Ha-ha, who cares?" she laughed to herself and put the blanket over her head. She looked like a mossy ghost.

Isabella pulled the blanket off. "I just am trying to find out a simple thing. I figured it would be of interest to you. I'm sure your life outside these walls can be rather boring, but I know the stories. I know how you shut yourself off. How you are determined to make yourself different. Surely there are parts of the family, the parts that speak to the old world, that must capture your attention."

"I hate history. It is dull. Every book is another chance to talk about how amazing we were. I don't believe it because they say that about us now and I know we're not. I can see it. Just a bunch of maroons."

"The world is like that in general. It isn't just your family. It takes time to appreciate them if that is your goal." Isabella felt like a parent and she didn't like that feeling. She looked around the room in all its somber qualities. The entire prison atmosphere offered a truly down and out mood.

56

"This is no place to have a conversation. If you ever want to have a real chat, you should visit me at my nightclub. It's called Le Chateau de Crawler and it's just on the east end of the Calliope across from the Herring Blue. You might enjoy it. It is—different."

"Oh, how very nice of you, little miss," smiled Chelsea, twisting up her lips and performing for someone not in the room. "A night out on the town. Come to think of it, I'm going to pass. I think, yes, I will pass. I find it, what is the word, boring. Yes, boring. You are boring and a plebian. I don't hang out with people like you. Didn't you know? You're worthless! Poor thing. She doesn't know she is worthless. Hahahaha!" Chelsea seemed to be talking to the room. She pranced about laughing.

Isabella was losing patience with the patient. She grabbed Chelsea's arm in an iron grip. Chelsea squealed and tried to pull away.

"Stop it!" barked Isabella. "Ever get Indian burns? I am going to give you little Indian burns until you cooperate."

"Stop it!" screamed Chelsea. She was a petulant teen. After struggling to resist, she became suddenly calm. "very well. You know who talks about old things," Chelsea smiled a cunning strange smile, "strange things . . . my favorite person on the planet. You want to meet her?", Chelsea looked all the more coy. Maybe crazy does exist, Isabella thought.

"Let go of my arm. You are filthy anyways. I can summon Aunty if you like. She can tell you all you ever wanted, hee hee. She said that if anyone tried to hurt me I could just summon her. Are you here to hurt me?"

Isabella really couldn't stand this little girl. She was all games and not the kind Isabella wanted to play.

"I might soon," Isabella mumbled beneath her lips.

"What?" screeched the girl, launching to her feet, pulling the blanket closer to her face. "What? You're here to hurt me?"

"I didn't mean that. You're just very annoying is all," said Isabella half bored. Now the girl was going into performative hysterics just to up the excitement of the situation. Suddenly Chelsea began to scream. The scream bounced off the metal walls. It was a kind of scream that only the most spoiled could do. The kind of scream that begged for something to control it because it was so unused to being controlled. Chelsea began stamping her feet on the mattress.

"Help me, Aunty! Help me! Help, help, help!"

Isabella felt the urge to stop the girl from screaming with a physical response. She focused her energy and did not submit. Let that creature scream. Chelsea continued to freak out in the corner of the room, letting tears cover her face. Her voice screeched painfully—each cathartic burst tearing at her larynx. Perhaps this aunt would show up and provide a change of atmosphere. This little number had certainly proven all it could.

The lights began to flicker in the building and the girl began to laugh.

"Hee, hee, hee. Now you've done it. Aunty is coming! Aunty will show you!"

Her voice screeched and cracked at the severity of her laughter and she began to wave the blanket around and around. Isabella could feel something shifting on the wind and in her body. A growing sense of something very unusual filled her being and her stomach took two turns for the worse. The sickness!

Saliva built up in the back of her throat and little beads of sweat emerged on her tiny forehead. A round and round spin cycle erupted in her gut with the flavor of gutter-puss. Whatever and whoever was coming, she knew one thing for sure—Marty did not want them to meet.

Minasha Darkglass arrived in an aromatic mist of wilted dandelions, molding cotton, desiccated leather and cinnamon sticks. She looked the spitting image of an older Chelsea, but with a face more stern, lined, gaunt and hollowed. Her eyes were painted in black, her hair a briar's nest of tangles. She wore a brown torn gown and a massive clunky necklace of animal bones shown prominently across her ratty flat chest. She entered the room in a burst, the door clanging wide open. Upon seeing Isabella, her posture tightened, her face contorted. She pressed her body against the wall and when she spoke, it seemed as though she hissed every word.

"Get backsss demonsss," Minasha hissed. She placed her hands in a strange cat's cradle configuration in front of her body and pushed it toward Isabella while sliding across the wall. Simultaneously, Chelsea shut her trap and slid her way behind her snake-like aunty.

Isabella stared at this woman while her stomach continued to churn. She was the witch of House Revan—the dark sister who scared the likes of the entire monarchy. Isabella could see why. She was demonstrably strange.

"I didn't hurt her. I came to ask questions," Isabella said plainly. She wasn't afraid of this woman, but she didn't like how she had become suddenly vulnerable.

"The demonsss always liesss. Thisss is a kind of conjuring, I am sure. Pick on a defenselesss girl. You have no shame. Stay back, I warn you!" Minasha moved along the wall and ushered Chelsea out the door behind her. She truly had arrived to rescue the strange girl. Isabella just stood there trying to keep her body calm. She breathed slowly and felt a slight relief to have a changing of the guard.

"My name is Isabella. It is very nice to meet you at last, Minasha Darkglass. I'm not a demon and I am not your enemy," said Isabella, and she reached out her hand in a kind of hello meets peace offering.

Minasha Darkglass twisted her face and stared at Isabella's hand. The offer clearly perplexed her and did nothing if not scare her all the more.

"Riddlesss. Always riddles you pose."

"We have never met. I have never posed a riddle to you and saying hello, in my book, doesn't constitute a true riddle. I also need to sit down. I don't feel good at all." Isabella did just that—her stomach taking five turns for the worse, her head pounding and her vision blurring. Marty's magic was strong.

Minasha Darkglass turned her eyes toward Isabella. A straight look and Isabella could see a tremendous amount of fear bouncing around in those sockets. She could see perspiration and feel the thud of Minasha's heart banging away, as her blood moved in an adrenaline-fueled panic.

"The demonsss is sick. Reminds me of myself when I first beganss, the feelings of the yousss and the usss colliding. Shape-shifter you are. Revenge is always your motive."

"I swear to you, " panted Isabella, suddenly very worried that she was losing consciousness. "I only want to know what I am."

"I don't trust this. It is a ploy. I can sssense you. You might be too much for me. I will not feel sympathy. Playing possum won't work, pretty kitty. I have retrieved what you came to take away and you won't take me either!" Minasha blew some dust into Isabella's eyes.

Her eyes stung and she smelled the witch dust of blackberries, duck feathers, and queen bee jelly. She scratched at her eyes and could hear the quick exit of the witch of House Revan. Tears fell from her tear ducts and her belly relented. Isabella vomited onto the floor of the room, her body shaking with weakness.

She heard the witch yell down the hall. "I'll see you again, Mire Witch!" then laughter.

Isabella submitted to the sleep of sickness that had been calling her name. As her eyes closed, she felt the sharp pain of something on her head—someone took a clump of her silken hair.

Chapter 6

Isabella woke to the sound of keys jangling down the hall. The institution was waking up. She shrugged to brush off the irritating sound and return to the world of blank that constituted her sleep. She didn't sleep like others. She didn't have dreams. As fantastic as her waking hours, her circadian rhythms brought to her mind nothing but the flat void. When the lights went out, no one remained home. She opened her eyes to the fluorescent lights of Chelsea Revan's cell. It appeared that Isabella had become the new inmate.

She sat up to see the pile of barf spilled out in front of her. She stared down in a haze wondering how long she had been out and then wiped her lips on the blanket. Her body was still quite weak from the attack that had made its way through her tummy. She got to her feet and found she continued to wobble far more than her liking. The earth seemed to shift and she was, uncomfortably so, a much weaker little creature.

Isabella scooted her way toward the massive steel door with the square plexiglass window. She could see the smudges of what must have been Chelsea's hands on the freshly painted institutional green door. Her hands shook as she attempted to pick the lock, but dexterity no longer accompanied her. She was stuck. Somehow, Marty's magic continued to work on her bones and the thought of being stuck troubled her deeply. What compelled him to assault her now? The feeling of helplessness was typically reserved for being around Marty, but this time it was in the homes of the deeply human.

She made her way back toward her bed and lay on her side. Nothing she could do but wait. The sickness in her appeared to be vaguely subsiding.

"I will just lay here and close my eyes. Time will be on my side."

She closed her eyes and fell straight into darkness. The next time she opened them, she saw a guard enter the door, his pants sagging, eyes wide awake from too much coffee. He placed a steel tray of food on the table near her. The smell of wheat toast, butter with lingonberry jam and a hard-boiled egg was like a conspiracy to make her vomit. She closed her eyes once again.

She woke to a new smell. It was a peculiar one indeed. Apple tobacco, gin, and root were the three flavors that floated in the air as she heard the presence of her new guest. She peeked between her blankets to spy him.

He sat across from her with his legs crossed and a notepad held in his left hand. He stared at her from behind small spectacles. He was older with a small black peppered beard and a shock of hair that seemed to spring out of the top of his head. He wore a laboratory coat only furthering Isabella's growing suspicion that she had inadvertently become a lab rat. His eyes looked troubled as he gazed down at Isabella.

"Wake up, Chelsea," he said with a strangely soothing sound in his voice.

Isabella kept her head covered with the blanket. She didn't feel like being discovered as an imposter just yet. Her stomach wasn't ready for any excitement. She did her best to imitate the young girl's high-born affectation.

"I want to talk to you from under the blanket this morning," she said. "Don't make me come out, doctor."

"Well, this is progress. So you now admit that I am a doctor. Fair enough, stay under the blanket. Do what you must," said the now confirmed doctor. Isabella could see him shift in his seat. He oozed control and she did wish she had enough strength to kick him off his chair. "The nurses tell me you were sick over the night. Are you feeling better?"

"I am. It was something I ate I think. I just need more sleep," said Isabella. She tried to muffle the sound of her voice but so far so good. The doctor seemed to not notice a thing. "So you know what I am going to ask you so tell me, what did you dream about last night?"

Isabella hated that she couldn't answer this question. It struck a nerve. The fact that humans could dream and she could not bothered her most terribly. This troubling point reminded her that as much as she and Fennel considered themselves superior, there were hints in the world that they lacked some basic qualities—dreaming being one of those most magical. Nevertheless, Chelsea Revan could most definitely sleep. She liked the idea of being Chelsea: a girl with problems, but a relatively normal girl nonetheless—one that could dream; one that, despite her position, was nevertheless lost in the drama of humanity; one that woke up in the morning and not the night; one that may have terrible parents, but not so bad that they'd stuff them in logs.

Isabella lay there on the bed. Glad to be confused, for a second at least, over a girl whose concerns were more bearable and down to earth. From her supine position, she could sense the electric nerves of the refined doctor. He could barely contain his excitement of having his new facility built. He still wished the rooms could be painted ochre and the dining services improved, but overall, he continued to be over the moon about it all.

It had been a dream of his since such a young age. The creation of the facility felt like the culmination of historic inevitability. He was born to cure. Ever since his days back at the school, he had dreamt of literally building on the new ideas that had been only hypothesized. He wanted to help people. This he knew. He had entered into psychology at the crisp era when this department had just begun to see the light of day—the science of mind and emotions. The entire discipline had ever fascinated him. His parents had always found him hard to read and at times, he was told he was emotionally inscrutable. So there was that. He continued to fall prey to the cliché that psychologists become that way because they wanted to solve themselves. But hey, people had to start somewhere.

Now he had this shiny new building with a renowned scrawny young woman of royalty as a celebrity patient. Her healing was paramount to his work and he knew what she needed. Daddy issues. They were all the same. He told himself that he wouldn't judge and would listen to the nuance of every word, but he had, up to that point, worked in so many test cases that patterns emerged. Remedies repeated. Young hysterical girls wild with emotion. The city may be predominately mad, but their cure remained basically the same.

That morning he had awakened before the sun as usual. The birds were chirping. He got his coffee and read the paper that showed up at his doorstep. He read about the building boom, the volunteer parade, the celebrity section that showed the faces of the *nouveau riche* that seemed to grow up in this town like weeds, and finally, the section that he was ever so pleased to see debut: *Out of the Box.*

This section, which he had lobbied for when he had met with the editors and the Mayor, Big Boy Charlie, focused on innovation. It was a space to highlight the ingenuity and intellectual prosperity that were the emerging face of the new Barrenwood. The articles focused on new innovations in electricity and gas power. But the doctor knew with great certainty that inevitably these pages would highlight the good work he had embarked on at Wellington Manor. Yes, he had chuckled to himself that morning he had truly become brilliant.

He was partially reflecting on this when the snaky words of Isabella pretending to be Chelsea Revan slipped back into his ear.

"I dreamt that you were a snake poisoning my ear. Whispering things that weren't true and trying to get me to become something I am most clearly not. I was naked in the woods and you were chasing me. The woods were wild with branches like claws and the clouds a mess of angry streaks. I ran toward a cave and hid in there. It was moist and mossy, there was lichen on the walls that I hid in and you could no longer find me in there. Then my aunty came. She was on a black horse. She rode up and her horse squashed your head. Your head splattered like a water balloon. Aunty took me away."

Isabella thought that sounded like a dream. She enjoyed making it up. She wished she could dream something like this.

"How does that dream make you feel?" inquired the doctor. That was often his go-to response to most things. It kept the patient talking and covered up the fact that he had been ruminating on the new newspaper section. He had trained his voice to sound calm teetering on the bored. Disinterest evinced the professional.

"Scared I suppose. And euphoric. I liked hiding in the cave and I liked seeing Aunty," Isabella responded. She liked talking about dreams.

"Did being naked in the woods make you feel vulnerable?"

"Is that a rhetorical question? Does sitting in that chair make you feel powerful?" Isabella snapped at Dr. Eldridge Never.

She didn't like this situation. Not only did she remain trapped in the room, but as she pretended to be Chelsea Revan, she also began to sympathize with the squirrely spoiled rich girl. They had her locked up in there with a doctor who threw questions upon her like coal into a steam engine. The imbalance of power in the situation was so evident that it exacerbated, not mollified, the extant tensions in the soft girl's daily life. Chelsea was just a girl with too many expectations and not enough self-agency. Like everyone, she suffered small in a big world. Chelsea just felt perhaps extra small.

This doctor sits there and studies as though his presence had nothing to do with the equation of power thought Isabella. His objectivity is a sham in the face of clearly tangible interpersonal dynamics. Isabella realized with clarity that this man was partly responsible for the removal of the mad. He was a scientist who confused his power with solutions. It made Isabella angry and nothing cured her sickness more than anger.

"Now, now, Chelsea," the doctor replied as though she had said nothing controversial whatsoever. "Just answer the questions. They are for your own good, believe me."

Isabella moaned out loud and lay back down on the bed. She didn't want to be interrogated and now that the doctor had already shifted to interpreting her fake dream, she had entered a very bored domain. Her stomach continued to make progress and she figured she would only have to remain in there for about a few hours more. Just as she had resigned herself, she sensed her brother coming down the hall. It brought a smile to her lips. She should have figured he would come for her, but the sickness had clouded her thoughts.

A knock at the door and a most timid voice.

"Excuse me, Doctor Never. Miss Revan has a guest. He said it was most urgent."

Eldridge Never got up from the chair. This interruption was not tolerated. They knew very well the protocols. He needed precise focus in these sessions.

He replied in a voice most stern and agitated, "Visiting hours are mid-day. I have made it very clear that my sessions are not to be interup . . . " before he could finish, in came Fennel with cane and top hat. He bowed low to the doctor and placed the end of his cane squarely on the lips of Doctor Eldridge, stopping the words at the edge of his beard.

"Shhh, good doctor. Good tidings are always bound to interrupt. You must open yourself up to the magic of the universe, my wise ol' chap. Open your heart and let the love shine in."

The Doctor pushed Fennel's cane to the side looking quite flustered. "What is the meaning of this? I will not be interrupted in my clinic."

"Untrue, good doctor. You have already been interrupted. It has happened. No going back now." Fennel turned to look over at Isabella. "Ah, the patient. She is looking much better, I must say. I was very concerned. We all were. Oh, you wouldn't believe the look of her good daddy and mummy. The worries! Alas. They are very concerned. These maladies afflict not only the delicate sense of a woman's emotional state but their entire nervous system."

Fennel leapt over nearly to the bed and sniffed in the air. "I see she has been sick of late. I knew it. This is the kind of illness one gets from behaving very poorly, don't you think, Doctor? Pardon me, my good sir, but let me introduce myself to you. Persifell Pemberton at your service, Duke of Junkmiser and Frankenfish.

"I've been asked by my cousins at Revan to pay a visit. Oh, don't look so thrown out of whack, good doctor. This is the way it goes with us royalty, you know. We aren't used to rules and regulations. I couldn't wait for your visiting hours. I have an extraordinarily important set of obligations this afternoon. I'm endowing a school for the study of hot dogs. It is most fascinating indeed. Oh, I mean you wouldn't understand. Oh, to live your life. One place. One thing to focus on. Haha, I envy you, doctor, I really do." Fennel made his creepy, squeally laugh and patted the doctor hard on his shoulder.

Eldridge Never had already experienced numerous unprofessional interruptions by the family Revan when it came to their daughter. They really weren't going to abide by his rules and he tolerated it because their daughter's presence remained such a boon for Wellington. However, this small strange chap slightly terrified him. If only he could study this one.

Isabella, on the other hand, in her haze of sick, just liad back under the blankets and enjoyed the show. Her brother had all the liveliness she wished she could have in her bones. He was dancing center stage for her and the show was most impressive. She managed to raise her voice, "So good to see you, cousin Pemberton."

Fennel winked at her while spinning his cane around in his hand. He spun around a chair from the corner, turned it to face the doctor and sat his small frame down. "You don't mind if I ask you a few questions before I go do you, good doc?"

The doctor clearly did mind, but that he also knew it mattered not. He sat silent and merely stared at the man-child calling himself Pemberton. Fennel enjoyed the doctor's silence. A battle of wills would only help the situation.

"Very well, I will take your stoic silence as a yes. I want to understand what it is you do exactly? You fix people in here? Like a mechanic fixing a buggy?"

Eldridge Never shook his head. The denizens of Barrenwood, wealthy or not, could never get their heads around what it was that he did. It was a miracle he had built this clinic at all as the city remained a backwoods encampment of ancient head-in-the-sand thinking.

"What I do as any professional in any field can tell you, depends. The goal, of course, is different in different situations. But to be short, the mind isn't like a buggy. It can't be fixed in that regard. I tell patients and their families this constantly, but the message rarely gets through. People think they can be magically cured, but the mind doesn't work like that," replied the doctor, crossing his legs and searching his jacket for a cigar.

"I couldn't agree more. The mind isn't a buggy, is it? People are so silly for thinking it is," Fennel stated back inquisitively. "But then, if I may be so bold, what is it that you actually do?"

The doctor found his cigar and lit it. The room filled with an unmistakable odor of cherry pits and tobacco. He took a puff and replied, "Well, again, like I said, it depends. For someone suffering from hysterical disorders like Chelsea here, we often continue a process of ongoing analysis. We let the patient open themselves up to past memories where traumas occur. Often, traumatic memories act as a sort of knot in the mind. They have a sort of echo effect that forces the mind to recoil when something gets near it. I try, through conversation, to find the source of this trauma and untangle the knot. First we require a map to the trauma. Thus, we often analyze dreams where traumas tend to reveal themselves."

Fennel thought about this for a second. "So all the people in here are undergoing this kind of conversational back and forth?" giggled Fennel, slapping the doctor on the knee. "How do you do it, you ol 'dog? I could

65

swear there were plenty of other folks, far more wild looking than our dear Chelsea who are in your care as well."

The doctor edged his seat further back so as to avoid another leg slap. "Like I said, our methods depend. Some are not nearly as healthy as Chelsea. Her disorder is curable if given time. Some of these others, we must treat in a manner more stop-gap if you will. Some traumas are too deep for the mind to hold. Bones can break and so too can the mind. We can at times mend a break, but other times, we must, by necessity, amputate—cut the wound out where it festers to protect the rest of the body. Such surgeries are an unfortunate part of this medical profession. Saving lives isn't always pretty."

Amputate? Fennel felt the anger build up in him. It welled up in his gut—the smug look on the doctor's face only encouraging his inner aggression. Fennel coughed up a large amount of phlegm and sent it flying onto the manicured face of the good doc. The viscous loogie caught hold of the doctor's prickly beard and hung there, a pendulum of bile. Fennel reached back to take a large swing at the doc only to find his sister tumbling on top of him. She had Fennel sprawling on the ground as the doctor sprang up from his chair and wiped his face with his handkerchief. The doctor then, finally, had the opportunity to realize that the girl he thought was Chelsea was, in fact, a young girl that looked far more like the strange Mr. Pemberton.

"You know, Persifell, now that you mention it, I feel entirely like a new person altogether. These therapies of dreams are a curative indeed. I think I need to stretch my legs out there in the world. Shall we be going?"

She put out her arm and Fennel grabbed it. The doctor rose robotically to block their passage, which, of course, is what Fennel had hoped he would do. Isabella stopped her brother yet again from whacking the doctor with his cane and blew some willow seeds into the doctor's face. The doctor fell to the ground instantly and the nurse went fleeing down the hall.

Fennel stepped over him and grabbed his sister roughly by the arm, "They don't need saving. sis. They will all pay dearly."

Isabella just kept quiet, glad to have stopped her brother from doing something a little too cruel with the misled therapist. They made their way out the door and headed down the hall. Fennel stopped by each door and peeked in the window. In each, stood a shriveled body waiting in a corner or someone staring, somewhat lost, out the small window to the exterior.

"Look at 'em, sis. They need our help. Can you feel it?"

And of course, Isabella could. As the sickness steadily faded from her gut, she could hear the hum of the mad—that familiar energy of water that fueled the clouds, the rain, the dirt, the bones.

"Yes," purred Isabella.

"They mustn't be penned up like this. They are meant to be wild and in the wild. This kind of fiasco will go on record like the tragic domestication of canines, one of the greater bad ideas of humanity."

Fennel closed his eyes and let the water flow around inside him. It churned rancorous and river-like. The rapids and the fury and the vast unrestrained flow of it all filled his mouth with saliva. He licked his lips and popped the lock on the door.

"These folks have got to go. They can't stay penned up here. I'm morally obligated to liberate, I'm afraid."

Isabella couldn't agree more and they both set about unlocking the doors and letting the lunatics, many of who were ill-prepared for the night ahead, out into the world. Some of them ran fast, straight toward the Mortestrate without a sense of direction or apprehension. A few others refused to exit their cells. And three final others just stood about the door of Wellington Manor, collecting their thoughts and thinking perhaps they could use a few provisions before they just went out into the night. Fennel opened up the storage locker and let them rummage around for blankets and the few belongings they had brought with them back when they had been interred.

Fennel went up to one of the three, a rather elderly man with a grey beard, missing teeth, a frightful smell and loony smiley eyes and sniffed at him as would a dog. The man just stood there, swaying in the breeze. Fennel sniffed the man from foot to elbow, from knee to belly, and the man just continued to wobble.

Fennel looked up, "You're a ripe ol' coot, ain't ya, boy?" The man just smiled wide at Fennel. "Aw, don't give me that look, ol' coot. You know what you're going to get!"

The man laughed out loud and jumped in the air. Fennel jumped up in the air as well and suddenly tackled the old man. They went flying into the dirt. Isabella looked down as she watched her brother wildly tickling the old man. The man howled laughter and they tumbled around like wild dogs in the grass. They wrestled around for some time while Isabella just looked on. Her brother was as insane as the old souls of the woods, she told herself. The old man and Fennel finally lay on the dirt earth, arms slightly wrapped around each other, panting loud and hard. Fennel bounded up, brushed himself off, and tipped his top hat at the three gents.

"Time for ya boys to be off, I say. The big city calls you."

The old coot got to his feet and the final three lunatics walked softly down the road together, shivering against the night—their mood not particularly joyful, the fear still raging in their sensitive veins, but the water, the water, flowed all the more.

Fennel closed his eyes and looked up into the sky. "Thank you for making me who I am," he whispered into the night, soaking up the water with as much capacity as his skin would allow.

After that, they headed back into Barrenwood. With every skip of her step, Isabella's strength continued to return. Rising up in her like carbonation, it bubbled in her blood. They were now back at the edge of the Mortestrate with the dirt roads and the missing toothed kids, banana peels, and Gatorade detritus. The sun was out and Isabella found it impressive that her brother had come out during day.

"You ventured into the sunlight for little me?" joked Isabella.

Fennel turned to her and smacked her against the head with his cane. It hurt.

"Didn't like that, did you, sis?" he said. His smile was gone and he looked at her with eyes much more drained. He hated sunlight. It bothered his skin and fatigued him. Whatever jocular display in Wellington had evaporated rather rapidly.

"You're heading off the reservation and doing things Marty wouldn't have you do."

Isabella held her hand to her face. Her cheek hurt. "Well aren't you? What makes me so different?"

"I'm just messing around, Iz! I don't know what you're up to, but it isn't right. Look at you. The sickness? Really? What caused that I wonder. When you go off on your own, you get in trouble and not the fun kind."

She looked at him. He was angry because he was worried. She could feel his tender crazy heart. It strangely made her love him all the more. She punched him in the jaw.

"Ouch!" he said.

"Okay, we're even. Now let's have fun together. I'm sorry for ditching you. We can have our hijinks as a duo if it pleases you," she said, putting her arm around him. Fennel shrugged her off.

"Don't get all lovey with me," he responded, still holding his face. "I don't like you going off on your own. It is true. But that said you did lead me to the most interesting of places. Did you notice—of course you did— that this austere establishment is built on the premise of healing? Isn't that hilarious?"

Isabella narrowed her eyes on her brother. Whatever mystery he was trying to solve would make little sense to most. "It is an absurdity, I agree. You sadly didn't arrive in time to hear my small dose of therapy. It was odd to say the least."

"I wish I could have heard it," said Fennel. He propped himself on a railing near a porch. "It is true that I am not the finest detective the world has ever seen. I will be the first to admit. I am easily distracted, but in my defense, the world is so distracting. That said, I couldn't help but notice that we once again have found ourselves in the presence of yet another attempt to quarantine the water. I knew it wasn't just me. There is a concerted effort to eradicate the thrill of life from the world."

Isabella looked at her brother. What did he expect to solve with this line of thinking? "I think we solved your mystery, I'm afraid. That doctor that you almost pummeled was responsible."

Fennel gave a loud squealing laugh and slapped his sister on the back. "Ah, Iz, you are quite the joker. One man does not a conspiracy make and this, I'm afraid, is a real conspiracy. Okay, so anyway, just know I am the Raven and the Raven stops at no single man. The Raven is also supposed to keep his evil eye on you, so yes, I think it is best if I accompany you. You need to be watched, I am afraid."

He meant it though he really just wanted to be in her company. He never really knew what to do without her around anyway.

They began to walk down the road together. The sun was out and Fennel handed her a pair of sunglasses and placed a pair on his face. "Damn sunlight. It is unbearable, isn't it? It's like rays of poison shooting down from the sky."

"But you do look good with those sunglasses, I must say. I don't know if I can handle this sunlight long enough to get back to the cave. I'm very tired."

"As am I, sister. Listen, let's find an alley to sleep in and then I do have a plan for us. Strangely, it is something I know that you will very much like to do."

They walked down along the streets looking for an appropriate place to get some rest. It wasn't that they couldn't be in the sun. They could. They just hated it. The sun removed shadows and shadows were their kinds of thing. They preferred darkness and perhaps in the darkness, in the world, the time of living got closer to the time of dreaming. Isabella spotted a boarded up building which wasn't all that uncommon in the Mortestrate. They scooted up to it and forced their way in a back door.

The building smelled of sadness and mold. Fennel was dead tired. He hadn't slept a wink, unlike Isabella. They climbed up the stairs and lay down on the wood floor. The cobwebs, dust bunnies, rat crap and beer bottles did nothing to interfere with the blank slate that moved across their minds as they kissed the world goodbye.

Chapter 7

They woke to the loaming—the sky a smear of salmon on lilac that crept through the boarded cracks in the window. Fennel dusted himself off with great fervency while Isabella smelled around the room. Such memories in these abandoned buildings. The desiccated remains lent tangible reminders of harried evictions, crowded dinner tables with mac and cheese, and the quiet moments of children staring at the cracked tin ceiling above. The twins found the pungent odor of families gone quite delicious. A sadness of the memory of places gone-gone.

They dusted themselves off and headed up to the roof where they could see the city getting ready for night to wash over them. The drunks were drunker. The workers were walking in the haze of a day of routine. And the wealthy—the oh so few—were preparing their minds for dinner and a future far beyond the now. At the edge of the Mortestrate, the twins could sit on the roof and watch the city play out.

Fennel found it hard to stay mad at his sister. Now that she was back with him, the world felt more relaxed. Looking over the city with her at his side, he watched with a rare calm. He loved the horses pulling the carts through the mud and the packs of dogs sniffing at the junk. The chimneys belched their black coal smoke and the street merchants raised their hands, getting hot snacks into the hands of the walking home commuters.

He sat there and thought about that doctor. The pit in his stomach grew with even the hint of that miscreant. That man didn't know what made the world magic. Such a pathetic creature. Diogenes was wrong. He thought people were as dumb as dogs, but Fennel knew they were much dumber. The human capacity for self-deception and amnesia to the obvious made him grit his teeth. That would be the point. Yes, that would be the entire overarching feeling of his sculpture. It would be massive. And it would remind. The thought of his sculpture always made Fennel wistful—a vengeful monument of agony. He couldn't wait.

He also could barely wait to tell Isabella of his sighting of the howling woman. Even though the news would tempt her toward her annoying path, as long as she stayed with him he could keep an eye on her. And he did like to make her smile. Marty wouldn't approve. Fennel had heard him slur it. He wanted Fennel to keep her in check, but that was how life had always been for Fennel, a tightrope between the drunk and the wanderer.

With the sickness dissipated, Isabella sat on the roof and took stock. She couldn't believe the new eve that spread out in front of her—the horizon never more distant, the sky never more vibrant, electric, possible, inviting. The world had started cracking open. Just a taste of it and she was salivating. Between the strange astral figure that rescued that screaming woman and the lisping words of Minasha Darkglass, she could taste the plane of heaven out there. The limitations of humanity foregone in hints of a vast network of metaphysical fraternization. A secret club. Sure, Isabella had her own secret club in the Chateau de Crawler, but this was a club of far more heft and vigor—one outside her control. She grinned ear to ear in vast rumination.

She regaled Fennel with her adventures of the night past: Wellington Manor and its correctional desires, the spooky Minasha Darkglass and her fragile niece Chelsea Revan. The story excited her with every word she spoke and Fennel, of course, took note. He did, in fact, find it interesting that there was a woman who spoke in voodoo gibberish. He just felt emotionally torn because every word of Isabella made him feel all the more nervous—as though she was going to leave or leave him. He felt his love for her so intensely it often manifested as deep anger if not hostility.

After Isabella finished her tale, Fennel jumped on after to tell of his own feats out on the town. He was eager to hold back the information of the howling woman to the very end. It was his little surprise.

"And so you wouldn't believe who I saw as I lay like a street side bum in the street with that preacher?" he laughed.

"Who? Tell me!",Her brother always got her laughing.

"That woman! That howling lady from the ship of fools. She was having a drink outside the tavern on the corner and I could have sworn she worked there. She was laughing at me as well."

Fennel didn't mention how the woman's laugh rang out with his. How she hummed at the same resonance as his most peculiar tragic pleasure. But the reaction in Isabella's eyes gave him both the pleasure he wanted and the fear he feared. She was over the moon.

"We have to go see her, Fennel. Right now," said Isabella. She was already up and getting ready to head out.

"Iz," said Fennel, reaching out to her. Isabella turned to face him. His face, for a split second, looked old, tired and perhaps his true age. "Just don't lose yourself, okay?"

"Alright, Fennel. I will keep my feet on the ground. I love you very much," she said and kissed him on the forehead.

He punched her in the arm and bounded out to the roof next door. "To the District of Jed! Last one there is an uncle's monkey!"

They bounded out, cutting past the Miser's Quarters and up over the edge of the Calliope toward the once again mud streets of Jed. Isabella giggled at the memory of the adventure with Doctor Seppy. Fennel could be such a weirdo. They sauntered through the streets, Fennel again whistling a song. Their feet took them across the path of a pair of workmen who were installing some large clock along the street. It was a beautiful ornate clock that told the time for all the public to see.

"Dear me, my good sir," said Fennel, bowing low toward the workman in saffron overalls. "Whatever are you doing?"

"What's it look like we're doing? We're putting this clock up."

Fennel pointed at the clock with his cane. "See that, sis. This is what I am talking about. Sir, do you hear me, do you hear me, sir?" Fennel gestured at the man who looked at Fennel quite annoyed.

"I'm right in front of you. I hear ya just fine."

"Is this the only clock or does this clock come with others that will stand on streets all through our fair city?"

"It's a big job. I think we got fifty or sixty of these things going all over the place."

"See that, Iz?" said Fennel again. "That there is what I like to refer to as a disciplinary mechanism. Sure it has its moments of Rococo. It is a beautiful object, a public form of jewelry, but that is just its disguise. That thing there is a water stealer. Not at all unlike that boat we saw earlier. It's a drought maker. An evaporator. These kinds of regimenters are just bad news for us. We really have got to get to the bottom of this." Fennel looked back up at the workman. "Sir? Can you hear me, sir?"

The workman looked down at Fennel. He wanted to ignore him, but he was just too odd.

"Sir, I won't beat you for this. Just go about your work. I'm feeling very kind this eve. I am glad to see my sister so I will let you live in obliviousness to your role in such insipid behavior." Fennel laughed and skipped along the road. Isabella agreed with him and skipped along as well. Those clocks were evaporators—another city initiative with the intention of stealing the water from the world by regimenting the masses. Alas! So little time.

Their skipping and whistling took them to the central square and they wandered down the street as the urchins they are. The preacher was no longer at his post, but the riffraff were already growing. Fennel pointed out the tavern. The Wayward Loon, its sign a pockmark of rain, hail and disrepair. They both slid toward a back table in a shroud of darkness. Upon entry, they could see the woman at the far end of the bar. She was smoking, a glass of red wine in front of her. Isabella's heart swooned at the sight.

They found a table in the far back and ordered some of the fine food options available at the ramshackle tavern.

Staring at the woman from her distant seat, Isabella could again feel the water pouring in the room. Like the sludging of mud and river sliding along the edge of a mossy rock, that familiar and longed for sensibility had returned with magnificent urgency. Isabella's mouth salivated at its arrival. It was a sound. It was a taste. It was an enchanted chorus that hummed in her body and it was most peculiarly strong. It was sharp and jagged— turbulent with rapids.

"She is something very special, Fennel. Surely you feel the water in the room," Isabella stated, gesturing with her porcelain hand toward the frenetic, nervous woman. Isabella's eyes narrowed and her forehead made the sign of a V in concentration. She was thoroughly transfixed.

"Oi, this is painful to witness. I do hear it, yes; but I am not such a flagrant hedonist," he laughed hesitantly. "I refuse to turn around. You know, I do have the sense the food here is sub-par, don't you? Let's see here. Oh, tater tots. It's been a while for me and the ol' tots. Perhaps that with chicken wings and nachos. Any thoughts? Hey! Snap out of it!"

Isabella could not. She was hypnotized. Now that the woman was no longer being assaulted by sailors, her day-to-day tragedy in all its subtle poetry was on the surface. She stood thin, possibly boney, in a slim tan evening dress. Her thin, blonde ratty hair hung over her face. Her cheeks were sallow and the skin under her eyes pulled heavy. A clunky elegance. She generally remained staring at the tablecloth, but at times she would look up, expectant. She smoked without interruption unless it was to finish her fourth glass of wine.

The howling woman had a name and it was Savina Lanthaur. She was in a state of despair, but despair it would seem was a constant companion. Nestled with feet propped up against boredom, despair had become nearly a central element of her skeletal structure. She was waiting for him. He had come into her life and had turned it upside down. He was not like a lot of the men that Savina knew. Yes, he was bigger. Yes, he was more sophisticated (not that sophistication was something she was much interested in, because she wasn't). He was passionate for the world in a form of hunger she loved and abhorred. As much as she was struggling to just make ends meet, she remained wary of the lure of such needy men.

As full of despair as she was, she was definitely not desperate. She had promised herself before she was eight years of age, living out of a caravan, that she would never be that. If anything, she was most happy when smoking cigarettes, drinking cheap table wine at home in the middle of the night and listening to a Gordon Lightfoot album. She liked to feel the night air on her skin and look at the moon make fun of her.

"Please stop, Isabella. We have a guest," Fennel said as the waitress came to their table. "I want the tater tots, please, with a side of steak. Haha. Yes, that will be delicious. And since my sister is in a trance, I will order for her. She will have the macaroni and cheese extra cheese. She really can't get enough. Oh, and if you have it, two glasses of grape juice. Oh, and thank you," said Fennel.

He seemed to be enjoying that they were not dining at Le Chevalier Noir. He too could feel the water. He wouldn't let it bother him, but it did make his head swoon thinking of that wailing sound of the lunatics on the boat—their howls tearing at the betrayal of the town they gave their grins to. Their faces so beautifully, undeniably lost in the call of the great fearful and glorious unknown.

"Oh, stop it, Iz," Fennel snapped, slamming his hand on the table. Isabella broke her concentration and placed her glowing eyes on Fennel. She looked as though she were on happy drugs. "I didn't tell you about our little prize so you could ignore me, you know. We are a dynamic duo and surely you know I missed you. You're looking like a cat at the fish market. I'll agree to whatever plan you concoct this eve, but do me a favor and let's at least have a meal together. There will be plenty of time to carve out this new piece of work. We can at least enjoy some tots and mac."

"Oh, Fennel," her voice was soft almost purring, "you're right. But my, oh my, she is something enchanting. I didn't expect it but she is better than when we saw her on the wharf. She is such an enchanting fortune cookie."

Of this, he already knew. She was enraptured. She liked people too much. She almost sank into them like jammies, bubble bath, or skin. She wore them. Got in their mind so fast and tried on their sorrow. She was still luxuriating in this one by the time the food was placed on the table. She wasn't completely inconsiderate; however, and once the food arrived, she set her attentions back to her chattering brother.

"So sorry, Fennel, but I am very bowled over by this one. She is a rare treat indeed."

"So are you, my dear sis. Rare and kind of dumb, sorry to say. You are unfortunate that way. A little dum dum. But you need to spread into the thinking of the collective sometimes. Yes, that is what I have been thinking about. Do you know that when I was that dog, I really could feel that the dogs thought like each other as one group. They had a collective consciousness like the patterns of birds in the sky. One hoard, one brain. I was part of a hoard brain. I liked it very much," Fennel continued while popping tater tots in his mouth.

Isabella knew Savina was waiting for something. She was anxious. Waiting. When the smell of gasoline crept into the room, her suspicions were confirmed. It was the creature from the sky.

He arrived barely fitting into the doorway, each hand larger than Isabella's entire cranium. Isabella gasped. In a haze of gasoline smell, she saw perhaps the largest man she had ever seen find his way to the bar stool next to Savina. She grasped Fennel's hand and made him turn around. Fennel's eyes lit up.

"Now ain't he a brute," snorted her brother.

This was not a creature from the sky, but a man. He had scruffy sideburns with boulder-like knuckles and his clothing was impeccable. His ermine jacket most probably requiring all the ermine in Barrenwood to tailor. He came with a heavy smell and like all things in the world, the twins loved smell the most.

"It's a gas smell, yes," said Fennel, sniffing at the air. "But one with coal to boot. Now, I will admit, while I find that howling woman interesting, this one is truly something. Can't say I've encountered anything the likes of this one."

"He's playing with her," mused Isabella, watching the two interact. She could see this man's words were obviously causing Savina much distress. His body so vast, the seat under him looked like a pin he precariously balanced on. They went straight into an argument. That much was clear as well. Savina's drinks kept coming and the back of her hand wiped her faded lips. His lurching, pleading, as clear as the frustration so evident in the tense arch of his back. The moment was quick, as the man didn't order a thing. He was there in a puff of gas and then exiting with the toothpick thin Savina held effortlessly in his grip. As they exited the door, Isabella felt the prickle of her ever-needy curiosity.

"Oh, this is wonderful. He's got her backed far, far into a corner. He is a force divine. I can't believe it. Such a wonderful accident—to witness this come to life," she said, placing her shaking hands in her pockets.

"It's no accident, sis," Fennel said, finishing off his meal. "I brought it about in my sleuthing, don't forget. You owe me one."

"I truly do, my brother," Isabella said as she patted his hand. "I believe we must follow them."

"Won't be hard to follow that smell. He isn't exactly under cover, I would say," laughed Fennel. The twins quickly finished their supper and crept out into the dripping streets.

Fennel launched into the square wishing the preacher would be there. He could use another go around with that ol' coot before he got drawn into Isabella's charade. But the square remained empty of the man of God and Fennel had to console himself by throwing a rock at a hobo asking for change. They scooted out toward the smell and sure enough found themselves standing outside the home of none other than Savina Lanthaur.

Her home, with a bent porch, lurched on its foundation. Desiccated wood rested modest and wee with a garden of sun-kissed daisies holding onto existence out front. The twins made their way up the rickety stairs. Under normal circumstances, these stairs would have wailed and whined from the pressure of any foot upon them, but the twins didn't make one jot of noise. Maybe they floated above them, maybe they stepped with delicate ninja steps, maybe Fennel had been sincere when he indicated he was a bird and their bones were hollow, but whatever the reason the stairs remained fast asleep. At the door, Isabella popped open the lock. It made a small pop and they slid within.

They entered into the kitchen. Pots and pans hung neatly overhead and the old gas stove was still warm.

"The Duke isn't here," said Fennel, sniffing at the air. He opened the refrigerator looking for a snack while Isabella poked her head around. Down the hall, she spotted the bedroom where a person was clearly in bed, passed out.

"Over here," she said, and they quickly and noiselessly darted to it.

Sure enough, Savina lay in bed, her arms twisted heavily around her pillow—the moonlight from outside settling through the blinds to rest on her sleepless sleep. The room was a mess. Clothes lay in a jumble about the room and from the chandelier above the bed hung little paper snowflakes painted in a wild tie-dye array.

Fennel reached into his robe and pulled out two vials of neon azure liquid. The color radiated in the room and reflected off the window. In an almost dance, they moved onto either side of the bed. They were ready. Fennel moved in and suddenly gripped the mouth of Savina. The sudden strength she exuded would have shocked anyone—had anyone been watching.

Savina suddenly awoke and made a quick startled sound. Without missing a beat, the blue liquid was whirling through the air and splattering against the back of her mouth. The awakened victim laid her head back on the pillow without sound, but her tired wild eyes remained open.

"That went well," Fennel said, taking off his gloves and jacket and reclining in a rocking chair. He sat back and finally took a good look at Savina. Isabella was right. Even in her trance-like state, she was enchanting. Her lithe body looked crooked and beautiful like a stick on a playground. Bony and twisted, her contorted frail frame held a magical allure in its unusual defiance. Her slightly crooked nose and long jaw held a grim visage. She was magic. Fennel smiled and resigned the evening to Isabella's designs.

Isabella lit one of the candles in the room and went into the kitchen. She placed the kettle on the stove and turned it on.

"Tea?" she inquired.

"Ahhh, good for you. Right-o. Do they have the Earl?"

"They yes they do."

"Oooh, delicious. Well, I don't suppose they have some pillows for my miserable bottom as well?"

Isabella just looked at him and shook her head. Her brother was just that—a brother. She felt she was only four steps ahead of him because he was always repeating the same steps.

She took the kettle off the stove, pulled two glasses out of a cupboard.

"Oh dear, Isabella, at least wash them!" Fennel yelled, his shoes and socks already kicked off and his little toes resting on Savina's.

She washed out the cups. He was such a little priss. She poured the tea, added the sugar and milk and came back over. They sipped merrily and Isabella went over to Savina. She placed her hand along Savina's face and gently felt her skin. Dry. She put her hand in her hair and petted her.

"Savina? Are you there?"

Savina answered as though hypnotized. "Yes."

Isabella looked at Fennel. He nodded.

"You seem to be having some kind of problems of late. I was wondering what those might be?"

"I don't feel like talking about it really."

Fennel laughed, sending some tea onto the blankets. Isabella was a little shocked as well.

"Don't feel like talking about it?" The solution had never failed them before. Isabella felt a cool wave of satisfaction sweep over her. Yes, she knew there was something about her. Just knew it.

"No, I don't. You must understand. I know what is happening. I know I will have to tell you . . . I know. I know." It sounded like she was about to cry. Her voice cracked. Her head shook in the pillow.

The twins were obviously startled. It was one thing to resist the solution, but to be aware of it? This was definitely turning into a strange affair. Isabella was lost in intrigue. Fennel scratched his head and squinted his eyes to focus.

"It's okay, Savina. Sit up, please." Isabella's voice had taken on a soft tone, warm, caring.

"Here, drink this tea. It will make you feel better as you talk. We're not who you might think we are. We're just angels here to help you."

She looked at Fennel in a joking plea. He rolled his eyes and wiggled his toes.

Savina sat up and took the tea into her hands. She began to sip and the words began to flow.

"Thank you. You're right. You're not them. You sound soft and, and young. Young like Beremel. She is probably your age now. There is no way that a voice so sweet could be injurious. No way. Anyway, I will tell you my problem, but please, I must get some sleep. Things have been so crazy of late. They are always crazy of course, but this week has been a doozy. You will go when I'm done? Okay? Good, as long as that is arranged. I just never sleep. I'm always so tired. That; yes, that would be my first problem. I'm tired. You know two men attacked me a few nights ago?"

"We actually saw that happen. I wanted to help you," said Isabella, petting Savina's now sweating head.

"Help me? Well, thank you, angel. Fortunately, or unfortunately enough, I don't need help. Not that that wasn't apparent. Did you see big man superstar come flying out of the sky and sending those ol 'boys out to sea? Ha-ha. Anyway, ya, I have a guardian, what would you call it? Guardian possessive man. Yes, it is the kind of guard that men can be that is a total mixed bag. Like, did I ask for one, angels? Huh? Did I? No. And let's not pretend it is because of him. It isn't. I have more worries than that. But the fact remains, I can't sleep. Or, I don't get any sleep. Or, once I go to bed I'm just getting back up. I'm always so tired. You realize insomnia is a disease? It is. It's horrible. And, right, it's because of him . . . Or is it?

"I did this to myself, I know it. I'm the problem. I'm the problem. I don't get any sleep because I can't sleep with myself. I feel wrong in my body now. Not that I have ever really liked my body. I don't even notice it really. I'm one of those oblivious types, ya know? Sort of a zombie walking around in a fog kind of lady. I'm sure people see me like that. I can't blame them. I could wear the same shirt for days and not know. I'm only partially on earth, ya know? That's probably why he likes me. Because I'm just barely here. He wouldn't like me if I was planted firmly in the earth. If I wasn't sleep deprived. No, he wouldn't like me then. Or maybe he would. Ha! Right, as though that is possible. No, that's not possible.

"Okay, so the problem . . ." she sat quietly for a little bit. Her body vibrated under her blankets as if a nervous tick had taken hold of her thighs and refused to let go. As she sat vibrating and staring off glass-eyed, the twins just waited her out.

" . . . the problem is hiding. I feel it. It doesn't want to be found. But you're an angel. You can help me, right? I'll help you. You help me. Okay, the problem is either A B or C. I don't know which one, but it is one or any combo of the three or all three or none. Right!!

"A: the Duke of Gasoline wasted his time coming into my life and sweeping me off my tired feet. Whew!" she laughed exasperated as though releasing some great weight. "B: the Duke of Fuel is an insidious insect dressed in the robes of a man—a big Brahma bull man, I might add—and out of sheer disgust for life has taken it upon himself to ruin the crappy life I had made for myself. C: my life is, in fact, exciting and it is only I who doesn't know it. The Duke is bored and wants a bite because he has chewed the rind off the rest. D: I am insane. E: the Duke is using me to appear more attractive to that witchy bitch Esther. It is I who is truly, truly in the dark!! Ha, ha! F: the Duke is actually a shadow of my true self in male form, hunting me down in some cosmic romance. I have always been just an audience member in the play of life and now, now, the Duke (that is me) will draw me vigorously onto center stage."

The twins listened intently, their arms propping up their heads. Isabella felt as though she had opened a fortune cookie—a fortune cookie stuffed with a black, luxurious liquid. It was spilling over the room out of this woman's mouth. She was bathing in it. Bathing. Though Savina's tale was rambling, Isabella listened as though it were the greatest of symphonies—twisting this way and that, crescendos and sobriety, the melody burst forth like fairy dust. Her words were an invitation, her invitation a game of Jenga.

"I, " she continued, "I am currently giving birth to a child that is feeding me tea and making me talk with glow-in-the-dark, black light potions!" Isabella looked at Fennel, purring. Meanwhile, Fennel had stopped listening. He had taken to making cat's cradle with some spindly yarn he had found lying on the floor. He wasn't much for this kind of chatter.

"Just get her to stick to the point. What a mess!"

"Savina," Isabella interrupted calmly, placing her hand on Savina's forehead.

"J: I'm ruined. Everything on this planet is born with the sole purpose of making my life miserable. I'm a victim of a worldwide conspiracy against me having a decent night's rest." Suddenly, Savina began to cry. (Not that tears ran. They never do with the solution.) But the twins could tell she was crying. The body would shake and the cheek muscles contort.

"Dear me, woman. You are a mess. Tell me about this Duke. Where did you meet him?"

"I met him at the Merchant's. It's just a dive bar along the Caripene River. I'm not a regular. I tend not to be a regular anywhere except the Loon. So, I was just having a drink or two or three. I was there just to . . . to get . . . what? Shit, I don't know. I was there to . . . I was there. I was talking to this man who claimed he was running this insurance scam. I swear, never met a bigger bore in my life. He couldn't stop talking. Blah, blah, blah, oooh . . . my take this year is la-dee-da, I spend my money on these wild parties, you should come by . . . blah, blah, blah . . . I'm a liar. I'm a drunk. Blah, blah, blah.

"I was letting him go on, just staring over at the bartenderess, watching her fetch drinks and running mad and envying her —she just could keep moving—if I could just pace or move from tap to bar to drawer and back . . . it would be more endurable. So, I was staring and out front I hear a carriage stop. Now, right? This is the District of Jed and this is the Merchant's and what is a carriage doing out front? Well, sound the damn horns, right? I mean who really cares anyway?

"There he is—Mr. Big Deal Kerosene—oh, pardon me, the Grand Duke of Izmir! He comes striding in, with his Chelton top hat and his Velenton cane and his cape flowing behind him. He's a huge guy. Just a beast! Looks like, well I told you, a Brahma bull! No lie. His body fills up the door and as he damn well knows it. Everybody in the bar is looking at him, right? And he thinks I can't figure that out? I swear that man takes way too much for granted! I mean, of course, he is at the Merchant's. And look at him! All gussied up, standing there like Mr. Intrigue. He looked pleased with himself. Well, I mean, I could tell he was. He pretended to be all somber and . . . dark. Oooh, the dark man at the bar! I wanted to vomit. No, I didn't. I just didn't buy it. But, at the same time, what am I going to do? He's obviously more entertaining than this insurance rat drunk bore slob? Right? Well, maybe he is.

"So, Kerosene sits up at the bar and orders a drink. I let him sit there for a while. I can tell he's looking around. I avoid his eyes. But he locks in on me quick. Didn't really even try to hide it, just kept his bushy eyes gleaming down at me. Let him wonder. Just let him. I swear. And he _is_ wondering. I can tell. Well, good. I get up to use the restroom. The insurance rat wants me to go home with him. I tell him to hold on and I head to the ladies room. I couldn't have been gone for more than five minutes . . . maybe three. I come back and he's gone. Just gone! Not that that's such a big stunt, I mean, he obviously thought that was so clever. Anyway, I go back to the table and my boring admirer is gone as well. In his chair is a note addressed to me, Savina Lanthaur. The penmanship is perfect. Flowing. The ink is even pretty. It soaks in the paper in black heavy splotches. I mean that does do something to you. If you have any class at all, little notes with gorgeous writing should be irresistible. And, right . . . the note says this:

Dear Lady Savina,

As you well noticed, I couldn't take my eyes off you. I am intrigued as I hope you are as well. If so, meet me tomorrow night at 11:00 at Alluvium's.
      Your admirer,
      The Duke of Izmir

"Now, there we are. That is where it all begins, because, you see, he knew. He knew!" She laughed and her hair flew back in the air. "Ha! He probably knew the whole thing from the second he walked in. So, he knew. He set that note down like it was the Serbonian Bog. Just ready. Ready to sink me right on in! And I did. I just sank. The second I got that note I was sinking through the peat and moss hag. Way on down into his decaying pit of a mind. You may even wonder where the piss drunk bum went, right? Shit, angels, I don't know. Just gone. He's like that. People tend to appear and disappear around him. He's not natural—mojo and fish eggs or something. But I'd heard of all that before. I don't worry. I've seen it. He knows I have, see? Ohh, Mr. Mystery thinks he's got it all figured out! But, see, he knows enough to know I know. See? I know as well. I know he's a damn liar. I know he's a damn sham, a regular Cagliostro, and I know about his games and I know about his tricks.

"Well, anyway, I know enough to keep him around. See and that's it. *I* keep *him* around. I won't let him leave. He's just such a man. Such a man. Ohh, why do I lie to you? Why? To angels? I lie to angels. He's beauty. He's what a delicate boy must become. Not that I have time for boys, mind you. He's just fire, that's all. He's just living fire—fire and coals and embers and lava and fire and coals and embers and lava . . . "

Savina began to mumble. Isabella grabbed the cup of tea from her and laid her back onto the pillow

"When do you meet the Duke again?"

"Two nights from tonight, 10 o'clock at de Vaca's."

Isabella sat back in her chair and wondered more about this Duke of Izmir. She knew this was the man from earlier. There was something about him—something so tempting. Yes, her feet squishing against the mud—she felt his pull like a tidal pull. It swirled around her knobby bones and gave resonance to the pond song—and this poor wreck of a woman. She was a spindly masochist. She was just turning the knife slowly more and more within. Like the darting schools of pollywogs, Savina's frantic resignation was the epicenter of marsh drama. Isabella smiled. She really had a gift. But something didn't sit right. She sensed that Savina wasn't telling her things.

"What are you hiding from us?" Isabella asked.

Savina's lips barely moved. "I've been hiding things all my life, little angel. I'm so tired I couldn't begin to answer that question. It's what I do, you see."

"I take it you did visit the Duke at Alluvium's. Tell me about that."

"No, I couldn't. Not now. Too exhausted. Now be a good girl and leave. I thought we had a deal."

Isabella got up slowly, slowly—so many emotions playing on her— the bottom muck swirling up and obscuring vision; the tadpoles hidden and just chaotic movement of dirt and glittering pebbles. She kicked her pond thoughts and they swooshed up and out.

"That's it?" Fennel asked.

Isabella looked into a figurine of an octopus on the counter, its arms stretched across the cabinet, its bulbous head jutting out. Stretched out. Suction cups. Spots. No answer. She felt as though she were in the company of someone other than Fennel. A woman. She looked longingly at Savina laying there, resigned to the bed finally. There was something here with her. Something.

"Hey, my dearest angel. We don't have to listen to her. I mean that dilapidated scenario regarding the Duke was entertaining, that much I will admit. I will also admit that she even, for a split pea second, had me concerned with her solution acumen. However, I think you have missed the most entertaining character of all. I want to have a chat with her bird."

"Be my guest," Isabella said quietly.

She began to rinse the cups in the sink. Oh, how strange and terrifying it was. She layered the images of de Vaca's over in her head. How would he act? Where would they go afterward? Where would Isabella hide? Then she thought of Savina drunk in bars talking to strangers—her bitterness spilling into her glass. The lonely Duke so calculating and dumb. Oh, what a beautiful night it was. People were such strange things. They seemed to sense their own tragedy, but were always being caught by surprise. They just forget and remember and forget. Savina seemed so beautifully aware of her tragedy. She was embracing her demise. She was lost in the poetry of it and relished the descent. What was it? The Serbonian Bog.

"And when was that?" said Fennel to the parakeet in the birdcage in the corner of the room. "You were five?"

He continued to pretend to talk to the bird, nodding his head in agreement. The bird stared blankly, occasionally ruffling its feathers, cricking its neck and staring back at Fennel with black-eyed nothingness. If only he had just let his sister come here alone. The Raven could be squawking and maligning the far corners of Barrenwood. How much time did he have left anyway? This could be the last free day for some time, and of all things, he was listening to the prattling of this codger mind.

Isabella signaled it was time to leave. Fennel said goodbye to the parakeet and gathered his top hat and cane. As they put their things together, they heard at the far end of their ears the sound of horses and a carriage—the clop of hooves and the pulling up of eight legs from mud—and with that sound came a most peculiar smell: gasoline. A door of the carriage opened, and as the heavy feet of the passenger made its way out of the carriage, they knew whoever it was was coming in the front door.

The twins looked at each other. They knew what to do. They rushed into the living room. Fennel flung his cane and top hat to the side and pulled off his jacket. Isabella pulled her robe up over her head. They rushed to sit on the divan just in time to witness the front door burst open in a hot rush of gas and heat.

Following fast behind the door, was the Duke of Izmir. He was massive. His muscles bulged against his clothing and his frame far exceeded the scale of the doorway itself. His face was red and the veins in his forehead were bursting. He came flying across the room, not even noticing the twins and barreled down the hall toward the bedroom, his body squished between its walls. Accompanying his entrance, mixed with the steam of petrol and the acrid stench of coal, came the twisted sensations of illness. Both Fennel and Isabella felt it. They looked at each other as perspiration hit their foreheads.

"The sickness." Fennel whispered.

"Get out of here!" they heard Savina scream, her voice harsh and terrifying, then the crash of something breaking against a wall, then something else breaking.

"Don't be so out of your mind, my love. I came for you. I can't be out there without you. Come with me. Come with me. I'm tired of living this lie. You are my everything."

The Duke's pleas came out low but desperate. He was distraught.

"I told you never come here! I told you that! Now get out! I need my sleep, you monster!"

"You are just drunk, my love. Such an angry drunk."

"No, you are! Look at you. Smell you. You're like a distillery at an oil refinery. Disgusting! Get out of here!"

"I need you. Come to my home and stay with me tonight. I am tired of this."

"I'm tired! I'm tired of everything. I'm tired of your pathetic pleas. I'm tired of the night. Just get out of here!"

There was silence interspersed with the faint sounds of sobbing—the rattle of a tired long sadness. Fennel wiped his brow with his handkerchief while Isabella snuck to the kitchen for a glass of water. This mysterious figure had arrived and she didn't want her soon-to-arrive hallucinations to put a damper on the moment.

"Let me put some music on for you."

The scratch of a needle on vinyl, and then amplified sound—the electric guitar twitting away on small semi-broken speakers. Fleetwood Mac began to fill the house, the voice of Stevie Nicks filling the halls as the temperature in the house got hotter. It was melodic, beautiful, sad and sensuous—the sordid dreams of the 1970s playing across the night in a dingy apartment in the District of Jed.

As the record player played, there was otherwise silence. Isabella and Fennel looked at each other. Had the pair gotten over their anger and found time for each other's sweet embrace? Before too much time had passed, the air screeched with the sound of Savina's voice.

"No! I said get out!"

They heard the two making their way down the hall in a quick pace. In a burst of hugeness, the Duke came into the diminutive living room with Savina trying to shove him out the door. His shirt hung open unbuttoned and a world of hair and sweat protruded. Savina stood tiny against the frame of this man and yet with every push, his body reeled. As he made his way backward into the living room, he nearly fell onto the gaunt twins. Suddenly his eyes looked back and for the first time, caught them in his sights. His eyes twisted in confusion and he picked up Fennel in the quickest of motions and held him in the air with one arm.

"Did you suddenly have more children, Savina?!" he said, a strange smile on his lips.

Savina took the sight of Fennel and Isabella into account, took a deep breath and looked straight back at the Duke.

"I took them in. They are mine. They are my new children." She stretched out her arms as though holding the world. "I'm the earth's most dissolute mother. I take it all in, my prince, the lonely, the cold and if you are good, even you. But tonight, I have these children—torn from the burden of the street without anyone to care for them. I alone took them in and I must care for them. They are my world. This is my home. Not yours. What I do here is for my life, not yours. You might hold the world in your hand, but this little grain of sand that you stand in has escaped. Has slipped. You cannot hold it and I will always own it. These are my children. Frighten them no longer. You're not to be here!"

"We're orphans, sir!" said Fennel, hanging from the Duke's one arm. It was everything he could muster to put a smile on his lips, but he did so all the same. This man was a no-go zone for Marty and his stomach knew it. While his face turned green, he looked like a puppet in the arms of a giant.

84

The Duke eyed Fennel curiously and then burped up a mouthful of smoke.

"Orphans," he laughed and put Fennel down on the Turkish rug in the living room. Fennel kicked his feet and did a small jig.

"We can dance for our accommodations if it will please you, sir!" he said. He did his best to put on his show, but his feet were sloppy under him. He fell on the floor and Isabella instantly noticed the rapidly shifting health of her brother. She lay back on the couch watching the light fade in the room.

Savina rushed her way between the twins and the Duke, casting her arms back in a protective position. Her voice suddenly went low. "Go, Sebastian. Our time will come," she said, kissing his sweaty forehead. "I told you there is much that you don't understand. I will see you soon, da Vaca's, one week's time and we will have our fun."

"Fun," smirked the Duke. "You are everything in the world to me except fun. I will leave you to your shabby orphans for now, but I can't tolerate this game much longer. You will be mine and that will be the end of it."

He leaned down to one knee and kissed Savina's hand. He looked over at the twins spilled out on the floor. They were a mess and he was dead drunk—but something, something wasn't right. He could sense it. He sniffed the air, took it in his nostrils and the twins watched them flare. His eyes creased and the look on his face changed.

"Wait a minute," he mumbled in a low tone.

"Get out!" screamed Savina.

She hit him on the side of the head making him snap out of whatever he was thinking. He looked back at her and smiled. He reached out and mussed her hair and then quick as a bat retreated out the tiny door. It thudded with such pressure that a sweet plaster trinket of a girl in a kimono fell off the mantel. Isabella caught it and handed it to Savina.

"Thank you for protecting us," she said. Isabella curtsied and Fennel bowed holding his stomach.

"We are forever in your debt," he joined in.

Savina waved her hands as though shooing them away. "Oh, little angels, the games you play. Not just with me but with yourselves. You're more lost than you know. I'm no earth mother. I'm just glad you were here to get that boozer outta the house."

Savina went to the kitchen and poured herself a glass of vodka. She threw it back in one motion, cleaned her lips with her forearm and lit up a cigarette. She stared at the twins as she made her way back into the room, her thin shadow like a knife in the fluorescent kitchen light.

"That big bum is now headed to his pretentious mansion and you two sit here haunting me as though the world would end."

Fennel gathered together his cane and his top hat. He walked up to her ever so delicately and tipped his hat. "You," he said with dramatic pause, "are not one to forget."

Savina coughed and smiled. "Neither are you two monsters. Now get outta here so I can get some sleep."

She pulled the robe from Isabella's head and then ever so gently, pushed them to the door.

"I must sleep. I truly must. I am sure I told you this numerous times. I'm tired." And she was. Her eyes were ever so low and her posture exhausted. Before shutting the door, she leaned down and looked into Isabella's eyes. "Such dark pools, my little girl. Remember, they don't know anything. They never will. Your truths are in you and you've always known 'em." And with that, she flicked her cigarette and slammed the door shut.

Suddenly the twins found themselves out the front door, in the night, wondering what exactly had just happened. Fennel walked straight out to the street and retched. Isabella didn't make it that far. She vomited off the side of the porch. Their bile blew out and sank into the garbage-strewn mud. Isabella stumbled over to her brother and patted him on the back. Besides their puking, the night was quiet. It was late. The District of Jed did not care about the twins' antics. Silently they made their way down the road until like all things, they came back to themselves and began their chatter.

"That Duke is bad news. I feel like crap, sis."

Isabella was shell-shocked. Her mind moved at a mile a minute. Even sick, her heart raced with excitement. "Can you believe it? That Duke is sure as fire. Did you notice he was sensing us at the end? He sniffed at the air. He literally put his nose in the air and took a big whiff. He was doing what we do! And Savina, she moved from the serum to waking without missing a beat. She seems to live in some netherworld. She didn't act at all surprised to see us in the house. She is altogether unique. Special. No wonder the Duke wants her so."

Fennel looked at her most cross. "He is rather pathetic, isn't he? All whiny and gropey for that tormented little number. I will not admit he is like us. That is something that you have to fool yourself into. I, for one, would never grope for a person like that. That kind of behavior is reserved for imbeciles if you ask me. And also, this sickness, I don't relish it."

Isabella hated this illness—their meeting with the Duke so brief yet she had almost left the realm of awareness. How could she continue her quest in this state? It was unfair—Marty chaining them so. And now, somehow, cracks had begun to appear in the invisible wall the corralled

86

her and her brother. Nothing had ever prepared her for this ; the fact that not only had Savina not been surprised by them, but also didn't really seem to care; the fact that in that instance of staring into Isabella's eyes, Isabella had, for the first time in her life, found someone who actually had something to tell her; and the fact that it had all happened so fast and so strangely without her being the slightest bit in control.

"It was amazing," she said in stupefied awe, walking like a zombie through the street.

"It was an amazing disaster!" said Fennel, clumsily clicking his heels together and pointing his cane at the moon. "That Duke is a behemoth, a Gollum! What kind of man is that size and what is that smell? What kind of uncanny world do they live in I wonder?"

"They are rather magical. I think they are deeply in love, Fennel. It is beautiful."

"I think it is rather beautiful, too, sweet sister. I'm no cynic, you know. I love, love just the same as any other good ol' love lover." Fennel kissed Isabella on the cheek and laughed. He was glad to be out with his sister. His health had already begun to churn in his veins and the eve's events had him feeling right as rain. Perhaps all was well after all. He could maybe leave her alone again. He did have much to attend to as well.

"I'm thinking of paying Derrilous a visit tomorrow. I have concerns about that solution. It seemed frail. I can't imagine he has been lax in his derivatives, yet the situation of our dear Savina's awareness begs to differ. Correct?"

"I don't think so. She is an exception, clearly. She has strength in ways we don't understand. Couldn't you see that?"

"Right. I see. Well, regardless, I will be stopping by. We have a new toxin in the tub! The toxin of the Toil! I truly can't wait. I've been waiting for this for some time. We could really get that sculpture we always wanted in the park. I just need to keep working on that committee. You see, Isabella, I wanted to surprise you, but I can't resist the temptation to talk about it. You see, well, this toxin, the Toxin of the Toil! "Fennel raised his arms as though presenting it to an audience. "Nice ring to the name, huh?"

"What does it mean, Fennel?"

"Oh, mean? Well, let's see, it is in reference to that magic I want unveiled! *Comprendo*? Now, this toxin will allow me to implant images in the architect's mind. I can actually show him diagrams and charts and blueprints, my bottom, whatever, and he will have it sitting in there like a monk—sitting in his mind refusing to leave. He will, of course, be convinced that this is divine inspiration! A message from God! A message from on high! He may even run to the cathedrals and basilicas and confess his new wisdom! And we will have our monument. He will build it for sure!"

"Sounds very inspiring. I hope this toxin is up to the task, but you realize, that will take some considerable time. And I must admit I have some reservations about the return of our dear benefactor."

Fennel's face became a little troubled. His brow creased. He was determined to not let this ruin his current jubilation. Oh, this Marty business!

"He won't know. How could he? He never pays attention to what's happening in town. Not to mention, once the seed is buried, I can just let it grow without assistance. I am the gardener! I'll just continue the service and da-da-da-lee, what's that? The Statue of the Toil!"

Isabella let it drop. Why should she bring up what they both knew? The day would come soon enough. There was a feeling about Marty that he simply knew. He would know. They both felt it. No real reason to ask why or how, he just would know. Let Fennel do as he will. She had given in as well. If only Marty would just stay at the carnival. If only he would stay in some whorehouse and never come out. Nope. No idea what he did there and so, no idea how long it required. Two more weeks was all she needed. Two more weeks and she was sure something would just crawl up on her lap.

They walked alone in silence and headed back to the boat. The night was ending. They crept inside, untied and set off from the dock. Isabella placed another soft Gypsy song of mourning on the phonograph and Fennel paddled. The crickets chirped along in the drizzle of the river. The boat rocked gently and the fireflies darted in and out along the banks. They watched the late night Vietnamese restaurants with butchered duck in the window; the beleaguered couples leaving the clubs and the rats scurry along the gutters beside them; the slippery salesmen on the corner with herbs and ointments and the mist along the hobos' legs.

As Barrenwood faded, they headed deep into the morass. The vines and Manzanita rose along the banks and the river widened its maw. The sound of mosquitos rose and the gurgle of the water returned. Isabella placed the film projector on the crane and raised it up into the air almost twenty feet above their heads. She pressed play and the black and white image projected onto the face of the black water. The films looked nice along the back of the water—granulated Cossacks danced jubilantly in a shoddy village center. Their dancing would vibrate and bend to the current and the feeling was soothing. They watched quietly and thoughtfully. The sound of the oboe played darkly with them.

Fennel cut some cheese and they ate and floated and listened. The moon overhead was envious and the night faded into light.

Chapter 8

They awoke with the night sitting on their chests. Their eyes popped open to stare into the shadows of clouds idling by on the cave ceiling above. Isabella woke to the sound of Savina's voice in her ear. It hummed like a scratchy Nina Simone with murmurings of oddball maternalisms. She could smell the Duke's gasoline—a cologne infernal. It hung in her nostrils as a mnemonic for her kin.

Fennel, on the other hand, had the whole thing out of sight and out of mind. He needed a circus. This much he knew. He had toyed with the idea of a lone travelling psychic or snake oil salesman, someone who was in the habit of deceiving the masses; but in the end, the circus—with its gear, tent, and folio of activitives—couldn't help but win out. He woke to the smell of catfish out in the water.

The cave seemed to go on and on into the mountain. A tunnel did lead out the back of the cave and crept far into the mountainside toward a place that only brought the twins more sickness. They basically stayed in the front entry area. A small plaid couch, a simple fire pit, a large bathtub, some desks, piles of books scattered here and there, and two wardrobes pretty much comprised their belongings. Fennel possessed an extensive wardrobe of which every item was black with an occasional hint of red. Isabella's clothes lay in a folded pile on the floor and were much more modest in quantity and taste.

Fennel began to prepare for the evening. Initially he took his bath, dried himself and spent twenty minutes deciding on his clothes. The clothes had to be perfect and tonight not only would they have to look impressive, but they would have to be fairly resistant to most acids and dyes.

For Isabella, the evening held out more opportunities to extend her ever-unfolding mission. The illustrious Persembes were scheduled to visit in all their regalia, and fortunately, their arrival fell on the day that Fennel planned on meeting with the alchemist. She had no intention of seeing that OCD nutjob. She was eager to further her investigations. Hopefully, they had come up with something.

"Don't forget the retardant leisurewear, dear sis." Fennel was now shining his shoes. Isabella was still writing and not even out of her pajamas.

"I'm hoping I won't have to attend."

"Why is that? Are you still intimidated by the brazen scientist? The last man of the enlightenment?"

"Yes. That's it. I'm terrified," she said sarcastically, trying to maintain concentration.

"Well, I can never understand your distaste for him. He's just a little mad. But, what is wrong with madness? I think humans tend to be more interesting and charming when they have had the strength to resign. Every time we visit he never fails in surprising me. And not to mention, he is the lifeblood of our schemes. Where would we be without him? Huh?"

Isabella put her book down and began to change her clothes. She had no desire to enter this conversation but didn't feel like listening to Fennel go on and on.

"It's not madness, first of all. He's simply crude not mysterious. As for his supposed genius, that is very true. He has been a great benefit to us, and that being the case we wouldn't want to lose his help because I am unable to restrain myself and say something I shouldn't? Right? I, personally, see no reason to respect the genius of invention. It hardly interests me personally. I simply utilize such things like I do a fork. Anyway, I am hoping the Persembes make an appearance. They should have arrived last night. I'm somewhat concerned."

"Ah, you're so sweet. Don't worry. I doubt much could trouble those demons that they haven't been through before. Yes, come to think of it, I think we may go our own ways tonight. It appears we have our own business to attend to."

Fennel chafed at his statement. He told himself that he meant it. Another night apart and she would probably be off moving toward that sickness. The thought of it still made his stomach turn. But, necessity called. He did have a lot to attend to. Can't live with 'em, can't live without 'em, as the saying goes.

There just wasn't much time left. Then again, he really didn't mind when Marty was around. Not as much as Isabella did. Marty could be funny if you appreciated his old world sense of ribald humor. Full to the brim with morbidity, his laughter struck Fennel as something to aspire to. The chores and missions he sent them on were generally of a business he could not comprehend, but he knew that behind every one lay a devilish plot. He was sure of it. But tonight, he needed to work on the statue. It must get off the ground. It would be a monument to his mind. Surely, he had a right to be a city planner amongst all those morons. Couldn't he present the world with a modicum of brilliance? They needed it.

"When that statue goes up, I think we will see ourselves differently, Isabella."

They set out in the boat and played their songs. The music drifted into the dripping leaves and piled undergrowth. Heinrich could hear them arriving before their boat appeared from around the bend.

"Good evening, monsieur and mademoiselle."

"Evening, Heinrich? What are the specials?" Fennel jumped from the boat and secured it.

"Tonight we have a phenomenal fresh Bronzino."

"Fresh? When did the fish arrive?"

"This morning."

"Oh, okay. I wish you could catch them as we arrived, Heinrich. That would be more to my liking. See if you can arrange that."

"I'll do what I can." Heinrich would endure Fennel's ludicrous demands. "The Persembes showed up an hour ago and I told them I wasn't sure if you would be in."

Isabella's eyes lit up. Thank goodness! "Very good, Heinrich, I appreciate your discretion. If you could take the ladies to the Burgundy Salon. Fennel and I will have our supper and I will accompany them once we are through."

"Very well. Shall we go?"

Isabella looked at Fennel and smiled. He looked so cute. Generally, his feelings were more apparent than his cravat, but she could tell he was unusually self-absorbed. It made her feel warm and compassionate toward him. She placed her napkin on her lap.

"You would make a wonderful architect. Have you ever considered it?"

"At times. Such things do require an enviable dedication to precision. I respect that in art forms, especially art forms of size. I have lately been fascinated with weight and size. I just want to be a part in creating very, very large objects. Objects that dominate the landscape and condemn the viewer. Art forms more akin to the cloak of evening and the ubiquitous of rain."

"Art forms more akin to battlefields?"

"Well, not as wretched, but definitely as devastating. I appreciate the design of cultural intention. It is my weak spot—just like a curvature of the road that moves rainwater to certain puddles; just like the layout of a home that has families walking a certain distance to use the restroom. It is the shaping hand. I simply want to place my own design into the scheme. But mine will not ease their conscience, such a dreaded occupation of theirs. I would remind and awaken. Sculptures of smelling salt that invigorate the blood."

"The tragedian. Are you having the special?"

"Yes, yes. I wanted to tell you, Isabella, that I hope all goes well with the Persembes."

Ah, Isabella thought, my brother is trying out being sympathetic. It was rare and when it did come, it came in awkward jolts. She appreciated it, of course.

"Thank you. I wish you luck with the Toxin of The Toil!"

He looked down quietly. They ordered dinner and talked of the past. They moved towards more usual topics and let the evening return to its languourous routine.

Soon it was time to head out into the evening. Isabella wished Fennel well on his project and made her way to the Burgundy Salon. She was very excited and had to concentrate to keep from running. The Persembes were perhaps (although they themselves did not know it) a primary part of her investigations into the machinations of Barrenwood. She had seduced these ladies of refinement into her service and their progress was essential to her plans. A city was a mystery and there was no mystery larger, more knackered, than Barrenwood—an urbanism resting outside of time, its foundation a bedrock of humanity and inhumanity. To solve the city, Isabella was ready to use whatever skills were at her disposal and these ebullient monarchical women were part of her forensics kit.

Heinrich accompanied her to the Burgundy Salon, past the velvet curtains and Do Not Enter signs. Upon entry, the Turkish women rose to their feet. Isabella took on her public look of contempt and nodded at them. There were three of them all adorned in the finest of gowns, glimmering with jewels and nearly reeking of perfume. Baroque and bedazzled, they presented a dangerous ensemble. There was Rana, Sibel, and Yosune. Isabella had known them for some time and their interest in her had never waned. She was a source of curiosity for them and Isabella did her utmost to maintain the mystique.

This trio was a constant source of attention throughout the great Houses in large part because, as three sisters in their teens, they could do nothing but cause attention—their every move bordered on scandal for the all too bored denizens of Barrenwood royalty. Rather than abhor it, the sisters adored the attention. They were troublemakers par excellence, moving from heartbreak to breakfast in an ever-pressing desire to escape the tedium that came with their position. They went from ball to ball, charity event to wedding, suffering through it all as if it was the most arduous of labors.

Isabelle could taste their ennui, their dry palates. It was in a sense the opposite of the water she cherished. Their tragedies were thin, flat, without calories. Their desires manifested as mere masquerades, their demonstrative tantrums barely raising their temperature. The boredom that rotted inside them was visible on the surface. They were dry, dry as a caked riverbed in the hot Georgia sun. A strange game of anxiety and desperation was always on their minds. In many ways, their parched qualities reminded Isabella ever so faintly of herself. At least she could sense it, but like them she craved it nonetheless. The tangy feeling in her mouth was the sign of a soulless dehydration.

The Persembe Family was the youngest of the great Houses. They had arrived in exile from the refuse of a good idea gone wrong—a people's revolution turned anti-aristocracy. Cries of "off with their heads" encouraged the extended family to head out with buckets of ducats. They had vast sums of money from a long line that had ruled the badlands of Xerxes so long ago. They were royalty and always intended to be so. Even if they were outside their original homeland, in Barrenwood they had set up camp a few generations back. The patriarchs were brutal before and they were brutal now. They knew, as Machiavelli had wisely stated, that fear was an emotion that exceeded love when it came to power—and thus fear was cultivated.

This reputation lived with them today although the sisters had not one drop of that attitude. They had been long removed from that tradition. These daughters were the apple of their father's menacing eye. In one hand he held an iron fist for those under him, and for his daughters an open pocket book.

The sisters were very much part of the inner workings of the city, but more importantly, society itself. What their father possessed in force, they compensated with social tenacity. Their father ruled with the assistance and might of his younger brother who strode the world as a giant. Gengils was his name—Gengils, as in Gengils Kahn, spreader of seed and conquest. His brother's infamy in the city was well known, but he merely stood behind every word of Anuk Persembe. Behind every word—a stick.

The four major houses were House Persembe, House Ellington, House Imbetta, and House Revan, which served as the leading house of them all. Like all ruling houses, they pretty much detested each other and yet also only saw each other. There remained under these great Houses, a vast array of minor houses, including Caliban, Percy, Darkglass, Gent, Nero, Chillbach, and Netherton.

Yosune was the eldest sister. A sandy brunette with sharp cheekbones and large chestnut eyes, her personality blended the arduous qualities of stern boredom. As the eldest, she had unfortunately found her role as the enforcer of order and sanity in a variety of situations untenable. Thus, her disposition moved toward the dependable yet moody. The ring on her finger told of an engagement awaited to a man she barely knew. She would stare at it often and wonder if that finger actually belonged to her. Just a finger with a ring. She would marry. She wouldn't complain. Going through the motions was her destiny and she had no urge to fight it.

Rana, on the other hand, was dark venom. With abundant black hair that seemed to not know which way to go, she was not only boy crazy, she was girl crazy and world crazy all at the same time. Her appetite was only matched by her fast moving anxiety. She could almost be described as incredibly beautiful, but her appetite for drink, cigarettes, food and everything else in life made her a little rounded on the edges. She laughed often even when she found nothing funny. She liked being disheveled because it often offended people and offending people was entertainment. She loved being royalty and hated it. She loved not having to work and knew if she weren't rich, she would be destitute. She had no skills to speak of. In fact, she avoided learning anything. Her attitude toward life was an almost negative form of learning. Isabella saw much of herself in Rana, but not necessarily the parts that she wanted to cultivate. If anything, Rana put forth elements many wanted to keep at bay.

And finally, Sibel, the youngest, the mouse, was assumed sweet because she rarely spoke. The darling of House Persembe, she was the apple of her father's bellicose eye. She always had a book in her bag and while the other two prattled on, she was often in the corner reading or writing in her journal about boys. Her eyes would stare at the page with an odd ferocity and her chittering teeth would be at work chewing on her nails nearly down to the quick.

"Good evening, ladies," Isabella stated coldly as she made her way into the Burgundy Salon to take her place at the front of the room. She shuffled onto her seat and set her shoulders straight. The sisters bowed low before her.

"Good evening, Lady Isabella," the sisters said in unison.

"Please grab a chair. Heinrich, could you please fetch me some grape juice? I trust Heinrich has provided all of you with drinks? Good. Before we get to the business at hand, let's get to the real point of this meeting. Gossip, anyone?"

The girls laughed and wiggled in their seats. It was all a little high school like, but the subject was dirt. They loved dirt.

"First, let me say, dear Isabella, that I am already drunk, said Rana, her hair whipping about the room in spasmodic shifts. "Yes, it is true. Drunk in that way when the first touch of alcohol hits your lips and the intoxication runs right through your veins. I have that feeling. Right now. That said, if I had to be a snob, which I don't have to be, but if I did, it must be said that they should import from Condillac Ranch which has a far superior collection. What is the gent's name? Hazmat?"

"Heinrich," Isabella corrected.

"Yes, Heinrich. I will let him know. This place deserves a far superior array."

Isabella stared blankly at the trio. "That isn't dirt. It's pretense."

Rana blushed. Her bold gallantry never usually backfired, but with Isabella, she was used to being put in her place.

"True enough," said Yosune piping up. "As you are most aware, Lady Isabella, we are sadly only privy to the rumors and innuendos of our tired houses up in the hills. It is for this very reason we are enjoying our precious time with you. So I hope you will indulge me if all we can say is what is happening up on high languishes in the realm of dullards."

"I don't expect any less. As boring as your rumors and lives are I am all ears for your situation. Rumors from the houses are more or less what I expect from you. Do you think I come to you to hear about actual meaningful subjects?" said Isabella. They didn't know if it was an insult or fact. For Isabella, there really was little difference. She looked down on them with her flat black eyes.

"Okay. Okay. Let me start," said Yosune. She didn't want to displease Isabella. She knew this small creature was more temperamental than she appeared. "Let's see, it is rumored that Faroos Imbetta is quite ill. He has been shut up in the attic of the home with the good doctor of Valencia."

"Oh, don't start with that," broke in Rana. Her impatience rarely surprised anyone. "That old man has been ill since we were born. That is just how he looks. It's not news to say an old man is ill, for god's sake. They are always ill. Ugh. If that is news I could shoot myself right now."

Yosune narrowed her eyes on her sister. It was a classic look that said keep-it-together. "I have it on good authority this time it isn't just a case of age. That would make their daughter Fereshteh the head of the house, which is only reasonable since she pretty much runs it anyway."

"I actually like her," said Sibel as though coming out of a daze. She had been staring at Isabella's chest to confirm that she actually breathed. As of now, she still couldn't tell.

"So do I," nodded back Yosune.

Rana interjected a little more quietly. "So now you know, there is an old man not well. Well, that is all fine and good, but I have heard that Minasha Darkglass has been even more strange than usual. The longstanding rumor, if longstanding rumors are okay to say in this room, is that she plays with dark magic, but let's face it, wearing bones around your neck certainly invites that kind of gossip, don't you think?"

95

Sibel giggled, "She sure smells like magic, doesn't she?"

The girls all laughed. Minasha Darkglass was, in fact, all magic after all.

Isabella raised her eyebrow. She hadn't expected the name of Minasha Darkglass to come up without her prodding and having it emerge on its own made things all the sweeter.

"I want to know more about this Minasha Darkglass. Besides the fact that she dresses odd, do you have anything else? Surely that is gossip, but it doesn't strike me as any with merit."

Yosune started in. "It is useful to note that most of the daughters of the great Houses have all spent a fairly significant amount of time together. While there are numerous families we have experienced enough get-togethers to have us all corralled together. We have played with Sasha and Melissa Revan, though they are much older than us; Carly Revan, who is more our age and a pretentious little twat; Marilyn and Chelsea Revan who are the children of mean man Blount (and didn't Chelsea get put in the loony bin? That is a different piece of gossip); Fereshteh Imbetta who is amazing, I think anyone would agree; Jane Ellington, although she has a new surname because she married that plebian . . . "

"Stop, it. I think it is romantic," interrupted Rana again.

". . . and Casper Caliban the closeted lesbian," continued Yosune. "Whew! And those are just a few of the ladies of some of the houses. Now this is all to say that we have spent plenty of time with Minasha as well (even if she is much older than us), and we have watched her get stranger and stranger over the years. She is daughter to the King, and the firstborn, but, believe me, no one in House Revan wishes anything more than to scoot her out of sight. Nevertheless, she is smart and vicious while her brother and heir is a fat childish runt. He garners no respect and it is common knowledge that no one wants him in charge when his daddy passes. But then again, they can't have the black witch Minasha in charge either, so no one is sure what to do.

"Minasha married the noble, and boring, Benjamin Darkglass. They have three kids: China, Money and Monkey. She has become all the more gaunt and strange, confirming perhaps one of the more juicy pieces of gossip that have circulated for many years. It is such common gossip among the houses I just realized someone like yourself might not know it."

For the record, Isabella did not know any of this. Barrenwood was still a little new to her. Marty being gone had given her an open invitation to the heart of the city and she was ready to dissect it several times. Here she had these ladies opening up to her and she would cultivate it enough to get to who knew what.

"Oh, I know!" said Rana excitedly. "Right, of course. That is actually something interesting. Perhaps Isabella could do something with this. Can I tell it? Please?" Rana put her hands together and began whispering in the ears of her sisters. It was all a bit of a show, but so grand they acquiesced out of sheer exhaustion.

"Go on then."

Rana continued, "Okay, okay, so here it is. The rumor, which is only part of nighttime stories that our parents told us and has long circulated in the rumors of us ladies, is that House Revan communicates with the other side. You know, like with ghosts and monsters and stuff. That's why people think Minasha is a witch as well. Because the house needs one."

"Why do they need one?" asked Isabella.

"Oh," responded Rana a little flustered. "Wait, why do they need one?"

"They need one," responded Yosune, ever exasperated by the idiocy of her sisters, "because the houses aren't what they used to be and in particular House Revan. Something has changed in Barrenwood and the tide is shifting away from the traditional lines of royalty. Desperate times deserve desperate measures and that is why people believe Minasha is a witch. They believe she is talking to the other side to assist House Revan in their time of need."

"Let me be to the point," said Isabella, pouring some grape juice and letting the room sit in silence for a moment in time. "A few weeks ago, when I met with you last, I presented you with quite a substantial sum with the understanding that you would return yesterday with some information. I realize it is only a day late and I am sure there is a lengthy explanation lurking in your minds, but let me remind you that I have little time to spare in this matter. I have treated the lot of you with great leniency and generosity over the last year. You Rana, in particular, would not be alive today if it were not for me. I think it is pointless to remind you of the benefits of maintaining my friendship. And so, please, don't tell me why I wasted a day expecting you. I just want the details of what I asked for and then I will assume this occurrence shall never repeat itself."

She looked into their faces without emotion. She was used to terrifying them. She enjoyed it. They did, in fact, look scared, and it was Yosune who came forth to provide what they had found.

"My dear Lady Isabella, allow me then to simply apologize," Yosune pleaded. "Your kindness has been appreciated by all of us. You will be pleased to know that, though we may have been inexcusably late, we managed to excavate some fascinating details. Our findings should prove to be most interesting." She paused and Isabella maintained a cold silence.

"We inquired as you asked regarding Big Boy Charley's attentions. Sibel has a dear friend who works in his office and so it was not difficult to monitor his actions throughout the working day. We followed him at night and made sure he stayed at home. We did this for two weeks and not much had come of it. We had become convinced he lived a relatively ordinary life, that is, for a mayor and all. He even appeared to be remarkably committed to his wife. We didn't catch him in the act of anything suspicious whatsoever. However, you did ask us to follow up on anyone he associated with that was unfamiliar to us. Well, strangely enough, we hit upon something. It may be nothing of course, but our guts tell us it is something.

"He heads way out of town to a remote farmhouse and has his driver wait outside. He goes in for some time and then comes back out. On the first visit we thought not much of it, but on the second, we decided, like the super sleuths that we are, to stick around and see whom it was that came out of the farmhouse as well. Luck would have it that two distinct groups emerged. One which we have designated the entourage of a Mr. Castilla as they all wear matching black suits and possess dark mysterious moustaches. And the other, more mysterious perhaps than Castilla, were these mysterious dark-robed men."

"Interesting." Isabella relaxed a little and picked up her eyebrows. "A secret rendezvous of the Mayor. Okay. This is something."

"That is correct, madam. We are truly enjoying our private detective work."

"How is it you know his name is Castilla and why call his entourage that?"

"Oh, it is just our guessing game," smiled Rana. "He is clearly the big dog of the group. He is much older and the rest treat him with great deference. We also heard the carriage driver say to him, 'Watch your step. Mr. Castilla,' which is kind of a giveaway."

"Any idea what was said at the meeting?"

"Unfortunately, not a clue. We did, however, have the great luck to notice that whatever the meeting was, it was not listed in his official calendar at work. We have plenty of contacts inside who could take a look. Whatever the mayor is up to, he is being rather clandestine."

Isabella looked at the Persembes. Bringing them into her strange world had been a good idea indeed. Isabella sat pleased with herself. They loved being her detectives and she loved scaring them. They were beautiful and bored and she found them to be a phenomenal adornment to her operatic lifestyle.

"This is quite interesting indeed. You three have done well. I have another request if you don't mind."

"Don't worry about us. This is the most exciting thing we have done in ages. We find it entirely enchanting!" exclaimed Rana. Isabella looked up to notice Rana had somehow managed to refill her glass.

"Enchanting," said Isabella somberly. "That is one way to put it."

"Yes. Oh, we had just begun to think we knew or could know everyone worth knowing in Barrenwood and then the evil eye seems to fall asleep. Sure, Serkan tries to keep us out of trouble, but he is younger than he would like to think. We are our own creatures. We really survive on mystery. You have been our most treasured friend for some time now because of that."

"Not because of my money, I suppose," said Isabella.

"Oh dear no, though it is appreciated. Money isn't exactly something we have need for. I hope you're not offended," replied Yosune concerned.

"Don't be stupid," said Isabella. She looked at the three women. "Allow me to benefit you with some free words of advice. Don't be so naïve as to believe society is aware of the true interworking of Barrenwood. There are many individuals behind the dark walls of this town. I suggest you invigorate your evil eye and for your own protection, don't let it fall asleep. I would very much appreciate it if you could find your way into the life of Minasha Darkglass. I'm not so much concerned with the city now. I have shifted my attentions to your world strangely enough—the great Houses. I want to know about this witch."

The girls' faces went a little white. They didn't mind investigating the mayor and the prospect of Castilla they found most compelling, but Minasha Darkglass scared them. This task had moved away from fun.

Isabella felt she needed to encourage them. "I realize she is a terrifying woman and I am sure that you do not relish her presence, but I must tell you that you have far more access to her than I do. You would not be questioned for questioning because it is to be expected of you. Can you do this for me, my sisters of three?"

"Oh, Isabella. We think so much of you. We will do whatever you want. Yes! The sisters of three will happily query the strange lady," Rana said, throwing back her glass. Her eyes were wild, but Isabella could tell the two other sisters had acquiesced. The hunt would continue.

"But we do have a small favor to ask in return. Would you please go out with us tonight? Please?" Rana laughed.

Isabella ignored the question. Her every meeting with these ladies felt the same way to her as she felt torn between enjoying them and detesting them. It was a pain that never let her jokes or demeanor come out right.

"Tell me, what do you know about a Duke of Izmir?"

"A duke you say?" Yosune's eyes squinted and she walked about the room.

"Yes. A very large man."

Yosune looked over at the other two in thought. "I have never heard of this man. I know the Duke of Imbetta, the Duke of Chillbach, the Duke of Ellington, the Duke . . . "

"But no Duke of Izmir?"

"No, I can't say that I do. Is there something we should look into? Oh, tell me about this duke."

"No. I am not sure he exists. Don't bother with it. If you do hear anything regarding that name please tell me."

Heinrich entered with a glass of grape juice and placed it next to Isabella.

"Can I retrieve anything for you, ladies?"

"I would like another Raki-Su," Rana stated, finishing off the glass she had.

"I would as well."

Isabella sipped her drink and thought about the rest of her night. She was without Fennel. She looked over at the Persembes—her darling informants, sisters who dazzled the eyes of men and women of the court and were ever so bored, so tired. The malaise of the thin life. Their thoughts on mystery perpetually eluding them. Isabella should bring them closer. Pull them in just a little more. And in her feeling toward them, she could sense the steamy breath of Marty right there, musky, on her neck. She needed them.

"Would you ladies be interested in a night out with me?"

The Persembes were now excited. "With you? Oh, well, of course! What did you have in mind?"

"I have a little function I put on secretly in the Calliope District. I think you might enjoy it."

"A little function?" said Rana, smiling. "You really are too much, Lady Isabella. Ha! Whatever it is that you do, I can only hope to know."

Isabella smiled at Rana. "You might benefit from actually doing something yourself. It truly isn't such a miraculous thing to invent things in the world. It just requires effort."

Rana squirmed at the suggestion. "Effort? I'm allergic to such a thing. Will there be cute boys and girls and toys and drinks and scandalous creatures in the night?"

"I should think so," responded Isabella.

"Lady Isabella," Rana burst in. "Do you like boys?"

"No."

"Do you like girls?" Rana giggled.

100

"No. Nor do I like men or women. I enjoy tragedy. Tragedy allows me to love the play but not the players."

"I can see that." Yosune grabbed her Raki-Su from Heinrich. "I aspire to gain your distance at some point."

"Don't be stupid, Yosune. It is a mistake to glorify such things."

"That, too."

Rana laughed. "I aspire to drunken shamelessness! Now, being one of the players in the play of tragedy, I will take my role seriously and present the most pathetic one. I am the foil to your profound majestic qualities, Isabella."

"Without question," Yosune said incredulously.

"Ha! We still have hours of night to tolerate each other, sister. It's a sin to rush." Rana threw back her drink. She was getting drunk and feeling more herself.

"Lady Isabella, let us cause some trouble this evening. These girls don't seem to have the appropriate zeal in their work."

"Ah, work. I do wonder what that means to you." Yosune was becoming annoyed.

"Work? Did I say work? My god, I don't like that word one lick. I guess by work I mean its opposite. You know, those sins: gluttony, lust, whatever else. Fun!" said Rana.

Isabella smiled and rose from her seat. "Very good. Now let's head out to this social game."

They headed out into the streets, Isabella striding beside these three women who towered over her in all their regalia. They loved having her as company and felt a strange sense of importance from it. Their chins picked up, their steps gained an excessive boost in confidence.

Isabella, on the other hand, felt a mixture of excitement and loathing. She preferred her solitude where she could slip along the shadows, but there was no avoiding attention with this company. They were extremely attractive and presented a ludicrous display. Their attire bordered on gaudy in their excessive grandeur. One could hear traffic accidents in their laughter.

Once they reached the Aliber Bridge, Yosune hailed a carriage. They all climbed in. They headed up Rue de Blunt with its collection of patisseries, cheese mongers, and vegetable stands. The smell of fresh bread hovered in the air, leaving an aroma of coziness amidst the trample of horse hooves. They were making their way toward the Calliope District along the harbor not all that far from where they spotted the Drunken Boat night last. Large frigates and galleons began to appear along the water. The silhouettes of people dining revealed themselves along the bows.

Isabella's eyes strayed to strangers who walked in solitude against the sea salt boardwalk. Her eyes spotted an old woman in a fur coat looking in a jeweler's window, her head kinked to the side staring. Isabella sensed this woman was the last of her family. She had outlived them all and was now left looking at clues left behind. She could feel the sad loneliness in her heart. It tasted good and made Isabella sad.

Up ahead she spotted the Drunken Boat continuing its loading. She could sense the sad movement of the crazies as they moaned their way up the planks to be shuttled below. At the head of the line, she again noticed the man of the night's past who Fennel had bitten with extreme hostility. His lavish robes and elegant mannerisms easily separated him from the smarmy hooligans commandeering the vessel. The moans and laughter of the inmates clamored through the air and into Isabella's ears. A torrent and eddy. She listened to scale and breadth of their sounds. The range so broad she swooned her head to get inside it. The sounds so unprotected. Oh, what a travesty to send them into the night, but what an amazing sight this boat must be as it careened along the misty banks of the cities—a wailing reminder of a town's betrayal.

They stopped outside a magnificent residence, the Chateau de Crawler, which carried the loud music of deep rumbling bass and beats into the streets. The bass was trembling the carriage and reminded them of a heavy cauldron boiling. Suddenly the excitement began to rise and course through their Turkish veins. They began to get the jitters. The house overlooked the water and a line into the building spread out along the sidewalk. People were dressed up in evening haunting wear—the clothing of the dreadful. Deathly pale men in mascara blended with women in silk suits. The brothers of Siam with their launch chests and the Kentucky Seven were all present. It was obviously a large to-do. The windows above were glowing in blood reds and lunar blues and the smell of spices flowed about as though cascading from the chimney. Isabella footed the bill for the carriage and they barreled out right toward the front of the line.

The doorman was a rotund, cabbage eating man. He weighed more than many and his arms seemed to squeeze against the air. The ladies just plowed right into his space—personal space of which he claimed a greater ratio than most. That was their way of being entertaining. They just zoomed in on people and played beguiling tricks on their retina. They showered him with glimmering smiles, lips puckering and whiteness of teeth. Their faces were both hypnotic and unnerving in their salacious charm. He grinned his ogre grin and gestured his arms in what appeared to be a failed bow.

"Welcome, my ladies," he bellowed. "Your presence confirms that I am somewhere. I thank you for that. Good evening, Lady Isabella. It's been a while."

"Good evening, Tugboat. I've been so busy lately. I'm glad to be back though." Isabella smiled and waved adieu at they sailed into the milieu.

The mansion or derelict ranch or whatever it was opened up enormous. Entering the main stairs into the foyer, one could see a maze of rooms down just the first hall. People were already smooshed together and the smell of perfumes and cigars was layering up.

Rana grabbed Isabella's hand and raced her through the labyrinth. The Persembes were enjoying the sights. They spotted a stage in one room where above it was an old woman covered in feathers and perched in a massive golden birdcage. Below her was a lone whistling farm boy in overalls. He was whistling and doing a jig. Below the stage, people were scattered about at tables talking and watching and drinking and chirping. Many sounds of laughs and caw caws caught Isabella's ears as she whirled by. In another room, they spotted people on their hands and knees crawling about through small dark tubes that littered the floor of a monstrous room—or was it a gymnasium? The tubes seemed to lead to little huts where Isabella could faintly make out the silhouettes of people smoking at tables inside. She heard the sound of hushed whispers and the darkness in the room seemed to make everyone a conspirator past their bedtime.

Finally, Rana stopped and turned to her almost panting. "We're here. We can stop. Oh, Isabella! You are so beautiful. I die. I die right now!" Rana all of a sudden collapsed on the floor. People spread apart and she bounded up laughing. "I die for you! Blood is on your hands! You're the greatest woman. I know it! I need to drink. Why aren't I drinking?"

"Follow me, kitties. I think you might enjoy this," Isabella said as she led them down some stairs and through a door. Inside the room was a large stage adorned with a big, beautiful, blaring brass band—horns wailed, hips jived, sweat was flung, a zoot-suited gangster leaned against a microphone and howled about "The dangers you'll find on Monkey Island." People were dancing at a maddening pace. Limber body parts flung every which way and the balmy air induced a fervent social jujitsu. High up above a few obviously well-mannered monkeys were swinging from vines. Howling and laughing they augmented the luau lunacies of this mad creation. The Tiki gods were descending from the heavens and demanding complete social calamities. The crowd was appropriately bending and bowing in complete submission to the blaring music of the brass band.

Isabella nodded emphatically in approval and led the enamored sisters through the crowd to a door positioned to the side of the stage.

"It is magic! I really have never in my life!" screamed Rana on her tiptoes, looking about the crowd. "I'm swooning, sister, swooning! There is nothing more I need nor want. Just give me this any night of the week!" She fled into the crowd with arms a flinging.

The blinking sign above the door read "The Hide Out." Another cabbage eating bucket of a man was at the door. He grinned wide and with strength. His large behemoth arms scooped Isabella up and placed her inside the room. "You, you, you!" his gravely voice gurgled. "I can't believe you are here. Ah, I am so glad. You have no idea. Isabella, the nights here aren't the same without its three ring master."

"I'm sure Capperwill has taken things along the appropriate invigorating course. I really liked the darling farm boy in the other room."

"Yes, a fairly recent acquisition. He is a charmer for sure. And the Ransacking Avengers?"

"Oh, of course, they are very good, aren't they? I think I might ask them to swap out that gold lamé, but, all in all, they are doing a great job," she replied.

The Persembes scuttled in past him, giggling, cackling and spilling drinks. They tumbled down into their booth and Yosune motioned a waiter over for their drinks. She noticed that across from their booth was a large window from which she could see into the chaotic dance hall.

"Is that a one-way mirror?" she asked.

"Absolutely. Tonight we window shop," said Isabella.

"Sibel, I want Raki-Su," Yosune said. "Window shopping. I do like this. All those rooms were so exciting."

"Yes, I think so as well. It is a sort of social experiment. I play with people. Right? I play. Like I play with you. Tubes, strange hallways, people crawling on the floor on their hands and knees, monkey mayhem high above. Oh, it is all so fun and there really are so many possibilities in this life. It's my attempt to give spice, liquor and adrenaline their proper respects," said Isabella, gazing through the one way mirror. Her reflection caught her and she reminded herself, "Yes, there are *so* many possibilities."

"There are so many faces I don't recognize here," said Sibel as she stared into the sea of people. They were all so fascinating to her. This world of people with lives and sorrows and beds and homes and meals and perversities all of which she would never know flowed like undulating waves before her—little dramas in each little face. Sibel chewed her nail and imagined kissing each and every one—her mouth touching their lips, the odor of their body.

"That's because we basically go to the same party every night of our life," Yosune threw in. "Hands and knees? Oh, like us?"

"Yes. I like to see the three of you groveling low and miserably." Isabella smiled.

"Ha! I'll do that for you, whenever! Now?" laughed Rana as she bounded back amongst them. Her face was perspiring and her wet hair stuck to her cheeks. Yosune couldn't believe how little time it took for her sister to look crazy.

"Rana, stop it and help me! I need a boy. We need to focus," replied Sibel.

"Yes, let's help our suffering sister out!" laughed Yosune as she banged her legs against the table.

"I want a little poet," said Sibel.

"A little wimp?" asked Rana, grabbing drinks from the waiter. "I want a drink."

"Yes, a frail petite poet that will cringe at me," said Sibel with an odd, nearly ugly, smile. "If we are in fact window shopping, find him for me, please. That's what I want."

"I want Isabella! Isabella is the best!" said Rana. She turned to look at Isabella and smiled wide and silly. Her lips were already very wet from gin and it made her look as though she were perpetually salivating.

"Please stop that, Rana!" said Yosune "You're making me ill. Look at something else would you?"

"It's true, Rana. Look out that window. Your sister needs you," said Isabella, smiling and playing with her hair.

"Fine. Fine. You're still the best. I'll look at your reflection," Rana said as she slouched in her seat.

"I'm sorry," said Yosune, turning to Isabella.

"Don't be dumb," said Isabella. "I like her sloppy like this. What about you, Yosune? What do you want this evening?"

"I don't know. I really don't know if I want anything."

They scanned their eyes across the crowd. Isabella's head was woozy from all the exasperating faces and hints she saw. It was always like this. She both loved the bevy of idiosyncratic guests and found it psychologically exhausting. Boots, gloves, furtiveness and remorse all slid across her view. She slipped past one face and onto another, watching hands twisting shirts and could feel toes curling in socks. Her acumen in minutia came in handy but made close proximity to crowds hard on her. She would just breathe slowly like Marty had showed her and let the murky water run through her.

"It's really too much. Large menu we have here. Sibel, what about that black boy with the valise?" asked Isabella. The boy was captivatingly feminine and obvious in affected sincerity. His hands softly clutched his valise and the golden buttons down his red vest glimmered. So plush. The boy was accompanied by none other than Barrister Bruno who constantly crammed his cigar in his mouth, puffing dramatically and talking incessantly.

"Is that Barrister Bruno he is with? I didn't realize he comes here as well," said Yosune. "They must be a couple. What an amazing pair these two make. I think there is no hope for you on this one, Sibel."

"They're not. I mean, they are not a couple that is," said Isabella. "I happen to know the Barrister quite well. I know him well enough to know that he would never deign to be in any kind of stated relationship. With him, everything is tentative, tendentious, and contingent. He doesn't like to hold on to things."

"The Barrister is truly one of Barrenwood's secret stars," said Yosune.

"It's no secret," said Sibel. "Everyone knows about him. He is quite the talk of the town, but I happen to be uninterested in him at this moment. I like his pretty friend."

"I believe his name is Gregory Daniels," whispered Isabella. "He is a young poet just as you requested and I am sure Sibel would have a wonderful evening with him."

"You know of this young man?" asked Yosune impressed. "How is it that you know so much about the people of this town?"

"You sound surprised. How telling that is. Yosune, I am simply observant. I can tell a lot about people rather quickly. Not to mention, of course, that both of these gentlemen are regulars here at the Crawler. I keep tabs, of course."

Isabella raised her hand and motioned for the waiter. "Hello. Could you be so kind as to invite Barrister Bruno and company to our table?"

The waiter ducked off into the crowd. The Barrister came barreling through the crowd. He was shaking hands along the way and slapping people on the back. He truly was a Barrenwood celebrity. Isabella had produced many of the night's activities in consultation with her literary colleague. The waiter brought him and his new friend over. They were laughing about some joke or other.

"I present Barrister Bruno and Mr. Gregory Daniels," said the waiter as he offered the two with chairs.

"Evening, Isabella. Didn't see you arrive. Our paths seem to cross more frequently of late," said Bruno. He took a puff on his cigar and put out his big hand. "I see you've got the Persembes with you. Evening, ladies. I didn't know you visited such low down dirty jamborees as this."

106

Yosune smiled. She put out her hand and he kissed it. She was used to people knowing who they were. Generally such familiarity would be seen as slanderous, but it was Barrister Bruno.

"Well, to be quite honest, we were never 'in the know' about this Chateau de Crawler. Frankly, we were surprised to see you here as well. You really should tell us about such things. Our lovely Isabella is surreptitious in the extreme."

"Indeed she is. A regular shadow, I tell ya. If ya don't mind me sayin', the place is going to crap without you, Isabella."

"I know, Bruno. I've been extremely busy. I wanted to put Capperwill in charge for a while."

"Bad idea, sugar. Real bad. Caperwill may be a great manager, but not a social alchemist. That's your bag. You're the tonic and the tobacco, know what I'm sayin'? Hey, but who am I? But I gotta say, remember the door cards? Remember? Now that was great. See, ladies, Isabella here had these cards you'd get at the door and they would have secret instructions to certain rooms that required these secret cards and certain advised secret topics of discussion. Like gods or war or sex and vegetables. Oh, I don't remember. Now if you had certain cards you would be asked to do certain things by the undercover insurgents at the doors to these secret rooms. People would end up just following these things—room to room— the whole party a mass of people blubbering about the most fantastic notions and meeting the most bizarre people. A beaker. Yes, a beaker. See, if that didn't make sense, well, you just got to try it. See?

"Isabella here is a real bona fide enigma. A visionary *tout corte*. She's got the most amazing cast in this house and they're all pioneers of social experience. Isn't that true? You know, I think I should make your experiments part of my upcoming book—something about a temporary space where the rules of society go astray and that this kind of structure is, in fact, critical to the production of the city," blustered Bruno emphatically. "The city would be a kind of canvas . . . "

"Bruno, you simply must stop. You're making no sense. I won't let you bore us."

"Ha, Isabella is too funny! Too funny! See, I need you! I don't know what I'm saying." Bruno slapped the table and laughed obnoxiously.

"You most certainly do not," intruded Sibel. "Now please stop for a second. I must talk with your friend Mr. Daniels. He seems so quiet back there." Sibel smiled sweetly at Gregory and he smiled back. Even reserved as he was, he didn't appear uncomfortable.

"Great move, Sibel!" yelled Rana. "Excellent maneuver! A cheers to Sibel!" Rana raised her glass and Bruno gave her a toast. They threw back their drinks smiling goofily.

The young Gregory Daniels leaned over to Bruno and whispered. Bruno laughed and said, "Don't be silly. Don't be silly. Yes, of course! Of course!"

"I'm fine back here," he said, leaning his chair back slightly.

"Are you a poet, Mr. Daniels. I get the feeling you are."

"You get the feeling I am? What kind of feeling is that may I ask?" Gregory said with a smile on his lips.

"A beautiful feeling. A feeling of Sambuca running down the back of my throat."

"Are you having that feeling right now?" he asked, still smiling.

"Yes, yes, I am."

"Then it is quite possible that I am a poet."

"He is a poet, ladies! This guy is a lexiconic demon! He will get you swooning and crooning, I know! I know ladies. You watch yourself. He'll get ya, like he got me! Yep, huh, Greg? Huh?" Bruno was smiling and shoving his hand into Gregory's shoulder. Pushing him around. "Oh, no. That's it. He's gone!"

"Woo me, please, Mr. Daniels," said Sibel in her little girl's voice. She leaned over the table and stared deeply into the eyes of the poet.

Gregory stood up from his chair. He placed his hands over his heart. "I believe that I would be a fool to not attempt such a wooing, but I hope it will be understood if first I get a drink to prepare myself."

"That will not do at all," said Sibel. "I need sufficient wooing now!"

Rana and Yosune laughed and began to woo like the bellowing horns of a train.

"Woo woo!" they sang.

"Wooing now?" he laughed. "Demanding, aren't we? I suppose that is what you like. I will not argue, my dear. I will give only what you need and nothing more."

His voice was the irresistible mix of sarcasm and sincerity that radiated excitement. He grabbed Rana's drink and threw it back into his mouth.

"You come to this place
A full deck but no ace
Bluffing vanity as a rule
But these cards aren't giving
And meanwhile you are living
On the words of an insufferable fool

"I raise my glass high
To your beautiful eye

For you are a princess no more no less
And with a quick swallow
I beckon tomorrow
When we recline in our mutual mess. "

The Persembes laughed and Sibel blushed. A poet he certainly was and a snarky one too. Sibel stood up and threw her drink back.

"Presumptuous most certainly, but daring and dashing, too."

Sibel looked him over. The smile of his lips unwavering, he held her look with earnest fascination. She put out her hand, which he kissed most gently. The touch put shivers down her spine. She loved attention. And she loved kisses.

The table erupted in laughs. "Bravo! Bravo!" the sisters laughed hysterically.

"You're a real dandy aren't you?" smiled Sibel. "Okay, you win. You won. I'm yours. Do with me what you will, but let us get away from these women from hell. I can't stand it! You can take me to the overlook, but I warn you; be a gentleman. I tire of this unflattering company."

They scooted out of their chairs and headed into the crowd. Gregory could be seen giving a last look of satisfaction to the Barrister Bruno. Bruno raised his glass and finished it off.

Chapter 9

Fennel was busy as a bee at Derrilous's den. Beakers were abounding and fire was a spurting. Bunsen burners and smoke. Boiling and sulfur. Electric zaps and occasional giggling from the radiator. Derrilous was a fuzzy little man. He was adorned in a splotched and stained apron and he stood at the same height as Fennel—just a couple of small folk. His hair was a morass of dreadlocks that piled in a crumpled tangle on his back. Fennel paced along the back of the laboratory with goggles on and his finest fire retardant leisurewear.

"If I place this here," said Derrilous. He was utilizing some thin pliers and was attempting to place a receptacle onto the slot. "No. No. Wait. Hold it. No."

"Too late. I know it. Oh of all the times . . . what is the use? Huh, Derrilous?"

Fennel was just pacing and mumbling. Derrilous barely listening to him.

"That's it, baby. That's it. You just need to sit. Sit, please. Sit there," Derrilous's voice was breathy and wispy—a man perpetually in the throes of asthma—wheezing words and wheezing theorems, wheezing his way into another mixture. Right now he was testing the solution that Fennel had complained about. He had used the proper combination of scopolamine, thiopental sodium, and even amobarbital. He felt sure as shinola that his solution was up to par, but if that's what he wanted. He had better because the Blue Goo hadn't been finished yet and Fennel was going nutty.

"And where else do I go? Where else do I wander off to? I'm just a pacer now. I just pace. I just move the legs to the whim of the foot. Am I a troublemaker? Am I an architect? Am I anything that would make me grin? No. No. Nopa. I am a pacer. The great pacer. The walker of yards. The treadmill boy scout. Call my name and I will move back and forth for ye. I travel by night but only back and forth. He is consistent. He just likes to cover his tracks. Yes, I do. I do it for you, Mr. D. I do it for you. I move there to here to there to back again and over for you, my good doctor."

"Tighten this knob when I say, Go!" Derrilous was yelling above the sound of steam. Fennel ran over and grabbed the knob.

More concentration on the placement. Derrilous had to be sure of placement—just putting this on the proper spot and catching the solution in the heat blast should do it, but it had to be in the right place.

"Gotta be in the right place, see?" yelled Derrilous.

"What?" barked Fennel.

"Right place! Right place! All about location here! Ok. Wait . . . Now one, two . . . ahh . . . shi-oooot! No, no. Never mind! Go back. I'll call you in a little bit!"

"What's the problem?"

"I said I'll call you in a little bit! I need space. Get, get!"

Fennel walked back to his spot and sat down at the desk. He was bored and depressed. He just wanted the Blue Toil Solution done in time. His project and her project. He perched his little feet up on the desk. They were doing their own thing tonight. Independence made Fennel sad. He missed his sister. As much as he had things to do, he didn't head into them with the same kind of dismissive zeal. That's fine. He did have things to do. If this project worked out—well, she is out with those horrific women. Could they be a part of her secret? That would really be a mistake. She wouldn't be so naïve. Well, maybe she would.

Fennel thought back to the Drunken Boat. The sound of the lunatics filled his heart with a twisted pleasure. He rubbed his tummy at the feel of it. But they were taking that away. He saw it with his own eyes. He wasn't a conspiracy theorist. No, he didn't need to be. He witnessed the conspiracy right there out in the open. They were literally hauling off the few creatures that really got it. He and Isabella had seen signs of this in the past. The emergence of clocks on the street, the growing belching factories with the line of beat down men in muck, the new murmurings of equality that got the idiots excited and the police force that made it illegal to have a good time. These growing provocations bothered him immensely and placed his heart in the hands of a slightly bad mood. This city was out to get rid of the little water they produced. Evaporators. All of them.

He wiggled his toes in his shoes and looked up into the ceiling. Pipes dripped and cracks abounded. The rust was peeling back. The dust was glittering with fragments of magnesium. He saw in the cracks the image of a cat—a snaking Siamese cat in the brush. He should really look into animal vision. Marty had mentioned that when they had been fishing together. Animal vision.

"Sure, you ken see da world from a cat's eye. Sure. Ol' ol' trick, Scratch. Can't believe ya never tried it. The things you waste yur time on, boy. Look, you gotta flick the wrist like this. A snap. Now see, yu can look from a Flounder eye too. Easy. I do all da time. Get in dat water and get to checkin' tings out. I do. I just put in some rat hair, tooth, and dat pride mix. Oh, I'll show ya one day. I bet you would love it, Scratch. He he. Be a Siamese. Dems da monkey barrel. You can look up ladies' skirts with it. Sure can. Would ya like dat? Heh? I wonder if you would. You still look

111

damn faggotish to me dough. Damn awful faggotish. But ya just might like a little peek-a-boo up a grown woman's dress. Yup. Just be a little ol' missy cat prowlin' about and then snoop . . . you be under the canopy, boy . . . You can bet I do it. I do and I like it. I like it plenty."

Marty knew so many beguiling tricks. If only he would teach Fennel animal vision. He would be a cat. No, not a cat; fish would be good if it was a fish in some mansion's indoor pond. A Coy! Yes, a Coy would be hilarious—plump and orange with a top hat. Oh, he would make little fish clothes. If he had felt gloves for his tiny fins that would be too much! Too much!

Or the Cawing Cretin? Yes, the Raven could strike! Strike down poppers and drunks! One fell swoop. Animal clothes. An easy year could be spent making animal clothes. The Cawing Cretin would get thin red fringes off the wings. Let them flap about as he sails in for the kill. Swoop! How hard would that be? Animal vision. Hmm.

"Hey, Mister, what would it take to look through the eyes of an animal?"

"Just a few more seconds!" replied Derrilous.

Isabella could be a tree frog and he could be a lemming. No. They would have to be creatures that traveled at the same pace—similar leg structures or something. Birds would be best. Birds of a feather. What if they could talk with animals? Fennel almost fell out of his chair. Dr. Doolittle. Was Dr. Doolittle really alive? Oh, if he talked with the animals, maybe, maybe, they were more interesting than these sub-humans. Maybe there were secret societies of elks and turkey vultures. Of course there were! They would gather in circles and discuss foreign policy. No, nothing as droll as that. They would discuss the style of their hikes. Yes. More haiku-like. Very zenny. He would just be one of them—with his top hat of course. Ohhh, too much!

"Hey, Mr. Animal Vision!"

"Okay, yes. It's time. Now, as I said, when I say 'Go!', just give that knob a big turn." Derrilous was bent over with his pliers, attempting proper placement. Fennel jumped up and ran over to the knob.

"Here we go. Ready? Wait. Okay. Ready? One, two, three . . . Go!" screamed Derrilous.

Fennel gave the knob a big turn with both hands and steam blasted into the room. *Pssssst!* He ran for the back of the room hoping his goggles hadn't been affected by the steam. He had paid good money for the goggles. The steam cleared and Derrilous was standing there smiling his uneven toothed smile.

"I told you! I told you! Look at this, Fennel! It's perfect." Derrilous waved a tube in the air and bounced around. "I don't lead you astray."

112

"Fine, fine. You're a master of mechanics and fluids. Now, Mr. D., this doesn't do much for the Blue Toil."

"All that work to verify and all I get is a change of subject." Derrilous shook his head. "Time. Your Blue Goo will take time. I thought I had the derivatives aligned, but I still need to work on it. You can't just come in here and rush me. What do you think I do with all my time? I just work. Isn't that enough? What's wrong with you?"

"Ahh, hop to it, Mr. D! I need my mixture! Hey, what do you know about animal vision?"

"Excuse me?"

"Animal Vision. For example, can you conjure up a solution that will let me see through the eyes of a fish or a bird?"

"Animal vision? Is that what you're jabbering about? First you come to me with this wacky notion of a monk in someone's head and now we have Beastmaster. Look, I don't think you understand how completely amazed I am that this Blue Goo is going to work. It's never been done before! Do you hear that, little snot? Never before! And now, you come in here, all impatient, and you're asking to be one with the jungle. I give up! You're an ingrate. Ingratitude, my friend."

"Oh, relax, Derrilous. It's just a question. I just heard it was possible."

"Did you? Well, I suppose one can hear all kinds of things when they go creeping through the night like a little miscreant. Now, why don't you get along and haunt that person for their supposed animal vision because I'll tell you right now, it's not possible. Not only isn't it possible, but it is possibly the stupidest thing I have ever heard you say."

"I doubt that is true," laughed Fennel.

Chapter 10

"You owe me, Isabella. Pilfering my pal. What kind of hospitality is that?" gurgled the Barrister. He unbuttoned the top button of his shirt and looked around the room. "The crowd here is changing, you know, darling. This place was once the house of the houses and now it's most probably the house of the unhoused. All this new money everywhere and well, from what I can tell, they know how to party. But I digress, since you have stolen my only friend, I suppose I'll have to peek about your V.I.P. room."

"Yes, do that. Peek about," said Isabella.

"That's great for Sibel. She's always timid. It's a wonder she meets boys at all. Daddy's little girl needs a helping hand at times," said Yosune to Isabella. "Isabella, tell me more about what you do here. This place. I do recall seeing it from the street, but never for the life of me did I imagine this."

"Yes, Isabella. Tell us more! I just can't be in the dark anymore! I just can't!" said Rana.

"I told you what she does here!" said Bruno. "She conducts this experiment. What else do you want to know? Isabella, how clear do I have to make this?"

"A little clearer would probably be more helpful. Why don't you tell them, Bruno?"

What was that? She had seen something. She scanned over Yosune's head. What was it? There. Back in the back of the dance hall she saw Chelsea Revan slide in the front door. She had died her hair red and her eyes were wide with excitement and fear. She covered her head in a black lace shawl with tiny glimmering rhinestones and tried her best to hide along the wall—her face a constant look of intrigued terror. It certainly wasn't easy being this young girl.

"Now, Rana, if you were to host a social experiment, what would you do?" asked Bruno.

"Ha! If I were to host a social experiment I would have confessionals galore. People getting it all out so they could really loosen up. And something dark—something that would cast off the feeling of innocence and make us have fun as though we were all complicit in something. A sacrifice. Yes! Maybe a chicken or something. And then, yes, and then lots of drugs and a ton, a ton of dancing."

"Isabella, put this woman in charge!" said Bruno.

"I need to go. Order what you want, kiddies. It's on the house," said Isabella, getting up.

"Where are you going?" asked Yosune.

Isabella didn't respond. She just walked out on them. Her mind was focused on something else far more important. She heard the bass and the drizzle—the back legs of frogs pushing out against the water. The call of water. She would go to her private den and invite her there. She gave Tugboat instructions on her way and then ascended the stone stairs to her office. The cacophony of horns and voices faded to the clip clop of her shoes. She opened the old oak door to her room—bookshelves and a lone chair facing a window that overlooked the dance floor—from where she could watch her social architecture.

It was interesting listening to Bruno try to explain what she did here. How could they really understand? How could they know it was just a heightening of the water sound? She could feel her plans feed the volume. These evenings here had captivated her a few years ago. The revelation that she could increase the volume of the glurb and bubble completely overwhelmed her.

With haste, she had built the evenings of Chateau de Crawler into a well-established cultural catalyst, but alas the sounds only went so high. There seemed to be a ceiling on the ecstatic possibilities she produced and, in fact, with every routine day, the sound of rapids and waves crashing turned to trickles and drips. The longer she held these parties, the less she cared. What did such things matter when the Drunken Boat had stolen her sounds with no effort at all? There was so much to learn and all she had were her acute ears. She would just listen so carefully. The sound of that boat came back to her. The vagabond symphony overwhelmed her—their gestures so uncontrolled, their pitches and degrees freed from the contaminated confines she continually ran up against. The water poured over the deck and drenched the sails. Waves toppled over the bow and the moon egged them on. The lunatics sang in a captivating harpy call. Their robes drenched. Their bedraggled smiles terrifying in their unrefined honesty.

A knock at the door.

"Come in," she said and stood up from her chair. In walked Tugboat with Chelsea Revan, his bulging arms juxtaposed to her spindly freckled limbs. She cowered behind his body trying to be cool, but her shaking cigarette betraying her. "Thank you, Tugboat. I'll be fine from here," said Isabella, gesturing with her hand that Tugboat should go. Tugboat exited and shut the oak door.

"So you have made your way to see me after all, Lady Revan?"

Chelsea Revan made her way to the couch and scooched into one of its corners. She was a timid aggressive little beast. She lit up another cigarette in adolescent defiance and seemed as though she were talking to the wall. "I am spying for Auntie. Don't think I came for a social call."

Isabella grabbed a crystal ashtray, walked across the room and set it on the edge of the couch. She walked back to her chair and turned it to face Chelsea.

"Not a very clandestine spy, are you? Your techniques are quite brazen."

"So I have been told," replied Chelsea. "Quite a party you throw here. I didn't realize it was the same stupid party I had been hearing about for some time."

Isabella winced at the comment—her disdain for the little runt coming back in a flash. This time she wasn't sick. These frantic rich kids. Nothing stuck in Isabella's craw more than entitlement. She detested it like a fart. She walked over and grabbed Chelsea's overly made up face with her little hand. The muscles in her hand scared Chelsea instantly.

"One more insult, little girl, and I will make you realize why your aunt was so afraid of me. I will hurt you, Chelsea Revan. I will enjoy it as well. I find your antics quite worthy of punishing. Now behave."

Isabella stared into Chelsea's eyes and saw pools of fear in there. She let go and walked back to her seat. Chelsea's tone did in fact change from there on.

"Who are you? Aunty wants to know."

Isabella looked closely at the nervous girl. She spoke with great effort. Each word a brave desire to push back her primary emotion of fear. Sometimes the bravery to overcome one's self, the ability to utter a single word, could be more heroic than any wartime effort or sporting act. For Chelsea, her interior struggles manifested visibly on her freckled visage.

Isabella could tell quite quickly that Chelsea's aunt, Minasha Darkglass, had not in fact asked Chelsea to visit. Chelsea couldn't help herself. She was curious beyond words. She had arrived on her own, stealing out into the night from a back window; the scrapes on her arms still visible from the branches of the tree she made her way down from her bedroom window; the mud on her shoes, a sign of her journey out across the backwoods to the gate; and the faint hint of horse hair, the sign that she had ridden a steed out of the Elegiac Hills into town. The tips of her fingers still were red from the hair dye that she had applied in a mad desire to go undercover (but also, of course, to enjoy changing her hair color). Isabella had a renegade on her hands.

"Answering who I am may prove most difficult as it is a rather large question, but let me make a deal with you. You tell me a few things and I

116

will tell you a few in trade. Some would call it getting to know each other. That sounds rather civil, doesn't it?"

Chelsea continued to stare at the wall and proceeded onto her second cigarette. "I'm here for Aunty," she said. "What family do you come from?"

Isabella had to laugh inside. When it came to her life, all the simple questions proved difficult and all the large metaphysical ones were answered with alacrity and grace. Perhaps the truth would be the quickest road.

"My family? It may come as a surprise to you, but in all honesty, that is a question that is hardest for me to answer. I have a brother my age who is rather precocious. I have a stepfather who is a most awful man. But my lineage is unknown to me. I suspect my stepfather may know it, but he bottles it up inside. That said, we don't come from any great line or anything like that. Most certainly not like you. If anything I would hazard to say we are refugees."

Chelsea nodded absent-mindedly. It was hard to tell if she was listening at all. Isabella spoke up. "I want to know about your aunt. I don't need to know anything super serious. Just basic things like what is on her mind. I find her most fascinating."

"She is, isn't she?" said Chelsea, looking over at Isabella. She looked so tired.

"She most certainly is," responded Isabella. "She seems unafraid of the world. A rather defiant figure. She doesn't look back. She doesn't trouble herself with the stupid antics of the monarchy and invests her time in larger questions. She isn't afraid of seeming strange."

"Exactly." Whispered Chelsea.

"So, what is on her mind of late?" asked Isabella. "Can I offer you something to drink?"

"One thing that people don't understand," said Chelsea, still looking at the wall and ignoring Isabella's second question. "If anyone, Aunty is the only one actually trying to save the great Houses. They think she is a renegade but she is actually the biggest patriot. Lord knows why. That is the part I don't understand. Who would spend so much time on people that vilify you? The kind of bile she has to tolerate. Makes you sick. But that is her way. She is actually the only one with enough sense to be preparing for the war to come. Is this your office?" Chelsea Revan got up from the couch and walked over to the bookshelves. She placed her red stained finger on the spines and read the titles.

"Yes. I am an avid reader. Books are mutators. Without them, power uses us as a vessel. Well, at least that is my opinion."

"Power uses you as a vessel without books." Chelsea stopped to think about that. "Is that my problem? Perhaps I should read more!" She laughed. "I will take a small glass of red wine if you have it."

Isabella went to the cabinet and poured the girl a glass. A girl like this could get most strange with a little alcohol in her.

"Aunty knows about you. She says you are dangerous and destructive; that you are moody and that you are not dependable; that you are powerful and that you are stupid. She says that people like you are important to us but that as soon as we depend on you, you betray us. She says I should stay as far away from you as possible. Haha."

Not a bad description thought Isabella. "I'm not the enemy she makes me out to be," said Isabella.

"I'll be the judge of that," replied Chelsea.

"Judge as you like, Chelsea Revan. What is this war that is to come?" Isabella couldn't tell if it was a euphemism or a reality. Yosune Persembe had mentioned that Minasha was being used because the great Houses were in trouble. That they believed she is 'talking to the other side to assist House Revan in their time of need'—because the great Houses were faltering.

"Ha-ha! I don't know. Aunty senses a war. She hints at it all the time. She says we are all in danger and that the enemy is in our midst—that the houses are asleep and that we are heading quickly into a state of war. That we must prepare."

"A war with who?" asked Isabella. Surely that is a piece of information worth knowing.

"Really? You ask me that?" laughed Chelsea Revan, throwing herself on the couch. "I thought it was with you!"

The comment caught Isabella off guard. She didn't know what to make of it. What bothered her perhaps more than anything was her inability to get a full read on this girl. She could play games with words and sometimes said them just to try out how they felt on her tongue. Rolled them around and then spit them out into the world, a raw pulp of syllables playing alongside the bass from the dance floor in the other room. It might be best to discount the interpretations of this mentally unfit lass.

"If you had a war with me," smiled Isabella. "You would know."

Chelsea Revan laughed at that. "What a strange little creature you are—all confident, proud and sure. You sit on your high throne and beckon the world like the Queen of Sheba. What on earth makes that possible? Hee hee. A war with you. A war with you! I don't even know what that might mean. Do you have a secret army you could summon to fight off our high guard? Do you have some evil spells that you could cast like Aunty and turn us all to rot?

"Actually, I think if a war did come, I would run. I'm not ashamed to say it. I don't even care if the families go down in flames. What is it to me? They had me locked up in that loony bin and they all eat pheasant and friseé. I can't stand them. If a war comes, we should both escape. Even if you have crazy spells, that isn't the point. You should run because there would be nothing in it for you either. You have no dog in the race as they say."

Chelsea got up from her seat and poured herself more wine. She was feeling energized. She waltzed across the room, caught her foot on the rug, and fell headfirst on the floor, wine going everywhere. Isabella shook her head. Perhaps the visit with Chelsea Revan was coming to a close. Isabella clapped her hand and Tugboat entered briskly. He went across the room and attempted to help up the small princess.

"Let go of me!" she squealed and squirmed. She seemed to want to stay lying on the ground. Tugboat looked at Isabella for a hint of what to do.

"Throw her out," said Isabella flatly. The rich girl had soiled her rug. It was time for her to go.

Chelsea looked over at Isabella from her supine position on the floor. "You can't throw me out. We are compatriots in a world of idiots. I haven't told you about Aunty and the war."

Isabella gave a flick of her wrist and Tugboat hauled the young girl over his shoulder and had her carted out of Isabella's chambers. Chelsea Revan let loose a bone-chilling scream and did her best to beat on Tugboat. Her punches falling like rolled up socks.

Isabella turned her back, as the door closed. She smiled to herself. She had enjoyed throwing the girl's presumptions back in her face. It gave her pleasure. She rang a bell and the cleaning man Bucknut came to the door.

"Could you clear away this wine? I will be heading out for the night."

She went to a small dresser and found a pair of diminutive black gloves. She placed them on her hands and bounded straight up to the ledge at the top of her room. She unlatched the window and exited onto the roof of Le Chateau de Crawler. The wind had picked up and the clouds were growing in the sky—a moody night for a sojourn, the hint of rain like garlic on a pre-dinner wind. She had best get moving if she were to get back to the cave before light. She ran to the roof's ledge just in time to see the final muddy shoe of Chelsea Revan enter her carriage. The driver whipped the horse and it began to make its way along the docks and out of the Calliope District. Isabella launched herself off the edge and glided across the wind, a flying squirrel, and landed ever so gently, on the carriage roof. The roof

119

made a slight *thud*. She gripped onto the edges and prepared herself for the ride.

Isabella let the carriage bump her around and she smiled to herself at the ludicrous nature of her mission—following this hyena of a girl toward Castle Yog Goth Makal, the home of the Revans. She watched the city pass by in the growing mist: so many adults with the mentalities of zombies—walking and bitter, torn asunder—their dreams a stain that shivered them as they walked, their agitated whispers falling dead as a groan in the ambivalent mess that was this manufactured age. Above, the smoke belched out of brick by brick industrial chimney stacks where the furnaces of the mighty engine of oil refinery ignited, blended and shook the contents of the earth's inner fluid.

These buildings too had begun to appear. These engines of the city that belched up black and made the city smell of coal. A metallic taste on the wind. These furnaces of energy were part of the gas lamp victory that felt slightly less than heroic. Isabella could see the lines of men heading out of work in the middle of night. Their bodies were bent over and exhausted. They were fuel as much as the coal that came loading in on the tramways—fodder for the grind. She could sense the workload, the cruel logic of it, sense the exhausted nothingness that hummed silently in their minds. This building was yet another water stealer, an evaporator. With each turn of its massive turbines, another body was cracked, another dream gone fallow. Barrenwood was under a spiritual assault. She knew. She could taste it in the saliva on her tongue.

Out toward the edge of the Mortestrate, she watched as the inner tensions of the populace became more frantically physical. She could feel the twisted anger of a group of drug addicts ambling on the unpoliced corner. The faint glow of streetlights illuminated the shadowy figures of people lost in agitated time—their mouths agape, their limbs loose. They walked in tight circles under the streetlights, mumbling to themselves with the pale blinking of the pharmacy sign above their heads, spasmodic muscle movements hinting at a physical revolt of bodies doped up beyond their sagging capacity—the sidewalk a runway for the mentally deceased and physically challenged.

The carriage ambled on, heading out across the back way toward the farmlands. Watching the city's sidewalk dollar stores shift to abandoned strip malls and then shift to large porches owning white Victorian homes with impressive yards to then, eventually, just green growing land—the stalks of the corn rising out of the earth like a waving gesture from the earth's body. The corn swayed in the wind, waving at Isabella a hello as she made her way toward the entrance of the Elegiac

Hills, the overlooking ridge where the monarchy stared down at the mess they ruled over.

The gate that guarded the long road was golden and guarded. Carved gryphons and shields adorned the massive gate with the crest of House Revan. Standing before the gate were men with red shiny metal helmets with white feathers, leathers straps made a tangle across their chests, white leather boots, and a long ceremonial sword hung low across their hips—plumes of adornment for men who had become a symbol of the work they no longer knew how to do.

"Stop!" they said.

The carriage came to a halt and Chelsea Revan poked her head out. The men shook their heads, opened the gate and waved them through. Isabella's body melted like ink into the carriage rooftop and she slid on by without a hitch.

The road up the Elegiac Hills bent this way and that with increasingly steep cliffs falling off the edge of the road, a windy journey across the lips of Barrenwood's territorial boundary. As they gained elevation, Isabella, for the first time that she could remember, could actually look down on the city from high above. This was not a rooftop. Something about staring down at the city gave it a boundary and a boundary gave it humility. Yes, it was a labyrinth but it was a labyrinth with exits and entrances—rivers that flowed out toward the sea, railroads barreled straight out toward the horizon without regret, a marsh that abutted the city and gave its northern edge the cushion of Manzanita and moss.

As it turned, House Castle Yog Goth Makal was the last of the great Houses on this journey. At first she encountered the guard houses that dotted the roadside with their gated entrances and men at arms. They stood staring out with faces most severe, cheeks drawn hard against their faces, in little shanty huts from which they monitored the guests and comings and goings of the town's elite.

As the road reached the top ridge, it wound its way into hilly garden homes of the minor houses: House Percy with the dandelions and marigolds, the gingerbread-style homes propped up on tall stilts with teakwood and the faces of their laughing mascots, the bird cages on the porches with the brilliant blue feathered Toucans and squawking Bumblebee Parrots; House Gent with stretched long ranch houses with horses grazing out in the yard, wood fences barricading the house so one had to look down the long gravel road to their massive Texas-style mansion simmering with bar-b-que and rotgut; House Nero with its neo-classical columns and its billowing large red banners; House Netherton with its overgrown front yard and gothic cathedral with gargoyles and black liquid belching front yard fountain—frogs, fireflies and honeydew made the tattered front yard their home.

"That could be my home," Isabella said to herself.

House Chillbach arrived with little fanfare—just a simple series of wood houses that littered the grounds, a central fireplace, the comings and goings of people dressed Shaker-style, wagons full of cheese, eggs and goose liver. The final minor house was that of House Calliban, a series of brilliant white alabaster domes, a land for looking at the night sky with the look-outs at the top of each dome opened up for the instruments of magnification and illumination.

After the numerous minor houses, the carriage headed up another ridge to the major houses. The road opened up with large oak trees lining the way—a parade of giants leading one to the final series of four estates. Deer, rabbits and the occasional fox appeared, stared and disappeared.

The first estate to present itself was that of Tacsim Station, the home of House Persembe. The rectangular hedges lining the property cut the view in half where one could see a large plot of green up to the massive Byzantine architecture on the horizon. Minarets towered into the sky and even from the long distance Isabella could spy the elaborate mosaics that decorated its exterior. She imagined the sisters growing up there causing trouble in the large field of grass and housing the amazing humanity that could get bored with anything.

Next came House Ellington with its modernist rectilinear homes. Again the hedges provided only the faintest view with another large plot of grass that stretched out toward the modernist homestead that worked its way into the very side of the mountain. Large glass windows combined with straight lines that moved across each other—a three-dimensional constructivist painting to live in. Then came House Imbetta whose imperious black-as-night front gates allowed little view of their home. The guards, dressed in black with the white-eyed monkey emblazoned on their chests, stood guard and denied entry to most.

The final home—and the one they were at last approaching—was that of House Revan, the greatest house of them all. The road seemed to grow even wider and the oaks all the taller. It continued across the grounds for a good while before reaching any semblance of living. They passed through a series of gates guarded by men clad in grey steel, with red cloaks hanging from their necks. The style of all the homes, and homes there were many, was that of Spanish Baroque. A maze of turns and twists riddled the surface of every building of stucco shells, flower petals and eagle claws. The cornices twisted and turned on the edges of the buildings, providing a fluid melting sensation with a barrage of details overwhelming the senses. There were many buildings that peppered the grounds as the carriage made its way across—past the Poseidon fountain, past the tower of the Gollum Eye, toward the central road that headed straight to the home of the inner circle of Revan.

As Isabella's eyes set on the most impressive mansion of them all, Yog Sogoth Makall, her stomach took a familiar twist. The sickness had returned. She swallowed hard.

"I won't let this deter me," she vowed.

She sniffed at the wind to sense the whereabouts of Minasha Darkglass. As she suspected, Minasha didn't live in the central home. She was too strange and too much of her own spirit to reside with the larger family of nincompoops. Instead, Minasha and her immediate family resided out in the dark woods just west of the main residence. The time of Isabella's stowaway adventure had come to an end. She launched herself off onto the roadside and tore across the grounds toward the black woods.

Much time had passed and the moon no longer haunted the sky. Her feet moved quickly as Isabella had no intention of greeting the sun from the grounds of House Revan. She ran as fast as she could until she found herself in a grove of aspens, the spindly white peeling necks of the trees reaching in a thick cluster all around her. Isabella didn't need her eyes. She could move by way of her stomach. Whatever direction made her feel worse was the way to go. Sure enough, that sick feeling brought her to the doorstep of a chestnut brown, towering gothic building, the massive arched door looking as though it dripped down from the mushy clouds above. Inside this very door, she knew, paced Minasha Darkglass.

Isabella couldn't be bothered with subterfuge. The time to be direct had arrived. She reached out and banged the large brass doorknocker. It thudded and clanged out. Perhaps, she thought, this was the first time anyone had ever come a knocking. A maid dressed in a black dress and a dark shadowy face opened the door.

Isabella smiled as best she could. "I'm here to see Minasha Darkglass."

The woman stared blankly as though not seeing her, forcing Isabella to wave her hand in front of the woman's face.

"Hello? Hello? Do you see me?"

The woman's eyes never moved, glazed over from who knows what, then slammed the door on Isabella. How rude, Isabella accurately thought. She waited for some time, listening as best she could to hear if any movement took place in the residence. She could faintly make out some banging of something or other. As she stood there and caught her breath, she realized her stomach was really turning to the worse. She didn't have long.

She was just about to let herself in when the door opened to reveal Minasha Darkglass. She stood there with her bone necklaces dangling over a white ruffled satin shirt with a black lace shawl. Her fingernails were black, her pointy shoes black, her lipstick, again, black, and her eyes as well, a smudge of black. Her hair was a bird's nest, and she stared at Isabella this time with a haze in her eyes. She was not quite right. She did not recoil or evade. Instead, she stood there with a feeling of blank.

Isabella jumped at the opportunity. "Good evening, Lady Darkglass. I realize it is a late hour, but I just had to come and see you. I think we got off on the wrong foot last time."

"The demonsss came as foretold. Come to my shack. Follow me," said Minasha.

She walked out the door, closing it behind her. Her feet moved miraculously fast. They walked through the fallen leaves in the yard toward a foreboding shack surreptitiously lingering in the wood. Isabella had to pause, her body was beginning to convulse from the sickness, the proximity to the woman in black not exactly helping. She bent over and threw up along the way. Minasha stared back without emotion, reached into a pocket in her blouse and pulled out an elixir. She sipped on it while staring without any hint of personality at Isabella getting sick in the woods.

Isabella waved at her, "No, really, I'm fine. Don't worry about me. Just throwing up over here." She wiped off her mouth and made her way toward the shack where Minasha held the door open.

A chill washed over Isabella as she entered. She could feel darkness in a way that she had never known. Something foul, rotten and cold lingered in the ways of this mortal soul. A small lantern in the corner made a flickering illumination of the workshop interior. A large workstation was evident with beakers, picks, pokers, and jars. Viscous fluids, samples of rotted milk, fetid mushrooms, boiled animal brains, bone dust, custard rot, junk noodle, blood sponge, and saliva pile were all categorized in small jars across the table. The room seemed to move as Isabella eyeballed small wooden crates holding pigeons, cats, mice, rats, toads, chickens, baby goats and even an iguana—a menagerie of magical sordid ingredients and sacrificial livestock.

Minasha grabbed a chicken by the neck. It squawked, cackled, and flapped in her hand but she gently petted its head until it calmed down. While she did this she continued to stare coldly at Isabella, her eyes not revealing a thing. Minasha pulled a long butler's knife from the worktable and slit open the chicken's stomach. Guts came spilling out onto the dusty shack floor and the bird squawked its final sound. Minasha flung the chicken's body onto a desiccated pile of trash in the corner of the room, bent over, and with her finger, drew a four-foot circle in blood on the floor. Isabella looked over at this strange woman. Magic.

She had seen Marty do it plenty of times. He loved it. Always joked about how good it felt to gut a creature and send its innards into mojo mayhem. "Dem gizzards got da glitter of da pearly gates." She didn't realize others were capable of such mystical enterprises, but here she stood, witnessing this morbid creature finger out a blood circle.

"Stand in it," whispered Minasha, pointing her dirty index finger at Isabella.

Isabella did her best to not laugh, but she was desperately holding on to health. Her stomach was getting the better of her and she realized she might have to cut this visit off.

"I would love to stay, Minasha Darkglass, but I'm afraid, I am, for whatever reason, allergic to you. My stomach gets sick the moment you come around. I'm afraid this nausea will prevent me from playing little miss witch."

Minasha stared intently at Isabella, "Sick when you get near me, you say?"

Isabella nodded, opened the shack door and threw up just outside. Minasha watched unblinkingly. She was thinking. She went over to her worktable and poured liquids into liquids. Her fingers moved at a furious pace. She looked in drawers, pulled out hairs and spices, and continued her work.

Isabella found herself on her hands and knees again. The darkness of the night began to fade into the pitch black of sleep. She couldn't hang on much longer. She just didn't have time and she had to confront her mysteries as they presented them. This is why she had come. Minasha was a key and Isabella had to grab it. She could see the wet of her puke in the wood chips of the surrounding earth. Small potato bugs were scuttling across the ground. Her puke was a mixture of fluids that had made their way through her body to provide nourishment and lubrication—through her veins, her stomach, her intestines, her esophagus, her body; a series of squishy wet tunnels that this fluid had explored. It now lay on the ground, released into the world. She wished she also could fold inside out and let the squishy tunnels inside her touch the night air. She passed out.

Isabella woke up inside the shack. Minasha made what appeared to be a smile, an ugly one at that, as Isabella raised her head. She was sitting inside the circle, as Minasha had desired. Minasha was feeding her some liquid from a jar, her bony fingers doing its best at a maternal role.

"It works," said Minasha, quite clearly proud of herself.

Isabella could feel her strength returning as she sipped the balm. It tasted of fish guts and grey hair. But no matter, having her strength meant the world to her. As she came to, so too did her senses. Minasha's words came out long, authoritative and somewhat, surprisingly, commanding.

"You are locked in the Zillinskin circle. Your actions circumscribed. Your mouth a moth hole. Your movement, perhaps, smaller. You are reduced to talking and for that I give thanks."

Minasha reached over to her table, grabbed some rose petals and flung them at a candle flittering light in some odd altar with a stone Pan head just out of sight. She flung them with a twist; her hair, for a brief moment, playing ballerina on the shed wind, playing fun on the moment, in a way Isabella found most peculiar.

Isabella took a moment. She inhaled her breath and took a beat. Here she was in this weird environment with this ever so odd witch of a woman. She was in a state of peculiar paradise. She didn't want much out of life. She really didn't. She just wanted life to live up to a remote sense of how amazing it was to be alive. The vast strangeness of it all! It had always struck her as wild, but more often than not people were amazing in their intransigent position that life was rudimentarily bland and obvious. She sensed their dull aching hearts wanting to constantly sleep, a beating so deep that it just wanted the cozy clothes of the grave—a life of pajamas and sodas—a body so worn, so tired, that its entire existence was hell-bent on not existing. This was Isabella's perception of humanity and one that found its monstrous counter-balance in the emphatic bone-laden woman named Minasha.

Minasha, on the other hand, was having a similar reckoning. She had met higher beings. Yes. They were foul-mouthed moody creatures that didn't give a rat's ass about her or anyone for that matter. More like children they were—cross and vindictive without parental supervision to put them in place. But none of them remotely had the mood, disposition or calm presence of this mystical cherub. Perhaps it was a trick. Certainly Minasha held a particular disdain that the cruel stupidity of her own people seemed to be matched by a similar myopia by those the coven held divine. Trust was about the last emotion left in her simmering skin. Nevertheless, she couldn't help feel completely threatened by this small girl.

Perhaps this was something altogether new. She had been waiting for a sign. Something had to happen. She had sensed for some time that the feud would soon arrive. She felt it alongside the agitated electrons on the evening breeze that spoke of a coming deluge. She had seen it foretold in the upturned possum belly and olive pits. The war. It threatened the great Houses and she knew not what side the higher beings would choose.

She had stopped asking why she cared for the houses long ago. She knew with every muscle in her being that she didn't. But it mattered not. It was her obligation. Her destiny. She was the true savior of the great Houses even if she alone knew it. If nothing else, she would do it for Money, Monkey and China, her beautifully wise progeny who already had dabbled with Ouija boards and alchemy. Even her husband, Benjamin, was worth saving. Kind stupidity did have its own rewards and virtues. Other than that, the individual members of the houses were worth less than that chicken on the trash heap. They were just mouths clucking away while the world spun out of control. Her brother, the king, perhaps, the cluckiest of them all.

She stared down at the girl. She should be trapped in the Zilliskin circle—so the books had stated. But then again, the books had been wrong about so many things.

"You are trapped in the Zilliskin circle."

"So you already said," said Isabella back, smiling. She loved having the calories moving and grooving in her body and it was not lost on her in the slightest that she had just ingested some kind of liquid that reduced Marty's sickness. She had just taken into her body the closest thing she had ever known to escape.

"Thanks so much for this healing balm. It is mighty delicious. Was that trout I tasted?"

Minasha squinted her eyes in an obvious attempt to try—desperately—to see the truth in Isabella's words. "It is a fish. Yes. Why have you come to visit me?"

Isabella made herself comfortable inside the circle. She crossed her legs. She couldn't believe that this little blood circle would actually work. It was tempting to put just the end of her pinkie outside the ring, but she figured that would stop the conversation, and frankly, wasn't conversation why she had come in the first place?

"I came to you for answers, Minasha. I get the feeling you think I am something I am not, or on the other side, you know things about me I do not. Either way, I feel very much in the dark. As you witnessed, I am cursed with a sickness that prevents me from coming into contact with you and that knowledge itself makes me want to know why."

Minasha shook her head and paced the room. "You come to me with questions. You want to know things. You are lost. Don't you see I am lost? I have been calling to you with questions. I don't know what is going on either. I can feel it but I can't place it. Something is about to break and I need your guidance."

Isabella found Minasha most curious indeed. "When you say that you have been calling to me, do you mean specifically me? Little me, sitting here on your floor? Or are you referring to some abstract desire from the universe? It's not like I received a letter from you or anything. I don't know you, Minasha. You know that, right?"

"I, oh, never mind. You confuse me with your words. You always do," mumbled Minasha, "but what can you tell me about the coming war? What starts it? Why does it come?"

Isabella was flustered as well. She had come with questions and not answers. She took a breath. Perhaps she knew something she didn't know she knew. "I can tell you one thing, that everyone, not just me, already knows. Barrenwood is changing. You can feel it. You can see it. It isn't an abstract change, but it is happening, not just in the streets of the city, not just in the new markets and docks, but in the very imagination of the city as well. People are changing. The city is mutating.

"If anything, I would say that the answer to your question resides in the carting away of the mad. Whatever force is behind that, is the force that is changing the world as we know it. And come to think of it, whatever changes the world as we know it, will inevitably lead to a shifting of powers which often means a war. Ha! Maybe I do have answers for you, Minasha Darkglass. I am an augur after all! Oracle Isabella, I like that."

Minasha's eyes lit up. "Your name is Isabella."

Isabella realized she didn't really want to have said her name. She didn't know why, but it had always felt like a bad idea to let a name get loose. She stayed quiet.

"A name is a powerful thing you know. Isabella. Words have weight and certain words more so. Your name gives me power. You aren't the brightest of your kin, are you? Maybe a young one. I can't tell." Minasha reached over to her chicken guts and dipped her finger in. She began writing Isabella's name on the shack floor. I, S, A.

Isabella felt suddenly panic-stricken. What if she had escaped Marty only to find a new master in this odd woman Minasha. She didn't like the way she was flaunting her power over her.

"Stop it! Don't you dare write my name on that ground!"

Minasha continued with a slight smile playing on her lips. And with that, Isabella, with her small little fist, punched Minasha Darkglass out with one clean blow. The witch woman took the hit straight to her temple and fell to the ground out cold. Isabella took a step outside the circle to find it had no power whatsoever. Perhaps it needed Minasha to be awake, or perhaps it didn't work at all.

Suddenly, Isabella found herself, alone in the back cabin. All the better. She didn't really need Minasha's mashed up wisdom. What she really needed was the ingredients to that balm. She grabbed a canvas bag off a peg and began throwing as many of the ingredient jars as she could into the bag. She also carefully put the top of the balm Minasha had made for her inside another jar, as this elixir was the Rosetta Stone of her liberation.

This escapade needed to come to a close anyway, Isabella thought. She could see the darkness of night giving way to hints of azure. She opened the cabin door and felt that shift in the wetness of wind when the air prepared to hand out the dew. Time to skedaddle. She ran out of the cabin toward the Yog Goth Makal and found a horse grazing out in the vast lands of grass.

"Get me on outta here," she whispered in the horse's ear.

They strode off and Isabella's heart soared. Flying along the ridge of the Elegiac Hills, she thought about one peculiar thing: Was she really going to escape just when the city of Barrenwood barreled headfirst into civil war?

Chapter 11

Fennel paced along Rue de Chartin. He had a night ahead of him and where would he go? He thought of tracking down Isabella. Yes. He would surprise her. He picked up his nose, smelled the wind and listened for clues. He put his hand on the ground and closed his eyes to feel tremors. She was in the Calliope District. Well, so that's how it is? He took out his handkerchief and wiped off his hand. Such filth. He stood up and made his way along the Aliber River. The streets were lively. People were out dining under the clouds. Newspapermen were screaming news of the coming election. Gypsy children were scurrying about trying to sell gum to strangers. Fennel found the festive mood to be distracting.

He whistled out, "Boy, boy, I need a shoe shine!"

A little gypsy kid pulled out his stool and promptly began wiping and shining.

Two more days. Why did it have to be so slow? These things take time. Maybe he could go spy on the shacker again. Oh, what was the point? He would just be snoring or drinking or writing. Not much fun to watch. What about Savina? He could tiptoe into their house and . . . no, that would upset Isabella and why go around that bore. Wait. Yes, he would surprise Isabella.

He looked down at his shoes. "No. That's horrible, boy. Look at that scuff. You've only exacerbated the problem. There. Polish there!"

How about a boat? He could sneak aboard a houseboat.

"No, no. Oh, here forget it. You don't know what you're doing. Damn idiot!"

Fennel kicked the shoeshine boy's stool and threw some coins in the street. He headed off along an alley.

A chilly draft blew along the cluttered ground. Coupons and glossy magazine ads swirled about his boots: half off fabric softner; Franklin's Coffee, all natural from whole organic beans from Sunsilet; a diet plan to slim those curves. Cats were up on trashcan lids. Rainwater poured out of pipes from tenements high up above. Fennel kicked a tin can and whistled to himself. It was the mourning song—the song he sang when he tried to drive people crazy. He would sing it to himself when he was depressed. His mind would ruminate on images of a white sand beach at night with a lost boy along its shore. He would stand there naked and pee into the black sea complacently crying. The world ebbed and flowed to the rhythm of his mourning song. It was sad. So sad.

That was the feeling he wanted in his statue. That was part of it—the toil and the longing, the tragedy of beauty that seemed to play on his heart all night long. Isabella knew it. She could touch the edge of this darkness with finality, presence. She didn't shirk or cower but stood resolute. Like the boy in his dream, relaxed in posture yet aware. Fennel suddenly turned to his left and banged through a door that led into one of the decrepit tenements. He found himself at the bottom of a stairwell and he noisily clanged his way up, up, up the stairs.

He was on the roof. The door shut behind him and from his vantage point he could see far along Barrenwood. He saw the looming bell tower of Cathedral Ogre, the lights glowing over the Jewelers Market, the lantern lit Market Street, and he could faintly make out the distant bend in the Aliber River near where the cave was. Barrenwood felt silent. He was glad to be up there. He stepped over to the edge and peered down. Seven stories. That could kill him.

He took a mighty leap and flew over the fifteen-foot gap between the buildings. His body seemed to just be given more consideration by the air. A pact seemed to have been formed. He just hovered longer like a flying squirrel. He landed and ran to the next gap and jumped again. Again and again he ran across the building tops. Time went by and finally Fennel was out of breath. He was panting and heaving and laughing to himself. It felt good to run, felt good to have sweat trickle along the brim of his hat.

Looking down he noticed a couple sitting in a tulip garden. Oh, what have we here? A couple in love. The woman was dressed in white with a bonnet and the man sat with his back straight. They were sitting on a rusted iron bench. The woman's feet swayed to and fro beneath her. Fennel looked up into the distant constellation of Corvus, which sat perched upon the back of the Hydra. Ah, the Raven must once again descend from his perch, he thought. He shimmied down the roof to the chimney where he could hear the couple talking. He smelled raspberry. He leaned back and began to file his nails.

"This tulip here is a Rembrandt. And this one here is a streaked Bizarre, my particular favorite. Did you know the word tulip is derived from the Turkish word for turban?" said the man. His voice was the shape of his moustache.

"No, I didn't. That is fascinating. You really know so much about flowers for a man," she said.

"Ha! I doubt that. I just know about tulips. That's all. When I was a boy, my mother and I would work in the garden. She was especially fond of tulips and so I have a modest knowledge."

"It is to your credit. Terrill, do you think a lot can be learned in a garden?" she asked

131

"What do you mean?" he asked.

"The garden. The garden as metaphor. Since the dawn of time, the garden has been such a metaphor for life's processes. I can only imagine that one would gain a far richer understanding of life by working in one," she said.

"Oh, I see. Hmm. I hadn't thought of it that way. I was more concerned about not making my mother angry." He laughed and clicked his heels. He really was impressed with himself.

"I can see that being the case."

"Ha! Do I seem like a mamma's boy to you?"

"A little," she giggled.

"Well, I can handle that. My mother was a good woman," he said.

"I'm sure she was. Isn't the painting in the living room of her?" she asked.

"That's right. I painted that two years before she died. I suppose it may not be healthy having her looming in my living room like that."

"Oh, don't be silly. It's perfectly fine. She was an important part of your life. It's good to have the past with you. Retains continuity."

"I guess so."

"Well, some things. Some things should be left behind."

Quiet. The faint sound of Fennel still working on his nails.

"Hey, did you see the Turrenbull Art Show at La Fievs?" he said excitedly.

"Oh, yes! I'm so glad you mentioned it. Did you see it?" she said excitedly.

"Of course. I wouldn't miss it. His use of texture."

"I know. I know. Very visceral. He has really come a long way. I saw a show of his two years ago."

"Really? Work that good can't help but be noticed. He's so aggressive."

"Yes, he sure is. Not my style, but I really appreciate it."

Fennel was becoming ill with this chatter. Oh, let the Raven strike! he thought. He leapt down into the garden with a pitter patter of feet and began to dance his way over to the couple.

"Dee-da-da-leee!" he sang. "Hidey-ho, folks! I'm the garden boy. How do ya do?" He tipped his hat in a highly overdramatic fashion and bowed low to the ground. His face was smiling. They were obviously startled.

"Excuse me?" stammered Terrill. He took his hand off of the woman's knee and repositioned himself on the bench.

"I said hidey-ho! It is a common tra-la-la sound one makes when meandering through a lovely garden. I did mention I am the garden boy, didn't I? There are those that would describe me as a symbol of life's processes. Isn't that right, Madame?" he said, still smiling. He gave the woman a wink. "No, no, I'm just joking with you guys." He laughed loud and long. His high squealing laugh sent shivers up the collective spine of the couple. It was like a slaughterhouse pig without the comfort of knowing it would soon be dinner.

"Isn't it past your bedtime, boy?" said Terrill, deciding to deal with the "Raven".

"Sure is. Feels late to me. I'm exhausted." Fennel yawned. "What is it you two are up to any who?"

"Could you please move along? We were having a chat," she said and she smiled affectionately at Terrill.

"Boy, don't I know it. I believe you were discussing the work of my uncle, Mr. Turrenbull. You said something about his use of texture," said Fennel placing his hand on his chin representing the idea of deep-in-thought.

"He is not your uncle," Terrill said incredulously.

"Fine. He's not. Whatever you say, team smarty pants. I just thought I would join in on the conversation, but apparently I am not invited."

"Well, it isn't polite to listen in on people," said the woman.

"I know. I'm truly sorry. I just heard the name of my uncle and how could I but not listen in?" said Fennel, frowning melodramatically. "Can you really blame me?"

"Oh, I suppose not, lad. The synchronicity is a bit hard to believe, you must admit."

"I admit. I bow down in the face of such questionable circumstances. But have at you, Mr. Terrill, I am not a liar. I am Percy Pendleton at your service." Once again he bowed low and held out a flame tulip for the woman. She reached to grab it and he let it drop to her feet. She reached down and Percy Pendleton whisked it away. "I believe it would be improper to not offer our dear Mr. Terrill this streaked Bizarre." He opened his hand and the tulip had lost all its petals. They lay forlorn in his tiny hand.

"What is this outrage? Boy, I said off with you!" Terrill rose to his feet in total consternation.

"I didn't mean to," Fennel whimpered "The petals just fell off. It's like love, Terrill. Just like love. You know that I'm sure. The petals just die away and you are left feeling abusive. Wait, Terrill, look at me." Fennel began to grin. "Lookie here. What do I see in those eyes of yours? Another! Ha, ha, ha!" Fennel's squeal rose up into the night air yet again. A howling pig. He jumped in the air and gave his heels a click. "You've abandoned someone, haven't you? You dirty dog. Dirty dirty dog!"

133

A look of shock came into Terrill's eyes. Fear. The look Fennel knew he would get if given an opening, the look that changed the currents in the air and the electricity on that bench. It was the wind Fennel always conjured. The swooping wind of insurrection. The woman went cold, her body reacting swiftly to a new, dangerous environment. Yes. Terrill was a liar and not a very good one.

"Right, Terrill?" Fennel scratched his head feigning concentration, "Who was she? A girlfriend? A wife?"

"I haven't the slightest idea what you're talking about," he said. His voice sounded false. The woman's face became grave.

"A wife! Ha! Terrill the down and dirty mutt! Look, don't be like that. You gotta do whatcha gotta do! Know what I mean? The dirty whore is probably still cryin' her stupid eyes out. Dumb, fucking bitch." Fennel lips curled in ferocity.

"Stop this!" barked Terrill. He threw himself at Fennel, lashing out with his cane. Fennel side stepped him easily and let him fall face first into the mud. He then gave him a quick kick to the jaw and left him bleeding in the dirt. The blood oozed into the earth and Fennel began to laugh hysterically. The woman sat sobbing on the bench. Fennel turned to leave, feeling his work had been sufficiently accomplished.

"Well, needless to say, you're not invited to the next Turrenbull show! Ha, ha! Sweet dreams, lovers!" yelled Fennel and he ran off into the night. Ahhh, the Raven. What would life be like without the Raven asserting justice wherever he goes?

Fennel ran across the rooftops laughing. He found the entire escapade funny in the extreme. Such pretenders they all were. Turrenbull, ha! Such haughty chitchat these foolish people toyed around in. He couldn't help it. Listening to them had been painfully gross. It would be an offense to his entire being to not interfere and so the Raven had been summoned. But just as fast as his laughter ebbed out of him at his most recent exploit, the last pants of air fell like dull thuds—his exuberance fading to a deeper ennui; like butterscotch candy on the tongue, the flavor fell out as fast as it came on. All that was left was spit.

He placed his tongue on the roof of his mouth and took in his current environs. Funny enough, he was staring back out at the Aliber River. The river bubbled in the twist of the bend as it careened its way toward the sea. How strange these waters in its tributaries fed the mouth of his cave where he had resided in ebullient obscurity. Now here he stood, leaning on the edge of the tile roof, staring down at the empty port where once stood Le Bateau Ivre—his feet having magically taken him without his knowledge toward the site of the crime. Unfortunately or, fortunately, the boat was not there. It had just left. He could just faintly hear their cries drifting far out now into the blue. The workmen were along the docks loading palettes into sea containers and the general stench of fish was still seeping into his refined nose. Yuck.

He sniffed at the wind again for just another hint of that delicious flavor of tragedy that these vagabonds of madness evoked, but alas, their entire aura had faded. They were gone. What now? He looked out over the city to see if he could see or sense any packs of dogs nearby. Perhaps he could run with them again. That could be fun he supposed, but then again, it would be strange if it were to become a pattern. It made him slightly excited and slightly uncomfortable the way that idea appealed to him. Nevertheless, no packs were nearby so the point remained moot. His sister was nearby. He could feel her. She was up to no good he was sure. He could interfere just as Marty had told him, but then he would just be a dilettante.

Fennel paced. Stared at the moon. He howled at it. Okay, he would head out and bother his sister. He motioned to jump off the roof when he noticed coming down the street that same man he had bitten a few nights past—the refined businessman in the silk suit. Today his suit was pinstripe, navy blue, with a peach handkerchief in the pocket. His sandy blonde hair blew in the breeze. His nose was literally held high. He seemed to not have a care in the world, except that the man now possessed a slight limp and the sight of it made Fennel smile.

"Sorry ol' boy, the Raven can really be a terror."

Something about such a gussied up fellow limping along really struck Fennel as absolutely wonderful. He hopped off the rooftop toward the wet ground below. His feet went slap as they landed. The man, Conner Deville, turned immediately as Fennel appeared not far from him on the other side of the street. The look of horror on his face gave Fennel pause.

"Fear not my good man," said Fennel as he waltzed his way up toward Conner. "I was in a foul mood a few nights past. I really shouldn't have done that to you. I'm sure the leg is on the mend. I don't have rabies, I can assure you. Nothing but the finest saliva from little ol' me." Fennel patted Conner on the back while Conner stared with wide-eyed horror.

"I dare say, you must get a grip. This is no time to lose one's tongue. Let me walk with you and shoot the breeze. The air is so very nice this time of year and at this time of night. Let us saunter for a moment."

Conner Deville didn't need this. His life it seemed was really turning a corner. Everything had fallen into place in the last few months, and if it weren't for this specter of a creature, his life could be described as absolutely perfect. Barrenwood had allowed him a fresh start and the chance to re-invent himself or perhaps to finally be himself. He had just left the Estuary Bistro with Jerry and Mike, his Nicoise salad had been incredible, he had lost at least six pounds in only two months, and he was returning home with a pocket full of ducats. The night had been beckoning him and then this strange creature appeared. Conner swallowed and did his best to converse with the monster. Indignation hadn't gone over well last time so he thought he would resort to a most pedestrian manner of talking.

"I won't belabor it, but it was very rude of you to bite me. I really don't know what that was all about," said Conner as he walked with a most assured and detached pace.

"Note taken," Fennel slapped himself on the wrist and looked up at Conner as they walked. "I get a bug in me, you see. I think I might have got it out of my system earlier so for now I think you are safe. I just saw that boat with all the dear folks of our town on it and it really got me angry. I have to tell you, when I am angry, I am most insane. I couldn't help myself. I really couldn't."

Conner picked up his pace and let the creature walk with him. He figured that as long as he stayed agreeable, he could make it to the Café Vivre where he could say he was meeting a friend. Jamal might be working the bar and he could easily pretend they were meeting. But for now, he would just walk briskly and chatter with the currently, agreeable miscreant.

"You really shouldn't take things so seriously, chap. It isn't good for your breathing or your health. Stress is a major cause of illnesses, you know. Relax. Be at one with your fate. It will be better that way. So, on a more serious note, you really don't think those lunatics should be taken away to a more hospitable place?" Conner stated, realizing as he finished that perhaps he shouldn't be bringing up the past.

Fennel felt the hairs on his back go up and he talked them down internally. The man was trying to be nice. He just was very dumb. No need to bring out the Raven right now.

"No, ol' chap. I don't. Do you want someone to drag you off to a more hospitable place?" asked Fennel, slapping Conner on the back with a little more aggression than either would have liked. "Of course, you don't. What you want, I am sure, is to eat nice food, do your thing and be left alone. Like all of us."

Conner gave up on this train of thought. The best tactic would be an agreement. "I'm sure you're right. I must admit it really isn't up to me anyway. I was just asked to facilitate this on behalf of the dockworkers and the medical advisors. I am no expert on mental treatments, believe me. In fact, I really don't know much of what I am doing. I hope I haven't offended you."

Fennel looked at the man. What he said really was true. Not only did he not know what he was working on, he really didn't care—a middleman, the world was just chock-full of middlemen, all little ants in an anthill with little pieces of leaves on their backs, just doing their jobs, in the morass of the mass. What did Mr. Conner DeVille know of anything? Nothing! And did that excuse him?

"You know, my good man, I believe you. You don't know anything of anything. You are just getting by now, aren't you?" asked Fennel. He closed one eye and looked quite fiercely at Conner. It was a most peculiar look. Enough so that Conner began to fear that the Raven creature might return.

"I am?" said Conner, unsure if that was the correct answer. He could see the lights of Café Vivre just around the next bend in the road.

"You are!" said Fennel, whacking Conner upside the head with his cane. Conner fell backward and landed on his back. Fennel twirled his cane and looked up in the night sky. The stars stared down in pure ambivalence at his sudden justice. "But I'm afraid it is not enough. Ignorance is bliss, but it remains guilty nonetheless. There was a war once, you know? A whole country of people wiped out masses of other people and they all claimed they were just doing their jobs. I'm sure you heard of it. Some trial, some lame argument where everyone was culpable because they were all dumb as rocks and frail as old teeth. I just won't buy it. I'm not even angry. I swear to you."

Conner held his head and lay on the ground. He was terrified. Why was this child haunting him? Fennel bent over him and got his minty breath right up close to Conner's delicate nose.

"Don't blame this on the Raven. Blame it on me. Fennel. That's my name and that's who is doing this to you. I won't hurt you too much, but I just can't let it go. I just can't."

Fennel pulled back Conner's pant leg as he writhed on the ground. The cobblestones were slick and they stained his silk suit. Fennel looked down at Conner's goose bumped leg to see the slightly red-stained bandage on the spot where he had bit the poor man last. He ripped off the tape and pulled back the bandage. Small holes still revealed the site of puncture where his tiny teeth had entered.

"Aw, it's like a photograph of us," said Fennel.

He put his mouth down and took yet another bite. Conner screamed into the night and Fennel let his incisors cut deep down into the meat. It was a hardy bite and he let the blood run into his small mouth. Iron, blood, salt, and what was that.

"Holy moly," said Fennel excited. "I would have never guessed. Is that coriander?"

Chapter 12

Despite their mutual big night out on the town, Isabella and Fennel had managed equally to get home before daybreak. As such, they lay on their mats as the sun moved from east to west in a boomerang shape across the sky. As the light bid the day *adieu* and hid itself behind the curtain of earth, the eyes of the twins equally opened up. With the opening of their eyes, the neurons in their brains equaled the buzz on the marsh, which occurred at that witching hour when all creatures took on a last frenzied attempt to take a bite out of the living, breathing world. And as much as they were eager to share their new odd insights, they mutually desired to keep to themselves, which meant they had to hide their excitement.

Isabella got up and shuffled her way to her desk. She sniffed herself. She smelled of horse. On her mind was that amazing balm—the key to her escape!—the end of that debilitating Marty illness. She could sense she was close. The end of this wretched chapter in her life was coming to an end. The excitement pushed through her veins as she set about at her desk to decode the sauce.

Fennel, on the other hand, shook the sleep out of his hair as he slipped on his slippers and made his way toward their library. He chuckled to himself about his last night's exploits. He really had an unquenchable thirst when it came to being pleased with himself. Last night had been on the verge of just being yet another night of purely stirring the pot, but that last bite into Conner Deville's leg had revealed something most telling: coriander.

They sat quietly for some time; Fennel reading and Isabella scrawling. She was trying as best she could to figure out what was in the liquid. She would taste a drop and make a note. She figured the best way to decode this balm would be in utilizing her amazing sense of taste. Surely all ingredients could present themselves to a slew of gumshoe taste buds.

Fennel turned the pages of his tome, *Heretofore, The Divine*. It was a chronology of the School of the Divine Line. Reading wasn't Fennel's forté and he flipped through the pages searching for the pretty historic illustrations. The School, which held no small presence in the city of Barrenwood, also happened to be the home of the ever so ubiquitously known Coriander Monks—exactly, coriander. Wherever the monks went they carried with them that extremely distinctive odor: a smell of spice, sweat, and lusciousness. Their robes also were the color of coriander and their presence had been a part of the fabric of Barrenwood for as long as people could remember.

The twins had only some knowledge of them, however. They had visited them quite frequently in the Billington Hills as Marty often had them deliver goods to their doorstep. The monks would answer the door with their hard drawn faces and barely evoke a word, just bow, take the package and disappear inside. Nevertheless, as boring as the visits tended to be, they also comprised a large part of their workload for Marty. Since Marty often had them delivering goods to different organizations and individuals in town, the School was clearly a large part of whatever he was up to. They also were quite aware that the sickness weighed on them as soon as they reached the doorway. Whatever lay beyond that door, was off limits for them (like so much else).

It should also be clarified that the School wasn't a real school—not in the proper pedagogic sense. The School of the Divine Line was the major religious order of Barrenwood. They had churches; they had books, scriptures, and psalms. From what Fennel knew, the scriptures were taught as the result of pure divine analysis. They professed a belief in God, but not a judgmental God, not a destroying God, not an angry God, but an even keeled sort of know-it-all God. A God that left clues to his presence in the divine natural laws of the universe of which the priests were adept. Kindness, virtue, benevolence and modesty were not simple dogma, but God's inherent presence in the laws of social construction. The celestial made its presence known in the perfect functioning of society. Their belief system could be interpreted as ecology, a series of various beliefs and values that wound its way from concepts of death to those of daily living.

Even with its hyper-rationalist methodology, the School of the Divine Line maintained an abundance of macabre rituals and weekly sermons. They loved paraphernalia and a baroque sense of adornment. Statues of wily eyed goats, cranky hawks, multi-armed blue women with their tongues out, black as night crocodile-headed men, and humble shrouded holy figures of antiquity riddled their many ministries. Their altars were rarely humble and their churches built with a deep sense of surplus: marble floors, velvet curtains, gold plated cornices, even the finest wine at sacrament. It was maintained that, just as humans, God enjoyed the finer things in life.

But, of course, what truly zapped around in Fennel's mind was the question of why that man Conner smelled of coriander. The obvious conclusion was the School had something to do with the removal of the mad. The idea bothered and excited Fennel greatly. Could the Raven's justice spread itself to those that arbitrated morality? The prospect sounded most sweet. He never liked that school in the first place. So arrogant they were. Tip-toeing through their contradictions, the monks hid in hoods but nevertheless provided so much sage advice. Silence would suit them better than their churches.

But being Fennel, he was—as usual—of two minds. He appreciated the churches as well. He had to admit it. He liked their visual sense of passion. They at least looked like something the world should provide. Why they chose to be dour in the face of their amazing buildings, he could not say. It often seemed to him when he would pass by the churches packed on a Sunday that in their own somber way, the School pointed toward a wild mad world—a world worthy of the lives they had been given. So why cart away the mad? The shamans of the lived lands.

The Coriander Monks could benefit greatly from thinking through the implications of their own teachings. The mad were the keepers and providers of water. They fueled the world with cosmic wanderlust and their psychic meanderings were poignant in the extreme. It made him angry just thinking about it. He slammed the book shut. He didn't need to read up on those monks. He knew plenty already. He looked over to watch Isabella walk out toward the river.

She was smiling to herself as she made her way barefoot through the mud. She was making progress. She had been right all along. Trout scales was a major ingredient. She had named it the fish sauce. Tadpoles swam about her feet. The pussy willows and rushes stretched around her. Isabella would soon possess a homeopathic remedy. It was a tonic. Dragonflies whizzed. Out on the shore, she noticed a package on the mail table. Seemed as though Marty had yet another round of deliveries for them today. She had planned on seeing the Persembes. Oh well.

She stared back toward the cave where her brother was curled up in the big chair with a candle lighting the massive tome on his lap. It made her smile all the more. Her brother reading. Such a funny thought. She could see how much it agitated him as he scanned for the pictures. She felt the river wash past her spindly legs and knew the feeling of sadness was going to shortly descend on her. Was she really going to go through with it? Leave all this?

She had only known the cave. She and Fennel had been there for as long as she could remember and loved much of it. Fennel would never leave. She knew it and she pushed that idea out of her mind. She had to talk him into it. Marty was a nightmare. Not just to her, but to him as well. Leaving could only be for their mutual benefit.

"Fennel," she called out over the sound of the gurgles in the water. "Come here, Fennel. Let's play in the river together."

"Ew! How can you pillage your feet like that? So disgusting! Isabella, you're fortunate I still appreciate you even with your hygienic inadequacies."

He jumped out of his chair and went to his closet.

"I don't relish the idea of playing in the water, I'm afraid. You will have to do so on your own."

"I am fortunate, Fennel. You are ever so understanding. How you put up with me, I'll never know."

She made her way back to the cave and began getting dressed. Fennel went over to her desk and scanned over her notes. Shouldn't he be allowed to take a look at what his sister was up to? No need for secrets.

"Iz, what are you working on?" he asked, seeing the words sea bass, bluegill, herring, fluke and monkfish crossed off, with the word TROUT in bold letters.

Isabella turned in a quick whirl and smiled widely. "Fennel, my brother, I think you should call me Derrilous. Yes, I am a bit of an alchemist myself. I am working on a cure for the sickness and I think I might be very close."

Fennel finished tying his bow tie and stood speaking to himself in the mirror.

"Isabella, why do you force me to be the wise one of the two of us? You have always seen that sickness as a curse, but I think it is a warning. Marty may be evil, but he reserves most of his vile behavior for the vile world outside. First of all, we both know you don't have the skills to prevent the sickness. Lord knows what you will talk yourself into. Please, when you do finally think you have cracked the code, don't take too much of that stuff. Sure enough it is going to have its own side effects. Second of all, what the hell do you think you are doing?"

Fennel was fuming. She could sense it. He had that wild look in his eye that scared even her.

"Fennel, this isn't for me. It is for both of us. Aren't you curious what is in the big beyond? Don't you want to find others like us? They are out there. We have seen them! We have seen them with our own eyes. Why are you so adamant that we have not! You are so curious about everything and yet you seem so determined to stay in your cage!"

Isabella's eyes were tearing up. This conversation made her sick with sadness. He was so infuriatingly stubborn. Her love for him at times overwhelmed her. It was an ocean that surrounded her. He was as much a part of her as air or water. He had to come with her when the time came.

"Enough!" shouted Fennel. "I warn you, sister. Don't push me. These are merely games and they will come to an end. Maybe you will have to

141

experience it because you sure aren't listening. But, whatever the case, your life is forever circumscribed. That is life. Period. You will find out."

Isabella stood still, staring at her brother's back. He hadn't even bothered to turn and face her. He would not bend and a slight chill went through her. She realized in a flash that not only would Fennel not come but, in fact, he might actively try to stop her. He wasn't just the brother she loved, he also was in cahoots with the devil himself. The thought was too much for her. She shook it out of her head.

"On another note, dear brother, it seems we have a package from Marty out there on the mail table."

"Really. Let's check it out."

Fennel ran out onto the shore to gather up the package. Isabella walked out to join him and she noticed quite clearly that something was wrong.

Her brother squished up his face. "He has duties for us again."

Isabella's heart sank. She had so much to do and none of her plans consisted of running around town delivering packages for Marty. It was almost as though he knew she was ever so close and he had intervened to keep her busy. Idle hands.

Fennel opened up the package on the shore, divvying out the small boxes that hid within. They were addressed to different bland addresses. Who knew why they handed over what they did? Fennel hoped for a few packages to the School and sure enough, they were there. Of course, they were. Not the worst news, he thought.

"Well, sis, looks like our reindeer games for the moment have come to an end." He gave his sister a wink.

Isabella turned away. "Let's get this over with," she grumbled.

For the next week, the twins were busy being the celestial UPS deliverymen of Barrenwood, handing out packages to the homes of the wealthy, surreptitious, and divine, but rarely the poor. Fennel did have a chance to visit the doorstep of the School of the Divine Line on a few occasions, but on each and every visit, the sickness welled up in him and prevented him from saying much of anything other than, "here are you packages, good monks." It was all he could do from not belching onto their coriander sandals.

Isabella tried her best to make progress in the small window between when they left and when they got back to the cave. But progress was not on her side. Try as she might, the fish sauce still just gave her indigestion and did nothing to prevent that wretched illness. Fennel found her exploits increasingly amusing as her failure confirmed in him the superiority of ol' master Marty.

During that week, Isabella became increasingly sullen. With the sauce fading and Marty's packages showing up every twilight, filling up her time, she felt the window of opportunity shutting most severely. Looking forward, she could only hope that she could follow that Duke of Izmir to some remote island where he could tell her the truth of her and Fennel's situation. He would sit them both down on a couch and regale them with tales of the true beginnings and their proper role in the universe. He would tell them what a fool Marty was and he would, with just a nod of his head, remove the sickness as though it was the most paltry of desiccated ropes. He would love the water as much as they did and they would go out at night and hunt to their heart's content, slurping on the traumatic joys of humanity. These thoughts helped her go on day to day.

It was on the eighth day that she woke to see Fennel holding a different kind of package from the mail table. She was just opening her eyes and Fennel was already dressed and ready. He had become all the more dutiful and Isabella already slipping into sloth.

"This is odd," said Fennel, turning the package around in his hand studying it. "This package isn't from Marty and more than that. It is addressed to us."

He handed the box to Isabella and sure enough, written on the side of the box, were the words:

To The Twins
Located at mouth of the Cave in the Southwest corner of the Aliber Swamps
A letter of most importance from the Guild

It was from the Guild—the order of assassins.

"The Guild writing us?" queried Fennel as he opened the box which held a single letter.

"Strange tidings," mused Isabella.

The letter read as follows:

Dear twins,
As you know it is not in our customary nature to either write you or your master, but we have had a unique opportunity present itself that we had to act on. Your participation in this venture is purely up to you without any obligation whatsoever. Our only task it to let you know of its potentiality. We have been approached by members of a renowned and lucrative business to set up a meeting with you. We can assure your total safety and assure you that if we didn't think this would be of great benefit to you, we would have

never broached this. They are interested in discussing business and felt that the nature of the meeting should be most candid. If you agree to join us, the meeting is this evening at 3 am at the Guild. We assure you that we have never confirmed your existence or that you would ever arrive, only indicating they would wait whether or not you existed at all. They are most determined. We will wait for you, but please feel no obligation to arrive. This is a matter that is completely up to you.
  —The Guild

  "How exciting!" said Fennel. "The Guild setting up a meeting with us and who? I am ever so eager to discuss business, of course. I say we make a pile of cash before Marty returns and we can even buy him a mansion instead of the squalid shack he resides in."
  Isabella shook her head. Her brother seemed to live in a constant present tense. Even his dreams of the future seemed to live in only instant gratification. Nevertheless, this was the only package. Marty's deliveries, at least for this eve, had stopped. They had a night to themselves and that was good news for both of them.
  "Fennel, Marty would never live in a mansion. We know this. And as for the business aspect of this, one can only wonder what kind of power these people must have to talk the Guild into contacting us? They seem to know already too much from what I can glean from this letter. Frankly, I am just glad that Marty's deliveries have stopped for now. I can't say I was enjoying that. I am up for attending this meeting if nothing else than to know who these people are."
  "Of course we are going to this meeting! Are you crazy? This is most exciting indeed. We can really get our fingers into some dirty dirt."
  "Don't get too excited. I have no intentions of doing anything they request. The whole thing assumes too much and our covert status remains of the highest priority."
  Fennel's smile faded as he realized not only was Isabella right but that he was also as impetuous and unprepared for most things just as Marty and Isabella had always indicated. But it wasn't exactly a surprise that the deliveries had stopped. He had asked Marty to give him a night off. Isabella didn't know and that was fine. He had plans tonight and he needed a break. Marty acquiesced. He really wasn't that bad. And now he had this letter from the Guild. Of all things!
  "What are you going to do on this night where we can actually get out into Barrenwood?"
  "As it turns out," Fennel said with a smirk on his lips. "This couldn't have been a more opportune night for Marty's deliveries to cease. As it turns out, I have been requested to join the Auxiliary Cultural Committee

for Barrenwood's annual festival. My humble opinion on matters of high culture has become of great interest to the state."

Fennel adjusted his bow tie. He pulled on each end and made a regal gesture with his eyebrows. Isabella squinted.

"Is that really such a good idea? Sheesh. You seem determined to out us in Barrenwood. Caution, dear brother. The city is not the friend you think it is."

"Wasn't it I that just made the same claim to you?" he responded. "Sister, I am a grown man. I don't think anyone, least of all you, would accuse me of considering this waste heap of a city my friend. I can make my own decisions. I will do as I see fit as you most surely do for yourself."

"I know, Fennel. You are truly your own person. I just worry. Try not to make too big a scene and be as discreet as possible."

"I am the Raven remember. I will swoop in and swoop out in the fit of night. No one will be the wiser and Barrenwood's cultural life will be ever so much better!" Fennel made a mock evil grin and guffawed. "We both know Marty will return soon and, dear sister, I too have my little plots. This one will be fine, I assure you. Nothing too dramatic will occur."

"Now that sounds like a lie if I ever heard one. Have your fun and be careful."

"As delicate as a child I am," he laughed.

The prospect of Fennel speaking in front of representatives of the city gave Isabella the chills. He was too wild. He would botch it for sure. Her brother's taste for mischief made him a clearly unreliable public servant.

"So it appears that with this window opening for us, we are again on our own, dear brother. That is fine with me. I have matters I need to attend to anyway. As far as I am concerned, a free half evening in Barrenwood without the interference of Marty is a gift I am ready to accept. I will miss you though. Please don't have too much fun. Let's rendezvous at the Guild as arranged at 3:00 AM."

Isabella smiled at her brother as she unmoored the boat from the dock. They both jumped in and made their way to Le Chevalier Noir.

Heinrich greeted them in his usual manner. Fennel jumped out.

"You will have to excuse me, my dear old chap," he said, grinning. "I have pressing matters of state to attend to. I am on my way to becoming a politician so prepare yourself, Heinrich. The world is about to experience politics in a manner it has long desperately attempted to avoid."

Heinrich creased his brow and said nothing. He knew no response was desired anyway. He helped Isabella out of the boat. The mosquitos were whizzing by the lanterns and the air was thick.

"It looks like we will meet later this eve, sis. Don't be surprised if you meet me as Mayor later this evening," Fennel smiled, tipping his hat.

Isabella just turned away. She was tired of Fennel at this moment.

"Good evening, brother," she said as she made her way toward the reception room. Heinrich whispered in her ear that the Persembes had come with an immediate request to see Isabella. Isabella felt a wave of comfort at the news. The universe seemed to be speaking to her. Even if she couldn't crack the code on that sauce, there was still more than one way to skin a cat.

"Yes, please, come, "she thought.

She whisked her way to the Burgundy Salon, waving goodbye to her brother who flew out toward the streets of Barrenwood with the energy of an excited rat. She scooted up onto her large throne where she could greet the gossiping sisters three. She sat on her chair and rang the bell for the ladies to enter. They rushed in a whirlwind of chatter dressed to the nines with their long hair pulled up into beehive towers above their heads. Upon seeing her, they hushed and bowed in reverence.

"Good evening, Miss Lady Isabella," they all said in unison. They gathered in front of her with their faces most smiling. They had experienced something over the last week that clearly was more interesting than Isabella.

"Evening, my dears," replied Isabella. "I suppose you have some news for me after our last soirée?"

"My goodness, do we! A more exasperating journey I could not imagine. Whatever have we done to deserve you, I shall never know," Rana gushed. "But here we are—rescued from the sybaritic nightmare of our family name and their toilsome dullerdry. Sibel, as per our last understanding, has become our personal private eye and lovebird. But she is not alone. Oh, no, not alone at all. We are sisters after all. We couldn't let her have all the fun."

Isabella just stared at Rana and sipped her grape juice. As sullen and stern as her face appeared, Isabella couldn't be happier. This was how the world was supposed to be. She was in her element. If Rana was rescued by her she felt equally rescued by them.

"Continue," she stated blankly.

Rana continued apace, "Sibel, forgive me, I know this is your story and I will be sure to stop shortly so you can fill in the juicy parts. For now, I just want it said that Yosune and I enquired further to all our various friends and family regarding the inner workings of the city, you know, to find out about this Castilla and more so, what the mayor might be up to in that little hut outside the Mortestrate."

Sibel burst in, as was the only way to talk when Rana was in the room, "I did as you said, but I must say that it has blossomed. I think I might have been sidetracked by love." (And love it was. More than she could express in the room. It had taken her heart by surprise and made her mad with passion. Every night she saw him. In her sleep, she smelled him. She was perhaps in pain. Yes, pain. The love was too intense. They would never understand.)

Isabella could sense it—a rare feeling from these Persembes—a trickle of the water issued from Sibel, her agony an awful awakening. Her fingernails were eaten down to nothing. Her agitation and vexation were palatable. Isabella licked her lips.

"Love! Your request to spend time with Minasha somehow turned into a double matchmaker extravaganza," laughed Rana.

"Enough, Rana, let Sibel tell her story," barked Yosune, and Rana, for a tiny shred of time, backed off.

"As I was saying, I, well, we, did as you said. It is all rather confusing. Perhaps you and Minasha Darkglass are secretly connected. We were about to set up a meeting with her when we found ourselves invited over to her place for tea. This kind of thing never happens. Anyway, we accepted, which perhaps had you not asked us to spy on her we may have refused, because, of course, being in the company of Minasha Darkglass is not exactly something we enjoy. Anyway, it matters not. For reasons that I cannot completely understand, when we arrived, Minasha Darkglass had a secret guest at her small gathering."

Even telling the story brought it all back. Sibel's blood rushed up into her face. Her cheeks became hot.

"Love at first sight. Yes, that is what happened. Instantaneous. Peter Wilkins is his name."

"And they are in love already!" laughed Rana.

"Shut up, Rana. Don't make me lock you out of this meeting," snapped Yosune.

"Yes, don't ruin my story. Isabella you have to take partial credit for my beating awful heart. He is so wonderful. The most romantic, soft-spoken dreamboat. Of course, he isn't from Barrenwood. I knew I needed something from not here. The men of this city are so beaten down. Not Peter. He is from a place called Gorsten or something like that. Anyway, it just so happens, he is from the same place where his employer, Mr. Castilla, is from. We have dined a few times since we spoke last and, in fact, I would say, we are in the midst of a glorious romance. He is everything. He is quiet, affable and possesses the most quaint, charming accent. This twang sound on his lips. It is so captivating. He is quiet, soft-spoken and very simple. Not a complicated boy, but a handsome one. I like him so much I must say I half feel guilty for saying all of this."

Isabella listened with what felt like electric pins tingling inside her. The city was speaking to her in a strange way. It led to Minasha Darkglass.

147

It led through these sisters. And now it led through love. Sibel was on fire and Isabella could nearly feed off the warmth. But what was it trying to say?

"So, Minasha Darkglass introduced you at tea?" queried Isabella.

"Yes, he was there as her guest which is odd considering he is only a carriage boy."

"Do they know each other, Minasha and Peter?"

"No," blushed Sibel. "We joke about it now. He received her request to tea as a complete surprise. It came out of the blue. He was extra uncomfortable at that meeting. He just sat in the corner stirring his tea uncontrollably as though he were trying to make a whirlpool inside it."

The girls laughed. It was very true.

"But that isn't the only way that you and Minasha are psychically connected," stated Yosune, "for her invitation has also allowed us to know more about this Mr. Castilla. As it turns out, Peter is extremely close to Mr. Castilla. He works as his carriage boy. It is almost as if you and Minasha both want us to find out about Castilla. Ha-ha, I'm joking. I don't see how Minasha Darkglass gets anything out of this, but it is all rather bizarre that you have us finding out more about this Castilla and then bam, here is this extremely proximitous source of information. Turns out Peter is orphaned, and Castilla has taken him on as a sort of pet project; a semi surrogate son, though what he is doing as a carriage boy is beyond me. That perhaps will be solved later in my investigations. As it turns out, Castilla works for a land company called Gaventas. They have been on an extended stay here for some time due to some business that Peter knew nothing about."

Sibel interrupted, "Peter knows very little at all. About not only Castilla but well, anything," she giggled. "I like them more that way, I think. Dumb as a rock and handsome. I might just marry him and make father crazy!"

Rana burst in as she had held her breath long enough. "If you married him, father might annihilate all of Castilla and this Gaventas and possibly even Big Boy Charlie. No, I don't think you should do that, sweet sis. I mean if you did that too, we would have nothing left to investigate. Everyone would be dead!"

The sisters laughed. They laughed because it was sort of true. Sibel's laughter was nearly hysterical as it touched too close to the agony inside her. Yes, it was funny she was in love with a dumb errand boy. But it was love. No question about it. And the thought of it made her miserable and wild.

Rana collected herself and continued, "Well, it shouldn't surprise our dear Isabella that she sniffed a rat and a rat she has found. For while no one knew of this Mr. Castilla, they did know about Gaventas. Our father, for one, was quite aware of him and he indicated—with little interest in telling us much more—that so, too, were the Houses Revan, Ellington, Imbetta and even Calliban. In fact, from what I gather, Gaventas is part of something that has been more than a thorn in the side of the great Houses.

"Father went on to ask where I had heard of them and I just lied and said I had heard about them from friends and was embarrassed to say I didn't know what they were talking about. To this father simply stated that all we needed to know about them was that if they had their way the great families would be begging for their dinner on a Mortestrate sidewalk. "

Isabella felt progress was being made, but perhaps it was trickling in all too slow. "News is news, I suppose. Things seem to be afoot in Barrenwood."

Yosune laughed, "I couldn't agree more. To find something that all the great Houses actually agree on is quite miraculous. It is, in fact, a gold mine of gossip if you will. Gaventas, it seems, will be the talk of the balls, galas, and dining rooms for the next few years to come I would imagine. And to think there is something out there that could threaten them enough for them to unite! It is exciting."

"What do you know of this Mayor," asked Isabella.

"As you may know," responded Yosune, "the Mayor has traditionally been hand-picked by the united efforts of our houses. They are capable administrators put in place to run the ever-complex arrangements that are the inner workings of civic life. This Mayor, Big Boy Charlie, we like to call him, has been in office for almost twenty years now which is basically our entire lives. He is as Barrenwood as they get. In general, I would say he has been the embodiment of capable corruption.—assuaging the right merchants, paying proper homage to the right houses, not letting the trash pile up, keeping the peace, but ultimately, not doing much of anything. In the last few years, however, I have heard it said that he has begun to—in a way most out of character—make waves in the sense that he has come to the table with some big ideas—new concepts of road management, public parks, public education and the like. I suppose he now considers himself a pudgy Renaissance man."

"Big Boy Charlie was at our house about a month ago. He comes by every so often and smokes cigars and talks shop with pop. He isn't the least bit interesting if you ask me," said Rana.

"I have heard about enough I suppose," said Isabella, getting up from her seat. "I would be pleased if you could continue your relationship with Peter. As you two possess mutual affections, this shouldn't prove too difficult for you. If it wouldn't be too much trouble and emotional turmoil, I would greatly appreciate it if you could at least allow the relationship to inform us all on the inner workings of Castilla himself. And you girls, perhaps you could keep your questions at a minimum to your parents and society. I get the feeling that we have wandered into something that might actually be interesting. I wouldn't want you getting your hair mussed over it or worse."

"What are you doing now?" asked Rana. "Are you heading over to the Chateau de Crawler again? That was ever so much fun."

"I'm afraid not this evening, my darlings. I have pressing matters. My time is running short, and I am forced to become more utilitarian than I am comfortable with." She pulled out a bag of coin and flung it toward Yosune. She then rang the bell and Heinrich stepped into the room. "Thanks again for your assistance."

"Ladies," Heinrich said as he opened the door for them to leave.

The Persembes bowed low and exited.

Chapter 13

Fennel could feel excitement at the evening ahead. He had always plotted to integrate himself into the inner workings of the city, but Marty had been very cautious to make sure he was never in arm's reach of it. In fact, he was sure that Marty used Isabella as both a sister and a security guard. Well, basta to all that! He was liberated. The city was his oyster and he was going to shuck it and swallow. Sure he had sort of tricked his way into this event, but he was convinced once they heard his thoughts on the festival, they might possibly embrace his wit and charm. And even if they didn't, they would have to be impressed with the results afterward. He was a social architect and that was all there was to it.

Marty lacked the proper faith in him. That was all there was to it. Fennel and Marty shared a mutual admiration for all things perverse and what could be more perverse than a festival planning meeting by the city? In a strange way, Fennel felt he was meant for things cultural. He was an artist in his own wetlands inspired way. He couldn't help but feel like the world was reverberating through him, singing its own convoluted tale. He just wanted to be true to its spirit. It was in acting in great harmony with it that he found most thrilling.

Of course, he was excited to participate in the planning of the city's festival. Not only did he already harbor machinations to unveil his statue during the festivities, but he also possessed a bold vision to catalyze a more frantic and exciting collective citizenry. The festival provided an opportunity to try out his own PT Barnum dreams. He would create a truly amazing carnival—a world where the multitudes of the tawdry could frolic together and be united in the dance of complex emotions and behaviors. It would be an opera full of fireworks, drinks, dancing, costumes, unexpected tragedies and anticipated revelries. He wanted so badly to choreograph the world's emotions like an epic song.

Costumes would prove critical. Revelry mixed with costumes stirred magic out of the core of the earth. It let people become foreign to themselves. Something about a mask allowed them—like a sort of societal pass— to let their more mutable selves drift outward. They became something altogether heavenly. And groups of people frantically becoming something else was all that a little PT Barnum social architect like Fennel could ever wish for. Which reminded him, he needed to find a circus.

Fennel bounded up to the rooftops to make his way to the City's Auxiliary Meeting Hall in Barrenwood's Garibaldi Plaza. He bounded across the tops, feeling each tile underfoot. He leapt like a flying squirrel, shooting himself as high as he could into the air and then landing ever so gently back onto another rooftop. He was quite the sight. It was his favorite kind of calisthenics, to feel the air flying past him; the humid soaked nights of Barrenwood moving across his spindly body.

Heading toward the center of town was easy enough. City Hall loomed large with a massive high beaux arts capital building that situated at the exact middle of Barrenwood. All four major roads met up at the office of the mayor. It was a city planning charade that made Fennel laugh. No matter how the city was designed, he thought, there is no way that the person in that building would rule the city. Nevertheless, City Hall itself made quite an impression. Its central tower rose up high into the sky with a triumphant statue of a young man holding up the crown of blessed victory. His young outstretched arms made Fennel roll his eyes.

Staring down at the city from his perch high above, he watched the people coming and going—their bodies lost in the maze of a built world. Before he even spied it with his eye, Fennel sensed it with his heart. Along a small road off the town square, an arrest had been made. The city's soldiers had in hand a man, handcuffed behind his back, and were forcibly walking him toward the paddy wagon. The man was angry and scared. Defiant and down. His eyes were opened wide with fright. He struggled unsuccessfully, his legs dragging behind him. Sure he was a drunk redhead, but he had juice inside him. Fennel could feel the water flowing from the man and watched in remorse as he was thrown headfirst into the back of the paddy wagon.

More internment of the water! The city was in a conspiracy. No doubt about it. A familiar anger rose up in him. Fennel took a breath. He bounded down to the street, dusted off his pants, and headed toward the large oak front door where a doorman, who smelled of mothballs and birdseed, waited.

"Greetings, good sir," said Fennel, tipping his hat.

"Business only I am afraid, lad. Move along."

As common as the doorman's greeting was and had always been in Fennel's life, it would never, ever fail to irk him. His smile grimaced just a bit.

"I'm on the list for the Auxiliary Cultural Committee. I believe I am under Fennel Highwater. Oh, and that lad stuff won't serve you well. Need I remind you that while I am going into this meeting of dignitaries, you are signing me in like a proletariat lowlife?"

Fennel could gauge from the look in the doorman's eyes that his comment went over like a lead balloon. This elder man from most probably the District of Jed wanted nothing more than for someone to hassle him. Over time, it had become his secret reason for going to work and Fennel had given him what he wanted. Why couldn't he just keep his mouth shut? Before they could get into an argument about whether or not Fennel would acquiesce to the power of the doorman, he winked his eye and flicked just the smallest amount of willow seed into the man's face. He blinked for a second and then, graciously conceded.

"My apologies, sir. You are expected."

The man bowed low and Fennel raised his chin and headed past. He really didn't want to get into an argument and ruin his day. He was looking forward to this exuberant meeting. He shook off his disappointment and got a smile back onto his lips.

As might be expected, meetings for the city were anything but glorious. Fennel entered a large banquet hall with chairs facing a central podium. People filled the room, rubbing shoulders and gathering around the snack table full of sugar cookies, smoked salmon, bruschetta, and teriyaki chicken on a skewer. He wasn't hungry. There were forty people at least hovering about the room in casual conversation. They were predominately the women of the great and minor houses as well as some of the up and coming merchant class—each one more lavishly dressed than the last. The attendees wore over-the-top gowns, blinking bright jewelry, designer clutches and for whatever reason, felt it necessary to drench themselves in perfume. What kind of meeting was this? They barely noticed Fennel's entrance. He knew no one.

In just a few milliseconds, his entire interest in the evening shifted from one of great anticipation to a terrifying feeling of dread. How much willow seed would he have to blow in order to get any attention around here? On his way there, he had imagined a table with a map and six dignitaries including himself at the helm gathered around making a plan as though it was a war. He pictured himself, of course, leading the meeting and impressing his new-found consorts with his brilliance in cultural planning. They were laughing at his jokes. An old colonel with a monocle was slapping him on the back boisterously.

But the reality, as usual, was not that. He pretended to want to eat food, grabbed some smoked salmon for a plate and stood helplessly in the corner, eating it with his fingers in the hopes of gaining an offended gasp from someone. Fortunately, the meeting started up not much later and he found a seat toward the front of the room.

"Can we have your attention please, friends?" said a portly woman into a microphone. She teetered on high heel shoes with pink bows at the ends, wearing pointy edged black glasses and a long unwieldy necklace of turquoise. She was, most obviously, a lady of society and clearly this was one of her numerous tasks at organizing her extremely bored cadre of friends. The microphone screeched with feedback and she smiled in a half awkward manner. The murmur of the crowd dwindled as they made their way to their seats.

"We are so pleased that so many of you have come to this auxiliary planning meeting for the annual festival. We couldn't be happier with the turnout. I know many of you and for those I don't know, please be sure to introduce yourselves to me later. Let's face it, this meeting is as much a chance to catch up as it is to plan this soiree." Defne Revan laughed and her face squished up into a tiny ball.

"You look glamorous, Defne!" yelled a woman from the back of the room.

"Oh be quiet!" giggled Defne. "Anyway, I am Defne Revan, Chair of the Mayor's Auxiliary Cultural Committee. We are pleased to have all of you here to provide your thoughts on our current thinking for the upcoming festival. Our evening's presentations should be very short as I know your time is quite valuable."

And so began the meeting.

As much as they had said it would be short, to Fennel it dragged on and on. They spent the first thirty minutes introducing different chairs of different committees who all said nothing and all looked about the same. Then he realized that all the people introduced were simply introduced for the purpose of introducing more people. After doing the math over the course of the first hour, Fennel began to feel as though the only person that hadn't been thanked or introduced was his lonely self. When it finally came time to discuss what the actual plan was, Fennel had nearly lost all interest.

"We are excited to say that we have hired the Barrenwood orchestra to play Debussy for the ball. We will also have the team of Richter and Sons to provide fireworks and they have assured us that this year, the grand finale will come off without a hitch."

"Boo, that's what they said last year!" someone barked from the back.

"I realize they have been a little less than reliable, but we have our best people on it, making sure they follow through this time. We will also be having the customary dance in the city center so let's all be sure to get the word out! We don't want to be out there dancing alone."

Fennel's feet twisted in his little shoes. It shouldn't have surprised him that these people were so boring, he told himself—but longwinded and boring? Did they not understand the power they possessed? Did they not appreciate what a festival could be? In most circumstances, he would have caused a scene in frustration, but he didn't want to mess this up. So he waited.

The public comment section of the night seemed to take forever to arrive. Many of the women seemed to know each other and routinely interrupted, thus forcing long digressions from the meeting—whether it was on the overcrowding of the stables, to the high cost of the orchestra, to the upcoming city meeting on the allocation of gas lamps. He was at his wit's end by the time they opened the microphone up for comment.

He was determined to not be first. That would seem out of line and diminish his respectability. So he waited for someone to go. Surely someone wanted to be heard. They were so loud anyway. He waved his hand in front of his face to alleviate the overwhelming smell of perfumes. Was he being poisoned? He had almost given up all hope.

"Anyone?" asked Defne. "Anyone at all? Come on people, I know you have opinions out there. I don't want to hear them suddenly while I have had two too many martinis. Let's get this sorted. Out with it!"

A grey-haired older woman stepped forward from the back of the room and got in front of the microphone.

"Ah, there we go. Ladies and gentlemen, Margaret Pierce has something to say," screeched Defne.

Margaret Pierce adjusted the scarf around her neck and fussed with her jacket for some time before she whispered in a cackling raspy voice.

"This year," she said with dramatic effect, "I want some young men with no shirts!"

The room erupted in laughter and howls. Fennel rolled his eyes. What a disaster. Was there no one who actually cared about the content of this meeting? Fortunately, the next woman to go to the microphone settled the tone. She was a regal woman with black olive eyes and deep hued skin. Perhaps she was Persian though he could not say for sure. She was introduced as Fereshteh Imbeta and her presence caused more than a little whispering from the back.

"Ladies and gentlemen of the auxiliary committee. I am so glad that we have the opportunity to plan such a festivity together. I would like to say, without any hesitation, that I think it would be wise for us to acknowledge some of the complications that come with this year's event." A noticeable rumble went up in the room. Fereshteh continued without the slightest hint of bother. "For as long as most of us can remember, and many here more elegant and refined than myself can remember even longer, the festival has been hosted by Barrenwood's esteemed families. The festival has served as a thank you to all of the people of Barrenwood no matter rich or poor. This year it seems certain interests—and we know who you are—have decided to transition this occasion away from its traditional roots. This festival—while of course a great and wonderful time for all of the city—is also our annual opportunity to remind everyone where we have all mutually come from. I see right through the new re-arrangements of the festival, and I believe most strongly that they are an attempt to move the narrative of the festival away from the families that are the progenitors of this great city. I want it said, here and now, by myself and by my family name, that a line must be drawn in the sand; for if it is not, it will be drawn too late. Yes, it is a festival, but it is the hint of things to come and the greatness of our houses must be on alert when things that have long been are beginning to be undone."

A few claps went up and a whistle as Fereshteh left the microphone, and then, a small regal Hindu woman, dressed in a crisp black suit, with dour dark eyes ascended to the microphone. Her eyes twinkled like a child's and her small feet moved like a phantom as she strode briskly to the microphone. She wore the shiniest pointy shoes ever seen. As she walked up to the microphone, a silence crept over the entire room.

Defne squeaked out, "And, of course, our new found friend from Golston, Ms. Vinessi Suleiman of Gaventas."

Vinessi's voice was punctuated with great clarity and her words came out in a vibrant quick paced staccato. "I realize that we have all not had the great opportunity to meet each other. I realize that our company has made quite a presence in your incredible city and I want to assure each and every one of you, that we mean nothing but the best for all the great Houses. As you know, Gaventas is a very large company with enormous holdings, but we got that way by taking care of our friends each and every step of the way. You are our friends. If there is suspicion, I do not blame you. We have been honored to pay for this year's event and to do so without asking much in return. We want what is best for Barrenwood, its families and look forward in making a return on an investment that will be of benefit to all here in this room."

Fennel was impressed. He had not noticed this woman in the room and now she was in front of the microphone. Perhaps to the rest of the ladies and gentlemen in the room, this silver tongued emissary was a monstrous miser with great political power (or something else he could not tell), but to Fennel, she was something he had not encountered in a long time. She was on the cusp of sinister magic. She smelled of tree moss and dried leaves. Her black mink coat hummed like eel laughter. Fennel could tell she was part water.

She sat back down from the microphone and Fennel could resist his urge no longer. He pranced up to the microphone and made a long bow.

The room erupted in laughter and *awws*. It threw Fennel's confidence off for a second, but he gathered his composure rapidly.

"I'm sorry," said Defne, "but I am unfamiliar with you, child. Who may I say that we have the pleasure of listening to this evening?"

"Sorry?" smiled Fennel. "Sorry is the state of the planning going on for this most of important of events. I am here to assist, and so fear not, all is not lost. Let me introduce myself. I am Fennel Highwater, at your service."

More laughter went up, although muted, as something in Fennel's appearance always blended the look of a child with the personality of a demon. The growing volume in the room clearly agitated Fennel.

He grabbed the microphone and shouted, "Respect is demanded at this moment!"

His brazen and clearly angry tone did what it needed. The room went quiet—at least for the moment. As opposed to throwing Fennel off script, it gave him the boost of confidence he needed.

"Good," he thought. "I knew propriety still had a place in this fine city."

It was at this point that Fennel went a little crazy. It wasn't often he had the chance to be in front of a microphone and for someone who thought about such an opportunity with such zeal and so often, he took up the chance with perhaps too much enthusiasm. He orated into the microphone for far too long, talking of the sordid problems of the human soul, mankind's capacity to forget, their weaknesses being both their greatest tragedy but also their greatest comedy. He talked at length about the thought power of muscle tissue and the mind/body divide being at the center of the crisis of the enlightenment—how a person's diet said more about them than their dumb ideas on the human condition. He talked about the festival and how through this basic social mechanism, the sheer power of the collective masses could produce new forms of being in the world that could make life for all more complex and beguiling. He talked about how dreams are made in the company of large masses of strangers being strange and how the light on a building at night, the smell of the Aliber River and the ready availability of alcohol are more important to the soul than any bedtime story. He talked of his statue and how it would be a marvelous addition to the festival. And he went on for just a bit longer about how the well-known fact that the problem of wealth is that it dimmed the spotlight of the soul. They must acknowledge their limitations when thinking and instead resort to the desires of those that have nothing left to lose.

By the time he finished, he realized he had walked the microphone in circles so much his feet were tangled in the cord and he was now at the back of the room. The seats were now half full and those that were present stared at him in stark terror. He wandered back to his seat in a daze, wondering if anyone at all had heard a thing he said. He had talked himself through numerous emotions and sat catching his breath in the front row. His voluble personality had even exhausted him.

When he finally looked up, he realized the only people left in the room were himself and Defne Revan. She was about to leave him he noticed. He shot up from his chair and zoomed right into her world.

"Oh ho ho," Defne laughed nervously. "What a marvelous speaker you are, Mr. Highwater. What you said about the human soul and all, it is so true. I really would love to talk, but I must attend to my children at home."

She was nervous beyond belief. Fennel could hear the clatter of her necklace as it banged back and forth on her chest as she rocked on her high heels. It felt like the thud of a judge's gavel, pounding, pounding down.

She nearly escaped his menacing smile when he puffed some willow seed into her face and said, "Oh, and how you do love everything I said. Yes, my dear, you truly, truly do. I look forward to our next meeting." He scampered out of the room in a blur.

Defne remained standing there, her necklace slowly but surely coming to a halt, her eyes now far away on a distant star not in the room nor the corroded exhaust pipe sky above.

Chapter 14

The twins each left their mutual meetings and headed separately toward their appointed rendezvous. Both were riding a little high from their previous surreptitious plotting and had their minds in the clouds.

Nevertheless, the journey to the Guild was neither easy nor simple—a drainage pipe along the harbor served as the entrance to the catacombs that fed the Guild's home. An enormous lock hung heavy on the entry gate. Long ago, the twins had been gifted with certain access to the world, and upon their arrival, its rusted hinges simply creaked open. A small creak of spillage seeped from its entrance making a stinky pool of dung and crud.

Inside the mouth, the tunnels went on beneath the entirety of the city—a labyrinth of steel and bilge that echoed in the movements of the few things besides rats that scurried about its subcutaneous surface. As light as their feet were, the twins still made tapping sounds that echoed down the dark maw of the metallic tubes.

Fennel arrived at last. Isabella could hear her him humming a little dityy as he skipped along:

> "Under, under, under the ground
> a place so sensuously unsound
> the earth's rotten center
> has never felt better
> then when its been scattered and battered around"

He made a summersaulting entrance into the central corridor that was their typical meeting spot. Isabella had been sitting rather silently, crocheting a hat for Sibel. She had not known who it was for at first, but as she knitted the idea of whom it was for, had come to her. The girl lost in the agony of love. And so they were at the Guild, the home of the assassins and the feral naughty mercenaries that were the pleasure of an occasional Marty assignment. As far as they could tell, the rest of Barrenwood was unaware of their existence and it was understood both in hinted terms by Marty, as well as an overall sense of candor, that the existence of the Guild was a secret to be kept with the utmost responsibility. The entrance corridor breathed a heavy odor of mildew and dank. The sides of the tunnel glimmered from the occasional torch in the slime of its covering.

Fennel approached Isabella and covered his face in a scarf, "My dear sister," he said in a slight growl, "I'm afraid that we are in a very dangerous place."

She smiled knowingly and pulled a knife from her sheath.

"*Mon frère*, I am ever ready for anything. Bring on the assassins of the Guild for tonight. I am most predatory."

She leapt at Fennel and he dodged back against the side of the tube. They laughed and then made their way toward the Guild's heavily locked door with a skunk clearly etched into the wood.

They knocked at the door with one large thud and waited. The door quickly opened and there stood a person with every inch of his body (except his eyes) covered in the black clothes of an assassin. Behind him, the room was black as night except one torch glimmering down the hall.

"The Guild greets you, messengers," he said with a slight hint of a lisp in his voice.

"And Marty McGuinn is ever so delighted to greet you," said Fennel.

The doorman opened the door further and ushered them into the foyer. It was a limited bare room with three chairs and a bare bulb. The round carpet in the center also had the imprint of the skunk.

"We won't be long," he said. "Make yourself comfortable. Another member shall join you shortly."

He left and there sat Isabella and Fennel on the chairs.

"As much as I like creepiness, these hooligans certainly set the bar," said Fennel. He tapped the walls of the little room as though looking for a hidden door.

Isabella sat motionless on the chair. She was eager for this meeting. Hoping against hope that before Marty returned she would have enough of a handle on the city to pry its lockjaw open—just enough information could add enough torque to wrench a hole big enough for her to slide her little body through. The thought of that nasty log came back to her—the millipedes and fungi stuffed up too close and the pain of her aches and cuts. Ugh. Marty was a pig indeed.

It wasn't long before another member, perhaps it was the same man, entered the room dressed all in black, his head again covered except his olive black eyes. They twinkled in the light and his voice came out in a heavy Russian accent.

"You have come."

Isabella stood up out of the chair.

"This entire ordeal is a severe breach in protocol," she said as stern as she could.

"We are aware of that. I hope that conveys its potential value to you."

"Whether or not the value, as you call it, exceeds the value of our relationship is something I have yet to determine. I am going to want more than just a meeting to understand this. Please let us know more about whom we are meeting with and how they approached you. What is the nature of your relationship with them?"

The member shrugged his shoulders. "I am not at liberty to divulge anything. I am here to walk you to the meeting and that is all."

Isabella could have expected as much. No one in the Guild knew more than what they were asked to do. Compartmentalized. Their knowledge cordoned off into small distinct boxes. Tucked away in the crevices of black ops bureaucracy.

"Show us to the room, please," she said.

The member opened a door in the cave and ushered them in. They followed through metal doors and tunnels deep into the labyrinth. It was a considerable journey and the length of it told Isabella that whomever they were meeting had entered in an entirely different manner.

Isabella whispered to her brother, "Please, Fennel, on this one let me do the talking. This is no joking matter and even Marty himself wouldn't want us screwing around."

Their journey led them to a dank, dripping small room with a large oak table illuminated by small burning torches in sconces on the walls. Otherwise, the room was empty. Sitting behind the table were three men in dark black suits with top hats each. The two figures in front, with what appeared to be mandatory black bushy moustaches and stern faces, were young yet old. Men of money. The crouched over man behind them was smoking a cigarette. He had a long wiry moustache and a thin severe body. He was timeless, in a sense. If they were young but old, he was old and perhaps had always been that way—bent, cracked, yet lithe in his tight skin, wearing gingham pantaloons and a pressed, buttoned chemise. The member ushered them in and sat them both at the table.

As they sat in their chairs, two members stood against the wall at one end and two members entered to stand against the wall at the other end. Either their safety was guaranteed, Isabella thought, or their demise was assured. They were in a very tricky predicament and the only assurance Isabella could tell herself was that no one in the Guild would reasonably double-cross Marty with any hope for survival. These stuffed suits must have paid a pretty penny to make this meeting happen. As she scanned the room, she could sense the power emanating from the smoking man in the back. His bent cool frame sent off an energy unmistakable.

161

"What is it you want?" asked Isabella with an icy cold air that she hoped would set the tone.

One of the two replied, "Greetings. My name is Tristan Bellequant. We would like to make arrangements. To set up business, if you will."

"Arrangements?" said Isabella. "How about you tell me who you are and what you want. Vagaries will get you nowhere and frankly, I am not at all pleased with the surprise nature of this visit."

"We would have done this differently if we thought there was any other way, but it appears that you like to exist at the periphery of civic life. Clandestine meetings seem to be the only meetings you have. We don't mean to offend. We merely want to make a proposal of mutual benefit to all."

The young gentleman Tristan was handsome to be sure. Isabella could sense ambition in his every move. He mistook his sycophantic nature for genuine personality. His confidence made Isabella ill with contempt for people. She could sense Fennel dying to speak so she kicked him under the table. This was no time for his maniacal mouth.

"You may have called this meeting, but I want to set the rules. I want the man in the back to do the talking. Yes, you, Castilla. You are the person holding this meeting anyway, aren't you?"

The old man's eyes perked up as he drew on his cigarette. He smiled at being called out and stood up from his chair. "

Very well," he coughed. "I'm not much for games myself so let's get this over with." His voice was raspy and cold. "There is a new game being played in the city."

"I suspect the game is bigger than you appreciate," quipped Isabella.

"Good. We agree. The game is big. There are many ways to get to the finish line, but it is such a long journey there really is no need to take the long road. Even with the most efficient route, the road is long. My name is Elinore Castilla, as I guess you know. I am chief executive at Gaventas, which as you may know, is a large holding company with many subdivisions. We have in the last few years focused our attentions on Barrenwood as a site for development and exploration. While we have done much advance work in terms of knowing the key players in the city, it has only been recent that we have become aware of you—and you are most interesting, aren't you?"

"We prefer to think that everyone is just boring in comparison."

Isabella didn't like where this was going. He was on to her. Her games were becoming reality and feeling her private world brush up against the ever real inner workings of the city felt uncomfortable. Fennel looked a little awestruck by all that was being said.

"Oh, I am sure that is most true," Castilla eyed them carefully. "I know about you people. I know about your pacts and your truces. I know about the war of seven hundred years ago. I know about the soft money, the laundering. I know much. I only tell you so you know I am serious. Your secrets, your histories, are safe with me. I have no interest in divulging them. It is of no concern to me. What I didn't know until recently is that you were in Barrenwood, but alas, I should not be surprised. Myself, I am a simple man who cannot imagine what your world is like. I don't know what makes you click. But then again, other people are just as inscrutable to me. Worrying about this will get me nowhere. What I can only say is that the basic things that make my world go round seem to turn yours as well. We represent large interests that far exceed those of simply Barrenwood itself."

Isabella stared blankly at this strange bent man. He was whispering with a force of something she could not comprehend. There was nothing remotely interesting about him except that he exuded a sense of vast determination. He was like an arrow flying straight through time. He was mentioning things about her that she herself had no idea about. What on earth were all those references?

"I am just one of many when it comes to importance, but the scale of Gaventas is an empirical fact. We will be moving into a considerable position in the city shortly and at this point, only the very naïve would ignore it."

"What do you want then?"

"You do business in the city. You conduct affairs. You are not with the great Houses. You are a force of your own and from what I can tell, an important one at that. Due to these kinds of triangulations, I see that a working relationship could be established. We might find common ground."

"Do you see the great Houses as your competitors?"

Castilla showed no emotion. "Quite frankly, most of them have lost touch with the times—so, no, they aren't competitors. They could easily be collaborators and some have been most helpful. They remain the major force in Barrenwood and thus a constant source of negotiation. I deal with them often."

"Do you need help in your dealings then?"

"Of course. We all do. Let me ask, do you?"

"We don't exist, I will remind you. We don't reckon with anyone."

"I know that isn't true. I have solid information that tells me you conduct business throughout Barrenwood."

Isabella found this entire ordeal strange in the extreme. If it was business that she and Fennel conducted, she was unaware of it. Marty used them as messengers and that was pretty much its extent. She longed to know what she actually was involved in and it bothered her to sit with Castilla and have him know more than she (about her). They had never negotiated a deal nor known what the contents of their packages and envelopes were. Nevertheless, upon numerous occasions they had delivered materials to the gates at the Elegiac Hills to the Guild, to the School and even to City Hall's receiving desk. They had picked up packages in the Miser's Quarters and watched mysterious packages delivered in the middle of the night by horseback by people eager to not be seen. So thinking of all of this as business was not such a crazy idea.

"Do you have anything specific in mind, or is this more of a general sort of meeting?"

"I need leverage on the holdings in the Mortestrate. If you could get the Duke of Revan to relent on the northern section of the city, we would be most appreciative. We have already had a reasonable offer on the table and he continues to flat out reject us for no good reason. I am concerned that the Houses are organizing against us. They feel threatened. But there is no need. We merely conduct business."

"I am no fool, Castilla. Business is violence by other means. The Houses are certainly aware of not only this fact, but how your growing status in Barrenwood reflects this."

"That is an unfortunate way to look at the situation. I would suggest you take note of which way the wind blows. A friend in Gaventas will certainly be of value over time."

Fennel, who had sat quietly for so long, could hold back no longer. He was irritated with how pushy Isabella was being. He wanted to strike a deal. To make a bargain. This gentleman wasn't wrong. The great Houses were asleep at the wheel with their annoying sense of propriety and lack of any inventiveness. The meeting he had just come from still wandered in his mind—a tawdry group of socialites oblivious to the magic of life itself. Zombies running the world. An overture from the likes of Gaventas felt like an opportunity that Marty surely would enjoy.

"Mr. Castilla, we are glad you came to us," interrupted Fennel.

He reached across the table to shake the man's hand and the Guild went for their weapons. Fennel backed off.

"Hold it now, gents. It's called a handshake. Surely meetings are meant to incorporate the international sign that says I hold no weapon. See, Castilla? I hold no weapon." Fennel showed him his empty hand.

Castilla looked down at Fennel's hand skeptically. "What is it we are shaking on?"

"Yes, brother," said Isabella, deeply annoyed with her brother, "what is it you are planning to shake on?"

164

Fennel smiled broadly still holding his hand out. "Why, we are shaking on the dream of better things. Surely that is what you came here for and that is what we want as well. The dream of better people, better relationships, better fortunes and ultimately, right, a better Barrenwood."

Isabella's stomach turned. Would her brother never stop making speeches? Lord knows what happened at that auxiliary meeting. She placed her hand on Fennel's shoulder to sit him down and he aggressively shook her off.

"No sister," Fennel said, turning to Isabella with eyes ablaze. "We are doing this my way." He turned back to Castilla and continued to hold out his hand. "Why do you not shake, Mr. Castilla? Do you have a weapon in your hand?"

Castilla relented and placed his small limp hand in Fennel's. They were magically about the same size as each other's. Fennel could feel his blood, his heart, through his fragile wiry grip. This old man was not a man at all. He was a force—a force of history. Fennel's eyes sparkled.

"That a boy, Elinore. I knew you had it in you." Fennel smiled and Elinore Gaventas took his hand back with a frown.

"I'm not accustomed to shaking for no apparent reason, but it seemed important to you, so very well. My time is limited. I must be gone. I expect an answer from you shortly."

Isabella stood up from the table, as the meeting seemed to be coming to a close.

"We can't answer just yet as we need time to consult our people, but we will get back to you shortly. Just look for a letter from us."

"Not to be too practical, but what kind of compensation will you be looking for if you decide to be of assistance?" said one of Castilla's assistants.

"That is entirely impractical," replied Isabella. "If we do you a favor, it would be just that—a favor. We work in the long-term and money is less of an interest for us than other matters."

"Well, then," said Castilla, "we will be off."

Isabella and Fennel got out of their chairs and left the room.

Chapter 15

The big night arrived and progress finally showed its ebullient face. By the time Fennel was out of the tub, Isabella was again at her desk, trying desperately to crack the code of the fish sauce. She had to finish tonight because this was the night. The big night when they were going to rendezvous with Savina and the Duke—the big man from the other side whose fifty-seven Chevy soul would lead her straight out of this nightmare. She could feel it. She could also feel the second hand of doom ticking in her sensitive ear. She did not relish the idea of falling flat on her face in a pile of puke just as the exit door opened up in front of her. No, she had to finish in the next few hours. She struggled with it. She could tell she was close, but something wasn't right: trout scales, pecan shells, tarragon, sawdust, milkweed, wet chub and Carolina salt. But still, something not there.

Her Eureka moment happened as it so often does by something completely unrelated. It was her annoying brother yet again. As usual, he resented her work on this venture and he had grabbed her by the hair to pull her away from her desk. They wrestled, scratched and fought and when they finally tore themselves apart, Fennel was standing there with a little black clump of her hair in his hands. She stared at him, her mind playing tricks on her and then it struck her.

"Hair!" she laughed. "Hair! It's hair! Don't you see, Fennel? You solved it. Your baby fits have saved the night after all. When I was down and out at the asylum, Minasha Darkglass grabbed a handful of my hair. She wanted to make a balm for me."

Fennel threw her little bits of hair in the air in exasperated fashion. Confetti of the head. "Gods, no! Can nothing make you stop?"

Isabella pulled out her hair and placed it in the mixture. Sipping it, she coughed and spit. Disgusting, if not outright vile. Meanwhile, Fennel paced inside the cave, thinking out loud.

"So, about our good friend, Mr. Castilla. I know you find me peculiar, I really do. I find myself that way as well, I must say, but this man Castilla, I admit a soft spot for the old crow. He is a wiry little thing, ain't he? A real wizened old shoe of a man. But he has got something. I could feel it. He was such a straight shooter. A real get-to-the-point negotiator and, I have no doubts, a can-do man. I like him, Isabella. I really do.

"I know Marty isn't around and I know he wouldn't like us dabbling these ways, but I am interested in taking up Mr. Castilla's proposal. Why not help the guy? No doubt he is smarter than those dullards in the high house. He is no-nonsense, but I think almost in a magical way. He is so boring, he is interesting! His lack of interest in being interesting is in fact interesting!"

Even though Isabella was predominantly ignoring him, she could sense him heading into speech mode—his being pleased with himself becoming a glowing sensation in the room.

"Who could blame me for moving to the highest bidder?" he continued. "You know, at the cultural meeting, which went very well by the way—thank you for not asking—there was a woman; I forget her name, who hinted at a brewing war in the city, a sort of reckoning that positioned all those pathetic houses on one side. Well, as you know, I am quite the sleuth, and I deduce with my uncanny aptitude for subtlety, that this war is with Castilla. He is the money man, the *real* can-do operator. He is getting stuff done and those high society vagabonds have got themselves all in a twist over it.

"I can't imagine that ol' coot giving some lame gossipy speech. It's impossible. No, he is a man who likes to stay on target. He is Mr. No-nonsense and now he is giving those perfumed hedgehogs a run for their money. Well, good for him, I say!"

Fennel banged his cane down on the table. Isabella was scurrying about the floor of the cave picking things up. Startled, she looked up at her brother. She smiled at Fennel most sincerely.

"Something about you finding that dried up old man interesting makes me love you all the more, dear brother. You are ever so full of surprises."

Fennel slammed his cane on the table again with a smile on his lips. He did love being a surprising person. He banged his cane a few more times.

"Here ye, here ye! I pronounce that the allegiance of this cave has shifted away from the Houses. We have new allies here in Barrenwood—allies more lucrative and allies more wise. We are like Switzerland over here. Machiavellian and stealthy. Ready to take on the highest bidder. Come on over, Mr. Moneybags, our bosom awaits your embrace."

"That's it!" Isabella interrupted. She was at her desk and had just finished drinking the fish sauce again. She danced around the room with a smile big and wide. She had cracked the code. "It was so easy. So very easy. I didn't need my hair, Fennel. Not mine! But Marty's! Of course! The balm is against Marty's magic and I needed his hair and there, there it is. These grey hardy wires are going to help us get the heck out of Dodge. Come on, Fennel, take a sip. Taste my genius!"

Isabella ran up to Fennel with her elixir in hand. She pushed it up toward him and he screwed up his face.

167

"Get that away from me! Yuck!"

Isabella laughed and tried again pushing the nasty wetness close to his lips.

"I said get it away!" he screamed and turned with great hostility, whacking the elixir out of her hand with his cane. It flew across the room exploding against the cave wall. Isabella turned away and made her way back to her desk.

"It doesn't matter. I can make more. And you should control yourself. I am on your team," she said.

Isabella steadily worked on another batch, trying her best to control her sadness and rage. Her brother's hostility did not bode well for the night to come, Now that she knew the formula, Isabella had a little arsenal to go. Her only concern was how many Marty hairs she could glean from the corners and crevices of the cave. So far she had nine and they should do fine for now. But if they ran out, which they just might, she would have to go to his shack. The prospect of that dirty hovel gave her the shivers. Marty wouldn't be oblivious in any way to her going there. She whipped up her batch and placed it in her pocket. She looked over to see Fennel with a small telescope in his hand. He was staring up into the night.

"What are you doing?"

Fennel looked back with a smile on his lips. "Who? Me? Why, your brother is preparing to hunt of course. We are out to catch a wildebeest if I am not mistaken. I have gathered together all the proper tools for our safari. I suspect this Duke will be more slippery than we anticipate. Off to the hunt!"

And with that Fennel hopped into the boat.

He was a moody little beast, Isabella thought. She smiled at her brother's inspired chatter and joined him in the boat. The marsh seemed louder than usual—the buzz filling the air with static most cacophonous. Perhaps it was applause from millions of insects moving their wings, or perhaps it was a million screams of warning. Isabella did her best to listen, but the marsh had been to her from the beginning, an inscrutable enigma. A madness of survival, wetness, and breeding.

Isabella pulled on the oars while Fennel used his telescope to search the brush. He enjoyed his toy. He spotted alligators, painted turtles and chorus frogs. He took note of them in his safari guide. While Fennel searched, Isabella thought about the secrets that were soon to be revealed.

They pulled up to the dock with Heinrich dutifully waiting for them. Lantern in one hand, he grabbed the rope as Fennel threw it and secured them to the dock.

"Good evening."

"Good evening, Heinrich. Expecting us?"

"It is your customary time, sir. I hope this evening is going well for the both of you?"

"I believe it will, Heinrich. The world seems full of possibility," Isabella replied still in a sort of daze of revelry.

Fennel, on the other hand, couldn't wait to break the good mood. "Indeed it does, Heinrich. If we never return again, don't be worried. It only means I have locked my sister in a vault and decided to be a monk back at the cave. Ha-ha."

"Don't listen to him," said Isabella, annoyed.

"I listen to Master Fennel with a degree of scrutiny," replied Heinrich with a slight smile.

"Yes, that's it. Master Fennel. A man deserving of scrutiny and subtlety. You got me pegged, mah boy," said Fennel, jumping onto the dock "I don't want to break your heart, but circumstances would have it that we will not be dining here this evening."

"Oh dear. I hope you haven't made a rival culinary pact," said Heinrich, leading the twins toward the back of the restaurant.

"No, no, business, Heinrich, business. Please secure the boat and we'll see you once again tomorrow night."

It was true. They did have business, and like most nights where they had something pressing, the most important way to kick it off was a game of Battle Ball in Scarlet Square. The twins had their priorities quite understood and in order. The evening was its usual creaking self. The alley was dripping. Isabella's boots were clomping. They scurried into the square and played for some time.

Cathedral Ogre, it should be noted, was not part of the School of the Divine Line. Its gothic interior had been abandoned by any religious order long ago and was now an art gallery. The twins often ruminated dreamily on the exquisite possible religious orders that had once haunted its halls. Whoever they were, they belonged to the glorious age of shadows and misery that the twins respected so affectionately. Ah, the old religions. How times change. It was a time of heavy fading tapestries and pursed lips. A time where people found it difficult to walk cocky because they could see their pet's sardonic smiles. Yes, a time where priests investigated intestines and rugged journeys promised dragons and spices.

They laughed and laughed—a ball bouncing along the cracks in the cement. After a good few rounds of perspiration and red rubber ball reindeer games, they headed toward the Miser's Quarter.

"Such a regal part of town for us," Fennel laughed as they bounded from rooftop to rooftop.

Fennel loved the Miser's Quarter only because he felt most at home causing problems there. It was a neighborhood so full of tragic ironies that just setting foot in it made him laugh. He loved to agonize the affluent. However, on most occasions their feet would tread the Miser's sprawling streets at a far later hour.

They flew past the red light district with its hobbling whores, past the downtrodden pariah center where hobos disobeyed traffic laws, past the Penom Po, the Vietnamese hub that screamed hints of contraband and down into the Miser's Quarter. They had been to de Vaca's before. Most people had.

Isabella was actually dressed up this evening. Her fur Russian hat and mink collar made her look like a mongoose. Well, at least Fennel thought so. She didn't dress up often and when she did, Fennel tried to show his best appreciation. She had to be encouraged. Fennel pulled out a Congo safari hat. He placed it on his head in triumph.

"You're not going to wear that hat inside are you?" she said to him.

"No, I guess not," said Fennel, putting it away in his satchel of tools. They both looked down at De Vaca's from the rooftop. "Down there those two love birds will dine."

They leapt down to join the rabble.

The restaurant was crowded as was typical. The twins knew this place was excessively austere on the exterior and failed to live up to it on the interior. The cuisine was very good as the cook had actually left Sardines and come across town to start up this place about ten years ago. It was hardly Le Chevalier Noir in the twin's opinion, but Le Chevalier Noir had faded in glory as it had been around for some time. It was a fading star chock-full of nostalgia and beef Bourgogne. De Vaca's was the new hot spot with fusion meals so intricate the menu read as alchemy. The twins liked basics—the glory of chicken noodle, basic broccoli with Parmesan or a classic macaroni and cheese. No, this place was that annoying kind of lavish restaurant that went out of its way to demonstrate how superior it was—the most non-superior form of superiority.

The twins were onto them even before they pulled on the rough iron door. They walked over to the host whose hair was slicked against his head and his eyes showed every nauseating glimmer of self-satisfied pretension. Isabella watched his strained posture displaying his physical effort at control. Some people are so painful to look at she thought.

"The name is Arrogance, monsieur," said Isabella, looking past him.

"Excuse me, Madame?" said the host, a bit taken back.

"Just look it up. Arrogance. I know it is there."

The gentleman tried to gather his wits without showing it. What were two children doing dining out so late at night? No parental supervision. It rankled him deeply to have anything happen at the restaurant that didn't look *au currant*. But then again, his mind suddenly began to consider the matter in an entirely new fashion. Perhaps two well-dressed children dining alone lent a certain chic element to the room. He pondered the idea, lost for a brief second in his genius sense of taste, and made his mind up that in this instance these twins would be a phenomenal addition. Arrogant. Yes, he decided, he liked that name. He looked down on them to see the twins smiling knowingly. The smell of willow seed somewhat caught in his nostrils.

He escorted them to their table suddenly head over heels at the gift of their presence. Isabella felt for the poor guy. He was really tortured. Not all unlike that guard at the asylum. Just people that wanted to love their jobs so much, they forgot who they were. Just because he waited on the rich, he somehow mistook himself for one of them. But that is the nature of one's life in the end. What one does often overtakes who one is. For better or worse such battles can wear on the soul. And for the pretentious host, such lessons were a battle long lost—forgot the fact that his mother was alone at home unable to care for herself, unwilling to think about his brother locked up in jail for the sixth time on some crime he once again swore he was framed for. His family was a mess. He blocked it out so deeply, he was a living shell of the now. It would be pathetic if it weren't so tragically, humanly sad.

Fennel sat in his seat and scanned the crowd for Savina and the Duke. Isabella was already well aware of where they were—in the back corner with the Duke's chair practically facing them. His gasoline smell had been a popcorn trail to Isabella before they had hopped down from the rooftops.

"Well, well," said Fennel, "there is our most masculine brute. I really needed to appreciate what a Brahma bull of a man he is. I thought money made people small. Look at him. He must have grown up wrestling mules and wildebeests. Yes, he is not of this earth that is most certain. We have something truly magisterial on our hands here."

Isabella watched the Duke intensely out of the corner of her eye. Did he notice her? Could he smell her like before? No. At least she didn't think so. He was probably already drunk enough to dull his acute senses. He was drinking his beer and Savina was sipping brandy. They looked happy together. Savina hardly showed any of the anxiety she seemed so consumed with last time. They were comfortable. Isabella noticed the way he intensely stared into Savina's eyes. Savina felt no compulsion to hide anything. She was his—as much as was possible. There was a part in her coarse demeanor that verified part of her soul had been nibbled away, a sort of seductive night of the living dead. Isabella knew that feeling. She had always considered herself a creature from beyond the grave. While Fennel relished in it as though it was pure freedom, she felt a peculiar pit.

171

She envied most human's capacity for amnesia. They could forget and thus get giddy at the most inane things.

Watching Savina, her heart crept up in her. She thought of earlier in the evening, the sound of the marsh—the mad mystery—pollywogs swirling about her white ankles and mud squishing up, up between her toes, the delicate sounds below where the mud squished and oozed. Yes, she heard that. It was that that attracted her to Savina. That sound. The rich depth of swirling and mush that was so glimmering in her. The water.

"Hear that? Hear that? That's their sound. Gish, I tell ya. Gish. And it ain't just gish. It's a jug of muddy give and more give. Now you listen to the Aliber. Just put your lil' perky ear right in the water. Get it wet. Get soppy, girl." Marty pushed her head into the water. Isabella didn't resist. She heard the sound. Swirls and slides. He pulled her out. Her hair splashed up against her face. "Now, ya get it? Listen to em. They're always sliding. You got to know that slide. Like ya feet on the floorboards to Granddaddy Fats. Just know where it's goin'. It's easy, but they'll never knowd it. Oh, but you knew that, didn't you? You knewd it maybe since ya born." She said nothing.

The vision of Marty first telling her about the water caused a shiver in her spine. Yes, it was that swirling she heard in the left part of Savina's body. It played on light notes like woodwinds with the thundering sea wavering behind. Yes, deep below the sound of soft, low noted bells. Bells so soft and ominous with their felt progression. An unappreciated sound indeed. The old churches had known. The sentimentality of low bells, cadences most Canterbury, and this was the ominous foundation of Savina's symphony—an undeniable carousel of emotion in the part of her body still alive.

Yes, it was that song that attracted the Duke. He was lapping her up like a kitten at a milk bowl. A deer at the glimmer pond. He sympathized with its strength and turned within his own drought. So dry. Isabella's lip quivered at his heavenly lack of moisture. He was thin for water like Fennel. Parched and very alive. His eyes played games of cat's cradle. Round and round he spun a nauseated delight. She knew his tortured mania. He was ill with strength. He shared his moments of weakness with Savina and this made so much sense. Yes, a hidden oasis. Isabella often felt the need for such a place and person. So inhuman. That was what bothered Isabella and invited her. Could he be different? Why must she and Fennel only share their disastrous birth with the soiled likes of Marty? There are others. Minasha knew it. Her mouth went dry. She drank some grape juice.

And as much as the twins were eating in public, they had tricks that for all intents and purposes made them invisible to the masses. The twins ate inconspicuously through movement, poise and sound. They just blended into a manneristic camo. They were used to it. People's eyes would scan over them as though they weren't there. They moved the air around them. Fennel would even entertain himself by flinging his peas across the room and hitting someone on the head. He would laugh and then suffer under Isabella's disapproving eyes.

It was not long before the Duke and Savina got up to go. The Duke helped Savina with her jacket. She was obviously pretty drunk. The twins maintained dining. The host said a few very gracious words with the Duke and they were out the door. There was no missing the smell of the Duke—gasoline.

"It's fuel?"

"Yes. I'm surprised he doesn't ignite."

They heard the carriage arrive and wiped their mouths. Isabella threw some money on the table and they were out the door. The street was crowded with shoppers and hoity toities. Fennel put his hand on the street. His head perked up into the air and his nose quivered like a badger. He pulled out his telescope and scanned the road ahead.

"Ahhhh, well, looks like he dropped Savina off at her house. We are following this Duke, right?" Fennel's eyes were lost in the clouds above. He was still sensing.

"Yes."

"Well, we should get some horses. The Bull is headed way out of town. I have no idea where he resides, but he is leading us on a glorious journey."

Fennel smiled. He was ready to hunt into the outskirts. The wildebeest had headed off into the brush. He positioned his hunting cap along his brow.

"Bring the horses!" he barked as he let out a loud ear-piercing whistle. "The hunt is on."

Chapter 16

Down the road, the horses came galloping. They often grazed in the tall grass wild lands that abutted the north end of the Pedigree District—out where even the hunters thought twice about setting foot. They were wild beasts with eyes of frantic delight. Fennel's horse, Zarathustra, was a black Arabian that glimmered in the night light. Strong, sleek, and elegant in its every motion, Zarathustra flew through the streets with madness, as though he had escaped from a time when horses, not people, dominated the world. The horse's arrogance and pride was a palpable energy as it flung Barrenwood muck off its hooves.

Following on Zarathustra's heels came galloping Isabella's trusty pinto, Elia, whose dust and milk bone coat made a camouflage of coffee and cream. Elia reigned in calm and for all Zarathustra's manic qualities; it had been Elia from day one so long ago that had kept order in their very open-ended horse lifestyle.

The horses trotted up and the twins felt wonderful to have an opportunity to again ride their steeds. Fennel reached up barely able to touch Zarathustra's mane.

"Wow. You are absolutely incredible, Zarathustra. Hope you have been enjoying so many days out in the woods, mah boy."

Fennel loved that horse more than any human; perhaps even more than Isabella or himself, which seemed nigh on impossible. He found perfection in the creature that he found lacking in so much else.

They leapt up on their horses and went galloping out toward the Duke's retreat. They had to wind their way back across the District of Jed out along the southern edge of the Calliope and then take the main road toward the mountains, which turned abruptly straight up along what a small yellow sign indicated was the Parakeet Path. The brick homes drifted away toward factory ruins and then quite rapidly to the oaks and birches that sunk roots into the base of the Bomberly Mountain Range.

Neither of the twins had actually gone this far and as they turned up the path, Isabella pulled up her horse to pause. The mountains were massive, stretching far up into the star-speckled sky, their haunted peaks an impenetrable wall for those outside, but also for those in the valley of Barrenwood below.

"The chase, dear sister, the chase. We must continue before he gets too far," said Fennel. His eyes were almost as wild as Zarathustra's who's foaming lips and panting were hard to ignore.

"Fennel, I know you can feel it. I sure can. The closer we get to the source of this gasoline, the stronger the acid pit in our stomachs. That spitting feeling is growing already and I shudder to think what it will do when we get up to the top of the road. We need to drink the fish sauce." Isabella put a sip into her mouth and felt instant relief. She reached out to hand it to her brother. He turned his horse and began galloping up the road.

"It hurts to know I am so much stronger than you! I don't feel a thing! Last one there is a rotten cat turd!" he yelled and Zarathustra had already galloped past the first bend in the road. Isabella spurred Elia and raced to catch up.

Traveling this far couldn't be more exhilarating. They had never seen nor heard of this path. It had almost magically opened up for them and they were now heading up into the maw of their favorite subject of all time—the unfamiliar.

"The unfamiliar is a clumsy toad on a malevolent road to a spooky abode.

The unfamiliar gives time its life and riddles the wise and steals their wife.

The unfamiliar is treacherous and coy like a codger's old toy or the knife-wielding boy.

The unfamiliar is a clumsy toad on a malevolent road to a spooky abode."

Isabella sang to herself. It was the song Marty would sing to her when she was a smaller, younger but no less frightful cherub. She loved that song. Marty was once so kind to her. He would rock her to sleep and tell her dark Grimm's fairy tales that made her shudder and slobber. He once took her on the walks that he now only shared with Fennel. He would tell her why some old women become obsessed with cats and how, in the old ways, you could tell the mood in a house by the softness of butter. But he had changed. Become afraid. Afraid of her and these very unfamiliar roads that had her spitting thick spit. She hocked a fat loogie into the brush and charged along. The road twisted up into the mountains where boulders and cliff faces dared the road. Fennel could still smell the Duke—lamp oil and propane. He pushed on.

After almost two hours, they reached a tunnel that went into the body of the mountain—a hole ominous and inviting. It just vanished deep into the interior. This was it. The entrance.

"Magnificent," whispered Fennel.

Even with the fish sauce, Isabella felt the stir in her stomach. She couldn't fathom how her brother felt. She looked over at him and besides the perspiration accumulating on his brow he seemed fine. His excitement if nothing else provided a powerful energy in him. Neither had any intention of turning back. They dismounted and told the horses to wander into the woods.

"We'll be back in a couple hours, so don't disappear," said Fennel to the faint sight of Zarathustra ducking its head into the grove.

The mouth of the tunnel was cracked, chipped and ancient. Above the entrance, carved into the melanoid mountain were the words *Incendiary*, which Fennel gasped happily, "Incinerate!" The road below their small feet showed signs of heavy use. As obscure the location, it was not without its inhabitants and those in-the-know. They grabbed each other's hand and walked delicately inside.

Darkness. It gave comfort to the twins. Their noses perked up to the unmistakable smell of smoke and gasoline—its dank odor undeniable. The air was thick with a corroded texture. They moved silently along the road, the wet towering walls hugging the vast darkness around them. The blackness enveloped their breathing. They could hear water trickling along the edges of the wall and a thin glistening stream made its progress to their right.

It wasn't all that long before they could see light flickering in the distance. As they came nearer they could see torches and then the carriages that they illuminated. Several carriages were parked with the horse stables just a little ways up. They approached. No one was around, but there was the carriage house. Horses shuffled at their approach but made nary a sound. The twins tread as lightly as they could, mustering as much internal magic as possible to shield their presence. Such things weren't easy when it came to animals. People were easier to fool.

Inside the carriage area, there were numerous tunnels offering the next path to travel. They opted for the one with the most flagrant aroma of petrol. The scale of the entire world around them made the already small twins all the smaller. The tunnels towered high up into the sky above them. Massive carved faces whose almost lack of adornment were compensated by the sheer impenetrable darkness. They scampered along the tunnel and began to smell the oxygen of the outside. They exited into a sprawling lush garden from which they could at last view something of which they had never seen anything remotely close to. Towering far up into the mountain, carved from the mountain's very body, stood a castle most extraordinary. Spiraling staircases wound across the architectural surface and the glimmering from the lights inside made an astrology of life across the mountain's surface. They could see people coming and going as though it was a hotel for thousands—a world outside their own carved into the body of the mountain itself. Fennel always eager to act before thinking ran as fast as he could up to the exterior wall of the building. He placed his hand on it and then showed it to Isabella.

"Unbelievable," he whispered. "It is coal. This fortress is made of coal. What a wonderful home. What a wonderful, wonderful home." He pulled out his handkerchief and wiped off his hand. "Though, I must say, I don't relish the effects this would have on one's apparel."

Isabella took another sip of her fish sauce and stared in wonder. "Here it is, Fennel. Proof of others. I knew it. I just knew it."

She felt a wave of satisfaction rolling through her. It almost made her cry, the feeling so big. An ocean of sensation so deep she could no longer register what emotion it was. Something big, like a world churning inside. She wasn't crazy after all. Whatever this home of the Duke was, it was a place outside of not only Barrenwood's geographic territory but its psychic and spiritual border as well. Isabella found herself getting on a knee and thanking the universe. It was almost too much for her.

Fennel came over and helped her back up. He was laughing. His face was noticeably gaunt but his laughter sincere. "You are a piece of work. Get on your feet, Miss Melodrama. We are just at the beginning."

They both walked across the garden with its blackberry bushes and calla lilies. They felt tiny in the face of such expanse and with their little black bodies they looked nearly like floral adornments. As mesmerized as the twins were, they could sense the Duke's presence in the vastness of the castle above. As much as there were hundreds of people inside, there was only one duke. He was a distinct entity for sure.

"The window. Up there" Isabella pointed to the closed dark window at a height of nearly fifty feet. This would be their front door. "We'll enter there."

She grabbed onto the surface of the wall, its chalky exterior making her hand instantly stained and climbed up spider-style. Her body, spread wide across the surface, moved stealthily up toward the window with alacrity. She popped the lock without difficulty and crept inside. Fennel, on the other hand, just leapt up in one jump, his little calves obviously being an ancestor of the kangaroo. He sat perched in the window, looking and smiling beguilingly at Isabella.

"Ha, ha, ha" he laughed quietly. "You really should learn to bound. Ha, ha, ha. Your face is covered in black. How hilarious you look."

Isabella was covered. Her face, hands, body, everything was dirty birdy. She paid little attention. Instead, it was Fennel who felt the need to slightly wipe her off. They had entered a darkened hallway that overlooked a giant banquet hall. The table below could fit almost forty people, but at present the room was abandoned. The chandelier candles were unlit but melted nonetheless.

"Lavish," said Fennell, "very lavish."

They crept along the hallway and slid down the banister into the banquet hall. Little children in a foreign home. The walls were adorned in giant paintings of battles, regal portraits, and red dripping canvases. A bearded man swinging a morning star charged almost out of the picture frame. His mouth contorted as he charged toward death or victory. A forlorn woman stared obliquely out her screen door into the silent evening outside, her hand loosely holding a small shovel. A canvas thick with paint was swathed in a charged umber with a heavy gaping incision across the left side. The paint clotted and richly textured created a landscape that made its way toward the oak floorboards below. Pouring down.

"Quite an atmosphere for dining. I shudder to think where this man digests," mused Fennel.

They walked around the room and Fennel couldn't help his slight kleptomaniac desires—the polished silver sitting without use on the table too tempting for him. He grabbed a spoon and knife and went to slip them in his pocket. They fell on the floor with a clang. It was the sickness. His hands were shaking. The twins jumped below the table just in time. A broad odd-looking man in a bow tie peeked his extremely bronze face into the room and then entered with a squadron of assistants in white scrubs.

"If those crows are in here looking for scraps again, I am going to resort to placing poison on the table," the man barked as he looked around the room. "That window up there. They got in that way. Sheldon, you need to close that and do find a way to get out whatever got in. I am sure it is a buzzard or some carrion eater of sorts, but it is dark as night in here and you are going to have a heck of a time finding it. You should head over to the supplies closet and grab that extended pole net. That is how I have done it in the past. We can't have these things flying around and relieving themselves on the sisters of the wet. That would go over fairly poorly, I would say."

The man, who it should be noted possessed a most nut brown skin with a head the shape of a bowling ball, disappeared back into the room with all the men except Sheldon who ran up to close the window. He locked it shut and then scooted down a hallway and out of the room.

Isabella looked at Fennel angrily. He was trying to stay chipper, but his stomach had begun to really turn on him. He made a faint gesture of apology, but his illness was getting the better of him. His hands had become harder to control. The arthritic shakes were setting in. She saw it in his face. A sound of movement emanated from the room on their left.

"We can't afford to be discovered, dear brother," said Isabella.

Fennel just stared at the floor. His face was paler than ever and perspiration had really accumulated. He was fading fast.

"Dear me, brother, take this fish sauce. You're going to end up getting sick in here and then you may never leave."

Isabella again offered the sauce to her brother, shoving it right under his nose. He mumbled something, laughed to himself and took a sip. He screwed up his face.

"Disgusting!" he said, but a slight bit of color returned. "Let's follow that sound." He moved fast toward a door.

Isabella just let the moment pass. She didn't need to rejoice on the small victory of her brother taking the sauce. He had sipped it instinctually and now he was off.

Isabella followed her brother toward the door. He wasn't being nearly stealthy enough; just operating on instinct, and Isabella was worried he was impossible to control. They were bulls in a china shop of coal.

Isabella followed Fennel back up the stairs and down an exit hall toward an increasing whirring sound. He sensed something. His acute hunting instinct had taken over. They took lefts, rights, lefts and lefts again to make their way through a heavy metallic door that said most invitingly, *Staff Only*. Isabella breathed a sigh of relief to see her brother on the other side of the door looking down over a metallic railing. She didn't want to lose him in this house.

What they looked down upon was hard to explain. Nearly thirty figures clad in bright blood red satin robes scribbled away on long oak tables. Piles of faded parchment with ink splatter littered the enormous desks. Old books, magnifying glasses, compasses, ink jars, and tan folders were everywhere. A series of massive tired mechanical fans spun overhead with ancient dust still sitting safely upon them. The scribes were diligently at work not looking up at all. Their faces were covered in red veils that gave them the look of devilish dervishes. A gigantic fireplace with a small tree inside burned ecstatically on the distant, distant west wall. The heat made the smell of coal all the more present. Urgent and ambitious, the sound of the pens scratching on the parchment mixed with the crackling sound of the burning wood. Smoke.

In the far corner of the room, they spied mechanical machines for copying. The machine belched black smoke and a man in mechanic gloves was in the guts of the machine fixing it as best he could. The paper coming out of the copier was a marred series of black streaks, the kind of photocopy that might not in the end serve its ultimate purpose of legibility.

Fennel leaned over the railing down onto the scribes. His face was gaunt again and he hocked a large loogie over the railing. He spit and then spit again. Isabella grabbed him by the arm and pulled him down out of sight.

"Don't do that!" she reprimanded him, but his eyes showed not a glint of recognition.

"Need to spit. Get the wet out," he mumbled. They needed to get to the Duke and soon. Time was running out.

Isabella grabbed her brother by the arm and led them both out the far end of the room. She could sense the Duke at the opposite end of the building on floors much higher up. She, fortunately, located a large spiraling staircase that they ascended in rapid fashion. It wound in and out of the building, allowing them a view of Barrenwood just barely visible in the distance. Isabella marveled that for her whole life, this home had been there in plain sight, melted into the mount.

They traveled further and further up, scuttling past hallways full of guests coming and going. Isabella could feel the strength of her brother waning. She stopped when they had finally reached nearly the top and looked him over. He was a worse mess than before.

"Fennel, drink up a little more," she said, placing the fish sauce again in front of his face.

"That stuff is disgusting. I don't want it," he said, waving it off and then suddenly reaching out to drink it. He nearly spit it up but swallowed nevertheless. Isabella then took a sip as well. Fennel's eyes suddenly looked sad.

"Iz," he whispered. "I don't think this sauce is for me."

Isabella paused. It had never occurred to her. She felt pretty good and her brother looked, well, terrible.

Fennel then smiled and punched her in the shoulder. "Ha-ha. Gotcha! Okay, people are down that hall. We will have to cloak ourselves. I will just refrain from grabbing cutlery."

The hallway was in the central building. A sensuous wine colored carpet made room for their fluid black feet. The castle reigned majestic. Ornate mirrors, candelabras, intricate mahogany shields adorned the cornices and doorknobs. It was a perpetual vertigo for one trying to stay surreptitious. Maids and guests and even kittens exited some doors and made their way through others. It was very crowded.

They stepped into the hall and walked along unobstructed. No one bothered them. It wasn't that they didn't see them. They would even receive courteous eye contact from people and smiles. It was as though they were familiar. Fennel would tip his hunting hat at the gentlemen and say, "Evening sir," in an exaggerated baritone. Isabella walked briskly along the hall. It felt good to be in this strange mansion with its own world of denizens and design. She peered at the paintings that adorned the walls.

They were paintings of duke's from time past. The resemblance to the Duke of Izmir was remarkable—all large men, and women, with burning eyes, immense hands and the intensity of an oryx.

It was in looking at these paintings that she came upon one in particular that captured her attention. "Fennel," she whispered. "Look at this."

There in the painting sat a refined, rotund couple, most probably the Duke's parents, as he stood resolute directly behind them. It was a family painting of sorts. But it wasn't the immediate lineage that captured their eye, but the company they kept. Alongside the Duke was a man black as night with a singular earring and a playful smile on his lips. His arm was wrapped around the back of the Duke. Next to him, were two female twins in their teens, with light pale skin, and their black hair pulled straight back against their head. They were beautiful, seductive and like the rest of those in the painting, odd in the extreme. They all possessed a look both divine and deformed. As though one couldn't tell if it was beauty they were gazing upon or the hideous pallor of dreams gone rot. And finally, the source that had made them come to the painting in the first place, at the far end of the picture as though he didn't want to be painted at all, smoking a pipe, sat none other than the gruesome Marty. He was turned sideways as though already walking out of frame, but it was unmistakably him.

"The ol' boy sure gets around, doesn't he?" laughed Fennel. "Never seen him in the luster of paint though. Doesn't strike me as something that appeals to him."

"Something about these people is unnatural. They are like the Duke. Like Marty. They are all, mysterious. Odd," Isabella mumbled, staring into the painting, hoping to catch more clues. And she did see them although they never registered in her mind as her eyes scanned its surface. There, in the background, just barely lit at the back of the room, stood two small silhouettes equally sized of boy and girl children, their diminutive stature barely recognizable in the illuminated portraits in the foreground.

But they had to carry on. Time was running thin and she was eager to make progress. She could sense easily where to go, the Duke's scent making an unmistakable track throughout the home. Her feet moved quicker and Fennel was far behind, bowing and even shaking hands with some of the guests.

"Yes, sir. And we know what a good lad he is," he laughed, holding his belly. He was enjoying himself most certainly.

Isabella felt the handle of a door. It was hot to the touch. He was in there. The Duke was behind the door. She put her ear to the mahogany and heard nothing. Silence. Fennel caught up with her as she battled in her mind what to do. Go in? Sneak in? Time was running down and she had to

181

know more. She had to burst in. She shouldn't, but she did. She quickly unlocked the door with her glass key and pushed the both of them in. Incense. Darkness. Smoke.

They slid into an extremely dark foyer. Their reflections played on a mirror across from them as they could hear the crackle of fire play on their ears. Candles in sconces lined the walls and a red velvet unattended couch with an inscrutable painting above it sat on their left. Across from them were two larger oak doors where the slightest hint of conversation could be heard.

"He's in there," Isabella whispered.

She opened the doors ever so slightly to peer in. A room of worship greeted her retina. Satin red pillows with gold stitching stretched across both walls and only fifty feet in front of her was the Duke bowed over in front of a large altar. It was an altar of the old church. He didn't turn around but lay prostrate on the ground.

The altar was glorious. Though many believed the old church to be long forgotten, there were still those insightful few who adhered to its call. The Duke was one, every muscle gone supine in honor of a quirky, rickety, aggressive altar. An altar designed to empower and obliterate objects and people. Small motors turned the figurines of naked children with small flames coming from their heads. Like dedicated cigarette lighters, they spouted small fires and turned a sysiphysian 360. Long, languorous strings of ruby beads and icy cobwebs reflected light and dangled along the edges. Hints of aubergine powders, seared grasshopper legs, jelly jars of priest breath and small scrolls of pathological eviction notices were some of the many gifts laid at its steel base.

The altar itself was a char pit where inside was only the dust and briquettes awaiting a high priestess's fiddling stick. The priestess was to stir the dust and light the bar-b-que and stare intently for futuristic trace elements. Crossing in front of the altar and then disappearing underneath it, ran a phantasmagoric chasm stretched across the chamber. Slowly moving within it was the viscous ooze of lava. The heavy radiance ignited every corner of the chamber in a pulsing heated glow. The lava was continuously churning, transforming, metamorphosing as it twisted its cryptic turtle pace.

The twins crept in along the back wall and slid inside a cloakroom. Hiding amidst broomsticks and mothball overcoats, they peered out to watch this adventure unfold.

The Duke lay there silently for some time. His mind bent inward; he concentrated on pure submission. He gave in so completely in order to hear the resounding crackling of those infinite flames. As they burned and chewed upon the chamber's oxygen, he heard them tell him the story of annihilation. How the sun was voracious for worlds, how the sinkhole gets its fill, how the great winds break the dead branches, how the riotous forest fires consume and revitalize the overgrown woodlands. Yes, this was the story he was born into.

Finally, he lumbered to his hairy, heavy feet. He was huge. His monstrous size made the enormous altar shrink in comparison. He whistled and made his way to the pillows where he reclined. He was tired. He pulled on his large knobby toes till each one popped like a cork. He pulled a glass pipe from his pockets and began to load it, his large fingers placing the weed in its bowl. He lit the underside with a nearby candle. The smell crept through the room. It lurched around, dancing along the altar. He lay there and smoked some more.

A woman dressed in a radiant indigo dress came in and sat alongside him. Her hair was pulled up and held by a chopstick in back. Her eyelashes spread wide from her eyes. Her fingers were thin and precise. She was barefoot. She sat next to him silently and took the pipe. She smoked. Exhaled. The smoke swirled around her face and then filtered amongst the lava. He moaned slightly and sank further into the pillows.

"What do you see in there?" she asked, as he stared hypnotically at the ceiling.

The Duke grunted and replied, "Sometimes nothing. Sometimes it is just a blank space that tells me to eat the world slowly. Like my mother telling me to slow down and chew on the bull bone. But this time, I did have a vision. It was odd really. They usually are. I dreamt of salt being poured like a waterfall into an ocean of soda. High up in the Bomberly Mountains it poured down a river of white sand. Below it poured and the mass of the syrupy water struggled to soak up the burden of so much saline. The salt piled into a pyramid taking the entire ocean into its ravenous body. I stood up above helpless, wanting to dive in and drink it all up into my body. I wanted to be a human sponge. I wanted to soak up more than the salt pyramid."

The twins found the Duke hard to hear. He mumbled at times and it didn't sound as though he was even communicating with the woman either. More like revelry.

She caressed his head. "You really need to sleep poor thing."

"The fact of the matter is, I can not endure this pace," he said, pulling her hand off and replacing his own hand to rest on his big head.

"I do everything anyway. Not sure why you worry so much. Pick up a hobby." She said.

"Hobby. Ha! Perhaps you are right. I could pick up crocheting or tidily winks." He said.

"Don't jest. I'm serious," she replied. She laid her head back into the pillows and stared into the lava. She took another hit off the pipe. "Or maybe you need a distraction. Why didn't you bring little miss nightmare with you?"

"Oh," he laughed to himself. He moved to his side and faced the woman. "Believe me I tried. I nearly became pathetic in my attempt, but she is a stubborn mule. Just dug in her heels and wouldn't budge. She pretty much threw me out with her own hands. She may be frail, but she has some might in those arms."

"I don't suppose you were sober?" she smiled and lit the pipe again.

"I was smashed. Drunk as a loon. I had thrown back far too much before I arrived. It was madness really. I wanted her to be here. But as much as I play with her, I fear she plays with me all the while. She torments me. Gods!" he threw his glass against the wall and it smashed with a crash. "When did it get to this? I am meant for grazing not delicate games of passion. I have fallen so low. Now I wait for her beck and call? Me? What? This is absurdity. She should be so pleased to know I have dared to even smile upon her, but she doesn't care in the slightest. She is up in the agonized mindset that is her life."

"She is all you have ever wanted, isn't she?"

He petted the woman's hair and smiled at her, his large hands enveloping her. The woman leaned back and stared at the ceiling. "I will get her back here soon. I am sure of it. I must let time work its magic. And when she is here, she will bring such wonder to our den."

"She will wreak havoc, Nicolai."

"Yes, she will be nothing but agony, but that will be our pleasure. I thirst, Esther. I thirst so badly."

"I know. I do as well. Your face has aged . . . there are so many lines." She put her hand up to his face. A world of hills and ravines pushed up against the texture of her index finger—his face a map full of the consternations of a man most hungry.

"Ha, lines." He brushed her away. "Those lines have been there for a long, long time, council. A long time, as you well know. I encourage the definition of my face. I encourage the sand of the world to batter my skin. I am not concerned about lines. I live to age with severity. But this . . . oh, this damn laboring. My father was never forced to such trifles."

Esther stood up and began to pace the floor, her bare feet sticking out from beneath her robe.

"It is true. These days are filled with far too many details of labor. I know your father was far more versed in the ways of social amenities than capital. It troubles me as well. I wish it could be different for you, but from what I can gauge that is simply not the case. We are a dying breed, Nikolai."

"Yes. At least there is glory in that. Glory in extinction."

"It is my job to prevent you from experiencing such glory. Sorry."

"It is your job to bring to light this madness. In that respect, you are failing miserably. I don't know what is going on. It's a dam waiting to burst. I'm just plugging holes throughout the years. It's this tiring and painfully sophomoric utilitarianism that is the present craze."

"I am doing what is possible, but you realize how absolutely impossible it really is." Esther walked over to the lava pit and stared into it. It was hypnotizing. If one thought the embers of a burning fire were entrancing, one has never been blessed with the radiance of lava on opium.

Her voice was husky, calm and soothing. Just the way she placed her delicate hands on his forehead made it apparent that she loved this duke. He stood up and walked with her to the chasm. He put his arm around her and stared into it.

"I listen to the lava," he whispered. "I was given a salt pile, Esther. Lord knows this body of mine doesn't need more to drink. Nothing. I pray for solutions. I receive destruction. I pray for answers and it opens its mouth. One might think it wants me to jump in sometimes. And I would. I would. But I believe it is dry in the grave—a sandstorm the likes of which I am not prepared to engage."

"I am pleased to hear that," she said. She rubbed his back and pulled him to the floor. He lay down with her. The Duke shook his head. He wished he could wake from his troubles. His red spotted eyes were glowing in the haze. He laid his head on the oak floor and looked into the ceiling. His hands went under her dress and he felt along the cool edge of her breast— his grainy forefinger against her equally grainy nipple.

Isabella's eyes opened wide. A knock at the door. The Duke looked up irritated.

"Can't they leave me alone?" he whispered.

"I'll take care of it," said Esther, putting on her robe. She walked over to the door and opened it. There at the door was one of the scribes who whispered to her. He handed her a piece of paper and left. Esther walked over to the Duke and handed him the paper.

He crooked his head as if listening to the wind. Silence. He stood up in an awkward way and remained standing contorted. After a short awkward silence, he inhaled broadly through his hairy bulbous nose—a vast inhalation that took in the follicles from the carpet and cinders from the fires. And then, following in musical succession, he exhaled the strangest sound—a low elk call that shook the floorboards. A sound primordial and soft. A calling to a tribe long lost. He put his nose in the air and his hand touched the oak floor. He stood up straight and smiled.

Before they could even react, he had opened the door the twins were listening from and held them each, by the throat, in his huge hands. Upon seeing them, his eyes grew wide.

"Ha, ha, ha!" he laughed, looking at Isabella and Fennel as though they were souvenirs just purchased. "If it isn't Savina's orphans! Just look how you have strayed from the path. You certainly are finding your way into my life just a little too frequently, I must say."

Before they had time to think, he flung them both into a closet. Their bodies banged against the wall and knocked them down to the floor. They tried to jump out, but he was already locking them in—the sound of metal clicking, clacking, locking and then, a fateful sound of him muttering some spell.

"Enjoy your stay," he laughed.

They could hear the Duke and Esther exit the room. It suddenly went quiet—just the sound of the lava slowly oozing its away in front of the altar and the faint sound of the Duke and Esther's feet going down the hall.

"Well this is rather unexpected but I have to admit, dearest Fennel, we are in the presence of something unlike anything we have ever encountered." said Isabella. She was enraptured. His grip on her neck had been strangely soft, barely able to reach around. She hadn't been frightened in the slightest but instead excited to meet his touch. It felt hauntingly similar to the passive visceral strength of Marty. "Fennel. Fennel!" She looked beside her. Fennel was sitting on the ground. His hands across his legs and his head buried between his knees. Isabella squatted down beside him. "Fennel are you okay?"

"Seasick," he mumbled. "I'm just seasick. Stop the boat."

Isabella tried her glass key on the lock. It didn't budge. Didn't budge? She tried it again and again, all to no avail. She kicked at the door. No luck. She squatted down beside him again. "Hey, my little hunter, you're not vomiting, are you?"

"Soon enough, crafty. Soon enough. Bile and filth will be spreading across this floor. This is horrible. Let's leave. I have to leave," he mumbled between his legs.

"Oh, Fennel. We can't. I think we're stuck here. I can't get this door to open."

Fennel looked up, his eyes wide with panic. "Can't get it open? What are you saying? Surely we can leave!"

He stood up and gave the doors a violent kick. The door held fast. He kicked again and again and again. The sound pounded through the room. The time for silence had gone. His face a deathly white. Perspiration saturated his hair.

"We can't be stuck here. What does that mean? We can't stay here. We must get home!"

"Calm down, Fennel. I'll figure something out."

"No, no, no! We're getting out of here. Now, Izzy! We're getting out of here now!"

He kicked at the door again. His ankle twisted on impact and he recoiled. He then doubled over and began to get sick in the corner. What a mess. Isabella sat down across from her brother. She should have left him behind. She should have known the sickness would have affected him so badly.

As if reading her mind, Fennel looked up at her. "Why on earth, Isabella, " he whispered in a gargled voice, "have I been so cursed as to suffer with this compromising malady while you are so fortunate as to sit there and gloat over me?" Dribble slipped off his lip and onto the floor.

"I am not gloating. I am ill as well."

"Sure, sure you are," he mumbled.

Isabella peeked through the slats, staring at the altar. The way he had bowed. Totally resigned. It had been sincere and evocative. He was channeling. There were secrets here—the face of this building and the chasm of lava, the paintings and the scribes, the painting with Marty, halls of people coming and going. It was true. She had always known. And now they were trapped. She laughed to herself. She was glad she was trapped. She almost hoped the doors wouldn't open. "Don't budge." Could he know who they were? No. No that wasn't possible. But what did he intend to do? It really didn't matter. She couldn't wait to find out. But Fennel. Yes, that was a problem. She looked over at him all curled up. He wasn't enjoying this at all.

"You seem to be feeling better," she said, handing him her handkerchief.

"For now. For at least this minute. I am simply exhausted. The sickness wears me down terribly." Fennel reached up and grabbed a giant jacket from off the hangers and placed it on top off his refuse. He sat on top of it. "This is horrible. What kind of purgatorial mayhem is this? I refuse to believe we are stuck in this coatroom like a pair of broomsticks. A coatroom? This is so beneath us. Ha, beneath us. I can't even believe what is beneath me right now. I'll destroy this Duke. Crush him!"

"Calm down, Fennel. I find the whole thing impressive so far. Aren't you amazed at this labyrinth? It is fantastical!"

"What amazes me, dear sister, is your apparent vitality," he said snidely.

"Hostility, Fennel?" she said.

"No. I simply believe that if you felt like I did you wouldn't be so bright-eyed about our supposed great fortune. That fish sauce doesn't really work on me. I don't know why. I didn't want it anyway. We shouldn't have come this far. This was a mistake." He looked at her. His eyes were sagging. It was breaking Isabella's heart. This was what she had feared.

"Drink more of the fish sauce," she said, pouring some of it into his mouth. She took a drink herself and felt some strength return to her. For Fennel, its effect seemed remote.

"Bleck, tastes like the guts of a salmon egg." Fennel spit into the corner.

"Oh, Fennel, don't you see this place? There are others out here. Don't you see?" Isabella put her hand on his knees emphatically. "Fennel, I can't live on a chain. I can't be the servant, the messenger with bouts of illness and perimeters. I always knew there were others and now . . . "

"There are no others," Fennell interrupted quietly. "There is me, you and Marty. That is all. That is all there ever will be. We are the only ones, Isabella. The way you romanticize these pathetic humans, it's embarrassing."

"Embarrassing? What about the way we're treated? Look at you. You're sick, suffering . . . you're sitting on your own vomit because of what Marty has done. And you talk about embarrassing."

"Marty is wiser than you know, Isabella. Generally I am the one guilty of hubris, but obviously your arrogance will cause you greater harm. He is a wise man. He knows a lot about the serendipitous maneuvering of this world."

"Yes, he does. He knows enough to hide things from us."

"Maybe. He also knows how to protect and teach us. He has plans for us, Isabella. He doesn't intend on keeping things this way."

"I wouldn't be so sure," Isabella said. "You don't think the Duke could be one of us?"

"Who? The fat Duke?" Fennel laughed. "Why? Because he prays to the old gods? Big whoop. Hurray for him. I'm gonna tear that guy to pieces when I get out of here. Lock *me* in here!"

"But you heard how he and that woman talked about Savina as water. That isn't human. That isn't the way they talk. That is us."

"Savina isn't water, Isabella," said Fennel. "How you have managed to come to this conclusion is beyond me."

"What? She most certainly is. Couldn't you hear it? Surely you must have!" gasped Isabella.

"No. I didn't. Why? Because there isn't any. The only fluid I heard was brandy. A particularly cheap brand as well. Now, when you talk of water I think of Zarathustra. That is the ocean thriving. That is a fluidity unbound! I have never heard the water run from a human. I shudder to think what it means that you have."

Silence. Both. Their hearts grew sad and sank.

"I love you, Fennel," said Isabella. She put her head on his lap and wrapped her arms around his stomach. He petted her silky hair.

"I love you, too, my sweet, dodo sister," he said. He began to whistle his mourning song. Laconic and delicate. His lips pressed softly against the musty closet air. The notes reached through the keyhole and along their future. Always tragic. Suffering and incomplete. Words can never bridge the human gaps and spaces and the song gracefully dispelled the soothing amnesia. He saw his boy peeing in the sea and watched him shed his tears. The sea rolled slowly without emotion against his feet. The black sky blended smoothly along the black water along the black horizon. Nothing. Just unresolved tears that could never, ever be stopped.

He rubbed along Isabella's nose. He touched her and felt the space still lingering along his skin. Always distance. More distance now than ever before. It terrified him. He closed his eyes. The illness began to rise up in him. It rose up out of the pond and made a sickening gesture toward his raft. He pushed slowly with his pole further along the Aliber River. The greasy raven landed next to him. He pushed into the mire and felt the pole sink deep into the silt below. He pushed slowly on and let the raft drift along in the direction of the sea. The sun rose over him and the algae collected around the raft wood. He lay down next to the raven and let the sun blanket him in a sheet of soot.

That sun went glittering below the belt of the Earth and the lids of our twins rose like a curtain. Voilá. They were awake in an instant and the clitter clatter of teeth chattering rattled the air. Fennel was now practically translucent. His hair was wet in sweat and his face sallow. The smell of his vomit permeated the air. Above them, staring down was one of the red robed scribes. His eyes peered without emotion, patient. He had obviously been standing there a long time.

He handed Fennel a wet cloth for his head and Fennel threw it out the door.

"Good evening," said the scribe. "Generally our guests stay in more comfortable quarters, but I hope you found your stay enjoyable."

Fennel mustered a portion of saliva and spit. The spittle failed to reach the gentleman's face and landed weakly at his waist.

"Pardon my brother. As you can probably tell, he is not feeling well."

"He doesn't look well at all," said the scribe.

"No. In fact, I am a little concerned," said Isabella, rising to her feet. "That being the case, I really think we should be going. No offense."

"No offense taken. Coincidentally enough, I am here to simply accompany you to the door." The scribe stepped back.

Isabella reached down and helped Fennel to his feet. He was shaky. She was very worried. She hadn't realized the sleep would aggravate his condition. With one arm under his, she followed the scribe along the burgundy halls and to the front door. The hallways were deserted and the mansion's previous charm dissipated under the weight of the twin's desire to return home.

They entered the carriage house where two scribes were caring for Zarathustra and Elia. The horses whinnied and whined and clopped jubilantly over to their masters. Fennel rubbed his cheek against Zarathustra's muzzle. Isabella pushed her brother's slouchy body onto the saddle.

"The Duke has asked that you present this note to your superiors. Oh, and he thought you might be needing this." The scribe handed over a singular fork. Isabella nodded and received the questionable gifts. She then gave Elia a quick whack and they charged out, away from the Duke's incinerating coal mansion.

Chapter 17

The ride took much longer than she had hoped. On several occasions, she had to go find Fennel by the side of the road and place him back on Zarathustra. His skin had gone lucent and not a word came out of his lips, just blubber and spit. Isabella rode and rode to get to the cave, blocking out of her mind her increasing nightmare that it was, in fact, her own hubris that had caused this. Blind ambition and myopic desire, she hadn't even considered that perhaps the fish sauce would work on her but not her brother. One night in that closet was too much for him up in that castle.

By the time they reached the cave, Fennel was curled up in a ball in the back of the boat, cradling the phonograph, lying there shivering. She lifted him from the boat and placed him on his mat, grabbing a wool blanket for some heat. He looked smaller than ever. The sickness was so much deeper in him and it showed in his fevered brow and his crumpled body.

Between the sounds of Fennel's shakes, she could hear the distant laughter of Marty. The twisted revenge that cut into her heart. Maybe she could leave but Fennel was forever bound to that drunk. Her brother's fate was far more intertwined in the inner workings of a man that placed gambling and hot dogs as priorities over simple kindness. Now he lay there like a wilted black dahlia, a signal of the retribution for all those that had forgotten.

She wanted to think about the magic of the castle—the Duke's mentioning of the water, the dreamy world beyond those of Barrenwood—but the stain of her brother's illness made such considerations indulgent, only reminding Isabella of her own selfish pursuits. She would heal him and go from there.

Isabella set up a fire and got a kettle on. A little tea should help. She went out into the brush and picked ephedra from her brother's lackluster garden. He loved gardening though knew little of its ways. She placed some in the tea. He just needs some rest. Isabella shuddered at her stupidity. His body shook as he slept and she put her hand to his forehead.

"I'm so sorry, Fennel," she said quietly. "I just wanted you to join me in this mission. To be together in this. I was naïve. So stupid. So stupid." Her tears fell from her eyes and wet his cheeks. She laid her head on his stomach and cried. The wind blew in the mouth of the cave and the candles went out.

For three nights, Isabella tended to her sick brother. What started out in Isabella's mind as a warning from Marty turned out to be far worse. Fennel's condition deteriorated, his fever not desisting. The order deliveries piled up as Isabella sat quietly by his mat, making tea and cooling his forehead. Fennel had always been under a much stronger medicine and maybe, Isabella was always intended to leave. Maybe Marty knew that she would resist his magic and let her get to this point. Fennel's slight betrayal was taking a major toll on him. He shivered and shook and even small patches of his hair were flaking onto his pillow. Like a pre-emptive fall, the hairs let loose and let their grip go limp. All Isabella could do was wait and hope. She would curl up next to him, spooning him with every inch of her body. Each shake of her brother moved through her body and she echoed a shake back.

The nights were long. She would hold her brother and then get up and walk into the river and stare into the sky. What did the universe want from her? As usual, the shrill buzz of the mosquitos filled her ears with a haunting franticness of a world at odds with itself. Chaos reigned supreme over harmony as the labyrinth of desire, hunger, resentment and ferocity seemed to outweigh the subtleties of compassion and mirth. She had spent her whole life hinged to the whims of a man hell-bent on the now with not a concern for a person in the world. How she and her brother had managed to be as well adapted as they were, she could not say. But surely there was more than just delivering his packages (the likes of which she had no doubt perpetuated desires most base) and living on the outskirts of a humanity most lost and dazed. The heroic of Barrenwood were a lost lot. Frantic and feverish, tragic and destitute, the kind of magic that stirred in Savina Lanthaur's heart spoke of a tragedy beyond time itself—a mortal condition of which great operas could barely scratch. But even that—even that in its own sordid way—did not truly touch upon the more glorious, something all the more wild, something all the more alive.

It was all too much for her. Her life was a trap and Marty had used her brother as the bars. She hated this and she held her head under the water trying to undo her plight. Alas, to no avail. She came up for air time and time again. The humidity of the wet night soaking into her small lungs and telling her that she must continue to live, even if she knew not why.

By the fourth night, Fennel's fever miraculously broke. Perspiration riddled his brow and a glint of light could be seen in his eyes. He had barely said a word in the last few days, which for Fennel was perhaps the greatest sign of illness. Now, his lips trembled as he peeked his glimmering eye out and whispered, "Iz, the Raven has returned." Isabella was so relieved. She could now rule out her brother's demise as an option.

She kissed him on the forehead. "Good to have you back," she whispered.

She made some solid food and even had some herself. While he had been ill her appetite had simply vanished.

It was night and the marsh was alive with frog sounds and the chirps of birds. Fennel lay on his mat in a daze while Isabella lit some candles. At the recovery of her brother, she finally had time to at least consider the events at the castle—the Parakeet Path that had led straight into the mouth of a coal mountain, men and women from who knows where all coming and going. She then remembered, much to her dismay that she still had not read the note handed to her as they departed. She pulled it from her pocket, realizing she hadn't changed her clothes. Her head was woozy from exhaustion and she tried to recollect the parting discussion at the Duke's castle. Her superiors? Is that what he had said? Could he have meant Marty? How strange. She unrolled the parchment and read.

> *To Mr. Castilla,*
> *I want to thank you for your gift, but I can not accept. Your two secret agents are a little young for my needs and so I will be returning them. Apparently, the boy seems to have a weak spot for silverware and so I have given him a complete set for his own culinary needs. As for you, you seem to have a weak spot for my plans of which, I am afraid, I am not at liberty to discuss with you. I find it unfortunate that you did not find it in your heart to pay a personal visit. Has your perspective become so inflated that you now send children? I warn you that it will take far more to gain control, let alone an accurate assessment of the situation. I would suggest a far more cordial and diplomatic approach. You are still young to this world, Mr. Castilla, so please try to not be so careless.*
> *With regards,*
> *The Duke of Izmir*

"Careless?" scoffed Isabella. "Who's the careless one, Nicholi?"

Isabella read the letter again. The events of the past few days were overwhelming her and she walked to the Aliber River to clear her head. Her body was tired. The night was warm and the air muggy. The smell of vegetation and decaying wood crept up her nose. She flicked off her shoes, took off her clothes and waded into the water. It wrapped around her waist and invited her skin. Rarely did she remain around the cave at dark, but what a pleasure it was to be here in the peculiar din of past midnight marsh. The water felt so good and she dunked her head. Underneath the music played in her ears. Gurgling sounds. She blew bubbles and listened to them *palunk* and rise to the flowing surface. She stood up and took in the thick air. Breathe. And back down she went. Feeling her thin hair play against her shoulders. She swam down the water following the current, letting it take her along. Eyes closed. She gave into the drift and floated. Like driftwood.

Her heart grew sad. Fennel's illness made it all too apparent for her. She floated on. Her feet catching on moss rocks and her hands catching lilies. She watched her knee floating above the black surface. The bone moon made it appear as if another lily floated on the water.

"I'm just a lily," she thought. "Just a bump in the flow."

She drifted, watching her bony body ebb to the current. Her mind cleared and filled with the sound and movement. Thoughts changed to a faith in her skin and ears. They ushered in the world and gave each particular motion its due course.

Suddenly, her head hit against some wood and she stood up. Her heart jumped. It was Marty's shack. The rocking chair was motionless on the deck next to the jugs and cages. She spotted the card table, the broken screen door, the cluttered shelves, discarded harmonicas and croc skulls that adorned the patio fence. The ashtray still held piles of tobacco from his pipe and empty bags of chips accumulated in the corner of the deck. She pulled herself up and dripped along the floorboards. The wood creaked and groaned. She peered through the dusty windows into the interior. The small home was vacated—Marty's simple cot unslept in for many moons. The floor was swept neatly and the moon glow illuminated the chalk dust that had settled upon the furniture. Upon first view, she felt the chill that accompanied his doorstep. It swept through her wet bones as though smelling a hint of a mother's youthful perfume or the hazy day aroma of wet pavement from childhoods gone underfoot. It was a mood that carried the sweet smell of his apple core tobacco and the dingy air of his dusty hair. Memories. They come through the nose. She shook it off and moved to the rocking chair.

There it sat unattended and still facing the giving groove of the Aliber—a place from which Marty crafted history with corkboard and mildew. She reclined in the chair and let her dripping butt press up against the splintering deep cracked cherry wood. Her hands gripped the knobby edges of the armrest and she stared out over the water.

Her mind turned to the altar that greeted the Duke of Izmir—its robotic eccentricity with children with flaming heads spinning in circles. She imagined them dancing on the water. A winding trail of lava wound its way around their ambulation and across the wind. She heard the call of the old gods—*Incineration*—the Duke's worshipping calling card. The dismantling of all that was. Fire the eater of oxygen. There was a charm in it. A foreboding hunger in it. He was a beast most primal, carved from an emotion refined and given flesh. He now worked his way across the fetid landscape of a humanity most uncertain. That castle as remote as it was remained too close to the idiocy of Barrenwood below. Isabella could see the Duke bowed down low. His back bent. A brute mighty man so fatigued. Tired. He could not keep pace he had said.

The war that was coming. It touched on Minasha, it touched on the mad, and it touched upon even this man beyond time that watched from a view most high. A war was brewing with Castilla. That bent man with an iron will had stirred the pot and set forces in motion. They were spilling out across the city and disrupting the order of things. Even the fire of the Duke could not eat the fire of this old man's relentless precision. The soulless will had a strength of its own.

Immediately she felt Marty's presence with her. Just like a dad's old suit or a grandmother's mothball wedding dress, the rocking chair issued forth its owner's posture and disposition. The crackle of the splinters curled around and against her skin.

She rocked back and forth as the sounds of crowds filled her ears. Her vision shifted from one of the altars to an image of muddied Barrenwood streets. Chanting. Marching. Masses of people moving. Now she could see them. Out of the fire, their shadowed bodies coagulated in unison. They moved as one being. Like ants at the mouth of an anthill, they pulsed and ebbed. She watched and gleaned. Their movements gained cohesion in the virulence of their shouts and clamor. Torches burned and startled eyes peered in sublime awakening from windows above. Water trickled from the window's hinges. The shouting continued and she rocked back and forth. The crowd moved up against the architecture and the cradled hand of the fairway. Collectively they pushed into parts of town not for them, their footsteps defiantly intruding on villainous cobblestones. Against the design of the city, they overtook the streets with their slip-shod cacophony. They riddled the air with demands and Isabella felt water seeping from the scabs in their lips and the strain sag under their eyes. Water seeped from their hardened old potato toes. Water from their raised angry fists. Water from the onlookers who shook in their shoes and stared in stained wonderment. It ran along the street and helped people's quaking feet gain confidence in the eye of the storm. The air above twisted in a phantasmagoric smoke. Yes, the sky caught fire and crackled in approval. Electric, the sizzling wind lifted the hair of cats and dogs on end. The torches caught the houses and the hands tore windows asunder. The cohesive flock split into pieces. Shards and splinters. Dirt clods and stones burst against the hooded police.

She felt a calling in the madness—the moving of bodies turning the heavens into earth, the fire into water. The sky rained lava and she felt something bigger, more majestic than a mere escape. It was a deep sound within her that surpassed curiosity. It was a revolution most divine. The wind stung the mouths and eyes of everyone. The fire and the streets descended into one raging movement of collision.

In the smoke filled mayhem, Isabella felt him make his way to her. His shadow pressed against the riotous mirage and she saw the silhouette of his bent hat and corncob pipe. His heart pulsed slowly and his heat pushed against her. Marty's eyes glinted in the morass of smoke and tinder and eclipsed the epic moment entirely. He stood there laughing and limping. His peculiar walk most definable as it slowly made its way toward her. Isabella sat, helpless, as his silhouette gained texture.

Silence. He was in front of her now. She could smell that sweet bourbon on his breath, the acrid stink of urine and the bacterial nastiness that always came with his appearance. His old eyes gleamed young despite being covered in creases caused by too many offensive jokes. He wore soiled overalls, the knees black from kneeling in muddy streets. His hands reached back behind his body where a very obvious pair of gleaming metallic sheers scraped the concrete earth. He rocked on his feet.

A ragged smile clung to his lips and his throaty voice spoke out to her.

"Clippers, darlin'. Clippers." He exhaled his smoke and shoved the clippers glistening blades against her nose. "Ya getting all da satisfied. All up and bustlin. Ain't ya? Now ya in ma chair and ya probly want ma pipe. Gotta clip ya. Gonna clip ya. Ya gonna get a sharp clippen and ya getten paired down to da stub." He gave her a wink and grabbed her by her hair. His nappy breath still humid in her nostrils. "Cocky ya are. Cocky bitch dat's all fired up. I knewd it happen. I always told ya. Ya just a mean whirlpool. Up against all da water in da land. Gonna hit yer head. Bump and go down. Down. Ya dat's right. There be more and more than ya ever shook ya noggin to. Lil girl getting a wake-up call, eh? That be fine, deary. But ya pushen up against boulders and the hills and doin it as reckless as a mountain goat on a mud slide."

She caught her breath and screamed at him. "Why didn't you tell me there were others? What are you afraid of that you keep it all locked up inside yourself?"

"Others? Heh, heh. Y'all twisted up on a clothesline, ain't ya? Gotta a big wind blowen through ya and ya tell yaself it's a hurricane. Well, well, ain't you just a curious one? Oughta put ya on my knee and give ya a whip from a tether, I ought." In one quick motion, Marty swiped with the clippers and clipped her right arm clean off. It fell to her bare wet feet and Isabella reached for it with her left. He clipped that as well and she stood their stubby and useless. "Now get outta ma chair and get a red eye for ma home comin." He grabbed her hair and flung her into the Aliber.

Breathe and swim. She coughed, reached out and was relieved to see her arms stretch out before her. They felt numb and pushed through the water faintly. Her mind twisted inside her and her thoughts were to crawl upon the cave floor and sleep. So away, away from the shack and to her home. Back against the slight current she swam, but the darkest part of the evening still lay before her.

As she approached the shore in front of the cave, the glimmer of fire played along the water's edge. The crackle of sticks and the flutter of wings grew nearer as her frail body pulled itself from the current. There, upon the banks of the Aliber danced her dear brother around and around a fire. His hands spun about in the night and the trees were filled with ravens and their beeswax eyes. They peered over him as he chanted, cawed and ran. Circling round and round, his pants were torn and his shirt burned upon the pyre. The language he spoke she could not comprehend and for a second she realized his eyes had turned yellow—the pestilent malaria of the Raven. She crawled upon the floor of the cave and gave herself to the morning.

Chapter 18

Evening came and with it the sordid package. The Stallhammer crew pulled their boat up upon the shore and were already playing cards on a foldout table. Their hands were permanently greasy; their orange overalls covered in mud. The table creaked back from the weight of their hirsute forearms. They flicked the cards into a pile, drank their jugs of Fenyan's Grey and chewed their tobacco.

"Evenin'," they grumbled as Isabella raised her head from the floor. Their mutton chops blew restlessly in the thick air. Her head was still dizzy from last night's events and she sat up to gain balance.

"Good evening, gentlemen," she mumbled. She pushed herself up onto her feet and realized she was still naked. The Stallhammers bickered over cards and lost interest in her as soon as they had said hello. Their stay would only be a few hours and then it would be back on the circuit. Sitting next to their plumber's boots was the package wrapped in the usual pale parchment with the red twine holding it together—yet another to add to the growing pile of things to do. Last night hadn't been a dream. She plodded over to the tub and slid in. She pulled her head from the water trying to rinse out the fog that had crept into her mind. What a mess.

Fennel, dressed in typical black cut-off shorts and t-shirt, walked briskly outside the cave and grabbed the package.

"Ah hah!" he laughed, tossing it into the air. "Business as usual boys?"

He danced into the cave and leaned against the tub.

"Just when things look as though they are about to shatter into a thousand pieces, the great god of routine and grind comes and knocks on our door. Iz, look at me! I'm better, sis. Bolder! Grander! Wiser! I'm better than ever. New and improved and twice the gangster I used to be. And lookie here, the big boss man seems to be putting our ship to sail again. It even includes a little letter addressed just to me."

He laughed his high squealing laugh and clicked his heels. He showed her a letter with the name *Scratch* penned on the front. He disappeared toward his desk and giggled merrily. He definitely did look better. The glint was back and the spring in his step as well. Isabella tucked last night's mad dance back into a deep pocket in her mind and got dressed.

The package was, of course, to be delivered to the School. Isabella took this as a sign that Marty was, in fact, returning any day. If she were going to make a break, it would have to happen any time now. The thought of leaving her brother made her sick and she put her head back under the water. There was only one way. She would have to be strong.

A sadness couldn't get out of her as she put on her clothes for the night. As she watched her brother dance around the edge of the cave enjoying his new burst of energy, she delivered the money to the Stallhammers.

"Here you are, gentleman," she said, looking them over. Their mouths, billowing with wet tobacco, moved up and down like laborious jackhammers.

"Yup," Gary said, his face a maze of wrinkles and warts. "Think we don't know. McFly is as undependable as he is screwy. First he heads out of town without even a note or nothin'. Now he can't stop pesterin' us."

"He is sending more?" Isabella asked, her head clearing up at the news.

"Sure is. You didn't know, little pigeon? Heh, heh, heh! I s'pose he keeps you out of the loop. Well, I wouldn't worry yer pretty lil head about that. Just remember to sign the stuff out, that's all."

"I'll be perfectly blunt, Mr. Stallhammer. It's very early in the evening and I am still waking up. My inability to appreciate your sarcasm, if that is what it is, could easily result in your maligning misfortune. I advise you to save yourself and your limbs as it appears we will be seeing each other the following evening as well."

The Stallhammers grumbled again and resumed playing cards. They were a sordid batch of boatmen. Part of the upriver delirium. Their shipments had been arriving at the cave as long as the Manzanita's bloomed and briared.

Isabella and Fennel waved goodbye to the gruff cadre and boarded their boat. The week's previous events played on Isabella's mind. She scratched her ankle from the mosquito bites and felt strange about heading into Barrenwood. Just as the town opened itself up, she could feel Marty's pipe coming down the river. Fennel, on the other hand, felt little apprehension. His vision had cleared and in the agony of his fevers he had found an eerie calm—a cruel oasis in which he perched his hat. The maladies of his sister were of little concern to him. He had signed the pact if you will, and his destination was assured. He nodded his head vigorously to his internal conversation and rowed the boat more eagerly than ever.

As they pulled in toward Le Chevalier Noir, Fennel cackled and leapt toward the other side. "Ha, ha, ha, Heinrich, surprised to see us?"

"It has been some time, I . . . " Heinrich mentioned as his varicose hands pulled the boat to shore.

"It has been some time because, my good sir, we are diversifying our portfolio. As you see, we are once again couriers. Paddling gods like

Mercury delivering the goods, the proverbial crap if you will, to the proverbial mob. But think you not—no, don't you think at all—that we are somehow burdened by the relegation to manufacturing plant workers. The assembly plant stratagems are entirely welcome to us. At least, in so much, as we have made peace with our treacherous fate. Have you made peace with your fate, Heinrich? Is your conscience clear?" Fennel squinted one eye, rose up on his tippy toes and stared at Heinrich. "Well, right, fate can be dull. Fate is cruel, my good man. And the ability to endure cruelty is a mixed bag that only the choice few are bestowed with. But the score still goes unsettled. You, Heinrich, are our unwilling accomplice in our escapades. Well, to be quite frank, both you and my sister are. Oh, we're all so unwilling! So unwillingly plodding along the line of fate! It really tears at the soul, doesn't it?"

"Terribly," Heinrich uninterestedly added. "Lady Isabella, the Persembes have sent urgent word to you. I have left the letters in the Red Room." His eyes caught Isabella's with a peculiar glint for a gnat wing second, but Isabella cast her eyes down and avoided anything more.

"Fennel, if you will allow me just a second," she responded with peculiar deference. He smirked, jumped in the air, and then tapped his wrist with his cane.

"Five minutes I give you, dear sis. Five is all. We have places to be and places to do. I'll not be delayed by the effete needs of your aristocratic coterie."

Isabella turned and quickly scuttled off to the Burgandy Salon. She could feel Fennel's cold eyes on her back. Everything was off. The balance had gone lopsided.

"Probably a hang nail, folks! Or, possibly an invitation to an ever so knotty potty! I swear the agony of piddling with such high-class morass! Isabella, five minutes, I tell you!"

She closed the door to find a letter awaiting her on the table. Isabella scanned it to see if there was news of Castilla or Minasha or Big Boy Charlie. But there was none. It was a letter from Sibel and it was a cry for help.

Dearest Isabella,

Help me. Please. I am tormented and my skin turns against me. This cannot be love because how could something be so cruel. The only thing cruel is me and my own pathetic mind turns the knife deeper into my gut. Peter is dumb as a widget and I adore him so tenderly. He comes to me every night. He loves me fully. He smells like wood chips and hair grease. His hands are rough and his lips soft as satin. He even sings to me, dear Isabella. He sings into my ear beautiful pop songs that would embarrass anyone but from his mouth they are angelic. He flutters and loves and holds me and when he does I shake. I shake with a fever. Is it hatred? Is it nausea? Is it love? It makes me sick.

I am a liar, Isabella. He can't even conceive of it. He doesn't understand why I would lie. I don't understand either. But I do. The more in love with Peter I am, the more I find myself forcing my strange desires on other men. I've been very naughty. Naughtier than ever. I compensate for Peter's adoration in strange dark ways. I'm getting strange to myself. I don't know why. Am I afraid? Am I evil? I am evil. You know this about me. You see it in me. You know this about me. You are evil, Isabella.

Free me. Please, Isabella. I can't take this.
With desperation,
Sibel

Isabella crumpled the paper in her hand. This wasn't the news she needed. Tormented love. The last thing she needed to hear about: Sibel caught in a fog of delirium while the world burns. It made Isabella's lips quiver. She hungered to eat it. Not in a kind way, but in a way that she knew would only make Sibel scream in terror. She scampered out of the room to find her brother staring directly at her as though he had only stood there and waited the entire time.

"The hand of thunder moves our wings! I do hope you enjoyed your brief moment, Isabella. Time is not on our side for any l'amore dalliances. As Mercury is ever so inclined, we are bound by duty to be lightening-fast in our potlatch. Diligence! Long live diligence and precious responsibility! Heinrich, adieu, adieu, adieu!"

Fennel bounded straight up to the roof—his calves eager to find the roof gutters and chimneys. He dashed madly to the streets with his cape curling against the wind. By the time Isabella had caught up with him, he had the horses in tow. He sat upright and magnificent on the back of Zarathustra who chewed on his bit with eager animosity. His bristling white teeth loomed with the unnerving gel of plaque setting the edges. The wind bustled madly in the air.

And so they rode. Rode and rode into the pitched black algae of Barrenwood. Penom Poe spit eggshells and banana residue into the gutters. Energetic children clambered on horse carts and tossed their plastic playthings at each other. Mothers swept the sidewalks with brooms made from the hair of walnut trees and grandfathers hobbled and bobbled their nuts. It was on to the Miser's Quarters then the Mortestrate where the city was under siege—bars clamped on windows and the wrecking crews bashed against the walls of section eight homes. Automotive rust, coal residue, paint shards and brick cinders rose up in the wind and cluttered their hair. Down along Maxwell Street they carried themselves. The neighborhood torn asunder by the city's tyrannical reconstruction.

Renew the breeze—the multitudinous banners read and the bright red paint of the words scorched the desiccated wood chips that once constructed the town. Homes piled upon each other and faint hobo camps lurked on the edge of their destruction. The fire picked up their black eyes and their songs sang against the back of the demolition crews.

"I ain't never been a rambler. It's never been up to me." They sang. "It's a sure bet it ain't an accident. Gimme a drink. Gimme some peace."

The Mortestrate in all its tragic up-ending also lent a steady flow of the water that both twins could taste. Water poured through the banjo and the exploding homes split against liquid sorrow. The force of the city was unleashing such a sad song and poverty was a riverbed. Isabella watched the hobo camps disappear against the skyline of cranes, steamrollers, and cones. She hoped to pick up the bricks with them one day. To reconnoiter with destruction. The brick dust air swirled into her mouth and left the sickness there. She sipped on her fish sauce and considered handing some to Fennel, but then retracted. He didn't look at her, but she could feel, quite clearly, his strong almost virulent disapproval. The ascent toward the top of the Billington Hills became increasingly barren with the flora and fauna going brown and thin as they rode.

The School of Divine Line lived in chalk and its hospice was flatly impressive. It stood on the top of Billington Hill where the sandstone cliffs and boulders began. Snake holes riddled the front path and the orange baked earth cast a dull brown light even under the moon. From the top of Billington Hill, Fennel and Isabella could overlook Barrenwood. A telescope sat perched on the Manifest Rock for visitors to peer through. The monks were known to follow the movement of the stars from here, but Fennel suspected they would be better suited looking in their own bedrooms down below. Fennel leapt over to the telescope and began searching.

"Somewhere, lookie lookie, somewhere," Fennel mumbled. "Iz, not all that long ago, I got myself a clue. Yes, a clue, to that villainous beast who was putting our dearly beloved lunatics out to sea. It's that doctor. The one at Wellington Manor. The one that smells of apple tobacco, gin, and root. He is out there, hunkered down and so proud. I can see his home tucked back in the hopes of hiding. But, oh, we can see now, can't we?" He turned to her and smiled wide. His eyes looked fierce and his teeth like steak knives. She managed a smile back.

"That doctor is nothing Fennel, but I'm glad you found him. He is a tool. Surely you know that. Would it be possible for me to give the telescope a whirl?" she asked.

He turned the telescope so she could use it. The gears bent and careened. She dialed in the glass and pointed toward where she figured the Duke's home must be. Only the most perceptive eye could detect it, but there, the deep grey against black revealed the silhouette of the coal mansion. The façade leaned against the horizon with cruel ramparts. She imagined the dusty scrolls, ruddy cherubs and fecund passings in the halls. She pretended the windows with their glowing coterie were opening up to her—the dizzying clamor of blood red scribes and edifices to incineration. In that instant, her blood burned her bones. The fog lifted and she was instantly on course. She must return. She must return now! This feeling rose up in her with such urgency it nearly scared her. Something in her told her to run now or lose it all. Marty's packages, plotting, and disciplinary folklore must surely wait. Her brother, too, sadly, must be left behind. He had made his choice. She looked up from the telescope and her blood dropped deep into the heels of her socks.

Fennel's eyes studied her with a slow piercing cruelty that startled her. It was menacing.

"Don't, " he slowly stated, "for an instant imagine it. Don't think it. We are staying the course. The loss of some of my hair has at least given me the enlightened understanding of my role in matters. I will lead for now. Just stay the course."

He walked back toward the entrance to the school. Isabella, subtly surprised by her own immediate adherence, found herself picking up the package and stepping in line.

As they headed to the door, Fennel did something he had never done before. It was new and it was odd and it was done without the slightest recognition of just how unique it was. Instead of knocking on the front door as they had done so many times in the past, her brother opened the front teak door and stepped inside. Instantly the smell of coriander filled the nose. Stained glass appeared everywhere with various scenes from the universal history of man's great voyage toward manifest destiny. The slaves of Egypt tugging on chiseled stone as architects ingeniously deduce what will be. Diagrams abounded with cartographies of ocean depths, mountain trails, urban planning, the circulatory system and the neurological matrix. Hardly a universe ruled by gods, but one where even the gods themselves submitted to depths, fathoms, and leagues. The distance between salivation and salvation were quite in demand at this temple. But yes, dragons were present as well. Quetzalcoatl, Vishnu, Lock Ness and even Brigham Young, all shown in miniature blue, green and golden glass. A shined mirror was above the mantle and Fennel took a gander. Yes, he was looking different, he thought. He grabbed some of the thin sand that littered the foyer floor and swirled it into his hair.

"For a more cunning and dynamic you, we suggest, New! Floor sand!" he smiled at his reflection. His hair was now pointing in every direction—a dusty tarantula black salad that so obviously pleased him. Soon enough, one of the many monks presented himself from the interior. He wore the coriander colored robe. His complexion was sallow with a tanned face and thinly trimmed eyebrows. The lines against his mouth were heavily creased and he stood with perfect posture.

"Evening is here," he said solemnly. A strange greeting indeed. He stiffly put out his hand and each of them shook it. Firmly. His face showed hardly a trace of resonance. Hardly even present. His eyes a pair of bark chips.

"We have brought you this package," said Isabella and she hoisted it up for him to see. Her arms held out the package and the monk slowly looked down.

"Yes," said the monk and he nimbly took it from her. He opened the envelope slowly. His delicate long fingers peeled the wax sealed sides of the envelope. It felt odd to Isabella that these monks in all their regalia were able to read Marty's drunken scrawl without consternation. His writing was a boy's stick in the mud. The monk put the letter back and looked up quickly.

"It appears that our transaction will be a little more lengthy than usual. We have some other matters that need attending as well. Let me direct you to our sitting area. Hang up your coats. Reading on the table."

He led them through the musty halls toward a back room. The walls lurched in and the coriander breath billowed upon them. They walked this way and that, twisting and turning as though the School was a massive musty cranium. With every turn, Isabella's sense of anxiety grew. As Fennel skipped ahead, Isabella felt fear rising up in her with ever footstep. Something was terribly wrong.

The next room revealed a large waiting area with dusty grand couches and various encyclopedias and epidemiology fanzines organized on the tables. The monk indicated that they should wait here and Isabella thought that her life might just consist of waiting rooms. Waiting for someone to arrive to say nothing. She sat on the couch and an ugly cloud of dust poofed right up. She coughed and Fennel laughed. She looked around the room more. A gargantuan stained glass window bent the moon glow to reveal the image of a torn husk of corn.

"What do you think that means?" asked Isabella.

"Corn," Fennel got up from the couch and paced in the dull light, "indicates commerce. Ducats gone awry. It's an apogee for the intellect. A plebeian's anxiety. Erect their effigies as they might, none of 'em. Not an iota of spaghotta of 'em, knows a nothin'. Tell ya that much. The Raven can take that corn and turn it into mud honey. Isabella, my dear, let me take this opportunity here in this rare occasion on the soil of Coriander Christendom to initiate a new age. Let us call it . . . the eternal return. Thank you. Thank you." He bowed to an imaginary audience. He then clicked his heels and did a forward flip. "No, really, thank you! Yes, Isabella, my ever so loving love, I am convinced that through our travails, we can once again set off to eek out the most delightful tragedy yet. We will take our recent escapades as certain proof that we were meant for more, well, more distilled enterprises."

"For now we must wait here," Isabella responded as she flipped through the pages of the myriad medical books and magazines. She felt the desire to calm her beating heart. It pounded in her chest. She had heard of panic attacks and perhaps this is what they felt like. Fear turned to physical convolution. She steadied her gaze on the magazines and tried to lose herself in their pages. Magazines were an odd invention. Pages of information piled together like a breakfast buffet. A little of this and a little of that. She grabbed a science magazine dedicated to slumber titled, *The Journal of Circadian Rhythms.* The pages were full of images of the brain, of people with their eyes closed, of cats with electrodes attached to their small furry heads, somnambulist studies, REM studies, biorhythms, theories on synapses and theories on digestion."

Fennel looked over at his sister ignoring him. What a bore she could be. This was all for the best anyway, he told himself. The sickness had changed him. This he knew. He was bolder now. Wiser. His feet stood more firmly on the earth and his wings, mental as they may be, were ever ready to fly. Yes, he had talked to Marty when Isabella had disappeared. It was by the fire as he held his routine incantation—fish eggs, dust bunny, chilled wart and rusted carburetor. Marty had appeared in the midst of the flames and told him what he must do. His teeth were razors and his eyes brilliant embers. Fennel had nodded wildly and laughed.

"Fear not, Marty, my boy, the Raven didn't even need you to give the word. My fever has broken and with it came wisdom. She is out of control and like a dog that bites its master, you just need to put it in the proverbial doghouse She's gonna get what's coming to her."

Marty had nodded his head and they both had laughed with the fire rising higher and higher. Marty had pulled out his banjo and Fennel had danced like a leprechaun around the flame. He felt the heat and excitement with every step—the bacchanalian urgency and victory that was his new, more mature way of being in the world. Now he had a fever in him and his sister continued to pretend he was of the old ways. A child. It bothered him immensely. He sat in the corner and picked the dirt out of his fingernails. His impatience was getting the better of him.

He hated her. She wasn't that different from so many other people. Superior, blind, boring. He continued to file his nails and considered, as he often did when he was down, just how amazing his statue would be. The Toil would offer him a chance to give shape to his unusual perspective. It would offer a monument to the limping mistake. It would bear down viscous and grumbling in low notes and manure.

Isabella would adore this one. He looked over at her. No, she wouldn't. She was idly flipping through the pages and away from the tragic fold. He knew it. The Raven had been right and his teeth gritted. What a self-absorbed monkey wrench she had become. Only a few weeks until Marty came back and she had decided to skip town. It was less than purity and more than he could stand. What is it that she can't see? What has blinded her emaciated nostrils?

"Put down that damn book and talk to me!" Fennel yelled. He rushed at her in a fit of anger and threw the magazine across the room. It sputtered across the floor and Isabella looked up, still bored. Her eyes met his and it was he that turned away.

"Ta-tee-ta, that's better," he said, skipping down the hall. He turned around. "Isabella, you've become a dolt and a bore. I do declare."

She sat there staring at him. Inside, her heart turned but she gave no hint of it. Her brother was off the chain. He had gone feral, as he ever was apt to do. She had sensed it earlier this evening and as he moved about the room, she could sense an inner meanness that was most dangerous. She said nothing.

"Exactly," he continued. "A perfect response for one who is a dolt and bore. Ya know, I realize that my role between the two of us has traditionally been too demure from the task of our sensitive emotions, but alas, oh Dolt and Bore, no longer. I am not afraid to get right to the task of untangling our relationship. I will not turn from the glaring light of your sudden . . . whatnot. I am not afraid to address the quite apparent fact that you and I are having some problems. I am not afraid whatsoever, D and B!" He clicked his heels and jumped onto the coffee table. "Admit it!" he said, pointing down at her.

"Yes, it's probably true but what can we do?" Isabella said, surprised to hear her brother addressing the issue of their inevitable demise. Her head was clouded. She reached into her jacket for more fish sauce only to find it was gone. She reached more frantically and her brother let out a disgusting screech of a laugh.

"Hee hee hee! Looking for this, sis?" he held the vial in his hands and he was dancing on the coffee table. "I'm afraid you've become a sauce addict. I'm here to intervene. No more for you, oh dolty of the bores."

Isabella was feeling the sickness much more tangible now. It rose up in her throat and constricted her lungs. She sat helplessly on the couch vaguely realizing that Fennel, for whatever reason, wasn't feeling the sickness at all. He stood above her with the Raven's complexion. His eyes looked wild and mad.

She reached out to him in desperation. "Fennel, sit down. You must understand. I love you dearly. I have to escape. I want us to escape. Please, don't do this. Come with me."

Fennel stepped off the coffee table and sat next to her. He put his childish arms around her and nuzzled his face right next to hers. "Aww, necessity really is the mother of invention. And you are ever so inventive, aren't you? So sweet all of a sudden. The tables turn and now you pretend at sympathy. Admit you are a dolt and bore and all will be well." Fennel patted her hand. "You see, we are not a pair but, in fact, a triad. A triangle is magic and is where all the strength of the universe derives. You are resisting strength because you are sinking into that bog that is your own plebness. You are plebbing it up."

"Why aren't you sick?" Isabella asked, as she bent over, her stomach surging in pain.

"Hahahaha, the Raven is becoming his own little bird." Fennel bounced up to stand again on the coffee table. "My little recovery has given me a small birth. It was a bit of a birthday that had to slide through the needle of malady to arrive. But arrive I have. This Raven doesn't get sick because ol' corncob pipe has decided to take me off my bird leash. I am free to fly and fly I shall."

Isabella had heard enough of this. Listening to her brother prattle on made her sick. Nothing made her more nauseous than hearing people defend their masters, least of all Fennel. She stood up and pushed him off the table. He fell back, knocking a pile of books over.

"How delusional are you? You think this little bit of freedom is your meal ticket? You think it's over? And now what? You are my little jailor? How tortured your little soul is to be so full of pathetic rationalizations. Get it into your head, it is only me and you."

She was already feeling bad. She loved him and he drove her crazy. How stubborn was he going to be? So ready to display his power, he could only do so if he submitted to the predatory logic of Marty. Isabella put out her hand and helped him to his feet. He sat next to her and put his arm around her.

"It is such a tragedy, isn't it, sis? Delusion? When we don't know what is best for us?" he asked mockingly. The smell of his sandy hair and freckled grin. His eyes glimmered mustard and she could feel the talons in his fingernails. "What can we do!" he asked, jumping back onto the coffee table. He slapped her hard right across the face. Before she knew what had happened, he followed up with a kick to her stomach. She careened backward. Blood splished across her nose and she found herself tossed into the corner. The snakes in her stomach turned into a beehive. Her blood ignited.

She swooped up from the floor and grabbed Fennel by the hair. Her fingers dug deep into his scalp and she swung him around furiously. He reached out with his arms to grab onto her, but her momentum was too much for him. She twisted and spun. Round and round. Her fingers released the precious twin blood from his skull that made dandelions turn to mercury. She sent him flying into the wall. As he fell to the floor, she grabbed a somnambulism book and bashed it into his head. *Blugh!*

She panted and panted—her head bleary with emotion and illness. Vomit was a marching band within her. She paced back and forth to get clarity. The blue cornhusk did a jig above her head. Fennel was getting to his feet. He was walking toward her. He was gentle now. He was a milk boy. He gave her the sad eye and whistled out the mourning song. It rode through her and the marching band in her stomach cascaded onto the floor. A day for a parade.

Chapter 19

Isabella awoke to the blonde moustache of a stranger. If his feathered hair and tan suit didn't make it obvious enough, the opal hourglass dangling from his neck confirmed it. He was a Coriander Monk. He was feeding her some onion soup. It tasted salty on her cherub lips and the fluffed pillows behind her head felt good. Teak struts extended across the ceiling above the gas lamps that burned with a smell so spicy.

"You're awake. Good. I am Monk Harrison," he said. He sat up and put his hand on her forehead. "You still have quite a fever. Looks like you will be spending some time in this bed."

She said nothing and looked him over—pale burgundy handkerchief folded in his front jacket pocket, smoke stains on the ends of his fingers, brown suede shoes. She looked up at him and said nothing, her eyes shrinking down to the contempt she loved to show. His eyes twinkled with a smile, but his face remained grim.

"I don't suppose you read," he said, standing up from the bed. "I would get you some books if that might make your stay a little more pleasant. We have an impressive collection here. I am sure you know this." He stared at her with unflinching eyes.

"Actually, as I am sure you know, this is my first time in your rumor mill," she said. Even speaking made her limbs hurt.

"I *wasn't* aware of that. How strange that is. So, what is it that brought you here then?" he asked.

"I . . . " She thought twice. No need to go into this. She shook her head. Never mind. She felt like a used sanitary napkin. So, as fate would have it, she has been hand delivered to the monks themselves. Not bad. She should beat the crap out of Fennel more often. Fennel. Where is Fennel? She looked up. Harrison was exiting the door.

"Excuse me," she peeped. He looked back from behind the door.

"Come to think of it, I would like a hardy book. I feel simply awful, but I suppose some words of wisdom would do me good. Can you suggest something for me?"

Harrison's eyes lit up slightly and he walked back into the room. "I would need a little more information than that if I were to choose you a decent book. Everyone has a point of entrance to every subject. Everyone is particular. A good book is a good book, don't get me wrong, but given all the cultural variables, it's hard to say what would be the best choice for you."

No doubt, Isabella thought to herself. "How about something that is of interest to you right now. That way, well, no I take it back, I have a better idea. You're one of those Coriander Monks I hear about, correct?"

He looked at her with that drawn grim face. The lines around his face were tremendous. Thoughtful eye wrinkles and creased grease. He didn't answer but looked down on her. Thinking.

"Is that such a hard question?" she asked. Even for Isabella, he was a bit unnerving—hard to read and strangely intense. He remained silent then suddenly looked up into the ceiling.

"I was thinking how strange you are. Yes, don't take offense. You wouldn't. I am sure. You know you are strange. But that wasn't the entirety of my thought. No, I was caught off guard by how you asked me about being a Coriander Monk, because, well, yes, of course, I am one. I mean it really is quite apparent. But something about the way you said it made me . . . question being one."

"Why, because a little girl isn't intimidated by you?" she asked straightforwardly.

He stared at her unblinking. His eyes still soft and stern. He sat there quiet for almost half a minute.

"Yes!" he guffawed suddenly. "That is absolutely correct. How perceptive of you." He laughed and then sat on the bed. His face back to its monkish appeal.

"Very well," said Isabella. "Now I don't suppose there is a current favorite reading topic among you monks, is there? Something that is piquing the collective interest at the moment? A lecture series of sorts?"

"What peculiar questions you ask. Well, of course, yes, there are always topics around here. That is why we are here in many regards. We are here to keep these topics moving through these halls. Let's see, what has been the favorite topics of the last month? Agriculture is always a big topic around here. I love it myself, but I wouldn't describe it as a particularly new sensation. There has been some fascination with bugs but in a way, the fascination is again linked to agriculture. You can't tear the thunder away from the lightening you know?"

He looked at her for an indication of her interest. "Yes, well, I suppose the big study these days is just population studies. Some results have recently come in regarding the correlation between geography and culture that are quite fascinating. Monk Gavin gave a fairly impressive lecture on his recent field studies with the Tyransie tribe. A completely different tribe than us, but could a heavy abundance of flood activity have something to do with it?"

"You call that an interesting study?" asked Isabella.

"You would have to see the data to really appreciate the study. A lot of our most recent findings reveal their greatness inside the data I suppose," said Harrison.

"I suppose," she grumbled. "What about the mind? Do you study the mind?"

"Yes, of course, we study the mind. What would the Coriander Monks be without a thorough investigation of our most important organ?" he said.

"That isn't our most important organ," said Isabella.

"And what is?" he asked.

"The nose, you moron," she said, "but I know plenty about that. Tell me about the mind, if you can."

Harrison took being called a moron very well. Not that there is a very well way to take such things. But if very well indicates that he just let it pass without much of a thought that is how it happened. Very well.

"I thought you wanted me to suggest a book," he said.

"I do, but I believe I like hearing you speak. Can you just tell me what the latest findings are on *the mind*?" Isabella used the phrase *the mind* in an affected manner. She didn't mean to. She couldn't help it. It was in her blood. Quite simply she would say *the monks* the same way she said *the mind*. That is to say, she held both phenomena with a judicious amount of humorous skepticism—just a trace element that always betrayed her. She had little faith in the Coriander Monks and all their hard work. The monks were a very prodigious clan with little time to waste. They were busybodies too busy to laugh at their most solemn of terms: *the mind*. And like all things they felt somber about, they mapped it—continuously mapping the mind, this foreign object that just sat out there like a dead pet dog run over by a buggy.

"Well, that is not an easy question to answer. The mind will forever beguile us. We are still in a dark ages in understanding how it works. Yes, I can tell you that. But progress is being made. If only the world were full of more phantom limb victims. I swear. No easier way to discover the various oddities of the mind than spending some time with someone who is experiencing phantom limb. They feel their limbs moving around even when they are gone. It's a good indication of how the mind works."

"Are you sure it works at all?" she asked.

"What do you mean by that? Of course the mind works. The interesting part occurs when it works wrong. When it programs itself in odd ways and the monk is able to gain a perspective on the true inner workings. Like phantom limb, see? Phantom limb is . . . "

"I love the name," said Isabella.

211

"Yes, it is charming. Anyway, phantom limb is this bizarre occurrence where someone who loses a limb still feels it there, even gets pain in it, even though it is gone. Bizarre really. But alas, a moment of inadequate programming, right? Right. The mind is donating clues to us monks, if we are listening, that is. So, we have done some studies to not only cure phantom limb but to investigate it. In some cases, you could rub a phantom limb victim on the nose with a cotton swab and they will feel it on their missing limb. Why is this? Aha! In other cases, victims are cured by seeing a mirrored reflection of their one remaining limb in the place of their lost limb. A simple optical illusion becomes therapeutic. These clues have led us to an amazing finding. Our recent studies have shown that much of what produces phantom limb is the result of the mapping of senses on the mind. I'm talking about the actual layout on the mind map, see? The figure of the homunculus being an easy depiction. The homunculus is a grotesque character who reflects the actual mind space dedicated to certain sensory areas on the body."

"Homunculus, huh? He is the embodiment of the mind map, is that what you said?"

"Well, yes, but it really is just a visual aid of course. Nothing rigorous. Anyway, his body is shaped with big feet, wide eyes and an enormous nose."

"An enormous nose, huh? So, your studies have told you that the mind is mostly dedicated to smell?"

"I suppose you could interpret it like that."

"I don't need to," Isabella said. "It's quite obvious to anyone who is paying attention."

"Well, anyway, that is what I mean by learning how the mind works. We are doing studies, but the mind is beguiling," he said.

"But what I mean is: how do you know the mind works at all?" she asked.

"Well, I suppose it depends on what you mean by the term 'works'. If you mean that your basis for criteria was that a person was still able to breathe and eat, then right, most people's minds work. If you mean that people are able to hold down a job and feed their children, then most but not all people's minds work. Or if you mean that people are able to know why we are in this marsh, then well, no one's mind works. So, to answer your question in classic Coriander style: it all depends."

"So, what is the collective feeling on that around here?" she asked.

Quiet again. He got up from the bed and moved to the door. "Personally, of course, we are all mad. I will grab you a Coriander guide to phantom limb."

Isabella slept a lot. The sickness had really taken a toll on her. Just a few days past it was her brother in sickness recovery. Now it was her turn, but without Fennel to take care of her—only this monk with a moustache, his inquisitive eyes and silence augmenting his good old attire. She wasn't accustomed to dreaming, but rolling about in the bed she lived somewhere between sleep and waking.

In her haze, her anxieties painted gruesome portraits: Fennel with yellow mad eyes, his sneer growing to consume his boyish face; the sounds of the mad making a chorus in the sea salt air; Savina drunk in her rickety home; the Duke supine in front of the altar, a bull in front of flame; Minasha painting a ring of blood, a stained finger of gristle and hair; the Persembes scampering around blind, a trio of lost frantic sea gulls; Castilla eating the city with fork and knife precision; Doctor Eldridge Never sitting in a high throne of manila folders, scribbling notes on this wrinkly skin; and Marty McGuinn, laughing hysterically in a rocking chair with the shears leaning against the broken wood porch railing. Isabella felt crazy. She had come so close. She had to leave. These fevered dreams haunted her waking life.

She rubbed her eyes to notice Harrison sitting in a chair quietly reading a book. She hadn't heard him come in, but that mattered not. As she came to the world, he put his book gently on the bedside table and lit up a pipe. The apple tobacco filled the room in a puff. He picked up a note from the table and looked it over.

"You can not leave," Harrison said plainly, scanning the note. "I am not sure what it is that you have done, but it is our direct command to retain you here in our care." His fingers held the note plainly, his eyes unmoved.

"So be it," Isabella said and shook the visions from her head. She pushed herself up on her pillows. "It is not as though I am eager to get back to my UPS duties anyway. Package delivery vs. resting in bed. Hmmm . . . I think I will go with sleep for now."

"Those are not quite your options," Harrison said, putting the note in his pocket. He went over to the bureau and pulled out a small mustard yellow robe. "You're to begin work with the order today. This life is short. The questions are tall. There is little time to waste."

"What about my book on phantom limb?" asked Isabella. She tried not to take too seriously Harrison's prognosis. There must be worse things than being a captive of the School of the Divine Line. She wasn't much for sleeping in any way and although being incarcerated wasn't necessarily pleasing, she was more than happy to learn about these prodigious monks.

"I have brought two books on that subject as well as the report on flooding. I believe you will see the beauty in this wisdom."

"You misunderstand me, Harrison, " Isabella said, snatching the robe from his hand. "I appreciate the beauty already. Humor and irony are not without its aesthetics. I am enamored. Now, if you will excuse me, I need to get ready for a productive work day."

Harrison left the room.

After he departed, Isabella gingerly placed her feet on the sandy floor. How long had she been in that bed? She couldn't say. Time seemed to be disappearing for her. The floor felt good on the contact with her toes and she lifted herself up to her petite feet. She was still weak, but not too weak to stand. She didn't want to be in that bed much longer. Lying around wasn't exactly her style. She lifted up the robe on the bed. It was small. She would look like a yellow Star Wars' Jawa. The thought made her laugh.

But it was short-lived. Her laughter lacked its echo. He would have loved this. The old Fennel. The one before the fever. But this new one? The vision of Fennel's psychotic yellow eyes terrified her and sent a shiver down her spine. What had he become?

She placed the robe over her body, tucked the thought away and headed out the door. And so began her ordeal with the School of the Divine Line. Isabella had been sent to work with the new recruits—the young acolytes of the School who had yet to graduate into actual Coriander monks. A prep school for the holy. They were proper and straight and boring and Isabella steered clear of them as much as possible. It helped, to some degree, that she could sense there had been some kind of order to steer clear of her as well. She was a pariah with her only companion the occasional visits and ruminations of Harrison.

There had been some odd moments in the beginning when the monks seemed determined to figure out who and what she was. They had tried their best to get their inventions to assist in their discovery of the truth.

"How old are you?"

"Twenty-six."

The polygraph's arm stretched long against the graph paper.

"Where were you born?"

"In a cave against moonlight in a pleasing spray of marshsong."

The line created a mountain.

Isabella was tickled purple by the ineffectiveness of the polygraph—steel arms and voltage that reached into her every word. She liked watching the polygraph make mountain ranges on the gridded paper. The monks stared at her with blank eyes. No reaction. But the machine was ever so different. Her answers seemed to provide it personality. She laughed as they asked their questions knowing that her humor was a one-way street.

They had also asked her to take a personality test. Using a series of questions, she had to fill in with a number two pencil whether the answer was A, B, C or none of the above. She did her best to answer the questions. Do you prefer many friends with brief contact or a few friends with more lengthy contact, you prefer to be alone, or none of the above? With every question, Isabella felt compelled, much to her and the monk's chagrin, to simply go with the only obvious answer: none of the above.

It wasn't long until the tests to figure her out came to a standstill and she found herself relegated to being a small workhorse on the digging routine. Her average workday, however, turned out to not be quite as exciting, nor as illuminating as she had hoped. The topic: dinosaur bones. Paleontology. A large dig way out in the Scanderville range. Each morning she had to wake up, head to the Charibean Hall for breakfast and go right on out on the mules toward the dig site. Yes, she had to be awake during the day—something that didn't sit well with her biology or psychology. She felt clouded. It took much work and the sun blinded her. Her skin was pale. It shouldn't see the sun. But it did, and it baked.

Each morning, she sat on the far side of the room away from the rest of the acolytes with a few older monks slurping soup in total boredom. And with each day, Isabella's boredom grew.

"Is it possible for me to walk out of here? Maybe take a walk to the Calliope district to get some decent grape juice?" she had asked a bald eagle-nosed monk during breakfast.

"You are to stay with us for one month. Be quiet now," the monk had said as though he was reading from a script.

Isabella focused her attention back on the grey soup. Okay. For now I will toe the line, she thought. She looked up as one of the monks gave notes for the day's dig: Bones, Digging, Sites, Schedules, Methods.

Did dinosaurs excite her? Initially yes, they did—large lumbering beasts that bordered on mythology. Their behemoth size and adoringly reptilian natures provided clues to entirely other forms of existence.

"Fennel obviously did not know what was in store for me here," she mused.

Her heart grew warm thinking of him. She pictured him listening to the descriptions of the brachiosaurus and its relentless spiked tail and appetite for plums. He would go bananas. That face of his, the Raven's had so maligned his thoughts of her. Would it remain? His newfound anger put chills in Isabella's heart. Ice cold.

Dinosaurs are all dead. Their skin has gone flakey and joined the sedimentary layers of the Earth's historical crust. By piercing the earth's skin, a digger travels in time, at least with a shovel or pick or hoe. Isabella realized this on her fourth day of shoveling in a small mining camp along the Scanderville Range. Her own skin, once a milkish pale, now was crimson and flaking much in the same manner as the dinosaurs she was trying to find.

Brontosaurus, terrasaurus, brachiosaurus, stegosaurus, these names, these phyla, these genomes, these species, ordering, number cataloguing, dating, arranging, codifying, milking the bone of time.

Somehow this repetitive and tiresome affair of dino digging had dragged Isabella off course (and she didn't seem to care). While she wondered how twisted Fennel's lips were becoming, she knew Marty was out there, squeezing lemons and boiling a broth of her eventual disciplining. The Duke and Savina were ghosts in her veins and the thought of them brought a fever in her heart. These monks and their digging! What a bucket of tools they were. Their infinitely deduced sensibilities managed to pick the locks of the world and not necessarily shut them down. She was fascinated with their hijinks. Nets could be used to bring down the most agile butterflies. Carved lenses could magnify the most remote region of saliva.

So far all that had been located were some cigarette packs and some fishing line. The plastic coating on the fishing line being so miraculously unbiodegradable that it acted as a time capsule in the soil, but to find some simple bone—four days and nothing substantial.

The crew captain's whistle blew and the day was officially coming to an end. Her hands were sore from the repetitive action. Blisters crept up on her tiny toes. Her eyelids were weighed down from the accumulation of red magnesium dirt in the air.

"It is time we rest now," said Monk Blethel. His eyes showed a hint of something incredible called nothing. "Your work is appreciated. Bone revelations take time."

The Monk picked her up and put her on his horse. They slowly trotted back to base camp. Isabella looked at her hands and appreciated their depleted state.

"I've really been such an aristocrat for far too long," she thought. "It's good I finally do something. I really am so stupid."

Her hands were blistered and her meals were crap. It wasn't enjoyable, and yet, it was. For now. Like all her adventures, she was dancing with its exoticism. But it was more. It was the call of those songs that Marty had taught her. It was the gurgle of the Aliber and trickle of the creeks that had summoned the olive juice joy in her eyes. She was its victim. And lately, she had found newer, weightier tributaries that were leading further from the porn shack grumbling of Marty (and Fennel). She had heard new symphonies far greater than the muddy carnivals and boatmen. The Duke knew. Savina knew. The boat knew. Parts of the world sang with such sweet tremulous sorrow, such a deep roar of the bottom of the sea, that she could only follow their call. But to where? She could not stay here with the monks. She had to get back to the castle.

Isabella looked up. The sun was rusted butter spread across the searing wafer sky. The *clink clank* of water cups being pulled from the monks' pouches mixed with the scratchy thud of horse hooves in dust. She wasn't going back to the cave. Ever again. A clear channel opened up inside her—a vacuous space that held no fear nor joy, a space of possibility that filled her and put electricity at the ends of her fingers. Where would she go? What would she do? Her thoughts turned to Savina. She would simply crawl in her bed, rest on her pillow and let Savina blow whiskey breath into her face.

On the tenth day, Harrison arrived to join the crew. He had arrived because a dinosaur had been found. Not a moment too soon either. Isabella was absolutely bored to tears with the digging plan. She had been mumbling to herself for the past three hours to pass the time.

"Good afternoon, Isabella," Harrison said, getting off his horse. "I thought you might want join me as we head over to the bone find."

"Bone find?" Isabella asked. "Does this mean we can quit? Harrison, I don't mind telling you that my patience for this field trip is quite at an end."

Harrison began walking over the ridge and Isabella followed. Her back was sore from digging and she couldn't care less about the bones of a dinosaur. Yet, alas, there it was. Big. Purple. Crystalline. Bone. She gazed at it down in the pit. Monks were dusting and dating in a whirl. Yellow ribbon was being laid out to provide a clear space. Harrison produced some instruments and began taking soil samples.

"Millions of years ago there was a large lake here in the midst of a massive desert—a massive feeding ground for creatures from far and wide. Barrenwood and its marshes were the furthest things from these dinosaurs' minds. And now, we have this incredible find. You realize, Isabella, that this bone find might be an important piece in our understanding of these long lost ages?"

Isabella was impressed. The bone was massive and its contours strong. It was a ligament of an enormous proportion. Of course, this would help the monks. A large nodular edge protruded from the magnesium soil and hinted at a landing accomplished long, long ago. The strange aubergine hue sparkled with crystalline elements and the entire feeling was of crushed time.

"It makes you want to fold time, Harrison," Isabella said as she leaned back on her heels. "This creature is still falling to the ground. It hasn't stopped. Its bones are pushing to get as deep into the molten core of the planet as possible and we are falling in with it. Harrison, I dearly respect the pursuit for this creature, but I suspect that an even more pleasurable task would be to dig up your own bones."

"Dear Isabella, I haven't the foggiest notion of what you are saying, but I am glad you can appreciate this find. There is something important I must tell you."

Isabella interrupted. "I will be honest with you, Harry. Understanding that dinosaurs walked the planet is indeed interesting, but, believe me, much of those answers that you look for are in already in your skin and nose. And while I find your pursuits enjoyably thorough, I find it completely in cahoots with all the other myopic forms of past time that seem to drive you people." She looked closely into his serene face and began to smirk. "You don't believe it either. Ah, that's funny, Harrison. You don't particularly know what you're doing and you spend more time trying to repress that than thinking about anything else. Well, if that is the case, you should at least not drag me into it. Surely, since this lump of calcium has been acquired, I am free to go."

He looked at her inquisitively and a dark look came into his eyes. "What you say may be true. I honestly can't say for sure. But this discovery, in fact, doesn't release you. I'm afraid to say, I have just received word that you are set to be a long term resident here at the School. It isn't in our nature to kidnap people, but it has been ordered that you are to remain in our care for the next few years. I am so sorry." He turned his head and headed back into the pit.

Isabella was stunned. She looked into the sky and saw the screaming ice blue of these overzealous men. Basta! Isabella kicked a rock at Harrison and laughed.

"The time has come for me to obliterate this charade. While you and your consorts while away picking the lint off your own tombstones, I am saying adieu. I do not say goodbye out of any anxiety for what you proverbially describe as an extended stay, but in fact because I have pressing matters to attend to back in that slum known as Barrenwood. I say to you in an earnestness so uncomplicated and true that I am bored to tears."

She picked up some rocks and hurled them into the bodies of the digging monks.

"Take your greedy paws off time!"

The monks and their security squadron descended upon Isabella. Her stomach still hurting from the illness, she fled into the hills towards who knows what. Her small feet trampled the red dirt and with each step, she felt a greater urgency to cross over the distant mountains stretching out along the edge of the horizon—an out there that seemed to never arrive soon enough. The sickness welled up in her with every step. She only had run two hundred yards when her stomach doubled over. This infernal nausea. The bile piled up like a compost mountain. Her eyes watered and she fell to the ground. As she lay on the dirt earth ground, with coriander robes surrounding her, she licked the salt off her lips and said, "You don't win. Don't ever think that. I just feel terrible. Perhaps I am a monk after all."

Chapter 20

So began, in earnest, Isabella's sojourn with her inadvertent boarding house. Whether the monk's sensed her internal acquiescence to her fate at the school or whether they had decided to shift to a more accommodating arrangement since her stay had become a long-term one, the monks relaxed many of the restrictions on her. She could now dine with the other acolytes. She received a bunk in the barracks. She was treated with a modicum of equality.

Being of a nimble mind, even when she was depressed, she remained curious. The specter of her lost brother never fled, never stopped haunting her, but she couldn't help but be intrigued by this sprawling world of study. The school loomed large as a labyrinth of possibilities. The School of the Divine Line turned out to be anything but a line. It was an entangled web the likes of which would make any spider envious. Lines of thought and history bent back across each other with such certainty that they hit each other with a profound resounding paradox. Whether it was the great ornate study halls for translation where the monks gathered around dug up Rosetta stones from times past to the alchemical laboratories where petri dishes and sulfur came together for the study of new forms of dynamite, each strand of research came with its own language, discoveries and axioms. Truth, it seems, is a web.

The building was more of a series of great lumbering brick buildings separated by fields of sand with wooden knobby walkways. Isabella and the acolytes resided on the distant west campus, which came with its own barracks, dining hall and classrooms. Further east, the actual Coriander Monks, with their peculiar hierarchies and systems of organization, were busy with their solemn lifelong pursuit of inquiry. The dining hall had a beautiful arched ceiling that stretched high overhead—gold flecked mosaics of Hermes, Vishnu, and Saint Anthony the Great mixed effortlessly with numerical formulas and chemical compositions, such as $H2SO4$. Hanging below were the ever-familiar bleach bright lights of the fluorescents, which always cast the room in an electric hum of purgatory. Under these lights, Isabella had been made to ingest far too much stone soup and sourdough bread.

Occasionally, the acolytes were allowed the freedom to stroll about the enormous campus. She had already become familiar with the Paleontology Guild, which sat not far from the acolyte barracks. She loved how upon entering the guild, she was greeted by skeletal displays of creatures enormous and vicious—massive teeth, jaws and bone.

Standing outside the Paleontology Guild, she could look out over the campus and see ever so many other red brick buildings that looked exactly alike—humble, stout, without expression. It was odd, Isabella thought. The only signs of difference among the guilds were the various architectural elements built into the cornices whether they were the stone howling baboons and elephant ears of the Animal Research enclave, the tomato plants of the Agrarian Annex, the corn husks of the economists or the scales of the Law Center. The campus reeked of a hidden excitement, thought Isabella.

They tried their best to hide it, but there was a fever on the campus; no matter that their churches looked so very different from the exterior of their houses of study; no matter that the acolytes were reprimanded for exhibiting anything that resembled normal childlike behavior and the older Coriander Monks that solemnly walked the sand paths were shadows of silence. Isabella knew that this place contained magnificent secrets. That said, the air was ever bitter and dust was always blowing into her face.

How many monks were there she could not say. Easily thousands. The acolytes alone were nearly a thousand told. She didn't have many opportunities to walk on the actual campus, but when she did head over, she occasionally spied the spectrum of monk's robes that hinted at their internal hierarchy. The majority of the population was Coriander Monks. They were the meat and potatoes of the school, the dusty tan robed men, who silently slipped into the halls, mixed the mixtures and transcribed the scrolls. Occasionally, Isabella spied monks who wore eggplant tinged robes with long dangling necklaces adorned with small magnifying glasses. These were the rectors—the heralded few that were the masters of disciplines. And finally, even fewer, and only rumored as Isabella had never seen them, were the monks in black robes with red stripes along their wrists with the dangling geometric measuring tools—these an inner circle of monks that only the students whispered about. And beyond even that, because surely existed many more colors, Isabella had neither heard nor seen a thing.

Now that Isabella could eat with the motley hoard of boys clad in mustard yellows, the image of which gave Isabella the distinct impression of a Van Gogh sea of blurry buttercups, she had a new hoop to cast herself through. The nervous energy of youthful boys around her made her stomach turn enough that she at times mistook it for Marty's magic. As much as they avoided her, she could sense their weird energy—little guffaws, bits of food flung, and the hum of minds that couldn't control themselves. She stared down at her stone soup wondering if she may have actually died at the hands of her brother and gone to what she considered the worst hell of all—the banality of adolescent anxiety.

Fortunately, she found herself rescued. He sat next to her. His energy was far more steady. His need for attention was far less tortured. He had sipped his soup quietly next to her and said not an iota. When she finished, Isabella had risen from her seat and headed to the dishwashing station. Leaving the table, she heard the boy mumble, "I agree, this place sucks." She couldn't tell if it was to her or someone else, but that small resistance felt wonderful to have some camaraderie.

The next day, he sat next to her again, still not saying anything but quietly working on his soup. Isabella knew it was no small thing to sit next to her. She was a pariah and even if this young man with shaggy brown hair and almond eyes did nothing but eat soup, his presence was noticed by all. In this case, actions did speak louder than words.

On the third day, it struck Isabella that this young man might win in the war of silence. She wasn't particularly the quiet type and this slow moving camaraderie had already begun to not appeal to her. Who was he to crowd into her space and then not say a thing?

"I'm not your friend, you know?" she said turning to the intruder. Her sudden whisper of words startled him and he looked up suddenly awake.

"Who said you were?" he whispered back. "I really could care less." He went back to slurping his soup.

They sat in silence with just the sound of liquid entering lips. Their bodies bent forward, the lack of anything interesting becoming a cacophony in Isabella's ear. Was that to be it? The conversation ended there? Isabella didn't like the way he had ended her breakthrough in such bland fashion.

"It's you that sat in my area, you realize? I didn't ask you to join me. How about you join your little buddies over there and talk about your lame ambitions or something."

If Isabella meant to insult the boy, it did not work. Her words made him smile. He looked over at Isabella and it startled her to find that she found him attractive. His nose looks like a bird's, she thought. He gave her a sly smile and said,

"It is just that kind of painful conversation that has me sitting near you. I didn't come here to be your friend. I just figured people wanted to avoid you so much, I could avoid them best by being near you."

This peculiar thought made her laugh, which received familiar *shhh* sounds from the monks.

"I'll take that as a compliment."

The boy went back to eating in silence and they took their soup bowls away without another word.

His name was Milliard Penn and though it took time, Isabella and he became friends. They shared an antipathy for the school, although Isabella found his a peculiar blend of something from childhood and arrogance whereas hers came from the predicament of being trapped and arrogance. He was a bit of a downer always grumbling about this or that, but he became Isabella's only friend. They were both bored and the optimism that seemed to fill the voices of his peers made them equally ill. The enemy of one's enemy.

As time was ever regulated, she would catch him on his walk to the Paleontology Guild and chat with him. They would wander off on the eastern path to take the long way around the Horology bunker, to arrive back in the classroom. He often talked about boredom, which Isabella found was something that could really be a source of conversation for people. Boredom, Isabella told Milliard, is the slow-winded agony of birthing an idea. She had imagined that he would have been forced through some family obligation to join the monkhood but instead she was surprised to find that membership to the Guild was far more guarded than that. He had tested well at a young age and been moved to school for potential acolytes. His entry into the church had not been assured but instead was the result of many years of study and competition.

"I was so focused on winning," he said as they kicked little basalt stones along the wooden walk. "I forgot to ask what the prize was."

"And here it is in all its splendor," Joked Isabella.

Milliard enjoyed the research on the dinosaurs, but the digs themselves felt like a prison sentence.

"This isn't actually about digging for dinosaurs," he told Isabella. "This is a training in obedience."

Isabella knew the truth of that although such training clearly had some unintended consequences in the dissatisfaction of Milliard and the overt intention of Isabella to run for the hills. It was the eyes of Milliard that made Isabella more than a little embarrassed each time she dropped her pick and bounded out into the wastelands, or the time she hijacked a waiting donkey and rode off at a snail's pace. There at the horizon she pictured herself through his eyes dropping to the ground, like the rotted limb of a tree careening toward the sand.

Milliard had grown up far outside Barrenwood and the idea of a place beyond Barrenwood filled Isabella with great fascination. For all her worldliness, she knew she was rather provincial. Milliard didn't think much of it. He said the world was all rather the same. There were places to eat, places to sleep, places to buy the basic functions of life and a few places to augment life to make it seem less boring. It was, all in all, a moribund perspective. He came from a prominent family in a village called Exington. Isabella could have guessed only because his particular blend of insouciance could only be bred through privilege. His father worked in making sales catalogues for the growing number of discount home goods stores. His mother was an avid reader and writer. He talked about her quite often. She was a suffragist in every sense. Extolling the merits of the female gender and railing against the patriarchy that she so clearly witnessed around her. For Milliard, it had clearly added to his already growing well of ambivalence.

"She's right, of course," he told Isabella. "Women get a raw deal. But strangely, the only woman allowed into this hellhole is you, Isabella. Men get the privilege of a pathetic work-life and entry into this sand pit of celestial education."

Milliard and Isabella studied in the same class of chronological mapping where the monk professors would replace plastic sheets on the overhead projector and discuss the various methods for dating their finds.

It was in this class that they met their nemesis: Walter Mayhew. It wasn't that he was particularly mean that made him a nemesis, but that he was particularly invested in the truth of the church. It was his fascistic determination to be right that made Isabella and Milliard find him a useful subject for a joke or two. Every question, his hand went up. Every opportunity to extol the virtues of the School's commandments, he would sing them out as though from a songbook. He was an acolyte through and through and perhaps it was this very quality that allowed Milliard and Isabella to focus much of their disdain for their surroundings on him. This is all to say that if looked at from a different direction, Isabella and Milliard were simply terribly frustrated people acting out their agony on a relatively simple, nice person.

Isabella, at first, had attempted to enter into a conversation with Walter, but he would kindly demur. Like everyone, he knew no good could come from associating with Isabella, nor would it come from making her an enemy, so he would kindly excuse himself. But Isabella was determined to make him decide. Friend or foe, either way, Walter would have to put his neck out a little bit. It was through some mutual plotting that Milliard and Isabella managed to switch out one of Walter's tests with another of their creation. Walter received a perfect score of A+. They then proceeded to do it yet again. Upon receiving his tests back, Walter began to see the light of it. He knew something was amiss and it only required one wink from Isabella to figure out what was going on. He was now in a bind. Should he accept her help and forever bind himself to her or should he out her, and thus, immerse himself in a painful and embarrassing series of conversations with higher-ups about why on earth someone would cheat on his behalf. It was torturous for Walter. Each direction was full of agony and as someone who actively sought out the most efficient route to respectability, he was at a crossroads of shame.

In the end, he outed Isabella and her plot. The anger that raged in him from his confusing situation forced a cathartic burst of confession. And just as he had foretold in his worst of imaginings, the affair required numerous meetings with him and Isabella and various other higher up entities at the School whose attentions he had hoped to gain in a far more laudatory light. Isabella, of course, couldn't get kicked out of the church and in the end, as counter-intuitive as cheating on someone else's behalf might be, the officials couldn't help but consider that anything was possible when it came to her. She was more than a wild card. She was a female prisoner in an all male research and religious center. They decided to absolve Walter of all responsibility. That said, his name remained associated with this bad bit of luck and his stellar reputation had now gained some ill-fated personality. He was not pleased. He had become a nemesis.

It was through Milliard that Isabella was able to make the acquaintance of Lamont, Calwyn, and Jada. They were friends of his from his studies in Exington. Lamont was in botany, Calwyn in death studies and Jada in biology. They found Milliard's interaction with the lone female on the premise a bit of a nuisance, but at the same time not surprising.

"Milliard has always been a strange duck," said Jada. They were very much boyhood chums and their jokes and jests reflected the adolescent qualities that made being young actually enjoyable (for them). For Isabella, she suffered through their encounters. To her, they were such boys—always hitting, joking, being dumb, and rarely, if at all, saying anything of substance. Even while what they studied was at the most interesting aspects of the known world, she found their approach absolutely miserable. How Calwyn could actually study death and have not a single insight into it? Isabella knew that only people invented absolutes, that the universe operated in the terrain of the obvious. The greatest mysteries were only that way because they sat so obliquely in front of you. The grave, if anything, pointed out the obvious fact that people weren't truly alive. Perhaps it was this insight about their lack of insights that Isabella took away most.

Yes, it is true that in some respects the School of the Divine Line had presented itself to Isabella as an opportunity to find a community of sorts. As austere as her setting was, the everyday foils and increasing number of acquaintances allowed her to briefly take her mind off all the pressing issues that had catapulted her into exile. Nevertheless, she hadn't forgotten her ultimate goal: to escape to the castle and learn about people like her. At this point, surely Marty had returned. He and Fennel were laughing back at the cave playing Texas Hold 'em while she remained stuck in this school? How strange and awful a thought. She wasn't miserable, but really? Her brother had just left her. How could he? It scared her to consider how deep his anger must be to do that. She had been abandoned to this dusty campus. And as much as she was enjoying it because in many ways she was, she also had no intention of staying. No, she would escape.

The sickness, yet again, had emerged as her biological corral. She was chained in essence by nausea and if she could just make the fish sauce, she could catch the first bus out of town. Thus, it came as a welcome surprise when in passing she heard Jada mention his upcoming class on rainbow trout anatomy. Fish! These underwater creatures had been on her mind most avidly since the day she entered. The meals at the church never had fish. There was not a spring or river in sight. The entire aquatic world it seemed had been banished from the studies of these monks. But finally, a piece of the recipe came into place and with impeccable timing.

"Rainbow trout?" asked Isabella, butting into a conversation that she almost always obviously ignored with indignation.

"Oh, hello. I didn't realize you were there," replied Jada and the boys all collectively laughed together. Even Milliard couldn't help but smile.

"Well, I am here. I'm right here. Did you say your class was doing something with Rainbow Trout?"

Jada pulled his book bag off his shoulder in an exaggerated way and sat onto one of the minimal wood blocks that served as seating in the courtyard. He pulled his cloak from his head and turned his sardonic eye on Isabella. He was handsome with black shaggy hair and piercing grey eyes.

"Yes, we are doing dissections for the purpose of learning fish anatomy. We have already dissected frogs, of course, but also ducks, lizards and chickens. Fish, it seems, are next."

"I need something from you," Isabella said. She was eager to get to the point.

"Of course you do," quipped Jada. "Why else would you be talking to me?"

"I thought you wanted something from Milliard," Calwyn threw in. "I had never guessed it would be Jada."

Isabella ignored them and continued.

"I am serious. We might not get along completely but in this matter I am most earnest. I need a handful of fish scales for some research I am conducting. I am sure it wouldn't be a big deal for you to gather them up in your class and hand them over to me. It would mean the world to me if you could help me out. I would be most assuredly in your debt."

As snarky as the boys were, they weren't completely dumb and Jada most of all. They all had some sneaking suspicions that Isabella was more than just a peculiar girl. She struck them as potentially non-human—something more bizarre and more supernatural than her personal appearance allowed. It was just a hunch. A hunch, of course, that was accurate.

"Let me think on it. I will let you know," said Jada. He turned back to the boys to continue their conversation on inanities. Milliard and Isabella walked off toward the paleontology building.

"Fish scales, huh?" asked Milliard. "What kind of research are you up to?"

"It's just a guess I have regarding their properties. I think they might help with this stomach pain I have," replied Isabella.

"Oh, right. Your stomach. I don't think Jada will help you, but let me see if I can talk him into it."

They continued to walk to class in silence. Isabella snickered to herself about Milliard's naiveté. She knew Jada would help her. She could see his eagerness in his eyes. If ever there was one, he was an opportunist. She expected and received his request to come in private later that evening. She also had no interest in telling Milliard about her plans to escape or about the exact nature of her stomach illness. It would invite too much speculation regarding her bizarre background. Talking about Marty, Fennel, the cave, the water, the Duke, it was all too much. She and Fennel had always kept their private life under wraps and some habits don't go away.

Later in the evening she was unsurprised to spy Jada making his way to her bunk. She had never completely adjusted to the night sleeping regimen and usually spent the first half of the night staring into the ceiling. Jada quietly made his way to her bunk and tapped her on the shoulder.

"Good evening, Jada," Isabella whispered. "I'm glad you decided to pay me a visit."

"Evening, Isabella," Jada whispered back. "I don't want to stay long. I have thought about your offer and I thought perhaps we could make a deal." Jada pulled from his robes an envelope. "I have here the fish scales you requested. They weren't easy to get. Monk Genuine kept a pretty close watch for whatever reason on the holding tubs that held all the dead fish. Not to mention that when he finally did leave the room, it took much longer than I anticipated to get the fish scales. They don't pluck out as fast as you might think."

Isabella smiled sweetly at Jada. His gruff demeanor in front of the boys had clearly switched to someone both intimidated and beseeching.

She found it cute in the extreme if not because it was also, to some degree, pathetic.

"But I need a favor first," he said as he held up the envelope in the air out of her reach.

"What do you have in mind?"

"I know that you and Milliard were able to swap out some tests for Walter. To get the fish scales, I need you to do the same for me. The finals for botany are coming up and I could use a stellar grade."

Isabella smiled. "Your imagination on favors is about as myopic as your skills in conversation, my dear Jada. Nevertheless, like the jinni in a bottle I am here to answer your prayers. In order for me to do as you say, however, I will need the fish scales up front."

"No, we trade one for one, once you have done your part. Now let's finish this so we don't cause too much more attention."

It didn't matter. Isabella had already stolen the envelope from Jada's hand. He looked up to see that it was no longer there though he couldn't recall her actually moving to take it. She held up the envelope for him to see from her small catlike hand. His eyes widened and her teeth glimmered. It was fun, on occasion, to surprise people with her skills.

"I have them right here. And thanks. I have great need for their fishy qualities. And don't try to get them back. I will scream and cause a ruckus and well, you don't want that now, do you? But don't worry. I will do your inane favor. I'm a woman of my word. You want an A and you will get an A. Go back to your bunk. When you open your eyes, you will find your test upon your desk. It will be as simple as that."

Jada blinked twice in stupefaction, creased his brows to think, and then shrugged his shoulders in resignation. What else could he do? He turned and made his way back across the barracks. At first sad, his posture moved toward confidence as he realized he was about to graduate with honors.

And there she had it—the major ingredient to stir into the balm. She opened the envelope to see them glistening like jewels in the sliver of moonlight. She placed one on her tongue and spit it out. Yes, they were real, but boy were they gross. Next up, hairs from Marty and she had a pretty clear idea where she might find some.

Chapter 21

"Be careful what you wish for," mumbled Fennel to himself as he piled yet another box into the boat. Sweat dripped from brow and he stopped to pat down his forehead with a handkerchief. He took off his jacket, delicately folded it and placed it in the corner of the boat. The night was more humid than ever and the boxes had begun really coming in. He looked back at the shore. Six more to go. Fennel shrugged his shoulders. They would just have to wait. He couldn't have yet another night filled to the brim with these menial tasks. He had done everything asked of him and still nothing but worse than before.

He grabbed the oars and made his way through the turns in the marsh. Since the incident, he had taken to docking down river behind an abandoned lubrication shop. He didn't feel like seeing Heinrich's disapproving eyes. "What does he know anyway? He will get his." Things were just going from bad to worse.

He pulled up behind the warehouse, watching the cats scatter from the backwater trashcans. Fennel leapt up onto the banks and quick as can be, had whirled an orange tabby cat by the tail straight out into the river. The sight of the freaked out cat flying out into the night provided him a brief comfort.

"Lesson 1. Don't be around me," he said to the large splash that erupted on the water.

As the soggy cat swam its way back to the shore and away from Fennel, he lugged the boxes onto the bank. The note had explicitly stated that all of the shipments were to go to the dripping guild entrance for pick-up. The other six were meant for a drop off spot out near Danderill. No way. The guild and Danderill were nowhere near proximitous and so half would wait. These other six that he now lugged on that bank were probably for Castilla, but Fennel would never know.

Forever in the dark. It wasn't right. He had demonstrated fealty and Marty had given him marching orders. These tasks would clearly be easier with two. But no—that was over.

He hauled the boxes onto the awaiting carriage and snapped at the horses to get his way onto the guild. The horses had a fever in them. That at least made Fennel smile. They came blasting through the streets, Fennel howling loud, his eyes still yellow from his new transformation into the Raven. He dropped the boxes off at the mouth of the tunnel entrance, doing his best to avoid the sewer drainage, but, unfortunately, stepped into it anyway.

"Dammit!" The smell filled his nose and his body shook at the nastiness of it all. It wasn't all that long ago that he and Isabella had descended these halls to visit the sinuous and calculating Castilla and company. Another exciting idea that had come to naught. Not only did Isabella not go for the offer but neither did Marty when Fennel had finally reported on the incident.

The fire had been higher than ever. Fennel had come back victorious—his eyes butter with fever and glory. Fish eggs, twine, children's teeth, bottle caps, bad way crumbs, coffee grounds, molding baby toys and fabric softener all went careening into the blaze. Fennel's voice grew to a feverish pitch, he ran about the fire wildly, summoning the absent Marty McGuinn.

Marty's janky body appeared in the flames, classic muddy overalls, Texas Ranger baseball hat he probably found on the floor of a casino, his old beater boots, and his tobacco spit.

"Ain't gotta lotta time der, Scratch. Get at it."

"Ha, ha, ha, Marty! I did as you asked. I am your humble servant after all. Iz, the bad news biz, is closed up tight in the Billington Hills. She won't be stirring the pot while you're out and about."

Marty laughed and scratched his arms. "Serves da bitch right," he said, clearly pre-occupied.

"Sure does!" answered Fennel back. He threw an extra handful of bad-way crumbs into the fire and they lit up firecracker. *Blam*! "Oh another thing, Marty, I didn't mention it last. Don't know why. We were approached by a man named Castilla."

Marty spit a wad of gross and shook his head. His face suddenly perturbed. "Shoulda neva happened. Caught wind a dat. Money man gettin outta line. Ah took care of it."

Fennel crooked his neck. "I thought maybe I could work the deal for you."

Marty laughed more to himself than Fennel. "Oh ya? Ya gonna work da deal, Scratch? Gonna pass on dat. New shipments a'comin. Ready yerself, boy. And don't get uppity. Ya find yaself up in dat snake pit to boot. Gotta get back to da table. On a streak."

And with that Marty's image disappeared. Not the party he wanted. Not that it ever was, but still.

That was many moons ago and the excitement of the pyre had given way to the strain of shipments. The Stallhammers were relentless in their deliveries. Fennel jumped back toward the carriage glad to be rid of his never-ending duties for the night. If Marty meant for him to simply take Isabella away and then double the workload something would have to be done.

"Yes," Fennel decided, "I am on a partial subtle strike. A slow down."

It had been much too long and he figured Derrilous would have to be done by now. He raced through the streets of Barrenwood far too excited and without Isabella there to oversee him, subtlety was an attribute in short supply. He chased after children and scared the elderly. He watched a bicycle messenger accidently go head first into a parked almond stand. Fennel laughed loud in his victory. Time, when he had it, would be action packed.

Inside Derrilous's Den, Fennel inhaled the acidic haze and placed his laboratory coat over his couture attire. Yes, steam again. The knobs were still turning and the room still groaning. Sulfuric crust clustered around the ends of cast iron pipes. Dust fell from the cement ceiling in broad sweeping sheets. The air sizzled in the highly ionized den. The desk was more cluttered than ever with hot candles accidently pouring wax onto books on the fall of the Roman Empire and daddy long-legs nurturing cobwebs in the dog-eared pages. Three steel bathtubs sat in the center of the room with very expensive halogen lights pouring rays of light onto their blue liquid interiors. Inside, the very sought after liquid bubbled and traveled up the thin clinical tubes. The tubes circled endlessly through the laboratory doing donuts until they eventually were cinched with plastic ties to glass beakers. They rattled back and forth from the steaming pressure. Exhaust. Intake. Pistons were being invented in here as well. Derrilous turned up his radio.

"Ya, ya, on this long, lasting caravan!" he sang in a raspy, wet cement melody. The wa-wa guitar blurping in and the deep bass line palunking along. His speakers boomed. He exhaled and the smoke moved through the dust along the pipes past the concrete staircase to the dead still dark waiting room. Lights out. Fennel threw himself on the couch. He was glad to be back in control of his life, even if just a little bit. Derrilous ran around the room working on something or other. Things hadn't turned out the way they were supposed to. Marty had shanghaied him. At least that was how it felt. Back when the Raven first came around, Marty's tone had been so very different.

"Git her in dare. Get in wit da monkeys and you get her good and locked. The door'll open for ya, Scratch, and that sickness'll take her by the tonsils. You'll be as fit as a fiddler's itch so don't ya worry bout dat. Get her good and bloated and she'll keel over for a bit a time. They'll knows what to do. Those monkeymen owe me more than a few good dances with the devil. They'll keep their crawdad claws on her till I get up an back. You sit tight there, numero uno. We'll put the charm back in the farm."

Where was the charm now? Fennel put his legs out straight in front of him. He was sore from the boxes. Sore! What was he, some kind of dockworker or something? Stiff legs. Stiff as a board. Did he want this? He was Marty's numero uno. He was just doing damage control until Marty could deprogram his resistor sister.

"Derrilous!" he shouted, jumping up from the couch and bounding into the lab. "Derrilous! Gimme the toxins, baby! Give it up and out of your dread bred head!"

Fennel spun around on his heel and threw an empty bicycle tire tube at Derrilous. It wrapped around his head causing him to spill some of the mysterious alchemical whatnot in his hand.

"Pa-lease, do not play the Lone Ranger game right now!" Derrilous yelled as he pulled the tire off. He walked over to Fennel fuming. "Playtime bad, Fennel. Understand? Understand playtime bad? Playtime not now. Be good boy. Go couch." He turned around and got back to work, his small knotty hands fiddling with pliers.

"How much longer?" yelled Fennel. He was bouncing on his heels. "Play time good until Fennel get Blue Goo from mini-Marley!" He walked like Frankenstein and shuffled toward Derrilous. "I am a stick man from the future!" He yelled in a robotic voice. "I need the goods!"

Derrilous turned around slowly. "Okay, Romper room. You have got to get out of here. You are exceptionally stupid tonight."

Fennel put his hands out in Frankenstein fashion and squeezed his hands around Derrilous's neck. "Ha, ha, ha!"

Derrilous pushed Fennel's arms away. "Such an imbecile! Listen, in all seriousness, I can have this stuff ready to go by the end of the night, but only if I can work constantly. Constantly! None of your pantomime shenanigans. Get out of here and give autistic children nightmares or something."

Fennel did just that and scampered out of the den of tubes and bubbles. Upon exiting, he let the entirety of Barrenwood come-a-crawling up his nose. He inhaled and smelled the faint scent of freedom. It filled in his lungs and he sensed its contagion. "A man could get used to this," he told himself.

Fennel was excited. He threw off the lab coat and thought about his new life. He would be a great conductor of the world. Time was opening up. No sister to stop him and no master to monitor. His arms would wind up with his mighty orchestra supporting him and with this blue goo in tow, and he would make such a delightfully tragic magical song wash over the restive lot-of-em. This upcoming hoopla was all he needed to kick his vertigo into gear. He already had seeded the ever-so-dour command of that innocuous cultural committee. The goo, if Derrilous would ever finish it, will get the sculptor on board. And then, he had to get that down and out circus up and running. He had so many pieces at work simultaneously across this wet city. What a busybody he was. Thank goodness Isabella was locked up in that school of deep boredom. And come to think of it, screw Marty McGuinn.

"I am no longer on board!" he shouted into the night. "I am the Raven and the Raven needs to peek his dirty eye down into the business of his marionettes. Let's be off!"

Fennel bounded across the rooftops toward the docks of the Calliope. He had heard them. They were out there. He had a demon in him and he hoped he could let it free tonight. As he bounced, he appreciated the madness that was Barrenwood. Tucked along the river, the Vietnamese restaurants were in full swing with their boats returning from the tucked away rice paddies out in the marsh.

The street vendors sold exotic soft fruits just past ripe, barrels of deep fried crickets and squid, and basics for the family like brooms, underwear, and flyswatters. Trucks erupted in gas convulsions as they tugged the cardboard boxed goods around, along with the trash that never seemed to ever stop piling up.

When Fennel landed on the roof, he half hoped to see another ship of fools at the dock again. He could really benefit from another opportunity to juggle and dunk some sailors and petty merchants into the Aliber. And much to his surprise, he was half right. The Ship of Fools was in view. It just happened to be far out on the Aliber. Safely out of range of his tomfoolery rage. He gnashed his teeth.

On the wind, he could feel the howling of the crazies on board. Their wailing stuck in his ear and made dung in his blood. They were wildly wild. He could feel it, sense it, wanted it. Fennel faintly eyed the muslin robes swaying in the night air—a field of lunatic wheat on the bow. The sailors were laughing, whipping and working. The whole scene made him sick with hate.

What did people know? They ran around jailing, judging, pointing, and hiding and all under the pathetic name of righteousness. The whole thing would be a comedy if there was anyone left in the audience to laugh. But the entirety of the population stood on the stage without a modicum of humility, just running around blind with clinical diagnosis and loophole law decrees. But the Raven had its own justice. If Fennel had a window of time, he should use it to correct the correctors. And just as boredom sows the seeds of inspiration, so too does the cauldron of antipathy. And out of his bubbling gut that spilled and seeped with maddening anger came an idea most simple and inspiring.

"He's gonna get it." Fennel whispered to himself as he wacked the roof hard with his cane. Old Mother Mellonow looked up from traditional evening boardwalk saunter in time to see a small boy, waving his hat in the air, fly through the sky in the direction of the Pedigree.

Fennel bounded across the rooftops with determination. He would let the energies of the night move through him and fuel this adventure. By the time he arrived at the doorstep of the Never family, he was in rare Raven form. The massive Victorian home sat at the outer edge of the Pedigree where the backyards stretched into plots of land and the porches competed by way of charm. Each porch swing was trying to outdo the last, each set of wicker chairs was more country than the last. Dr. Eldridge Never most certainly did not want. The lights were still glowing inside the home where the entire family—as the family was large indeed—hustled and bustled about. Marisa Never folded clothes in the basement. Her two small boys were upstairs in their beds pretending to sleep but, in fact, were telling each other stories about a fat man that ate everything he came in contact with. Granddad Toby Never sat on the couch, listening to the radio, which had on a radio play of *The Great Gatsby*. Dr. Eldridge Never sat at his desk, reading the memoirs of Wilhelm Reich. The read entertained him and he laughed frequently.

The Raven waits for no-one. Fennel bashed through the front door, the sound of which scared the entire occupants.

"Gather round, gather round. A Eureka moment has happened!" screeched Fennel.

He ran to the radio and turned it off. He rushed down to the basement and took the clothes out of the mother's hands, he ran up the stairs and shook the children out of bed, and then he ran down into the living room and proceeded to bang his cane on the floor.

"Gather round I say!" the Raven screeched and the family didn't quite know what was going on. Granddad Toby remained on the couch. His eyes squinted and he stared at Fennel as though in a dream. Marisa Never came running up the stairs and the kids came running down the stairs to stare at Fennel from their perch. No one said a thing but instead just stared intently at the strange young boy causing a scene in their living room.

"Dr. Never! You are being summoned to the family gathering!" shouted Fennel and sure enough Dr. Eldridge Never made his way past his two boys to the living room. He immediately recognized the odd child from many nights' past.

"Persifell Pemberton?" said the doctor in a bit of shock.

Fennel looked up to see his prey standing dead in his sights. There he was—the jailer, the teacher, the brother's keeper, standing in all his deadpan pretension. The sight of him stirred the Raven into full bloom.

Fennel raised his arms and swirled around in a circle in the living room as though he was, in fact, a bird.

One didn't have to be a doctor to know something wasn't quite right about Persifell Pemberton. Eldridge Never could feel fear rising up inside him. Something primeval had been let loose in his sanctuary.

He took a breath. "Children, go back to your room. Marisa, could you please take granddad upstairs. Mr. Pemberton and I have business to discuss."

Fennel grabbed one of the small boys, Davie, by the hand. "Be a good lad, will you? Sit right there on the couch. I think you should see this. Daddy is going to finally grow up. Don't you want to see that?"

"Don't touch my boy!" shouted the doctor rushing in to take Fennel's hands off his child.

Fennel's eyes were as yellow as smeared sun at sunset and gave the doc a good whack across the head with his cane. The doctor went tumbling to the floor and the room erupted with the wailing of the children and Marisa Never. Davey went running up the stairs, his small feet playing a beat of retreat.

"Stop it, you beast!" shouted Marisa.

The volume only made Fennel's fury grow. Marisa Never came running at Fennel and he twisted his body to let her momentum carry her across the room. She bounced off the wall and fell, a sack, to the floor.

"Tut, tut, Little Miss Muffet, you really don't want to tempt the Raven. Not at this moment. You are not my quarry, but I am unpredictable. Do that again, and I will punish you as equally as I will your pedantic spouse."

The two boys sat at the top of the stairs, hands covering their sweet frightened faces, and looked down at Fennel as he paced over the body of the fallen Dr. Never.

"I won't regret this, you realize. I am a force of nature and you only pretend to be one. Justice isn't cruel. It is just a force that acts down on you. I am not after you, Dr. Never. I'm following a trail of popcorn and you are but one kernel. I am eating you now. Are you or aren't you responsible for the carting off of the mad onto the drunken boat? Is it your organization that is doing the rounding up?"

The doctor looked up from his sprawled out position on the floor. "Was one of them your relation or associate? We can always track them down for you if you have a grievance, Mr. Pemberton."

"I do have a grievance!" said Fennel, slamming his cane onto the floor near Dr. Never's head. "The entire flock is my relation as they are yours, you myopic fool. You need not answer, I know it is you that is coordinating this massacre."

The doctor shifted to sit up on his legs. He was rubbing his head as it pained him most severely. "If I may interrupt, it is entirely the opposite of a massacre. These are patients that we are retrieving. They need proper medical consideration."

"Dr. Never. This word medical, it is misleading so often. Who needs it and who doesn't. If all need it, then none do as well. You can't cure the mind, my friend. But it matters not. Tell me, please, I would very much enjoy knowing, who is it that pays the bills at your institute? This isn't entirely your idea. I know that much."

The doctor looked up from his sprawled out position on the floor. His eyes were sad. The fight in him was already gone. He was a deflated balloon. It made Fennel laugh.

"Such a wussy you are. Okay. You don't want this to continue I know. Just tell me, who pays the bills? I'm following a trail here. I'm a detective, but I am investigating crimes that humanity commits without knowing it. Your laws, your health codes, your curriculum, your mores, they are of no concern to me. Well, that isn't true. They are of concern to me in that many of them go against any higher sense of reason. Be that as it may, I leave most of that up to you to do as you will. What do I care if idiot number one ruins the life of idiot number two? That is not the kind of skirmish I tend to intercede on. But I will not sit by while people like you haul off the brilliant, the dreamers, those in touch with the actual free spirit that gives the earth its juice and flavor. I can't tolerate the arrogance, the hypocrisy, the pathetic claims of benevolence. I am the Raven and I am here to place on trial those responsible for robbing the world of its mystery. It is a crime that must be met with punitive actions much like you feel on your saggy frame. So tell me, who pays the bills?"

The doctor tried his best to shake the cobwebs out of his head. He couldn't comprehend what was happening, but he knew that he had to get this ferocious child out of his house. He had to protect his family and all he had ever possessed as a weapon were his words.

"My underwriters are straightforward. It is on public record. It isn't even a secret. You didn't need to come here to find out who pays the bills. Our receptionist could have told you. It is written on our building for the love of god!"

Fennel laughed loud and monstrous. As much as it scared everyone, whether lying on the floor or sitting on the stairs, the laughter came from a genuine place of humor. Fennel really hadn't thought about looking in the obvious place such as what was written on the front door of Wellington Manor. Maybe he wasn't really a detective. He shrugged his shoulders. The Raven was really in the mood for justice with just a taste for detective work. So what if he had taken the long road?

236

"A god's love indeed. Nothing makes punishment more tasty than one enacted with a sense of absurdist irony. Do me a favor ol' wise father of the floor, tell me, what does it say written in big black letters across the front of your impressive new building? I really don't have the time to go and pay a visit."

The doctor looked up exasperated. He wanted to move to the couch just to be more presentable. He hated what was happening in a very deep way. Every therapist secretly fears the wrath of their patients and though Persifell Pemberton wasn't specifically a patient, the idea remained the same.

"It says Gaventas. This is an initiative of the company Gaventas. I dearly hope that is what you are looking for. Please leave my family alone. They don't deserve this."

"Gaventas," Fennel whispered. Castilla, that lucrative little twit that Fennel so admired was a water stealer. Fennel felt dumb again and it made him angry. And with that Fennel gave the doctor a good whack accompanied by the sounds of the wailing of the entire family. It was a horrible scene and when it was over, the doctor was still alive, but his body was damaged most extreme.

Fennel cleaned himself off with his handkerchief and bid the family adieu.

"Justice, dear family Never, has been served."

Chapter 22

"Time for some ninja work," Isabella thought. She placed her pillows under her blanket to mimic her tiny body and slid out of the room. Her cot was in a maze of many acolytes. Their little boy snores a chorus of bad breath. She snuck out of the barracks and made her way, ever so gently, toward the welcome hall from whence she had arrived many moons ago. It felt good to walk about at night. The air up in these mountains was much drier, but the smell of sage on the wind awoke her senses. The sand below her feet spoke of a non-marsh world—a world dry with ideas. She kicked the sand and felt the familiar, yet annoying, sickness tucked inside her. She could not bound, nor walk lightly like a bird, nor disappear into the folds of darkness. Instead, she was forced to rely on her more human skills. Prowling about the grounds like a cat, she made her gentle way toward the entry home.

The path wound around the entire campus. Perhaps they wanted to keep the acolytes as far from escape as possible (unless they wanted to run wild into the Scanderville Range as she had tried). She walked across the campus, staring at each different building, wondering what amazing subjects they were studying inside. Architecture, botany, metaphysics, cynics, theology, engineering. As wrong as she found some of the impulses here, she also appreciated the pursuit. The subjects fascinated her. She couldn't deny that. She imagined that if she were in charge she would just re-arrange things a little—the theology of botany, the metaphysics of architecture, just some tweaking to keep the big spirit ingrained inside the mix of the real.

The route wound far out along the western edge of the grounds, where the sagebrush pushed against the upward slope of the foothills. Tucked up on the range, she spied a gated area with barbed wire fences, surveillance cameras and, for the first time, men with weapons. She could make out Coriander Monks, bayonettes in hand, stationed at a distance around a large sign that read *Research and Development*. The monks stood in their robes in the darkness—pacing. Behind the gates, Isabella could hear the murmur of machines with gears grinding and furnaces burning, the gears turning with great momentum and fury.

It was tempting to shift her gears and set upon the R&D facility, but she was in a hurry. Not only that but her entire adventure felt like something she and Fennel would have done together. Two peas in a pod. Her heart sank briefly, but she continued on. She walked away from the range and toward the entrance hall. With every step, she was getting closer to potential escape. The illness continued to grow inside her.

The entrance hall was not guarded. Its innocuous front door opened with ease and she was surprised to find the halls unattended. The monks, it seemed, were asleep. Perhaps the monks didn't really need all that much security. It was a school after all. She poked her head in different rooms recognizing at one point the depressing interrogation office where they had attached the electrodes to her to discover the truth. The thought made her laugh. People are so strange. She continued to poke about until she found what she was looking for—the lockers where they stored the incoming acolytes clothes. She inhaled, trying to hold back the growing bubbling in her stomach and located her robe. Strange, how things are left. They just sit there until something moves them. Her robe just sat in this locker waiting for her. She eyed her clothes carefully, hoping against hope to find them. And there they were—four slight, sparkly, luminescent wires that came from that nasty head of Marty McGuinn. She had stuffed some in her pocket back when she was free. There were just enough to get her the heck out of here.

The sickness rose up in her. She had no desire to linger. Isabella scampered her way back out of the entrance hall to start winding her way back to the barracks. A few paces in she spied the biology building. She had quite a lot to accomplish in that dour place of inquiry. Between her deal with Jada and making the fish sauce, she had to get it all done before morning. She patted her pocket with Marty's hairs and the fish scales and got a move on.

Again, security, in general, was not a top priority. She opened the massive front door and immediately smelled formaldehyde. It crept up her nose in putrescence of science. She could sense the prowling fingers of the anatomists and dissectors, the prying eyes of the doctors to be and the numerous skeletons hung up like a bearskin on a post for the world to view. The School was a place of vast voyeurism—ever looking deeper and deeper into the subcutaneous possibilities that were the body. Each room was a place of scopic investigation and wonderfully shiny metallic tools for digging, scraping, cutting, and folding.

She had her pick of empty laboratories. She didn't need much: Bunsen burner, volumetric flask, Buchner funnel and her fairly extensive list of ingredients that were now in her pocket. The time of chemistry had arrived. She put on a lab coat hanging up on the wall. It was too big, but it would work. She placed goggles on her little beautiful face and got to work. This with that and that with this. The hours whiled away as she heated things, up, separated them and placed them. In a few hours' time, the sauce came together without a hitch. She had another batch and her freedom, again, was in her grasp. She took a nice gulp and found her body twitch and preen at the sudden surge of strength in her. The almighty stirred in her bones.

Now she was off to task number three. Jada's test scores. As up to no good as she was, she remained true to her word. She could sense monks awake in the building. She was not alone. As she journeyed up the large stairs, she could sense the footsteps of thousands of solemn monk feet over time. She spied the familiar flicker of fluorescent lights. They buzzed and sputtered, causing a strobe effect in the halls. Inside, two rectors sat muddling over some papers. Their hoods pulled back, their sandy hair descended over their faces. The lines in their faces ran deep and the concentration in their brows were ever on point.

"Such are the findings. There is little disputing it. The entire matrix of the body circulates around this code. A simple collection of complex amino acids grouped into a complex formula is clearly the source of our inquiry. The next attempt is simply translation."

The monks shifted on their feet. They stood in front of a strange sculpture that twisted with metal rods in a rotating circle. Small red and yellow orbs adorned the rods in what would be known as a double helix.

"What a ton of work it is. I can't even think about that. I just need some sleep."

The other monk got up from his chair and paced the room, the creases in his face growing impossibly deeper still.

"Time enough to sleep in the grave, Galston. We have done our duty. That is what we are asked to do. We still need those last batches of formulae gone over and then the Beta studies."

Galston laughed and pushed a red orb along the wire sculpture. "Don't I know it. This is a long journey we are on. I swear I see these little twisting shapes in my sleep. You know I'm not one to complain, but I'm tired. It's not like Teddy does any of our work. But you can bet he will be pretending he was with us in the wee hours like now, sweating over combinations."

"Such as it has always been. We both know the Rectors have been taking credit for the work of the monks for as long as the school has been around. That is the way of the world. I just don't question it. Nose to the grindstone."

"So you tell yourself. Frankly, I have heard this project is going straight up into the Restoration shortly. It might skip Teddy altogether." Galston snorted a strange laugh.

"I would enjoy that," said the other monk and he got up from his seat.

Isabella thought he might be exiting the room and snuck her way further down the hall. She felt as though she liked these monks. Working on odd formulae late at night complaining about work. She could get into that. She hurried down the musty hall where bookshelves lined the walls and water fountains spit water in the corners. The hum of the building was noticeable even with the fluorescents out and the windows open. The building was the body electric. She spotted the obvious sign of biology— the skeleton with a heart—picked the lock with just but a flick of the wrist and she was in.

The test answers were easy enough to find. They rested on the top of what could only be the professor's writing desk in the second room to the back. But since she was there, she thought she would look around. See what she might find. The files were endless with names of what must be the last twenty years of monks' names. Boring. Fortunately, the bottom drawer of the rector's desk had a lock on it, a sure sign of worthwhile adventure. She popped the lock to find file upon file regarding budgets— vast paperwork of numbers in rows totaling up the cost of one initiative or another. It barely interested Isabella except in the general sense that biology seemed to have a lucrative component. Pure science in the real world never felt all that pure.

Isabella shrugged her shoulders, placed the folder and its contents back in the drawer and skipped back down the hall. Money. What a strange phenomenon that was. She never seemed to worry about. Marty had paid for everything for so long. It hadn't even occurred to her that she would ever need such a thing. She sort of looked at money as this odd naïve phenomenon that people dealt with, but what did she know? She lived in a cave with her mean-spirited brother ruining people's lives as they tried their hardest just to get by. She decided then and there not to be mad at the monks for being involved with money. Perhaps she would need to know more before making some kind of authoritative decision on it.

She made her way quickly out of the biology building and scampered down the trail back toward the barracks. The night had proven most edifying. It was at that moment as she was fiddling about the grounds as the first rays of sun began to lightly tinge the sky that she noticed, as if out of nowhere, the presence of Harrison.

"I won't ask why you aren't in the barracks, but I do hope you are returning," he said. He was smoking a pipe, sitting on a bench, and reading Kurt Vonnegut's *Galapagos*.

"As it turns out, Harrison," smirked Isabella, "I was heading home. I really missed it in fact. But now that I have you here, I am eager to ask you something. I want to ask you something so obvious that perhaps it will be difficult for you to answer in all your wisdom. Nevertheless, you must answer it. You must because if you can't, then you will be caught in a clever confession that you know little of—not only the world but more sadly your own choices. What is the purpose of the Coriander Monks, Harrison?"

She sat down next to him, most pleased with herself, and stared in his eyes. She was being too cocky she knew and she should probably hide the fact that she was clearly no longer sick, but she couldn't completely contain her pleasure.

Harrison took a puff and slowly put down his book. He stared out into the fading stars and sat quietly for some time.

"The monks simply discover, Isabella. We are here to question, observe, and consider. For us, this simple pursuit, in all its wonder, is the sacred dreams of Yog Soggoth and his numerous avatars and minions."

"But what about the doing? What about the building? What about the making? The monks don't just consider right, they do, don't they?" she leaned back and stared into the night with him. It was cold out there. The night sometimes so inviting, felt bleak as she watched the sky slowly lighting up. A new day was ever an option to repeat old mistakes.

"The monks should not make black magic, Isabella. They are not the shapers of people or of worlds. That has always been my teaching and philosophy. Nevertheless, it is a big church with numerous tentacles. There are those who do here. Indeed, the makers. They are a small group but a growing part of the doctrine. The times we are in will see their emergence, I suspect. But, hush now, you should get to bed and most certainly not be talking to me at this hour."

Isabella got up and skipped toward the barracks. She laughed out loud and sang out, "I'm not staying here. No one can make me." She laughed and scampered off. She was quite out of earshot when Harrison mumbled to himself, "I know that all too well, my girl."

Sleep was not to be her friend the next day as she had barely closed her eyes after handing off Jada's prize when she had the hand of Milliard pushing her to get up.

"Get up, Isabella. We have yet another dig to attend."

She could almost feel herself sliding into a determination to not only sleep, but, now that she was feeling better, to take on the entirety of the Coriander Monks. But such a battle would prove less than strategic. No, she would escape and escapes require surprise. So with a steady sense of discipline, she opened her eyes, put on her desert flats, grabbed her pick, and headed out to the caravan with Milliard.

They would ride out to the dig sites on camels and donkeys these days as the more fresh finds were increasingly further out. Lately, they traveled nearly a seven-hour ride so that they could dig for a few days and then return to shower up. It was exhausting work. The world, it seemed, stretched out from the edge of Barrenwood into a stark plane of basalt, sand, stone, and creosote. The barren back of the earth scorched by sun and the yucca plants, sage bushes and occasional cactus acted as a geological grammar to the starkness that were these desert plains.

Out on the plains, the wind picked up a furious pace. This work had done quite a job on her skin. She looked at it. Flakey. Dry. Her team of acolytes had found some pot shards, arrowheads and a few beads of jewelry, but nothing from the millions of years previous. The monks had roped off sections of land as far as the eye could see. Their digging into the earth acted as a collective journey toward memory. But the past, the idea of a world beyond all imaginable presents, provided a grounding narrative—a place from where the monks could look back upon an assured place in history.

Milliard and Isabella were boiling a pot of water over their fire. They looked out over the twenty other fires that amassed across their camps with silhouettes of the monks crouched in front of them. The sky above looked down with the twinkling of stars mirroring each other. Milliard rubbed a pot shard in his hand.

"To think, there were people living in huts here at some point. They must have lived an awfully difficult life."

"It's truly a wonder to see these bits and pieces of a society lost. The ruins of a culture whose time was up. It's like the dirty room of a society who simply never came home again," said Isabella.

"I wonder if the same thing will happen to our society. One day it will only be carriages and fluorescent lights around for some confused bunch of folks to wonder what we were up to," giggled Milliard. His eyes shifted to Isabella. She was a mystery beyond mysteries. When he spoke to her he felt like the world could fall apart because all he would ever need to know would come from her. "Where did you come from before you came here? You know about me, but I still know so little about you."

Isabella knew the truth of that. Reserved was an understatement when it came to her privacy. But what did it matter? This time was coming to a close.

"You wouldn't believe me if I told you. I hardly believe it myself. I have a brother out there. Somewhere. We used to sleep in a cave together. He has a fire in him. He would love digging for these dinosaurs. Oh, I could see him really enjoying that. Maybe not the monks, but paleontology; he would love that. Anyway, I am from outside Barrenwood like you. I just happen to be from a cave."

Milliard eyed her. "Is that an allegory? A cave? Come on, Isabella, you never tell me anything about yourself."

243

Isabella looked at the ground. The truth sounded like a lie. What could she do? "I told you that you wouldn't believe me. It is hard to believe, I know, but there you have it. I didn't attend a prep school or border house or any of your typically upper crust growing up things. I was born like this and have been like this for longer than I can remember." Isabella found telling the truth liberating. Even if it was strange, it hit home for her. She needed to talk—with Fennel so much was pent up. Milliard's words seemed to trigger something deep in her.

"What does that mean, you have been like this for longer than you can remember?" he asked. He found asking these most basic of questions fascinating as he could tell that instead of denial, they actually triggered in Isabella profound self-questioning.

Isabella paused. She looked at Milliard and for a second. He thought he could see tears welling up in her eyes. They disappeared fast, but he held her soft hand in his and stayed quiet. The silence drifted across the range, wind spilling through the cracks in the creosote mud.

"I . . . I . . ." she said through pressed lips, "I don't know how long I've been alive. I don't really know how long I have been in that cave. I don't know how I know what I know. I don't know who I am, Milliard. I am utterly without a clue."

Saying that out loud sounded absolutely odd for her. She realized in a flash that saying such things out loud made them conscious as though she suddenly knew it for the first time—one part of her mind communicating with another. A transference had occurred. The idea that she had so little knowledge of who she was struck her as a profound existential mystery. She was a foreigner on a planet with no past. All she had was her deep love for her horrible sibling and her fear of her master, and neither of them cared one iota to reflect on that fact that the three of them had no idea where they came from.

Milliard placed his arms around her. His scrawny embrace felt warm against the sage filled chill. They swayed on the earth looking up at the stars. They were lonely as well.

"I know you're not going to stay long," Milliard whispered. Isabella looked at him. His blue eyes sparkled under the stars. "I am going to miss you."

Isabella shook the chill out of herself. The reminder of her departure switched her mood rapidly. "Funny you mention it. I'm leaving tonight, right after a drink of tea actually. I have my bag packed. No moon tonight means no way to see me when I head right out into that wasteland."

Milliard grabbed her hand beseechingly. "Take me with you, please. I don't want to do this monk thing anymore. I am not cut out for this. I have lost all admiration for the School. Let them do their digs without me."

She patted his hand in a motherly fashion. "You are wrong, Milliard. If anyone is to be a monk around here, it is you. From what I can tell, you possess the kind of disillusion that can only help the School stay on track. Your thoughts are wild but they are on point. I have come around to thinking that the monks aren't half bad. Not that I would ever be one. No one here I believe is under that delusion. But you do. You have ideas. You are a thinker. Yes, you are a bit whiny and childish and a slight coward but that will go out of style for you at some point. Look to Harrison and get in his good graces. He is wise around here and you would benefit from learning from one of the more reflective monks. Plus, you can't go with me. You are slow and a liability. I have a lot of work to do and I really don't feel like worrying about you. We will meet again I am sure."

She stood up and poured some tea for the both of them. They sipped quietly and Isabella wished she could get in a game of Battle Ball.

As they sipped their tea, Isabella noticed the growing ranks of monks just outside of sight. They were sitting with none other than Walter Mayhew and these monks were particularly large. She saw their coiled ropes and heard their whispered plots. Isabella sipped her tea and spoke ever so quietly to Milliard.

"It appears our friend Walter has discovered my plans. Lord knows how, but I suspect we are about to be descended upon. Milliard, you are a dear friend. I will not be gone forever. When they attack, just run. They won't hurt me."

Isabella leaned over and kissed Milliard on the forehead, her lips touching his skin with the magic of saturated ink. Then, with the speed of a bobcat, she dashed toward the tent and grabbed her bag. She could hear the lurch of their feet as the monks dove to intercept her. She was much faster.

Milliard blinked in surprise, got himself to his feet and ran toward the monks. He was not a heroic boy but he also was deeply unafraid of getting hurt, which is a sort of heroism. He threw his spindly body on one of the monks as it tried desperately to get the little girl into his paws. The rest of the monks came in fast. Muscles and fists struck out clobbering Milliard and grasping at the wisp of darkness that was Isabella. She bounded out of arms' reach and bounded far beyond their grip, already folding into the darkness. She looked back to see the monks turn their attention on Milliard and begin to take their anger and frustrations out on him. He pathetically tried to fight back but he was outnumbered and basically, a weakling. She watched as they tied him up, bloodied and bruised.

"Goodbye Milliard." She sent a kiss into the night with the sound of crickets caressing her words. She wasn't sure he would be okay, but there wasn't much she could do. She most certainly wouldn't be returning. This was her one chance at escape and she had made a good first break.

The night and desert stretched out before her. She took a large sip of the fish sauce and felt strength surge into her socks. She had no horse and a long way to go. The sound of the monks racing toward her caught her ear and she bounded out over the brush and hills. That was good. She needed them. As strong as her little legs were with the help of her mojo balm, she had miles upon miles of barren wasteland to go and she didn't want to get caught in it come sun up. The heat would bake the liquid from her diminutive head. She had to force herself to move just slow enough so the monks could keep her in sight. She needed a horse. When they were nearly two miles from the camp, she bounded to the top of a small butte and waited for their arrival. They came on her quick. These monks were not the kind she was used to seeing. They were strong. They were immense. The heat in their eyes spoke of far too many years of training, discipline and focus. They would not be easy to fool.

But Isabella was Isabella and at least for this quiet moment in the night, on this night, she was fueled and ready. Her strength and wits were at a maximum. She saw them flying their lassos to catch her and she dodged them with the agility of a sparrow. A net flew out which just barely missed. As they regrouped for another pass, Isabella folded into the night, completely disappearing from their sight. They reared back their horses trying to get a perspective on her whereabouts. She quickly tiptoed up to one of the horses and whispered a wilding into its ear. The horse reared back, whinnying and whining. The monk tried to hold on but to no avail. His body catapulted into the brush as she threw herself onto the horse's back. She charged forward, leaving the monks mystified in the utter darkness of the desert night.

She was free. She charged forward on the horse heading straight out toward Barrenwood across the top of Billington Hill. The pace would be frenetic but she would get there. As much as she was eager to return home, she felt a pang of remorse for not saying goodbye to Harrison. He was a curious soul, he was.

Isabella stared down over the twinkling evening lights of Barrenwood at the top of a boulder on top of the hills. The familiar smell of coal smoke filled her nose and at a distance she could hear the horse hooves of the carriages making their way over cobblestones. Most people were sleeping, but others were drinking themselves into fantasy or plodding away by candlelight trying to make ends meet. Somewhere down there Fennel was up to no good either haunting some poor sod too delusional to appreciate the limited time they have on earth, or perhaps, working on some larger plan to remind humanity of their more collective awkwardness. He most surely worried about her—but how much? What had come between them? Somewhere down there Savina was smoking a thousand cigarettes and torturing the souls of the men around her. And somewhere out there, beyond the Manzanita and aphids, lurked the shore of the cave—her home that was no longer home. The thought brought her back to herself. Where was she going?

When she had considered leaving, she had never truly made up her mind as to where she would go. In some sense of denial, even though she knew it wasn't possible, she had thought she might return to the cave. She missed it. For better or worse, it was home. Her ultimate plan was to get back to the Duke's, but she was already at the end of her fish sauce. She would need another dose just to make it half way up the Parakeet Path. No, she just needed to regroup. Get her senses together and make a plan.

The only safe bet at this point was the Chateau de Crawler. It was her hideout and hang out. She ruled the nest there and even if Fennel was on the hunt for her, she had developed enough of an infrastructure to fend off him and Marty for some time. Surely she had bought and cajoled enough favors in Barrenwood to give her a few days peace before the true hunt began.

She charged forward into the city at a fast clip. She rode straight down the road and into the farmlands where the corn stalks waved a hello. She moved past the acres of produce to the muddied beat up streets of the Mortestrate, cut across the upper edge of the Miser's Quarters to descend into the warehouse district of the Calliope. The alley cats with their furtive eyes gave her a questionable greeting and she returned with her own dubious glare. As she slowed the horse, whose panting heaved heavy, she saw the fisherman already returning from their evening catch. Rows of slaughtered tuna were laid out on the docks for the vendors to purchase. Amidst the sound of their wet galoshes hitting the sea salt docks, she could hear the rumbling bass of her sneaky evening haunt. She tethered the horse whose mouth was a mess of froth.

She hopped onto the street and felt the earth beneath her. She had escaped at last. She opened the door at the back of the Pho restaurant. The washman mopped the floor and the owner was doing the final round of dishes. He winked at her as she quickly made her way through the backroom to the stairway in the back. The room smelled of peanuts and seaweed. She snuck up the backstairs where the walls were covered with graffiti of parties so long ago. She opened the door to her office. Sitting at the table, covered in papers and ink jars, sat the very tired figure of Caperwill.

He looked up from his work, and upon seeing Isabella, his face went white. "Isabella?" he said with a gasp. He got up from the desk, ran across the room and gave her a huge, inappropriate, hug.

She shook him off and said, "Evening, Caperwill. I trust the bills are piling up and you are half out of your mind at this point?'

Caperwill's face flushed with embarrassment, "That much is true, Isabella. I knew you would appear at some point, but my god, your timing is greatly welcomed. I know I don't usually ask, but where have you been?"

Isabella poured herself some grape juice from the cabinet and made her way to the window overlooking the party below. She could see people dancing and laser lights flashing. The hot steamy nightclub was still at its epic pace even though it would be closing in the next hour or so.

"Strange business is afoot, Caperwill. I'm afraid that no matter what we want, things around here are going to be changing." She gulped down her grape juice and lay down on the sofa. Her little legs kicked out to rest on the edge. She was utterly exhausted.

"Your words couldn't be more true. I have received some terribly troubling news in the mail. I went over to the Court of Appeals to make sense of all this but to no avail. I'm afraid we are being evicted."

Caperwill thrashed through the papers on his desk. He gathered up a pile, wobbled over to Isabella and handed it to her. She looked through the papers and there it was in black and white. The Chateau de Crawler was being evicted due to some order of eminent domain. Some large construction project along the waterfront was to put her nightclub shenanigans out on its butt. They were going to buy the place at market value in a month's time at which point she would be out on her own. She put the papers down on the floor and walked over to the window again to look over the night club where only a few souls remained. Closing time.

"This is indeed troubling news. We will have to fight this, but a month's time? Seems I am going to need you to locate a new residence for us."

Caperwill rubbed his head and cleaned his glasses. He had already been working on this with great enthusiasm. "I didn't want to jump the gun until your return but time was running out. I have already located an impressive underground location in the Mortestrate. It is without question larger than our current residence, but of course, would require a vast architectural redesign. The site is in bad shape and would need not only a lot of repair, but walls taken out, an office made with one-way mirror, and on and on. I have gone so far as to have some architectural plans made up. " He reached over to his desk to the plans lying there.

"I will look at them come next evening. It's too much for me right now," said Isabella. The idea of moving her entire enterprise was too much.

She just needed some rest. Perhaps she would wake up and find her attitude had shifted. Perhaps she would find this an exciting challenge. All she wanted right now was for the world to at best improve and at worst remain the same.

Caperwill could see Isabella was tired. He gathered together a few biscuits with sugar from the cabinet and came to her with them on a plate.

"Barrister Bruno sent flowers to you upon your return, but that was so long ago, I'm afraid they have wilted." He pointed toward the corner of the room where a vase stood with drooping desiccated sunflowers. "Oh and there is this invitation to the Mayor's annual gala. This might be a bit of fun," he said, handing her a card.

It was an announcement for the City Celebration for the Gas Lamp Victory to be held in the Elindale Plaza—a great city-wide costume ball to applaud the great progress of the city's renowned industrialists. *Come enjoy the libations, dance to the band, and watch the unveiling of a new statue for all the city to see.*

Hopefully, she could last that long. She put a kettle on for tea. Her stomach was queasy again. Little fish sauce was left and she had already begun conserving. Not this again, she thought.

She patted Caperwill's head and gave him a weak smile. "I appreciate what you have done. I am, however, completely tired from my journeys. I need to get some rest. If you could do me the smallest favor in the interim? I need you to send a note to the Persembes immediately. I need their presence here."

"The Persembes?" said Caperwill, his face going blank. He paced back across the room suddenly in a nervous fit. He reached over to the bar and poured himself a drink. Whiskey. A long tall whiskey at that. He gulped at it and looked back at Isabella.

"Yes, the Persembes. Why, what is it?" she asked.

"Isabella, I thought you would have heard already. Sibel Persembe is dead."

Chapter 23

The world spoke to him. He listened into the wet wind and heard the song of a thousand applauses. They were proud of him out there. Families were holding close together, cheering. A mother wept in awe. He was most certainly a sensation, or so his night dreams told him as he considered the future. "Thank you," Fennel whispered into the wet wind. The dripping hyacinth waved back.

Things were coming together at last. Fennel looked over at the shore where the boxes piled up, a growing altar to procrastination. The Aliber waters lapped against the pile, turning the cardboard to milky pulp. He really had no time for that. Liberation came with a cost. So what if the deliveries didn't arrive and the School and the Guild were without their proper materials. So what if the Stallhammers shook their heads, spit their tobacco, and grunted as they piled more and more boxes upon each other. So be it. Priorities had to be produced. They were not a given. Fennel had become a master of his world.

Night previous, Fennel had poured the elixir down Chesterfield Breakfast's gullet. He had chugged it like a child with a milk jug. The esteemed sculptor of so many heroes on horseback's bronze statue had been the subject of Fennel's dreams for so long. He was a superb craftsman with a massive studio. He had been commissioned to adorn Ellingdale Plaza and his choice in subject matter was his and his alone. Such a profound responsibility and one that Fennel had long coveted. And now, Fennel's dreams were becoming those of Mr. Breakfast's. Derrilous had come through at long last. The blue goo had finally been cracked and handed over—its azure phosphorescence sizzling in the midst of the steamy laboratory. The goo was hot and ready and not without a certain amount of timeliness. The City Celebration of the Gas Lamp Victory was a few nights hence and this sculptor would have to work overtime to get the monstrous totem produced for the people of Barrenwood to gaze upon. Fennel's dreams were coming together.

Fennel hopped in the tub and gave himself a good wash. Fingers, toes, cracks, and ears. He hummed a little song while washing the blood off his little hands—the umber crust let loose dissolving into the greater tub water. These men and their resistance! Who did they think they were battling with? He still could hear their whimpering cries that mingled with the steaming water exiting the drain. Fennel hopped out of the tub and dried himself off. He looked over to Isabella's desk. No one there. He shook the thought off and skipped to the closet putting on his tuxedo for the day.

"Regal as a beagle, my good man," Fennel said as he winked at himself in the mirror.

The fire outside the cave burned low during the day and rose up at twilight—cooking slow herbs in tin foil packets the twins often placed there, heating the kettle for tea and at times heating the cave on the few chilly nights. As Fennel straightened his bow tie, he saw the flash of light that meant the coming. Fennel hadn't summoned him and he knew this was going to try to be rain on his parade. Fear shook in his bones, but he smiled in the mirror again.

"Don't worry. No one rains on this parade." He gave himself a wink and skipped out of the cave to meet the summoning of Marty McGuinn.

"Der be some duties ya be remiss on, lil' Scratch. Dem boxes just pilin up and dem Stallhams a tellin me ya givem nuttin but da evil eye. Ya got me soupen up ya fire and haven to come down on ya like a bad uncle. I woulda waged a good wager or so dat now that de she bitch is out on her ass, you was gonna go soldier like and keep da hen house tight. But you ain't done like dat, is ya? Ya just as rowdy and restless as she always did warn. You need a leash more den she ever did. Now ya sitten round bowing and preenin' a righteous little twot on da high top. Look at choo. Just look at choo." Marty made a scrunched up cute face. His lips pursed together and he pointed strange at Fennel. His ugly teeth wiggled in his mouth and his body swooshed nasty in his overalls.

"You such a big boy now. All smilin in da mirra, laughin ta nobod. Y'aint got nuttin ya know? Nuttin. Ya can preten. I do know ya like dat. But pretenen aint happnen. Now ya got me runnin from a big run, just so I can hop into dis shamble called a pyre to give ya a last repriman."

Fennel listened to the monster's words. He was back and mad and all that progress was slipping away. Isabella was gone and Fennel was in less of a place than when she was even around. Everything gets messed up. No other way to describe it. Fennel landed on his knees and placed his hands in the air. He didn't want to lose momentum. He wanted this episode to go away. He only had a few days. He must keep Marty at bay.

"Marty, I'm sorry. You must forgive me. Better yet, I beg you to forgive me. I truly do. These boxes just kept coming. The Stallhammers were relentless. They just kept showing up. I have things to attend to."

Marty spit a wad of gross into the pit and gave Fennel the one eye. "Sure ya do. Always up to sometin. She-bitch was right. She had ya lil number all along. Said ya could neva do dis on ya own. Dat ya were too wild. I can see it now. A legitimized child maniacal. Dats your modo operando. Don't know betta. Ya just a babe, scratch. And ya know what I do to da babes. I whip em scratch. And I take a wire and I strike em hard on der baby rear. You gonna get a whippen. Mark me. A good whippen a comin." Marty had a belt in his hand and he swung it around his head. He started laughing and whipping at the air. He loved whipping those kids. Fennel knew it. Fennel hated it.

He couldn't listen anymore. It was just a mirage anyway—Marty's image shaped in flame, riding high above the kettle and herb packets. He couldn't listen to this drunk slob tell him right from wrong. Not now. He had given him freedom, only to make him a bigger servant than ever.

"What about Castilla, Marty? Tell me about him. He is stealing the water, you know? Isabella knew it. She sensed it first. He is carting all the mad off in boats. That's right. The water is being eviscerated. All for profit. The down and out carted off to prison. Barrenwood is getting rid of our lifeblood while you gamble away our savings. Isabella was right. She always is. She was always right about these things. That soulless merchant is out to take the water. Don't you see? Why do you do business with him?"

Marty spit again. He took a snap at the fire with his belt whip and the fire crackled in echo. Fennel's words really got him giggling. He laughed and laughed. Whatever Fennel had said really struck a chord with him as he nearly buckled over in hysterics.

"Scratch, I gotta hand it to ya. Ya bout da stupidest ding I seen in a long, long time and I gotta say, dis here Muddy Carnival is full the brim wit um. Der be here a boy born so dum, he only make da sound of a donkey when ya poor him a sip. Oh he love dat sip and he sing dat donkey song all night long. I buy him drink after drink just ta hear him snort. Der be an utta lass dat just open up her twot legs when ya wanna poke. She got a scar on her face and she be dum as a sock puppet. But she love dat Marty party. She come a slurpen for a burpen and I give it to her just good and a plenty. But neither he nor her evuh questioned da value of a man dat sets his sights on some cash money when he can get it. Way of da world, mah boy.

"But ya so dum it confuses you. I spoiled ya. Dat I did. If ya had to go beg for it da way I do, every night, ya would like money more. If you woke up in da mud, covered in da last nights bad ideas, not a ha'penny in ya pocket, jonesen for a lil somethin somethin, you would love money. You would dream of it. It would make ya pesky heart sing. You would worship it. Ya would get on yer hands and knees and rub your milk bones on it. Cash moves everything around me. So da sayen goes.

"Now get dees boxes over to der deliveries. And stop ya nasty boy tirades around town beetin and maulin low level nuttins. Dem boys night last, dey aint got nutt to do wit nutt. Once ya start maulin the rabble, da police start snoopen, the mayor start a callin, do rumor mill start a churnin . . . I put a good amount a work in ta not let dat all start up again. I knewd if

252

I took da twos a yas in I was riskin a bit o'dat cover. But I told em, and I tell em again, if either you or dat hellion start messin with my beau vivant, yas outs on ya ass. Can't helps ya. Now you gone runnin yer anger round town like a drunken Irish bum, beaten and a maimen townfolks. Can't have it, Scratch."

Fennel listened to Marty. He bowed his head and felt the desire to say yes sir the entire time. It made him crazy. His subservience drove him nuts. His hands were now clean. He was embarrassed slightly how he had run around last night placing a hurt on those involved. But he couldn't help it. They had deserved it. Now Marty had come challenging him and he felt like a boy. He didn't like that feeling. The Raven had awoken he reminded himself. The Raven had liberated him from Isabella and from Marty. Neither of them should place their mitts on his plots and plans.

"Stop yer yammering!" Fennel barked. He threw on the slang he had learned so long ago. His eyes were glowing yellow and the words juggled in his mouth with nervous Raven excitement. "Dose boxes gonna stay where dey may. Tell dem Stallhammers to hold up. Ah got plans, Marty McGuinn. Ah got me a super plan. And you're wrong 'bout money. Don't tink I don't know it. Ya sit der just whilin away dem ducats but you want em plenty. Ah know its allure. But ya don't get how dis Castilla is different, do you? You're too dumb to see it. Blinded by de now.

"De water won't always be around. It's finite, Marty. Dis taking away of de lunatics is more dan you tink. You tink I care about a slack jawed loony tune? No. I dun. Ain't nothin' but somethin' to laugh at. But ah see it. Dang, ah feel it. It's part of a bigger plan. It's a mega plan. Dey are puttin mechanisms of control 'round town. It's not just 'bout money, it's 'bout control, and control is 'bout dreams, Marty. Dreams. Our food. Our lunch. Our meals. You have never had any strategic sense. Ya just a small time crime boss always out on vacation. But dis Castilla is out to rinse de world of de water. Ah know it. Ah can taste it. You're too drunk. You don't know squat. You tink tings will always be de same. Lay low, and scrape the money off the top. You're goin to get cut out, buddy boy."

Marty laughed and spit again. He shook his head and snapped his belt in the air. It went crack and sparks from the fire went flying. "Get that ass of yours ready, Scratch. You're gettin a whippin and den ahma gonna watch your body burn baby burn on da fire roast chicken-style."

Marty laughed and laughed. His image slowly faded from the fire and Fennel was left shaking in his shoes. The Raven was strong in him, but he could feel the fear rising inside as well. They battled for control and he felt he was outside himself looking back. He was a battleground of submission and freedom. He wasn't sure which way to turn.

"Enough!" he shouted into the night air. "The Raven has spoken and the Raven shall speak again. What I said was true and these boxes are nothing but a sign of my incompetent docility. Isabella might have been right to some degree, but I'm right by all degrees. Justice must be served. Castilla will die at my hands and when Marty comes to town, so too shall he!"

Perhaps this was the night he had avoided for so long. He certainly couldn't stay there, not with Marty sure enough coming back so soon, whip in hand. He had a party to plan. He skipped over the cave feeling light on his feet, grabbed a suitcase and packed a few items. It occurred to him that he couldn't remotely carry all the clothes that he wanted. That idea bothered him. Living out of a suitcase wasn't his idea of a good time. He told himself that he would just have to get settled and buy an entire new wardrobe. These items were going to be a thing of the past. The concept agreed with him. He chucked his old clothes into the fire and watched them burn. They sizzled and cracked and he hummed to himself. He was off to join the circus.

Chapter 24

The moon had returned and its slivered toenail caught the cracked paint edge of the windowsill showing down onto Isabella's small breath. She woke with a start to an empty room. The boom of the nightclub was a rumbling factory engine. It rolled through her like the vibrating of the bottom of the ocean. She would often let it hold her in the palm of its hand. The world is a rhythm. She needed to wake. She knew that. The needs of the present couldn't be more urgent. She strained to pull herself from the couch. How she missed her mat in the cave. Her eyes immediately set upon the work desk. It was littered with bills, but all in all, things were in order. Caperwill was more than capable.

As consciousness sewed its way back into her body, the shudder of Caperwill's words took hold of her again. Could it be true? Sibel was dead? A pit opened up in her. The face of that beautiful young girl that had smiled upon her so was no longer around. Death had eaten her—a girl jumping off a diving board to be swallowed, so silently, in the mass of the universe's soft mouth, never to be seen again. The thought chilled her. The tragedy of it grew against her tongue. It tasted so good, so sweet—the aria of the horrible end singing delicious pleasure in her, the sadness of the living making her heart swoon. Her own appreciation of this universal grieving made her ill. How could she enjoy what was so horribly depressing? Isabella threw the papers off the desk. They fluttered in the air and fell lightly to the floor.

Isabella walked to the mirror. Her small feet felt already tired and the night had just begun. She stared hard at herself. Was she evil? Her mind was a mystery to her. The sadder the occasion, the more she felt inside her. She had feelings for Sibel and the news of her death only exacerbated Isabella's internal tension. Isabella bowed to her reflection unable to stare herself in the eyes. She was evil. Of this, she had no doubt. Her feelings were sadistic, brutal, cold and desirous—a hunger malicious. As much as she hated that her friend had passed, she also felt an overwhelming sensation of pleasure. Death, it seemed, was a meal for her.

To make matters worse, the sickness had returned. She looked at her vial of fish sauce to see mere dregs remaining—small flecks in a drip of silt. It seemed her freedom would be celebrated in a pile of vomit and remorse.

Caperwill came flying into the room. He was ever in a state of business and tonight he looked exceptionally exasperated. His long grey hair flew in every direction and his spectacles hung low across his nose.

"I have delivered the flowers and message, but I am afraid they will not be coming," he said, panting as he rushed in the door. "Rana and Yosune are locked up tight at Tacsim Station. The doors are strictly guarded and they are not receiving anyone."

"I am sure they are scared out of their minds and deep in mourning," whispered Isabella. The pain from her stomach made her wince. She needed more Marty hair. The days ahead were not going to be easy she thought. She sipped gingerly on the fish sauce dregs and headed out the door.

"The architectural plans for the new building!" yelled Caperwill as she hurried out the door.

"Just build it!" Isabella yelled back as she made her way to Tacsim Station.

The city was not her friend. This reunion was a tragic disaster. While she was digging bones out of the belly of the earth, a conspiracy had hatched against her in Barrenwood. How could it be a coincidence? Did Isabella's prodding lead to this tragic fate? Isabella prayed to gods above that such was not the case. She bounded across the rooftops toward the Elegiac Hills hovering above the city. Marty ever warned her about going up there and her last visit with Minasha Darkglass certainly gave his cautionary anecdotes credence.

"Dem high faloots ain't for ya. Dey just a bunch o scaredy cats with der wiskers caught in dar coffers. Don't you be goin up der. You and Scratch need ta lay low as a wet rug and don be catchin der glances."

Marty hobbled over to the corner of the room and opened up a burlap sack, untying the wires wrapped around the top. His hands reached in and pulled out handfuls of gold coins. They rattled in his hand and he gave Isabella one of those peculiarly gross smiles that indicated his own sense of happiness. "Dis. Dis. Dis what dey good for. We gotta keep em rich cause der ducats be our ducats. I gets up in dat hill only once in a blue moon and when I do, I come back with the riches dat keep us a eatin and fishin." Marty then laughed and sucked on his bottle of rum. Whatever insights he had wanted to tell Isabella were somewhat lost on her.

She had originally planned on going to Marty's cabin—come what may. She needed more Marty hair. But this news about Sibel. She couldn't just let that pass. She had to see them immediately. Tacsim Station housed the Persembe family in all its glory. High on the hill, it was a fortress with spiraling minarets and doors with ogee arches. The journey to Tacsim Station and up Elegiac Hills was not easy.

She borrowed a mule from Capperwill so she could make the journey without having to walk. Her legs were turning to jelly even with the fish sauce draining along her gullet. She would need to save her strength if she was to sneak into their mansion. It wasn't a bad idea in the end and she enjoyed slowly moving through the city. It was like a slow motion rotoscope and she watched the city get slowly poorer and stranger. The streets filled with the songs of the gypsies and vagabonds, the bars still rambling with the mighty laughter of times no one will remember.

Heading up the base of Elegiac Hills, she could see the distant silhouettes of the mansions of the families. They looked down at Barrenwood as though the homes themselves were staying at arm's length. Not committing to living in the urban sprawl of the city, they preferred a view that only looked out upon the distant marshlands where tucked within Fennel and Isabella had hidden from many a sunrise. Isabella could imagine Marty making his way up this hill every once in a while. Probably just like her on a mule. He would come like a beggar with a stick, threatening, laughing and cajoling some blood money off the families to keep his strange habits afloat. And now, here she came as well. A soft haggard woman hoping her words could soothe the agony of some sisters she loved dearly. She crossed her fingers that her return would be at least welcome enough to be of some use for the distraught pair.

Something had changed. As she passed the first series of gates at the bottom of the mountain with a tossed mist of willow seed, she found herself confronted by yet another set of gates at the top of the road. And then, after yet another poof of willow seed and an accompanying nod from the officer's helmeted head, she found yet another gate at the entry to Tacsim Station. The Elegiac Hills, it seemed, had been placed on an ever so rare moment of alert.

Isabella had planned on rationing out her final days of the fish sauce but her need to get to the Persembes took precedence. She took another large sip from her quickly diminishing bottle and folded into night, passing the first guard without him noticing. She bounded as hard as she could over the gates and onto the roof of the enormous mansion. She landed with the faint sound of a leaf falling from the jicama tree. Her feet stealthily tread the ledge as she peered in through the large stained glass of a Siamese cat with three eyes. She peeked through to see the hallways guarded as well. The family was in lock down. Paranoia had become the new norm.

Isabella tinkered with a small bathroom window and managed to unhinge it and slide her lithe little shadow of a body inside onto the tile floor. As she rose up she saw the reflection of herself in the mirror. She was extra pale. The shadows under her eyes were all the more pronounced and the toll of Marty's mojo made her wince at her unbecoming visage. No time to worry about that now. She peeked her head out the doorway to spy the guards in front of what she sensed was the room that the two lasses had hidden themselves away. She could sense their peculiar energy a mile away. It was sinuous and bubbly.

Isabella mewed a catcall and three Siamese cats came prancing out from different nooks in the house. The Persembes did love their kittens. She whispered her plot into their ears and the trio wiggled their whiskers in approval. Why didn't Isabella ever run away with the animals? Perhaps that was more Fennel's calling than hers, but she did like them. The three cats went flying down the hall in a fanatical brawl. Their hair on end and their talons a flying, they rolled around in a frantic tumble past the guards and then bumped down the stairs. The guards bored out of their minds, couldn't help but run over to the stairs to take a look and with that, Isabella slid herself through the ornate bedroom door.

As she entered, she at first went unnoticed. Rana was dancing with herself in the corner of the room singing some song of romance to a daydream. She was dressed in black and it seemed as though she may have not taken the dress off since Sibel's funeral. Her mouth was stained purple from the wine she now suckled on like a baby. Yosune remained lying on the bed, her feet hanging over as she stared at the ceiling saying nothing. Isabella decided to announce herself.

"Good evening, ladies. I snuck into your chambers. You will have to forgive me, but it was the only way to see you. You have clearly taken yourself out of circulation. I am so sorry to hear about Sibel. I came as soon as I could." Isabella had decided to not prattle with subtleties. She was determined to get to the bottom of this and condolences would feel fake. Her appearance startled them out of their revelries. Yosune sat up and Rana turned abruptly, her hair spinning wildly in tangles.

Rana turned to Isabella with fire in her eyes; a mixture of rage, pain and madness in between. She was hostile and beyond her sense of self. She had fever in her. One she couldn't control. Isabella knew this kind of temperament. She had seen it in herself and she knew what it needed. It needed an equally insane temperament and so she met Rana's stare with an eye more fierce and terrifying. Rana stared back and the two of them were locked in a strange stare down as Yosune looked at the both of them as though they were insane. At last, Rana turned her eyes away.

"Isabella!" Rana cried, after a momentary silence. "What are we to do? Where were you? How could you disappear at this time? How could she be dead? My sister? My dear, dear sister . . . and you! Where were you? Her body is cold in the ground and you are nowhere to be found. She died on some stupid mission for you and you go away?"

She was ranting. Isabella grabbed her hand and sat her on the bed next to Yosune, caressing her hair with her hand.

"Shhhhh, my dear. I would have come if I could. Believe me. But I was, more or less, imprisoned for the last few weeks. Tragedies inexplicable have prevented me from not only coming to your aid but knowing anything at all. I received the news last night and I came as soon as I possibly could. I am thunderstruck by this terrible tragedy. Sibel meant the world to me and I never intended to put her in harm's way. But I swear those responsible will pay dearly. I promise that."

She gripped Rana's hand as Rana leaned against her and sobbed. Isabella felt Rana's tears. They soaked into her body like memory—the crisp air of awareness that life is a massive tragedy. She hated the pleasure of Rana's pain brought her. It wasn't right.

Rana tore her head from Isabella as though sensing her secret enjoyment. Her eyes flashed, "What are you?" she asked, disgust in her voice. "What are we to you? Pawns? Playthings in your strange secretive game? I find it disgusting. My sister was an angel and you are straight from hell. You're not like us and you know it. You're some sick beast. I see it in you. Your eyes are evil."

Isabella's heart sank and her blood rose up in her. Rana was right. Her instincts wanted to tear Rana's eyes out, to rip her hair from her head and laugh in her face and say, "Yes, you are right! I am straight from the bowels of hell and best you remember that!" But she managed somewhere in her to push her rage down. It hurt her immensely to know how right Rana was. She didn't know what she was doing. This tragedy again seemed to feed her bones and the perverse irony of it only made her all the more convinced of the truth of Rana's statements.

She looked at Rana with cold eyes. "I am different than you, but I loved Sibel, too. I didn't ask so much of her."

"Get out of here demon! Be gone !" Rana yelled and threw her wine glass against the door. It smashed into a thousand crystal pieces with wine splaying the floral wallpapered walls. Yosune moved to quiet her, but Rana shook her off and stomped around the room.

Yosune sat up. "It isn't Isabella's fault. I have told Rana that numerous times, but blame has a way of being the balm for death. I thought you were dead as well, Isabella."

"I thought you were dead, too! Now I realize I had hoped you were dead," sobbed Rana.

Yosune's eyes teared up and she hugged Isabella. Rana remained steadfast on the other side of the room. Yosune and Isabella sat on the bed in a pile of sadness, consoling each other with tenderness and remorse. Again Isabella began to sink into the pleasure of another's tears.

"No! I said I want you out!" Rana rushed over to Isabella to grab her by the sleeve. Isabella stared at her with the most terrifying of looks and

259

again Rana demurred. She backed off and then in a whirlwind of confusion ran out the door, slamming it.

Yosune rushed over to the doors and locked them. "Dear god that stupid girl is going to make things worse. The guards really can't know you are here and I'm afraid I don't know what she is going to do. You are going to need to leave soon, Isabella. Our father is extremely distraught and wild with plans of revenge. His anger exceeds anything we have ever seen. We told him of Sibel's relationship with Peter. How they had fallen madly in love. Now they live in love's embrace on the other side of life like Romeo and Juliet."

"Peter is dead as well?" Isabella gasped.

Yosune's eyes opened wide. "Why yes! You did not know? They were found together lying below the Grand Oak near the railway station at Quelling. They wore matching silver rings that night. We guess they may have become engaged. They loved each other so. Their throats, their bodies . . . I can't say it. Yes, they died together. Oh, Isabella, there is so much to know. Sibel loved him dearly. The fire between them had grown so bright. But they were cut down. Our sister." Yosune went over to the bar and poured herself some wine. From the look of her, this had become a regular habit of late.

"Isabella, there is nothing for us to do. I do not even care. Our investigations into Castilla were a bit of mischief. We were playing with fire. Now, I just wish life could go back to the way it was. Father has taken up where we left off. He is enraged beyond all sense of rationality. You need not worry about revenge for I am sure that all hell will be brought to bear on Castilla."

Isabella took a second to collect her thoughts. So much had happened while she was locked away in that infernal school. Sibel and Peter were dead, and now the families were lining up to see Castilla's head on a plate.

"So your father now knows of Castilla?" asked Isabella.

Yosune looked up. Her eyes in shock. "You really have been gone a long time. Everyone knows about Castilla. He quickly became the source of every malicious joke in society—the wretched *nouveau riche* that are going to be the bane and demise of our livelihoods. The crooked man of rabble town. The bent hack. I don't know if anyone ever has gained such disdain so fast—and so well deserved. He is evil. Pure evil. And his evil musty laugh! After Sibel passed, we told Father about our own investigations. How Sibel had met Peter while trying to learn about him. I promise we have never revealed anything about you, even while we thought you might be dead. I guess we thought maybe that somehow, you were beyond death itself. It appears we might be right. You are a little black angel. I may be hallucinating you right now, I can't say. But anyway, we told Father about our childish games and Sibel's romance. It infuriated him. He may never speak to us again. I can't say. It is for the best though. He has lost his mind."

"How do you know what Castilla's laugh is like?" asked Isabella. Uncovering what had happened was making her stomach turn. Perhaps it was the sickness, or perhaps, for one of the few times in her life, it was nerves. All of this had become too much.

"Because we can hear it when we sleep? No, but really, we have seen him numerous times. Oh right. Dear me, so much has changed. Castilla is less of a mystery and more of a living nightmare for us now. Sibel's death has brought him far too close into our lives. Three weeks back, we would see him regularly in the judicial room at City Hall. When Sibel passed, Father rushed immediately over to the magistrate and a full investigation was put in place. Maybe he was too hasty. It has become immediately evident that there is absolutely no evidence linking Castilla to the murder and if anything it has only made our father more angry and distraught.

"After looking over the facts of her death, I must even admit personally, I can't see why Castilla would do this. If it weren't for the fact that his presence exudes an absolute darkness, I would perhaps have agreed with the findings. Who knows? He hates the houses and the houses hate him. He is ruthless and horrifying, but I have no time to play detective. I don't care. Many of the families it seems are perhaps overzealous to burn him at the stake.

"And our dear brother Serkan can't stop him. He tries to cool Father's temperament, but he is impossible to control. The rift this causes is palatable. Big Boy Charlie came over several times to cool Father's temper, but he barely wants to speak to him because he is now angry at Charlie for not telling him about his meetings with Castilla—who is apparently quite distraught over the slaying of Peter though to look upon him, one wouldn't know. Castilla claims the entire thing is an attempt by someone to besmirch his good name and has placed a reward, twice that which father offered, for any information that might lead to discovering who killed Peter and Sibel. It all makes me sick."

Rana suddenly came banging back into the room. She had clearly been listening at the door. "But it is worse than this, " she said. "There is a killer loose. There have been other homicides. All through the city. Much in the same gross manner as Peter and Sebby. Maybe it is a vampire or a ghoul. I cannot say. But the similarities even the police can't help but make a connection. Why would Castilla go on a killing rampage? Makes no sense. Something hellish is out there. I thought it was you!"

All of this news made Isabella's head swim, not to mention her body was already in a deplorable state. She doubled over from the pain in her stomach. Yosune jumped to help her. Isabella looked up. A slight hint of sweat covered her brow, "I'm fine."

Rana went over to the bureau and poured herself another drink. "Well, I'm not fine. I'm not fine at all. I hate that this has happened. It tears me up. Sibel is gone and here we sit like little detectives. It is embarrassing. Sibel was a dreamer, more full of life than any of us, and more tender to its ways. She was light and delicate. A strong wind has picked her up and blown her away. Isabella you must not let this go unpunished!" Rana drank the rest of her wine and poured herself another glass.

Even Yosune was having a hard time holding it together. It made Isabella sad. What would it take for her own self to lose it? Such things were harder for her. She tried desperately to get to the heart of sadness and always saw it playing about her like mist sifting through hands. She remained an outsider, watching the world at her short arm's distance. As her stomach once again turned on itself, she wondered if perhaps, in this case, it was her agony at existing at such a remove, that made her wince.

"You will make yourself sick if you continue to drink like that. It won't heal your pain either."

A knock came at the door followed by a bellowing voice. "Ladies, we hear you talking to someone in there! Open the door at once or we will be forced to knock it down by orders of your father!"

"Don't be stupid, Osgrove. No one is here. I am just talking to myself!" Yosune said as she opened a window motioning to Isabella. Isabella walked to Yosune and kissed her on the cheek.

She whispered to Yosune, "If there is any consolation, it is only that the grave will meet you as well." She then crept up onto the windowsill, winked at Yosune and Rana, and leapt six floors down to the courtyard below.

She landed on the ground with a thud and not a whoosh. The earth was heavier under her feet. Her stomach began to make the familiar twist as she scaled the outer wall to begin her descent into the city. She was going to have to solve this. What was she going to do when Marty's hair runs out? She knew she would either have to return to his cabin and search the nooks and crannies for some remnant of him, or she would have to confront him head on and somehow snip off some of his hair. Either way, the options seemed radically implausible. She was too weak to confront him and entering his home, at this point, wasn't much different than smelling his rum soaked breath. Such a possibility wasn't actually a possibility at all which left her facing other, perhaps more stark, futures.

For the other future she saw was one where she writhed in pain at the Chateau de Crawler and rode it out, the illness piling up in her until it either dissipated or ate her alive. She imagined herself lying in a bed, losing the little weight she had, and sweating and exhausted coming to. But what then? While she once thought of the sickness as an active spell sent by Marty to make her return, she had also begun to conceive of it as the disappearance of her powers—her gradual transformation into a plebian of Barrenwood. The one future she did not imagine, however, was ever returning into the fold of Marty. "I will die free," she told herself.

Isabella was so lost in her thoughts that when she came to, she didn't know where she was. As she looked around, she noticed the street heaved up in a pile of rubble. A massive bulldozer in stained yellow equipped with rusted, muddy gears, sat unattended, its front scoop still dug deep into the earth. The entire world around here had been upended, bottom gone top, built gone broken. Four houses were now torn asunder, their architectural frames splintered up, the faint remnants of wallpaper, a bed, a lamp, and chairs, sticking out of the pile of wreckage that was this reverse excavation. Further south along the road, an army of construction vehicles sat in waiting. The armada of this construction crew sat still without their drivers under the moonlight waiting in the calm silence of a pause of battle, to head out again to continue their aggressive redevelopment.

The building's corpses had been bulldozed to make way for something. And just at the edge, where the rubble ended and the street continued on as though not a thing had changed, like a family having a picnic in front of a tidal wave, the neighborhood continued on. The buildings were creaking on their foundations, lanterns hung on pegs out front of porches, and the streets moved with the bodies of people wandering in the heat of the night. A lone brick wall had become home to numerous splashes of spray paint with one of the more bold statements reading, *Death to the king.*

Isabella's eye wandered toward the homes where people gathered in groups sitting around on porches laughing, singing, drinking and arguing. The air danced with the sounds of humanity, and as Isabella listened even closer, she could hear a melodic banjo playing underneath it all. She wandered over to a corner where men and woman were laughing and drinking leaning on a pouring fire hydrant. The water gushed gallons upon gallons of water into the cracked black roadway making a refractive river that danced in the reflection of the dark bodies in motion. Children danced in the water even though it was the middle of the night, their limbs moving in a somnambulist dance. They laughed and pranced as though it were mid-day, their giggles like carbonation in the ecstatic extraction of the water lines below. The rusted and decayed infrastructure of Barrenwood's plumbing belched dreams of renewal into the fresh spray. The couples, strangers, and families, that gathered near the hydrant leaned back as though resting on the evening's humidity, their bodies holding against a different sense of time as though the world had nowhere to go—as though here was as good as anywhere and now was as glorious and as sorrowful as any now could ever be.

"Hey lil' lady, have a drink," said an older man with a bottle of whiskey in hand.

Isabella, who never drank, took a sip. The liquid felt warm as it slid down her throat and made a bed in her stomach. She pulled down her hood and stared into the moonlight. It caught the side of her face as if she was sunbathing and she leaned into the glow as it cooled and warmed her.

An elderly black woman said to her, "You sure are proper to be spending a while. Isn't it past your bedtime?"

The elder man with the bourbon, handkerchief wrapped around his neck and overalls suspended over his shoulders, snickered, "Regina, lil' miss can be out whenever she wants. Your kids have been whooping it up here since sunrise. It's too hot for anyone as far as I can tell. Like asphalt in a firefight." He wiped his forehead with his handkerchief and took the bottle back from Isabella and took a pull. Isabella, just sat silent, shared the back of the fire hydrant with her friend.

"Fact is, Freddy, your great aunt would rue what they've done to this street," said the old woman. "My aunt, her aunt, their aunt, and on back, they all grew up around here and I know the day is soon coming when we'll be kissing this town goodbye for good."

"Aw now, Regina. Don't get all worked up about it. This place has given us as much heartache as it has anything else. Maybe it's time to move on."

"The heartache is what I'll miss most," Regina said, staring out over the cock-eyed bulldozers, their muscular arms buried into the cracked asphalt of her memories.

"It doesn't much matter what we miss, the world around us rolls along. The winds that blow over us are the winds that have blown over all time. They move without a concern. God up there is a cruel strange man who spends most of his time drunk. I'll tell you that."

"The Lord is watching out for us. That I know. He speaks to me at night and in these hours he keeps me from the demons. He is up there with my two boys right now. Looking down on me and holding my hand through this valley of death."

Freddy snickered, "The good Reverend will be pleased to hear you say that. If staying in the good list is what you want, that is what you do. I remember us playing just like these kids at this very corner. I swear the days were never this hot back then, but we played and played in the fire hydrant. I will miss this street, too. Take a drink and relax. Or put your head in the water like this!" Freddy bent over and put his whole head into the spray of water. A burst of water shot out splashing Isabella and Regina.

They passed the bottle back and forth, listening to the friends and family, whoever they were, talk and laugh as the night went on. People would wander up, some bringing drinks, some sharing snacks—maybe dried mango or salted beef—some hanging around just hoping the bottle might end up in their hands, some talking too much and some not saying a word.

The circle would expand and contract like an organ of the city, just contracting and retracting with the pulse of people who couldn't sleep because their homes were too hot and the sticky air would not relent. Some people were friends and some were tolerated, but most had known each other for a very long time—through good times and bad, drunken brawls, romances gone south, surprise pregnancies, time spent in prison, and more times than not, scraping together money to just hold this torn fabric together. The rollercoaster of living had been a lot bumpier in the Mortestrate, and the neighborhoods took the hits together. It left them close and it left them hard. It is a bizarre gift to suffer together and for that few of them were thankful.

As the night grew on, Isabella leaned back into the fire hydrant, listening to the sound of the water pouring into the street. It gurgled and chimed along with the laughter and occasional argument of her present company. Sipping Freddy's bourbon, she dreamed a little too far out and came to herself to find just her and Freddy standing alone on that corner in the wee hours.

She sniffed the air. Something was moving. She felt it at the edge of her senses. Something familiar. Something rank. It rang a little bell in her deep inside. The bell said danger, but she couldn't stop listening to the water.

"Darlin'," said Freddy. "You better find some shelter. The Mortestrate isn't safe for the likes of you. Not at the hour you showed up, and definitely not now. Do you need a place to stay?"

"No, no, I'm fine," she said. "I can take care of myself."

She leaned up from the fire hydrant and adjusted herself. Her head was dizzy. She was drunk for one of the few times in her life. The night opened up with a terrifying scream. It was Regina. She came running frantic out into the street from her home.

"Come quick!" she yelled.

Isabella and Freddy ran over. Neighbors exited their homes to join. They followed Regina to a teetering house with a soft wood porch.

"The Mayberries! The Mayberries! All of em. They've been killed!" she screamed and then fell onto the porch overcome with grief. Isabella's nose told her more than her eyes. She smelled the gore. The blood. The guts. She also smelled swine—lots of little pig feet, which defied explanation. And urine. And the rank odor of unwashed oldness.

The sight of the killing in the living room was beyond description. They had been severely destroyed, some kind of extremely sharp object decapitating the bodies and leaving their innards torn out for the world to witness. The insides going outside. A family of four united into one massive mess of viscera and rot. Men howled. Women screamed. Freddy grabbed Isabella and led her out of the room.

"You shouldn't have seen that, darlin'. That is too much for about anyone," he said, holding her around the shoulders. "Can't believe it. The Mayberries. They have been here longer than most. It's their connection to the PRM. That's what's done it to them. No doubt about it."

Isabella had a lot of emotions running through her. The scene of violence had come so quickly, her body so fueled up on alcohol, she had trouble gaining her senses with so much happening around her. She could sense her inner demons wanting to go back in that room. She strangely salivated to taste that blood—to feel it on her tongue. She felt Freddy's arms around her.

"Who would do this? " asked Isabella in a daze.

"The monarchies would do this. They know the people are moving against them and they are trying to take us out. The Mayberries. I can't believe it. There is a war brewing lil' lady. Blood will beget blood."

Isabella shook Freddie's arms off her shoulder. "I have to go, Freddy. It is too late already."

Freddy wanted to stop her. It seemed to him that it was too dangerous for such a small girl to head out into the night. He wasn't half wrong, but she was off in a flash, her small feet catching the wind and the rooftops. She hopped not all that far away to the Mayberry rooftop. She had to—one last time—take the scene in through her nose. She inhaled deeply, the fragrance of death filling her nostrils. Swine, most definitely swine. And then, a thought chilled her to the bone, as it took hold of her with evidence most clear. This wasn't just a massacre. It was a massacre committed by someone like herself. Someone from the other side.

Her mind wandered in the clouds as she bounded back to the Chateau de Crawler. She tried to make sense of it all. Sibel's death. These strangers massacred. The hint of some foul creature set loose on the city. And her own time was running out as the fish sauce came dangerously to an end. She wished Fennel would come to her aid, but had he gone off the deep end? Had he given in to the Raven and left her for good? She couldn't believe it.

She was alone and soon to be very weak. She found herself wishing for the Duke. She needed to be rescued. He was large. He was a force. He could take control of the world in a way she found herself unable to do. For one of the few times in her life, she felt uncontrollably vulnerable. It was almost a human feeling—that feeling of no mastery and no wisdom, nothing but a stick in the ocean going this way and that.

As she made her way across Barrenwood, a unique feeling rose up in her that replaced vulnerability. Fear. Isabella felt a growing fear rising in her as she exited the District of Jed and cut over to the Calliope. Something was following her. She hadn't sensed it at first, but the feeling grew with each new rooftop. She quickened her pace as her stomach also began to turn over. Not now. The sickness had terrible timing. She ran through the streets as weakness began to set into her bones. Whatever it was that was chasing her was faster. And since no human was faster than she, she could feel it was the slayer of the Mayberries. A netherworld creature was fast on her heels.

She was outgunned, woozy and sick. She would have to retreat. Anger and curiosity surged in with mixed emotions. The right thing to do would be to run as fast as she could, but she wanted so desperately to know what this creature looked like. Why was it after her? She turned to run, slipped and plummeted off the roof to the ground below.

She landed with a thud and blood crept out of her nose. The creature was moving fast on her. She scrambled to her feet and darted as fast as she could toward the Calliope District. The chase was heavy and her breath was short. She ran for miles with her pursuer not tiring in the slightest. Over rooftops, through alleyways, through abandoned homes and across the Serengeti Park. Still it kept coming on. She was tiring and her body ached from her fall. Panic was beginning to set in and she tried to think while she ran.

She could only think of one escape and the thought of it didn't please her. She made her way toward the waterfront, her legs beginning to ache, the sickness having returned and oozing in her stomach. She didn't have it in her to make it to the Chateau de Crawler. She gave up on that plan as she crouched behind a barrel along the docks, knowing full well that this creature, with its pig smell, would be on her in minutes. What had become of her? She was becoming powerless—her skills disappearing, her body a haven for pain, her face smeared with blood from her fall and her lungs straining for oxygen. As she heard the pitter patter of the beast, she resigned herself to the only idea she had left and flung herself into the Aliber River.

The water was ice cold and it froze her bones as she sank deep into the black mire. The river moved slowly and the smell of algae and pond played hopscotch in her nose. She held her breath in her little lungs and swam under water downriver and to the other side. The creature may be able to beat her on land, but under water she was another creature. It exhausted her and her lungs felt as though they might burst. But she knew she had to stay down. If this didn't work, she was finished and that thought, strangely enough, somewhat excited her. She swam down the river nearly two miles before she came up for air, pulling herself soaking onto the muddy, rocky riverbank. Driftwood lay scattered about her as she coughed and coughed, freezing against the air. The smell of the creature seemed to have faded.

From there, in a haze, she dragged herself through the streets to make it to the Chateau de Crawler. She entered the noodle house, opened the back door, literally fell onto her office floor, and passed out, her body shaking feverishly. Her teeth small hammers tapping on the eggshell surface of dawn.

Chapter 25

Fennel kissed the boat goodbye. He placed his small red lips on its wooden bones and gave it a lip-smacking adieu. It had served them well over the years. He could still see Isabella in the corner, staring out into the night—a dreamer of worlds beyond the here. He sat wondering which one to take. The projector or the phonograph? He opted for the projector. He grabbed the tin cans of 8 mm film and snuck the projector into his already too full duffle bag. Goodbye phonograph. Things would have to go by the wayside. He was on the run. And he felt it.

Somewhere, out there, that monstrous master was packing his bags and making way for the marsh. Fennel couldn't imagine that he was joking on this account. No, Marty McGuinn was coming back. He could feel it in every drop of his malcontent blood. He would be none too happy either. Cutting his trip off short to play angry dad had never been his calling card. He may be a master, but he was no paternal figure. It truly scared Fennel to consider what it all meant, and he hopped out of the boat with an invigorated sense of urgency.

He gave a hardy whistle and sat on the docks and waited. He had docked the boat further down river on the off chance that he could come back sometime and retrieve these items. Fennel looked up river. He really could use the help of Heinrich right now, but he had, unfortunately, put an end to that. Burning bridges was apparently a pastime for him. That odd old fellow did come in handy at times, but Fennel had dismissed him without a thought. For a brief moment of rage, anyone with any knowledge of Isabella would be enemy number one. But that was no longer the case. He found a reserve of sympathy up in his throat—his own desperation bringing that rare attribute of humility to his top hat. Maybe he would rehire Heinrich if given the opportunity again.

Zarathustra eventually came trotting up—his immense nostrils flaring in the wet fog. Fennel jumped on his back and whispered his instructions. They were off to the Calliope where the warehouses provided a great opportunity for a circus to rehearse. The signs were literally in the air. Hanging from every lamppost and electric lines were banners preparing the city for the upcoming festival. Time was coming to a head. Fennel interpreted every banner as though they were announcing his own birthday. A celebration of Fennel. Of course, the banners merely featured Big Boy Charlie holding up a sudsy beer mug with an illuminated lamp shining brightly behind. Nothing specifically mentioned Fennel, but he knew better. This event was to be his and his alone.

Zarathustra let Fennel off in front of the warehouse. The hour was late, but he could hear the rumbling of the cast of circus crew moving behind the corrugated steel roll door. Fennel banged his hand against the door. A small door to the left opened up and out came a small adolescent with long, bright green hair and more than his fair share of tattoos. A tattooed noose was wrapped around his neck and his eyes immediately spoke of an old soul in a young body—a body like Savina's that had seen so much that heaven and hell and earth co-mingled without surprise or awe. A spirituality of it is what it is.

"Can I help ya?" said the boy. "You're banging awfully loud."

Fennel gave the kid a creased eye stare. He decided he liked the kid for reasons that weren't clear. He tipped his hat.

"The name is Fennel. I am here to see Phineas Welch, master of the Peanut Family Circus. As it turns out, I am the benefactor of the upcoming performance in Barrenwood. And who may I ask are you?"

"I'm Caesar. Follow me," said the boy.

He walked Fennel through the small door and into the immense warehouse. The room was full of a circus in mid-training. A high wire trapeze careened across the room with leotard wearing acrobats flinging themselves back and forth. A metal sphere held inside it some motorcycles that swirled in a blinding circle. At the far end, Fennel could see the contortionists bending themselves this way and that. He closed his eyes and took a smell. Sweat, peanuts and lion turds. It was amazing and Fennel tried to calm himself. A thing like this could send him into an adrenaline-fueled tizzy the likes of which no one would want to be around.

Caesar walked Fennel across the space to an old man with a long grey beard in a shabby overcoat who had his head deep in the gears of some odd machine. Cesar tapped the man on the shoulder and the old man abruptly banged his head. Cesar whispered to him and the man turned around with a big broad smile.

"So it is you!" he said, rapidly grasping Fennel's hand. Fennel pulled it back as fast as he could. He could see the oil stains on the man's fingers and smell the sweat of a man not bathed for many moons. "We didn't know if we would ever be graced with your presence." The man wiped his hands on his pants and smiled broadly. He had the face of an aged squash, squishy and grooved.

"Well, I'm here, Phineas Welch," said Fennel. He did a twirl of his cane. "The name is Fennel and I am, at last, on site. I know you have received my correspondences, but I had to see for myself how things are going."

270

"No need to say who are you are, my good man. I know all too well. So glad to finally meet you. I had no idea you were so young but alas, a surprise or two is never something to be scared of. As you can see we are in the midst of training for the big event. Look around!" Phineas motioned with his arm the entirety of the vast warehouse. There truly was much going on.

The Peanut Circus came at the most reduced cost possible. Fennel had been desperate for something and had searched the papers for any sign of a visiting circus. He had sent word to the Creole Knights whose tours were legendary with the largest elephant in the world, but they never responded. He had sent a carrier pigeon as far out as Edgerton to the Gundergrass Playpen, but the reply came back with a fee far too exorbitant for his coffers. Instead, Fennel had to break the bank on the lost tribe of Eskisehir. This Peanut Family Circus had actually run aground in this industrial city where the air smelled of coal and the entire city dipped into the mines during the day only to come out hungry for food, drink and forgetting at night. The circus had set up shop on the dirt lot at the edge of the city, a place where no permit was needed and no timeline necessary. They could be there as long as they liked. And they were. For far too long.

The crowds died off fairly rapidly as repeat customers have never been the strong suit of a circus. The lion tamer, the acrobats, and the clowns became an unnecessary sideshow as the runway games and gambling rapidly took over the bulk of the business. Phineas had suffered inside for the fate that had befallen them. He was a fourth generation Welch whose only mission in life was to keep this circus on the move. And there in Eskeshir he had thought, perhaps, his luck had run out.

But Fennel's letter had arrived just in the nick of time. As it turned out, they were desperate for each other. While it was true that Fennel's letter came with more than its fair share of caveats and addendums the likes of which none of them had remotely ever heard of, it mattered not. They had been saved. The money could get the circus back on its feet and headed back again to the remote reaches of Twin from whence they had came.

"What's that you are working on?" asked Fennel taking a peek at the big red mechanical machine that had certainly caused Phineas more than his fair share of consternation.

"Oh, this ol' dog?" laughed Phineas. "It's a double machine. I've been working on them for some time now. You might like it. It's a cotton candy maker and penny squisher loaded up into one creation. See, you press down on this bar, well at least that is how it is supposed to work." Phineas got right into demonstration mode. Grabbing Fennel's hand, he placed it on a large iron bar. "Now place a penny in the slot. There you go. Okay, now

271

we pull down on this bar and the engine turns and the cotton candy whirls."

As Phineas spoke, Fennel watched a candied mist of tasty spindly cotton come flinging about inside. It was a magical display. Something akin to an edible Tesla Coil, the wisps of pink hairy candy came swirling around in a circle while the metal bar in the center simultaneously squished his penny. A spark went flying and the machine came to a sudden halt.

"Dammit," lamented Phineas. He pulled off the windowed top and reached in with his hand. It was covered in cotton candy and he pushed it forward to Fennel's face. "Have some. It's delicious."

Fennel demurred. This whole business was disgusting. Somehow Phineas Welch had managed to touch him with his nasty greasy hands. Phineas continued to eat the candy and flicked the squished penny at Fennel. Fennel instinctively caught it in the air.

"Read it," said Phineas, smiling.

Fennel looked down on the penny. Instead of Abraham Lincoln's face, he now saw the face of a clown with simple words surrounding it. PINK WONDER

"Nice trick," said Fennel, giving the penny a flick with his finger. It went twirling in the air, heads over tail, falling gently back into his well-lotioned palm. "Now if you don't mind, I would like to take a gander at the goings on here."

"Oh, haha, of course! Let me help you out on that," said Phineas. He again wiped his hands on his pants and ran to the center ring. "Cesar, can you give me some amplification on the mic?" Phineas grabbed a beat-up microphone dangling from a long chord in the center of the room. The microphone screeched and the feedback quickly got everyone's attention. They stopped mid-somersault, twist or death-defying act.

"Pardon the interruption friends, foes, and villains, but we have in our presence our most esteemed benefactor. He is eager to see what we have been up to. He may even have a few tips regarding our upcoming performance that I strongly encourage you to pay attention to."

Phineas clapped his hand and Fennel decided that his first stop would be the clowns. They were gathered around each other in the back of the warehouse sitting on a row of barrels and trading drinks from a large bottle. "It's their lunch break," whispered Phineas. "Don't mind them."

Fennel turned to Phineas. "How about you go back and fix that penny squisher? I would like to say hello in private if you don't mind."

"Of course, of course. Be my guest," said Phineas, as he bowed low and headed back to the sticky contraption.

Fennel couldn't be happier. Yes, the Peanut Circus was ragtag, but so be it. It was better, he figured than a too professional circus—at least for his purposes. And now here he was in the center of a most glorious plot. Marty was out there lost in some haze of bad news while Fennel was currently in the midst of embarking on something altogether of his making. He was surrounded by a clunky cast of characters who were amenable to his every whim and creative choice. He was able to make life come sailing back into recognition of something worth living. He inhaled. Peanuts and glory.

The clowns were cranky. They nearly snarled in their fire-engine red smudged lipstick and saturated white cake faces. Fennel could see them making jokes at his expense as he approached with his typical cane a-twirling.

"Evenin', gents," said Fennel. "Thought I would pop over and give a hello. How go the routines?"

The clowns gave a brief laugh and whispered to each other something that was probably not all that funny, but funny enough to get them laughing. Fennel hopped up on one of the barrels and began laughing as well. He laughed and laughed far longer than any of the clowns. His laugh was a squeal, a hideous screech that even the clowns found disconcerting.

"Boys, boys. Don't make me do it. I'm eager to be nice. More eager than you know. But don't make me use the big stick. It's right here in my hand and I can give each and every one of you the boot. No money for no love. Who wants that in the end? Not you. Not me. Let me use my carrot instead. It's your lunchtime after all. How about I throw out ten ducats to the first clown to get a move on? I need to see me some routines out here."

Fennel flicked ten ducats to the floor in front of them and the clowns sat quietly staring at the money. For a second, not a motion and then a clown clad in dandelion overalls and puffy blue hair went flying onto the floor. He did a pratfall to come tumbling into the middle of the room. He picked up the coins like a groveling fool and placed them eagerly in his pocket. The clowns laughed at his antics and another clown came tumbling out trying to wrestle the ducats from the first. They wrestled like idiots, squirming on the floor. Fennel was entirely entertained. He tried his best to jump up and stand on the clowns as they wrestled, but they were a slippery lot. Fennel fell down on the floor and then got up laughing.

"Ain't y'all funny?" he said, holding his belly like a fat man. He stared at the clowns while the wrestlers two below him got back onto their spots on the barrels. "Now listen to me, and do forgive my size, I am your boss. I'm a privileged little brat, it's true, but I'm smart beyond my years and that is true too. What you need to know, what everyone needs to know, is that I have a dream for this upcoming circus. It's a dream big and wide. So wide it's a mouth that will swallow you whole.

"I want a clumsy nightmare, a stumbling homicide, a death on a banana peel so absolutely fantastic that everyone will know, they will all finally know, that life, this stupid, messed up horrifying nightmare of the profane and prosaic, is only made magical by the man that lays a big fart when he cries. Hahaha! If only it were that simple but you get the point—a big disgusting embarrassment in the midst of the most somber pit of hell. That is the juicy spot. That is the root of your comedy and your clowning. That is the root of our big act and sometimes, sometimes I think—bear with me, I'm new to this—I feel like, yes, your field has deserted its values. It knew them once. Somewhere, out there, buried in the blowing sands of history, is a solitary clown the likes of which the Bodhisattva would envy. He saw the inner brilliance of comedy and it humbled him.

"I can only be sure of it out of a sense of nostalgia, but yes, the ancients must have known. But time has a way of making us forget and forget you have. For now, you have all become professionals, all suited up and swelling in false arrogance at your stupid alacrity. You embarrass your faith, dear boys! Nothing more stupid than a professional clown, wouldn't you say? I don't want clowns pretending at being in a big car and being professionals at falling down in front of people. I hate that. Nothing worse than the simulation of the pathetic. Nothing could be more arrogant. I want you to demonstrate a man trying to be a master of the pathetic who at the same time is absolutely pathetic at pulling it off. That is much more funny. More true to the art form. Otherwise, what are you? A charlotte? There are so many others that pull that off so much better than you. You are so lame at being the professional faker of embarrassment. A stupid switch in the gear. Stop it. Wake up! You aren't fooling me and in their hearts you aren't fooling them. That is the kind of meta hilarity that will get those awful things known as children to really laugh. They will laugh and laugh 'cause they will enjoy how stupid you really are. Do you hear me, boys? Do you hear me? A true clown must embrace what a joke they are all the way down into the inner pit of their dirty, nappy souls."

Fennel was on a tear. The clowns stared at him in a strange drunken stupor. For a clown, and let's face it, a clown of the Peanut Family Circus, was as best as one could describe a clown; but a clown that knew what it meant to be a pathetic clown, in their hearts, each and every one of these clowns could relate to where Fennel's brain was going. Perhaps the alcohol helped. Perhaps in a sudden haze of convolution, they confused their practice with their living and it all rang like a clanging monstrosity of humiliation. But it clangs so deep and so true. They knew, better than anyone, what got the laughs. They knew, better than anyone, what sold people on the reality of the game. Yes, they held back. The little brat wasn't wrong there. They held back for fear of the pit of despair when they finally gave in—because after the lights went out and the lion went back in the cage, they had to sleep with themselves again. But it called them nonetheless.

Fennel's words strangely inspired them. They weren't an easy crowd to win over, but these clowns were an odd lot. They had a sweet spot for their craft and were bored to tears with the way things had gone down in Eskeshir. This upcoming festival was something altogether new. So they did as they were requested. They tried out new routines that included taking off their makeup, fighting with each other, making strangers clowns and the telling of town secrets out loud. They brainstormed on methods to get their comedy closer to that thing perversely called the real.

Fennel found it thrilling to be in the role of head coach. He found himself in the midst of the intramural sport of life. He was coaching his way through the fog and it felt glorious. The clowns were actually a funny prickly lot—their entire humor clad in a tone of sadness that touched Fennel's sympathies. This is all to say, they got along.

By the time Fennel felt the clowns were sufficiently on their way, he headed over to the contortionists. The hour was very late and many of the performers had snuck off to bed. Phineas Welch had disappeared as well. The only folks left were three young girls who were placing their legs behind their heads and doing their ninth yoga routine. Fennel bowed low to them and they informed him that they were about to retire. The morning was due upon them soon.

"Okay. Okay. You have to sleep. I get it. But listen to me. I am sure Phineas has mentioned this, but we are up to something altogether different here. You can't do your normal routine. No more putting your heads backward to stare out between your legs. No more wrapping your arm behind your head and popping it out of socket. That kind of trick, while good, is not what we are up to. Think of this as the drunken master version of what you normally do."

The contortionists stared at him with big-eyed bewilderment. They were tired and frankly they were never coached. No one usually spoke to them. For as long as they could remember, they had just done their stretches, pulled their bodies out of position and then let them settle for the world to see. It had started as jokes in the mirror and then when the family had run out of money during the war effort, it had become streetside income. Most everyone in the circus thought they were mute, but Fennel was not privy to this information. Instead, he was in their inner circle and he wanted them to shift gears.

"Okay, you girls are the quiet types. I can respect that. Just don't give up on listening. I can see you listening. So fine. Good. We have work to do. I have an idea. It's an odd one, but that is kind of my style. Bare with me for a second."

Fennel rifled around in his bag and pulled out the projector. He set it on a table and got a film canister out. He smiled at his wisdom of taking the projector with him. It had already come in handy. He cranked the hand lever to show the film he wanted these three limber sisters to learn from.

"What you are seeing here is the choreography of a most special freak of nature. Her name is Pina Bausch. She is so German it is almost painful to look at. All that awkward physicality is a bit much. I get that. But look at these moves. Where did they come from?"

Flickering in black and white in granular spotty imagery came the collective effort of a most frantic dance performance. Women and men flailed their arms against themselves, their bodies ran into objects and their heads twitched in odd spasmodic motions. Their bodies writhed in the emphatic excitement of living, but the sight was almost gruesome. The contortionists were hypnotized. It spoke a language of the body they had known inside themselves. They had never seen such a performance before and it was as though a door to another planet had just opened up for them to walk through.

Fennel stared at them and smiled. He had been right again. This was all they needed. They could take it from here. They would now know what to do. The performance of their bodies must be a wrestling with the excitement of living and the trappings of awkward embodiment. These contortionists could invent a new way to bend the body that pushed harder against the edge of their being. Fennel clapped his hands.

"Okay, I will just let you watch this for a while. I can see I have touched a nerve."

Fennel bowed low and one of the sisters, Nina Bird, placed a kiss on his cheek. Fennel wasn't sure what to do with that. He wasn't used to affection from anyone other than Isabella and the touch of it brought a bit of sentimentality into his misanthropic temperament. Fennel smiled and made his way toward the lighting board. It was time to shut down for the night.

He found Caesar reading a comic book. His eyes were drooping.

"Done yet?" asked the little green haired circus assistant.

Fennel nodded.

"Good, cause these folks could really use some sleep," said Caesar. He hit the lights and the warehouse went dark with the exception of the film projector in the corner where the contortionists continued to watch.

"It occurs to me that I don't actually have a place to sleep," said Fennel, realizing, that he really didn't have much of a plan.

276

Cesar looked Fennel up and down. The idea that Fennel was a vagabond who was paying all their wages struck him as amusing and strange. "Well, it turns out, you managed to surprise me. You can always bunk in my quarters. They are over there in the corner."

Fennel slung his duffle bag over his shoulder. "Show me the way, if you don't mind."

They made their way toward the corner of the room where a massive pile of hay pushed up against the wall. Caesar climbed up into his and squished his body around to make a place to sleep. Fennel joined him, taking the smell deep into his nostrils. He was literally hitting the hay.

He stared up at the ceiling and felt a wave of satisfaction roll over him. He was in his element and the world was finally what it should be. All he had left to do was to enact his grand performance and finish it off with his long overdue cherry on top. He would soon be killing Marty McGuinn and Elinore Castilla.

Chapter 26

When Isabella woke, she felt like crud. Her head pounded and it wasn't just the amplified bass coming from her churning nightclub in the adjacent room. Perspiration settled on her brow and awful shakes had set in her skin. Perhaps, this is what it was like to be human after all. She tossed and turned but after a while, she had to open her eyes.

As she imagined, there sat Caperwill. He was her bedside fellow and he tended to her with a wet rag. He patted her forehead and whispered to her that everything was going to be okay. His wild grey hair hovered above his head, a cobweb of his life's anxieties. Isabella tried her best to smile at him, but such things rarely came naturally. It looked bent in her mouth and Caperwill said, "shhh."

Time seemed to be diminishing—the curtain of the world about to drop. Last night's insane run through the streets with some foul demon chasing her just wasn't fair. That homicidal creature was most surely the beast that had laid Sibel and her sweet crush Peter to waste. Isabella shuddered at what surely must have been a gruesome scene. It was a monster divine and it had come for her as well. She could sense in the way it chased her that it possessed a kind of hunting sensibility reserved for an ilk beyond this nuanced land. It was pure in its aggression. Of that she had no doubt.

But the answer to why it killed Sibel still bothered her tossing and turning condition. It made little sense and while Isabella could perfectly accept that the world worked in unanswerable chaotic ways, she found it hard to believe that that particular crime scene was the result of pure coincidence. No, that creature had come for them and it had come for Isabella as well. It may have fed and bled along the way, hiding in old farmhouses and slaying an impoverished family here and there, but some of its actions were not without premeditation. There were larger hands on the game board and Isabella could feel them.

But for now she was a mess and the way seemed beyond her control. Last night, the water of the Aliber had soaked into her bones and she had just barely managed to crawl up through the noodle shop and lay on the floor, a sopping pile of sad moss. She had no energy and the tasks against her were too much as is. And she could feel out there, something faint on the back of her throat, that Marty had returned from his trip. He was out there, too, whittling some stick to poke her eyes out while singing on the porch the party was over (and it had just barely begun). The deck was most certainly stacked against her.

As it turns out, she had escaped the School only to jump into another trap—from kidnap victim to prisoner to wounded. Each environment turned out to be uniquely more constraining than the last. Now here she lay on the couch in the VIP room of her wildly popular secret nightclub. Nothing about Le Chateau De Crawler appealed to her at this moment—catering to the bored elite who ignored the suffering of the city only to wear costumes and play junior high school together. The pounding music so fanatical it drowned out the mystery that was already churning in everyday life. If she weren't so sick, her face would have turned red in embarrassment at the hubris of it all. She closed her eyes again and told herself that she had to focus.

Focus came in spurts and not rivers. She had moments of clarity, only to have them consumed by waves of nausea. In the interim, as she lay forlorn on her couch, she played limp host to some of her more concerned guests. Barrister Bruno came by several times bearing flowers—his large arms full of Dutch chocolates, dried apricots, and fresh oranges. He sat by her bedside and told her war stories from his time as a journalist and anarcho-syndicalist sympathizer. He told her how Barrenwood had only escaped total destruction in the war because of their insidious support for both sides. Their duplicitous neutrality was their tragic saving grace. How he had heard of a world's fair where electricity could be seen shooting around a giant orb and that people were even making machines to fly. The world was changing, he told her, and the sybaritic life they enjoyed here was most probably temporary. He told her about his limp and how it was the result of a bayonet from a child of only seventeen years, who surprised him as they sat waiting for a bridge to explode from dynamite they planted. How the kid and he had become friends after the war and they actually spent time together now in a way most romantic.

Isabella asked many times about the water. He would shake his head and not know what she was saying, but as he told her about the burgeoning development of the arcades in the Miser's Quarters, where the elaborate window displays with mechanical trains and tiny twinkling light bulbs (small stars erupting in a shop window) were garnering vast crowds of children, Isabella tugged his arm. "This," she would say. "This is the beginning of it."

Isabella could feel it, too. The city had a bad love affair coming. The markets weren't only dream makers, but slow dream stealers—a bathtub drain for sorrow that slowly but surely synthesized dreams toward a universal un-ending logic. It was the kind of anti-curiosity that she sensed in parts of the School. The kind Harrison warned about—the anti-enlightenment enlightenment, where all sorrows, heartache, romance and salivated dream could be reduced to a banal schematic to be read, ingested, and crapped out.

Bruno, in his own way, understood this. He complained about the clocks that were being installed on corners. The city's timekeepers.

"Clocks are not our friends," guffawed Bruno. "They look pretty and all, but they also remind everyone they should get out of the bars."

While Bruno regaled her with stories, Caperwill busied himself getting the plans together to move their establishment. Movers were coming in and out the door with boxes, and carriages were pulling up. Le Chateau de Crawler would be moving somewhere in the Mortestrate. Even Isabella was a tiny bit of a real estate speculator.

Yosune came by once with some homemade soup (but she was a terrible cook. It tasted like moldy water.) Rana was still furious, descending into madness. She was blind with rage and depression and wouldn't leave her home. Yosune was worried about her, but she didn't want to bother Isabella with it all in her sick state. Isabella again promised to find the killer even though, in a sense, she believed she knew who it was. Now wasn't the time to open that can of worms.

Yosune put a cloth on her brow and told her to rest. She told her how the great Houses were in a panic, that the festival was coming and that they had lost any role in it. How House Revan was furious with the increased power of Castilla and that the great Houses were refusing to contribute any money to the festival. How she had seen her father spending time with people most unsavory and that she suspected that violence was in the air. That blood was soon to be shed.

Nevertheless, Isabella's fever raged on and to make matters worse, her stomach pains intensified. In her haze, she missed her life in the cave, her trips in the boat with the record player and film projector, Battle Ball at Cathedral Ogre, Fennel's laughter and his chilling sense of humor. She had always planned to escape, for as long as she could remember, but she had never thought what it would be like to be without her brother. He was the laughter at her side. Without his cajoling malevolence, the world was a colder more rock-like expanse. Humorless.

As far as she could tell, this world, with its sad myopic emotions, was not all that different than making friends with a mud pit. So many were on the treadmill. Just walking about. Doing what they should do. Feeling the way they should feel. Even the Chateau de Crawler was losing its luster once she had now made her escape. As the boom of the nightclub interfered with her sleep, the antics she orchestrated for people felt like a hollow joke—a mirage to shelter people from the tragedy of their days. Maybe Fennel was right. His malicious sensibility had always struck her as tragically caustic, lacking in robust sympathy, but now she looked upon him in the light of fascination. He was so steadfast in his earnest desire to destroy and remind. If memory was destruction, his was the most acute.

On her feverish bed, she could hear his mourning song drifting in and out—the sad song of tears that fed his heart. It scared and soothed her as she longed to be back in the boat, drifting along the marshes, feeling the gnats play along the slight breeze and Manzanita with lightening bugs and lily pads crisscrossing on a moonlit sorrow.

She knew Fennel hadn't meant to keep her away forever. His betrayal at the School had just been following orders. He was perhaps the most obedient malcontent the universe would ever know. Isabella couldn't bring herself to believe that he would send her to permanent banishment at the School. He loved her. And she loved him. She missed him so.

And even that love had fallen apart. Fennel, not at all unlike Barrenwood. This city was limping along like a lemming off the cliff. Even in its sordid chaotic sensibilities, she could sense the forces of the city joining up to sweep away the magic. The water was disappearing. She had even heard Minasha lisp it. But she didn't need to hear it to know it. She and Fennel had sensed it some time ago. The dreams were getting thinner. The mad were getting carted away. The work-week was growing stronger. The arcades that lined the streets channeled dreams into limp patterns. She felt nostalgic for a city she didn't really know. Just as she was getting to know this place that she had for so long been a simple servant to, she was finding it hell bent on its own evisceration. The torn up streets of the Mortestrate pushed its way to the front of Isabella's delirious imagination—the water pouring across the cracks as the Gaventas construction crews took apart house and home.

She woke from her stupor with parched lips. Her head was woozy. Coming into focus, leaning over her, was none other than Heinrich, his bushy eyebrows barely visible through the mist of the hot tea he poured past her lips.

"Drink this, dear Isabella."

"Heinrich," she muttered. "What are you doing here? Shouldn't you be at work?"

"I'm afraid I have been dismissed. My last day on the job was some time ago, but I am already set up at a new establishment. I will be fine. Don't worry about me. I'm just glad to see you alive. You have been gone for some time and your wicked brother has made no reference to you at all. It was almost a cruel joke the way he avoided any mention of you. I had thought the worst, but fortunately Caperwill has tracked me down to come see you."

"I will be fine, Heinrich. This is just a passing fad. Don't blame my brother. He is an idiot."

"He is dangerous. I tell you that now, but I know you love him as a sibling should. Now don't bother your thoughts and just rest."

"There is time to rest in the grave, Heinrich. I need you to make one last return to your post to give Fennel this letter. I wrote it for him and I just need him to know I am thinking of him. Will you do that for me?"

Heinrich frowned. Caperwill came over and handed Heinrich an envelope. She had written the letter a few nights ago, worried sick that Fennel thought she was dead.

Dearest Brother,

As you may or may not know, I am no longer at the School. I escaped. It wasn't easy, but I did and frankly you would have as well. While it is impressively interesting there, they are more than a little too excited to get you to play by their rules. Talk about Dolt and Bore. It is a militarist approach to education that makes me terribly bored. Automatons masquerading as pedagogues. So I ran away and I am now in what you could describe as hiding. I am also very sick. I can't seem to shake Marty's power and I am afraid it is tearing me apart. I think I might be dying, but I can't be sure. Maybe this is what normal people feel like. I at times have a flare for the melodramatic so maybe this is just a passing spell. But I assure you, no matter how awful and bile covered I get, I will never return to the whims and desires of our insipid master. As much as the sickness seems to be overtaking me, it isn't nearly as bad as my longing to see you again. I miss you. I miss your stupid jokes and I even miss the Raven. I am also sure you have a mustard stain somewhere on your clothes that you can't see. I need to clean it off. We were meant to be together and I dearly hope you will leave the side of our crooked toothed tyrant to join me out here in this tawdry but ever so real world. I saw that the town fair is this week and that your sculpture is to be unveiled. I'm very much looking forward to seeing it. Of course, please don't tell Marty I will be there. I think he is out for blood.

Your sister,

Izzy

Heinrich took the envelope and got up from his seat near her bed.

"Of course, I will deliver the letter."

"If he asks where I am . . . "

"I will say one of your messengers handed me the letter at my new place of employment."

"Thank you, Heinrich. I will see you soon."

Heinrich leaned over and kissed her on the forehead, his wiry moustache making her forehead itch.

"Good evening, Lady Isabella." And with that, he exited the room.

Isabella was nervous that Marty could track her down. Fennel had never known about her Chateau de Crawler side project, but the Persembes certainly did and something about recent events had shaken her faith in them. The death of their sister could make anyone do anything and Isabella's shrouded anonymity may not be at the top of their concerns.

The Barrenwood Festival was set for the end of the week and Isabella's head reeled with how she was going to pull herself together enough to attend. She knew she shouldn't have told Fennel she would be there, but she was desperate to see him again. In her hazy daze, she thought that perhaps what was really ailing her was the lack of her other and the momentary rejoining of the two would set her anew. She wondered if he actually had managed to get his statue built—if he had actually gotten far enough along in his bizarre plans. He often set his sights even further beyond things even he could achieve.

In essence, Isabella was a mess of anxieties that tossed and turned on a couch in the back of a nightclub. She could lay here and deteriorate or she could make a move.

In a moment of clarity, an interesting thought occurred to her: "If I stay on this couch much longer, I might actually pass away."

Chapter 27

"I need to leave, Caperwill," Isabella muttered through slobbery lips.

"What you need to do, Lady Isabella, is rest and cure yourself of this sickness," said Caperwill, again patting her forehead.

This wasn't that kind of sickness. It wouldn't work like that. It would only grow and Isabella knew it. As counter-intuitive as it seemed, she had to get on her feet and move before the grip of this mojo took full control of her. She had two options. (There were probably better plans but at this point and she didn't have the luxury of time to craft some masterful initiative.) She could either escape to the Duke or—and this plan seemed flawed from the get-go—gather some Marty hairs to produce more fish sauce. What she hoped for was that big beast of a man who had locked her and Fennel in a closet would swoop into the room, bash it apart like he had back on the docks, and rescue her from her fate.

When she had seen him last, his eyes were molten from too much smoke, his senses were dulled and his brain operating on paranoia more than reality. Had he not been so bogged down in drug-induced revelry, she knew he would have understood immediately whom she and Fennel were. He would have smelled their kinship. But that had not come to pass. Escape had presented itself and somehow, she had been cast back into the fire.

But the next time around, Isabella would not allow that to happen. She would make it quite clear who and what she was. She would demand some kind of sanctuary. There must be a law or some kind of oath that had been taken for such things. She could see him now, bent low in front of that fire, praying to the old gods with their mercurial magic. The fever of fire burnt so bright in him—a hunger everlasting. She knew she did not have the strength to make it all the way up the Parakeet Path. Marty's mojo seemed to thicken with every step outside the territory of Barrenwood. The trip would be too much for her. She would end up some forlorn log by the roadside for some traveling salesman to notice months from now. Such a fate did not appeal to her. No, she would have to go to Savina's and hope for the best.

If that didn't work out, the alternative . . . well, it chilled her to the bone . . . she would have to enter straight into the mouth of the monster. There really was no other way because option three was to stay in bed and die.

Isabella did her best to jump out of the bed and fell slightly on the floor. Caperwell found no humor in it, but Isabella did manage to find her false start amusing. She coughed out a laugh. "Keep the machine here running, Cap. I have to again head out into the night."

Caperwell did his best to object, but Isabella was already out, down the back stairs of the noodle house and out along the hubbub of the streets in Barrenwood. The trip down the stairs already exhausted her and she leaned back against the steamy window where the bodies of bar-b-qued duck hung in a row behind her and a mechanical cat had an arm that moved back and forth to the pulse of the distant bass of Le Chateau de Crawler.

Isabella whistled for Elia. Wherever that wild horse was grazing, it would need to make its way to the Calliope—and soon. Isabella was already tired and all she had done was run down the stairs. She felt like an old woman. She stared at the passing bodies of people making their way past. Her sickness brought a strange sense of empathy. She could see the frailty of all their bones—the nicks and scratches that the world makes on a human so small.

She looked at the passing faces and closed her eyes to sense them in truth. She took into her mind a young man scooting by making his way home. He was running late, worried about the wrath of his estranged mother and full to the brim with anxieties. She sensed his cloudy thinking. The pressure of his inescapable fate from the job laid out by his family, his alienated sense that he didn't really belong in this city, his confusion over the fact that he had paid too much for the rice bag that he was delivering, and his overall sense that none of his life made much sense. It weighed heavy on her. Isabella opened her eyes. So many faces and so much burden. The faces of these people were mostly lost in a wilderness, which they found terrifying.

"I'm part of the problem," Isabella muttered out loud.

A little girl noticed Isabella talking to herself, but the mother pulled her along into the flow of bodies on the move. Isabella felt sympathy for people. They were lost and all she and her brother could do was make fun of them for it. Where did such hostility come from? It pained her to think of herself as such a monster—a terror in the world teaching people a lesson in the courage of death when both of them knew so little about the operatic pain of life. Perhaps she deserved to die.

A series of screams came rising up through the street and sure enough, Elia came galloping up at full speed. She reared on her hind legs and then landed right in front of Isabella. She knelt down on one knee and Isabella gingerly crawled onto the horse's back. She whispered their destination into Elia's ear and they galloped at full speed toward the District of Jed.

Something magical happens when one is sick and since Isabella was so rarely sick, she noticed its effects most tangibly. The body may lose personality, but it notices small details so much more. Imperfections in a person's skin become more noticeable and the contrast between light and dark more stark. The city of Barrenwood seemed to speak to her in a way it had never done before. She noticed the state of disrepair of many of the buildings, the way many of the roofs were in such poor condition their interiors must surely be leaking, the numerous potholes in the streets that Elia had to jump over and around like some video game, and the growing array of graffiti whose contents most surely had an increasing narrative of revolution in them: *Death to the Houses*, *Up with the PRM*, *I Never Forget*. The police were out more. Tension was in the air. Isabella could feel it. The city was a growing stew pot of discontent.

They rode through the muddy streets of the District of Jed to arrive at the Savina's rickety grotto. The lights were out in the house and the porch held an ashtray partially full of rainwater and cigarette butts. She had been gone for many days. It was tempting for Isabella to get off the back of Elia and just go hide in the house. She could lie down in Savina's bed and wait for her to come back. It may not be the worst idea, but she felt that if she were to lie in that bed, she might never wake up. She would just slumber her way into oblivion. Savina would find her many months from now, a small skeleton holding on to her pillow. She would wonder why the small orphan girl would come here to die and would chock it up to the cruel mysteries of the universe.

This wasn't good news. The next step was something that she had wanted to push out of her mind as a possibility. She knew she didn't have the strength to pull it off. She gave Elia a kick and said as loud as she could, "Le Chevalier Noir!"

They flew through the streets and out toward the edge of the Aliber River. Once again riding at full pace, even the bumps from riding on the back of the horse, caused Isabella some pain. She groaned as they traveled and made their way through the Capital District, out along the docks and finally to the tucked away crocodile-strewn inlet that greeted the edge of the marshes to the north, she found herself relieved to see Le Chevalier Noir. Elia bent down to let her dismount. She crawled off and threw her a fortune cookie. The horse ate it, fortune and all.

"Not a bad idea," said Isabella petting Elia on the nose. "Perhaps it is best to eat the future after all. Now be a good horse and find some unprivatized grasslands to feed in."

She bid Elia adieu and snuck her way around the side to the back entrance, which for so long had been her and Fennel's welcomed beginning each night. The restaurant was in full swing. The odd out-of-towners were clearly excited at their stopover in Barrenwood. Their nightgowns and tuxedos were an odd juxtaposition to the macabre wetlands that issued north from the back door. Unsurprisingly, neither the boat nor Heinrich was present. Her heart sank to consider where they both might be.

Isabella knew only one other way to get where she was going and as bad an idea as it seemed it was the only one. Time was wasting. She put her toe in the marsh. It wasn't warm, but it wasn't cold—just a slightly below room temperature bath. She didn't bother taking her outfit off but instead just slipped into the water off the dock. From a distance, she looked like a large nutria ducking below a wharf.

As sick as she was, her body was lithe in the water. She could swim with great agility, and the water surrounding her body felt good. She could feel the sideways glances of the crocodiles and the catfish, but she just let them wonder. She wasn't an alien in these environs. She felt very much one of them.

Isabella kicked and wiggled her way through the bends of the marsh toward Marty's shack. It was the only place she could think of to find more Marty hairs, even though she was absolutely positive that Marty had returned from the Muddy Carnival. It didn't take long before the lights of Barrenwood faded and the brilliance of the canopy of stars above made themselves known. Isabella lay on her back to stare up at them. She could see the constellation of Gemini. The twins. Yin and Yang. They were up to their own individual plots but seemingly unable to leave each other.

She continued to swim until she could spot the glow of the porch lamp of Marty's shack shining bright in the night. So, she was right. Marty was home after all. The porch still had his rocking chair and a fresh crop of beer cans, potato chip bags and booze bottles already piling up. Isabella kept herself submerged as much as possible. Her smell didn't travel as fast under the water. If Marty was drunk and she kept her distance, perhaps she could stay out of his strangely acute senses.

As she got closer to the porch, she saw movement inside the shack—the flicker of shadows and the rising sound of voices. Marty wasn't alone. The din of animated discussion came issuing from the cracked door. Now was as good a time as ever and Isabella slowly made her way up to the porch. She wasn't there to spy, only to gather some hairs and be gone. She would just need enough fish sauce to get herself up the Parakeet Path into that coal mansion again, and she would kiss Marty McGuinn goodbye.

As luck would have it, Marty came flying out of the house, laughing hysterically. Isabella instinctively swam across the water to the other side.

The good news was that Marty was drunk as a dog. She could smell his bourbon breath floating between the gnat wings on the water. Marty picked up one of the bottles on the porch and tilted it upside down. He was looking for a sip. He went through the bottles, one by one, until he found one still half full. He took a big gulp. It clearly tasted delicious.

"Ya betta lookin wit out dem bones. Not dat I give a rat's ass. If I knewd dis wassa waitin for me, I mighta come back all de faster." Marty laughed aloud as he tied up his belt. He then hobbled across the porch and settled himself into his rocking chair. He pulled his pipe from his pocket and began to load it nice and slow.

A voice came from inside. It was slithering and faint. "You owesss me. Don't forgetsss our bargain, Marty McGuinn."

Marty snickered to himself and took a puff on his pipe. He stared out in the night and for a second Isabella could tell he smelled her. He scrunched up his nose and gave another whiff. It was faint and before he could take much notice the inhabitant from inside the shack became known. It was Minasha Darkglass. She was messing with her clothes and clearly rattled. Her bone necklace as always was banging against her chest—a macabre percussion. She leaned against the porch railing.

"Tellsss me," she slithered.

Marty looked over at her and laughed again. Isabella wasn't sure what was going on, but she could tell instantly that he was being horrible per usual. She could see the smug toying on his face and that nasty air of superiority.

"Sorry. What ya yappin about? I dun recall no deal."

"Don't play gamesss, McGuinn. Ya know the deal."

Marty rolled his eyes. "Oh ya, da deal. I tink I recall sometin. Maybe if I could get a lil' more a dat black magic kitty I could set meself right." Marty reached over to Minasha and she slapped his hand down quick as lightning. "Ouch! Fearsome lil' wench, ya are."

"Talksss . . . " said Minasha, in a clearly threatening voice.

Marty obviously didn't think much of it. He reached down and pulled some fungus or something from between his toes. He took his time and the sound of the mosquito marsh filled the air. Finally, he spoke up.

"Okay, ya lil' she bitch, I gives it ta ya. But ye stupid as da workday. Ya know, ya would be betta off if ya just did nuttin. What am I for anywho? Just ta help ya untie da knots ya already make?"

Minasha rolled her eyes. These creatures were exhausting. Their circular logic and elliptical phrasings were enough to try the patience of a twig.

"Okay, I may be a son of a bitch, but I keeps ma word. Tell me 'bout it again."

Minasha exhaled in exasperated fashion and then told her tale. "You are right. It is a messs, but it isn't just from my doingsss. Your peoplesss twist me and the fate of the Houssses along with them. I came to her as I told you. I asked to make the families seesss who the true enemy was. That they could finally see the real troublesss that Gaventasss posed to usss. But the way she got there isn't clear."

Marty chuckled. "It never is."

"She told me to introduce that Persembe girl to the carriage boy. Said, it would be a love that would bring thingsss to a head. I didn't think much of it. That isss until the next timesss when she had me open the gatesss."

Marty looked up with a rare hint of surprise. "The what? The gates? Stupid! Stupid girl. You don not know what ya do. Ya opened da gates? Okay. And who I do wonder came a ridin through?"

Minasha's head was bent down. It clearly pained her to come to some kind of wetland confessional where she could tell of her true pain and hopefully be rid of some guilt, and, at the very least, know what to do next.

"I don't know his namesss. He comesss riding with an odor that smellsss of the pitsss of hell itself."

Marty raised an eyebrow. "Does he come a ridin wit a whole load a chitlins?"

Minasha looked at Marty confused. "He ridesss with pigsss."

Marty smacked his head and then stood up from the chair. "Jesse Ilks! You unleashed Jesse Ilks on da Barrenwood. Oh, ho ho! Now dat is a mess I dun relish a cleanin! Oh boy!"

"He killed them! He butchered the children most terribly!" cried Minasha, almost sounding as if she were in tears. It was hard to tell. She was a slithering sort of lady. Marty went over to Minasha and patted her on the head.

"Dat's what he does, deary. He's a killer, dat one. Eats blood like its mornin sunnyside up. Dun ya worry. I can do da math from here. Dat lil Persembe gal's poppy is hot as a whip. Wants revenge. Goes after Gaventas. And dat money maker Castilla has his back agin da wall and misses dat carriage boy Peter and he push back. Dat war you be wantin is a comin. It's an ugly road but da witch gave ya what ya wanted, Lil' Miss Muffet."

Isabella listened as she floated like a toad in the river. She could scarcely believe what she was hearing. She had somehow solved the killing of Sibel and Peter and it still made little sense—just more meddling from the higher powers that barely knew what they were up to. Pawns in a poorly planned master plan, their blood spilled down into the earth without rhyme nor reason. Minasha, looking crushed, slumped down on the porch. Her body said that she was tired of being a pawn but knew not what to do. These creatures, they toyed with malicious intent and yet, here she was, hoping for a helping hand from a drunken pervert.

"So what da ya want?" said Marty, sitting back down.

"I wantsss help. Help for House Revan and then, maybe, help for the Housssesss."

"I guess I coulda guessed dat," said Marty, puffing again.

"You are a friend to the housssesss. You should come to usss in our time of need," said Minasha. "Thisss has been the way for hundredsss of yearsss and generationsss before."

"Don't need to yap dat at me," snapped Marty. "I been der de whole time. Listenen to y'all complainin for longer than you or your granny do know. I don know da future. Never have. But I do know ya people. I can see possible futures a twistin up in each other. And I can see that ya aren't crazy for a wantin to wake up your sleepin house. Dey don't know what's about to happen. And darlin, if I were ya, I'd get ready for much worse to come."

Minasha stood up. "Thanks! Thanks a whole lot! I don't need to knows it's going to get worse. I need to know what you are going to do to help usss! And it isn't just usss, you know. I am in touch with forcesss even you don't know, Marty McGuinn. They tell me about the water. Yesss, you know of what I speak. They tell me about the drought coming. Your spiritual fluidsss are disappearing and you, like the Housssesss perhaps, are cluelessss about whats about to happen!"

Marty blew smoke rings and rocked in his chair. It seemed the angrier Minasha got, the more relaxed Marty became. Isabella knew it was his way of making her more angry, but it was also an instinctual thing. He was a master of manipulation, so much so his every reaction could skip his brain and go straight to muscle.

"What ya need to know bout da water is, it's a gonna be round forever. I don't care what you people do. You always gonna fear da grave and ya always gonna be cryin in your pants. Dat just da way you been and always will be. I get mah juice from a never-endin river and I always will. Y'all, on da other hand, are not forevers. Ya tink just cause ya got a banner and a big ol' castle, you gonna stick around forevers. But it just ain't so. Never has been."

"But I don't think that! They do! I need your help and you are bound to give it to me!" railed Minasha. She was up and standing right in front of Marty. Isabella cringed at what she thought would come next. Standing up to Marty like that was never a good idea. But Marty didn't react. He just rocked back and forth and smiled his gummy, loose tooth smile.

"So, whatcha want me to do, lil' Revan?"

"I want you to kill Elinore Castilla. He is the ssource of all these troublesss. Cut the head off the snake."

Marty laughed again. He clearly found Minasha very entertaining. He got up from his rocking chair, slightly pushing Minasha out of the way and leaned out facing the water. His squirrely hazy eyes pretty much stared straight at the bobbing up and down head of Isabella.

"Fraid I can't do dat. Too many ducats coming from dat lil man. How bout I give ya some advice instead? How about you make a deal with da businessman before its too late? It's the only way, lil Revan."

"You swore an oath!" yelled Minasha.

Marty turned to her with his fingers on his lips. "Shhhh. I tink we gotta water lilly out der dat needs a reelin in."

He had spied her! Or smelled her. It didn't matter. Isabella knew that she had to run. There would be no Marty hairs caught here this eve. Isabella ducked down toward the bottom of the river while Marty crossed the porch to his fishing line. He cast out his line. The hook sailed out and over the river to go straight down below and catch on Isabella's clothes. She felt his strong tug as it pulled her, flailing, bluefish style, through the water. She struggled with her clothes to pull them off. Marty was reeling her in fast. She got her clothes off just in time to feel them give way and come slapping onto the porch.

Isabella was naked now—truly a fish swimming in the stream—and she swam as hard and fast as she could. Her body could stay underwater. She hadn't lived in the marshes for nothing. She heard the splash behind her and figured Marty was swimming somewhere behind her, coming fast. Isabella had to do something. She couldn't outswim the man. She found a small hollowed out log and shoved her small self inside. Apparently seeing Marty meant folding origami style into a river log. She covered her body in the moss mud and closed her eyes. She would sleep here until he was gone. Isabella closed her eyes. It was all too much.

Chapter 28

Isabella successfully escaped yet again. Caperwill found her naked as a babe lying in the middle of the VIP room with a stinky pool of vomit around her head, a halo of gross. She had snuck her way through Barrenwood and taken a few moments to retch in this dark alley or that. Her journey was not only a failure but a colossal setback. She had nowhere to go. Nowhere to turn.

It had been a few days and her fever and chills were worse. She was a tiny mess getting smaller by the hour. She tossed and turned, trying to add up the facts, but all she could get were mumbled impressions of corncob pipes and bone necklaces. She had managed to gain some knowledge on the houses, on Marty, on the demise of Sibel, and confirmation that it wasn't just her, but that the water was in fact disappearing. It all seemed to be such a faint concern at this point. She hadn't retrieved those Marty hairs. Her sickness was completely overwhelming and now she wasn't sure if she was in hospice or not.

She lay on the couch telling herself that she didn't mind death. Let it come. She didn't want to fight for life like the rest. She wasn't so clingy as to have to have it. It seemed at every turn, her liberation eluded her. Perhaps she was meant for this kind of small existence. A crumb on the sofa.

When she woke at twilight, she could hear the drums from the parade. The crowd sounds played against the muggy night along with the occasional boom and crack of fireworks. The city was alive. Like static electricity, the air had ions bursting and exciting the hairs on the skin. Isabella could feel it and even felt a cosmic lift in her spirits. She put her tongue out of her mouth and tasted the air. Fun was out there. The day of the festival had at last arrived.

She dressed in a black lace evening dress and put on her most elegant red ruby jewels. She pulled her hair up on her head into a tall beehive and dressed her lips red. Looking in the mirror, she knew she couldn't cover up the terrible feeling that was now herself, but she winked at her reflection anyway.

"Even in death," she whispered.

Isabella had invited Barrister Bruno for company, as she couldn't possibly imagine going alone (and she didn't have much of a plan). Caperwill, who continued to sleep on a cot in the corner of the room, was adamant she not go, but she was determined. With the knock at the door, Caperwill jumped up and greeted the Barrister. He arrived in his buttoned up white cotton suit with a bow tie and cigar. He was puffing away madly and she thought he might already be drunk.

"Isabella, my dear. You look incredible. A queen of the ball, I must say!" he bowed low and kissed her hand. He then presented her with a singular plucked blue lily. Isabella took it and smiled.

"Ever the gentleman, Bruno. I am pleased you will be my date to the Barrenwood gala."

"I wouldn't miss it for the world. It's the one time of year that the city is of some interest. And I get the feeling this is really going to be a rumpus. People are already wildly drunk. The bars are overflowing and the parade is a mob scene. I got us a place in one of the penthouses across the square from the festival. Friend of mine I met on some business. Speculator. Nice guy who just made a ton of dough. Anyway, he has a great home where we can look at the party, eat caviar and not get our fine clothes sullied by the pabulum that is the masses." Bruno winked at her and took her by the arm. Isabella grabbed her cane and they both wished Caperwill good evening.

Caperwill looked up from his scattered papers. "Are you sure, Lady Isabella, you should go? You are terribly ill, you know." She looked at him with her gentle defiant eyes.

"Good night, Caperwill."

"Good evening, Lady Isabella."

"Caperwill?" said Lady Isabella before the day closed.

"Yes?"

"If I don't return anytime soon, please continue Le Chateau de Crawler in the Mortestrate. You will know what to do."

Barrister Bruno laughed loud and low. "Such a flare for the melodramatic. Don't worry, Cap. I will have her back on that sofa in no time."

They headed through the noodle house and to the awaiting carriage outside. Bruno helped her in—her body the weight of a Persian cat, all hair but skin and bones beneath. The smell of gunpowder and booze hung heavy on the air. The streets were as Bruno described: a drunken mayhem with just the hint of violence mixed in with the joy. The people of Barrenwood were descending into the Capital district and the streets were chock-full of hooligans, children, grandparents and gentry. It was the medley of the civic and it thrilled Isabella to see it. This festival was an orchestrated movement of the masses that brought waves of nostalgia, desire, hunger and wonder. Getting to the central square became increasingly difficult as throngs of people pushed off the sidewalks and into the streets. Isabella stared blankly out the carriage window. The mobs of humanity looked like one of her black and white films playing quietly behind the glass—an aquarium of pathetic madness.

Her reverie was interrupted with a big red splat. A tomato exploded on the window and the seeds and guts made a sinuous mess. A gravelly voice yelled out, "Die, monarchical scum!"

Bruno laughed. "I should say thank you. They take me for a regent. Being part of the royal family is just not what it used to be, I guess. These people have no idea how cheap these carriages really are."

As they got to the Rue de Blunt, the carriage could go no further. They would have to walk. It suited Isabella fine. She didn't like being cut off from the people anyway. That tomato had acted as a punctuation mark, reminding her that this was no time for a carriage. Bruno picked Isabella up onto his shoulders (she would have usually never allowed such a thing, but she found it a terrifying prospect to navigate the mob of bodies with her cane).

The pair of them pushed through the sweating bodies. The smell of alcohol soaked laughter, beer lined gutters over ripe bananas and rotting garbage mixed with the fetid humidity that was Barrenwood at this time of year. The streets were a spa of urbanity. Barrister Bruno laughed his way through the crowd, enjoying the frenzy of the night atmosphere. Eventually, they made their way to the large oak door of the residence in question that sat opposite of the Ellindale Plaza: quite the esteemed residence.

The door opened to reveal a well-dressed doorman who upon seeing the two, proceeded to give Bruno a big hug. Bruno said an enjoyable joke or two while he took Isabella off his shoulders and then they both made their way up six flights of steps to the penthouse apartment. The trip was nearly all Isabella and the Barrister could take. They were panting and heaving at the top of the stairs.

"My god," he said, "the view just isn't worth it. Give me a first-floor apartment any day. I will use a telescope if I need a view."

He lit another cigar at the top of the stairs and collected himself. Perspiration covered his brow and Isabella felt the irony of her feeling sorry for him.

"Okay let's do this."

Bruno opened the door to an extremely lavish apartment. A place along Ellindale Plaza really could be nothing else. Men and women in the finest attire were smoking and drinking throughout the flat. Bruno led her through the crowd, occasionally greeting someone or other and found his way to their host.

"Isabella, I would like you to meet Conner Deville"

Isabella looked up to see the man from many moons ago that Fennel had accosted near the Drunken Boat—the night that had in many ways triggered the series of events that now had her sick as a dog. This man, whoever he was, was just another part in the displaced conspiracy to rid the city of the mad. She gazed at him. He was a charming man who cared little about the implications of being a cog in the machine. She was too sick to protest and put out her hand.

"It is a pleasure to meet you," she said, curtseying. Conner looked down at her with a wrinkle in his brow.

Conner kissed Isabella's hand. "It is a pleasure to have you here, my lady. Any friend of the good Barrister. Please allow me to get some seats for you so you will have a spectacular view of the festivities."

Conner made his way to the balcony and quickly negotiated some guests out of their seats. On her way, she couldn't help but notice the faint aroma of coriander on the air. She spied around for monks or any familiar face from the School, but not a face appeared. Instead, the home was just a world of young entrepreneurs whose trajectories must surely match those of Conner.

"Please sit here, Lady Isabella and Bruno. I think this might be a show one won't want to miss. Can I get either of you something?"

"Scotch, an ashtray and a young hot man for my pleasure," gruffed Bruno.

"I'm fine with grape juice, please. And Conner," she said with a slight smirk, "don't be long."

Isabella went back to looking over the crowd who packed themselves into the smooshed plaza below. They were pushing and shoving each other to get closer to center stage where the jazz band was blasting their District of Jed-inspired party songs. The songs were rough. Already something new.

In general, the bands were orchestras playing traditional music with the square filled with couples of the gentry, a meeting and a greeting. But that was not possible this year as the square heaved with the bodies of the populace. The jazz band wore the bright pink feather headdresses and dangly glittery beads of the Harpy's Parades. The men in beards full of food and laughter were giggling madly as they wailed on their horns and banged on their drums. The tuba player, a rotund beer swilling mechanic of a man, held a 40 oz. beer in one hand and the tuba in another as between blurts he wailed songs about the rise and fall of the lobster tail as the boat creaks and groans from the hungry couple on its deck.

> And that boat gonna rock cause ya love wail wide
> Crawdads and peanut shells mystery tales

Crawdads as chums, gumbo in ya gums
And that boat gonna rock, cause ya drunk in da tide

These Jed-songs were hugely popular and there were moments when the entire plaza was singing along—a singular voice coming out in a frazzled mass of sound reverberating off the walls of the elite and ricocheting back into the ears of the adrenaline masses, wailing glorious soccer songs bouncing around the city in the excitement of some class barrier being hurdled in the midst of celebration. Some men in the band were dressed in skirts and every so often they would waddle their way to the front of the stage and flash their dangling balls to the squeezed up crowd. Taffeta, testicle hair, brass, and sweat were the callings on the big stage.

Isabella looked down with pleasure to see the rabble that was ensuing. She and Fennel had never been allowed to come to the festival. They had only caught whispers of it from Marty as he ever loved a good time. He would indicate that the finest wine and most beautiful women had made themselves available to him in some alcove of desire that must have manifested late into the night in some questionable grotto. He said they were too precocious for such an environment, that they would make a mess of it, and that above everything else, their existence needed to remain a secret.

"Ya gonna catch one sniff o da sweat and booze and ya gonna do some dum-dum trick. Ya gonna give it ups to dem and den wats we gots will be gone. Wat we got, we gotta keep it hush. We gotta keep it low down. If dey knowd, they be a comin and dey hungrier den dey knowd."

Nevertheless, they had always dreamed and imagined the whirl of the river that would spill out in the height of human revelry. And the truth of it made its imprint on Isabella immediately. She had tasted it at Le Chateau de Crawler, and now she was in the midst of its feast. And even though this was her first taste of the collective bacchanal, she could sense quite clearly that something on this particular occasion was amiss.

She leaned over the railing of the balcony to see the other balconies that lined the square's edge. Leaning out, drinking wine and anise, were the dressed up coteries of the ruling classes. Their aspirations to rule ever so evident in the painful way they huddled together on the tittering balconies. They looked over the rabble and couldn't help but feel small; their sense of scale making it all the more clear to them that on this particular occasion they were a minority most palpable. And being outnumbered, it must be admitted, is a very visceral feeling. Something the skin informs the brain. The elites laughed all the more nervous as they tried to shout over the chants of songs from the District of Jed, which rose up like a wave in the center of town.

Across the plaza, Isabella could see the great Houses gathered together. She could see Rana and Yosune together in what was probably to be an evolving dynamic. Rana had her arms around a young woman and was clearly talking as fast as she could while Yosune stared off clearly perturbed. On the next balcony, standing resolute was what must be the House Imbetta as their colors were gold and black. A young, incredibly beautiful woman stood prominently at the center. She was hypnotic and stoic. Her black smeared eyes glistened next to her jewelry, as did her golden gown that reflected with great luminescence the fireworks exploding in the night. Next to her were the Revans in all their magenta and gold. They possessed three balconies next to each other and were clearly having a wonderful time even as the night was already obviously a complete disaster.

The younger Gerald Revan was drinking his fill of wine and enjoying being the center of attention. Tucked in the corner Isabella spied the now familiar sight of Minasha Darkglass. She sat in a corner with the fire-red-haired Chelsea Revan who was clearly chatting wildly. Minasha looked deeply pre-occupied and Isabella could spy the faintest sign of her talking to herself on occasion. Isabella imagined those from the houses saw her as mad as can be, but little did they know that she might be their only hope at salvation. And noticeably absent, was the bright blue of House Ellington—the one house who, it seems, felt no need to demonstrate fealty to this most regular of occasions.

On the balconies stretching to the west of them were the throngs of minor houses whose numbers went on and on—the Callibans, the Chillbachs, the Nethertons, the Neros and the Ghents. Their coteries stretched out vast and long, painting a picture of some out-of-touch society who knows little of the agony of the people below. As a grouping, all the houses appeared as a series of color swatches against the immense gothic architecture, their bodies some tribal testament to the self-organizational needs of some primitive society. For the people below, there perhaps were not enough tomatoes in all the farms of Barrenwood.

But the music, masses and monarchy were not all that was on display, for the festivities were beginning and the Peanut Family Circus was just about to begin. Stretched across the central plaza, high up in the air, an acrobat danced with flames on a high wire. She balanced ever so gingerly, her feet of the koala, as the wire itself moved quite visibly from the shaking that was the movement of the masses. She hovered above the crowd, throwing sticks of fire lithely one after the other. Upon each catch, the fire would erupt just a bit more. If she were to fall, it seemed as though she would either careen to her death and splatter on the cobblestone, be caught like a pillow by the drunken mob, or simply float away into the heavens, a guest to the terrestrial plane.

On either side of the acrobat, were two children dressed as pigs. They waddled their way to either side of the tightrope and came back with mud pies. They flung them at each other across the body of the acrobat. The mud pies going splat at times on each other's clumsy paper mache' bodies, or, in general, descend down into the crowd, often landing on someone's consternated head. How the children stayed on the tightrope was hard to say as it looked as though they could fall at any second. Their clumsy steps, as they muscularly wrestled with their awkward costumes, made their trick all the more tenuous and death defying. Their vulnerability was an aesthetic that only heightened the frantic fueled night. For the acrobat and pig children were a collective display of terror as agent of amusement. Their hovering above death was a physical steroid to the drunken masses below.

Next arrived the clown car. It separated the crowd as it came moving up. The clowns piled out in half painted makeup. They went into the crowd and grabbed volunteers who they then quickly painted to look just as dumb as they did. Smeared red with white with smiles and tear drops. People couldn't help but laugh at the clowns as they stumbled over themselves to get the volunteers to juggle with them. Bowling pins went up then came clumsily down, falling to the cobblestone below. When the volunteers failed to be of much amusement, the clowns proceeded to pelt them with old vegetables and beer cans. The crowd laughed wildly as the clowns berated one of their own.

Next came the contortionists, whose appearance was made known by a spotlight shining bright on a rooftop. They leapt and hurtled and ended with their heads facing the crowd as they bent over backwards and stared out with blank-eyed faces between their legs. The crowd applauded as the contortionists then began a strange display of frantic bending combined with banal positions. Their legs miraculously folded back behind their heads while another scratched at their toes, getting the lint and crust out. Two contortionists grappled each other's legs to make a perfect circle and roll about the edge of the roof, a rolling tire of taut exercised flesh, while the third scratched their head vigorously as though infected by fleas. The girls then each placed one leg behind their head and hopped up and down on the remaining leg. They each hopped in unison and proceeded to enact their awkward Pina Bausch routine. Gesticulating wildly with their hands, they moved in a heated display of modern dance that appealed to the audience below not one bit. The crowd began to get bored and then suddenly the girls launched themselves off the roof to land safely in the net below. The crowd laughed and applauded.

Popping and snapping in the grey clouds above, fireworks burst. They were strange colors of greys, mauves, puke yellow and Pepto Bismol pink. As opposed to the usual flower style of explosion, these fireworks predominately streaked slowly across the night sky. Slowly descending as though the night sky was a sink with the fireworks toothpaste draining down the side—a dripping affair of gunpowder and heavenly drear. Occasionally, the fireworks would shoot up in that knowing sound of a rocket launched from a tube and then explode into words that smeared above. *Nightmare, nail biter, cheese-head, clumsy clumsy* and *doo doo party* were all words that glittered above in a pale reminder that perhaps anything with enough sparkle could be embraced.

He had done a great job. Wherever Fennel was at this moment, Isabella could only imagine the state of delirium he must have reached at this point. It was a choreographed clumsy work of genius. The sound of water was rising up in the din of the festivities. It was a babbling brook at this point. It gave Isabella a lift in her skin that oozed against the termites in her tummy—the sound so flowing. Fennel was putting his best work to work on this night and Isabella had a front row seat to enjoy it. She scooted herself up to appreciate it all the more.

On the stage, at the far right, Isabella saw a giant tarp covering what most surely be Fennel's statue. It rose two stories in an awkward shape that barely gave the impression of a human figure. It was such a monstrosity of scale and tarp one could only wonder how Fennel had managed the affair—how one could talk the entire city into lumbering it as a central element on their stage of glory.

She spied Castilla standing with the Duke of Revan on the stage and alongside them were a group of city politicians that included Big Boy Charlie. Castilla's bent and emaciated frame looked terribly uncomfortable in the company of the large bellied men of governance with white moustaches and monocles. It was clearly a show of force and Isabella saw the fights of the city standing together as though they were all the closest of friends.

Conner arrived with their drinks and took a seat next to them.

"Thanks for this, Conner," said the Barrister. "You are most definitely going to have a cameo in my next book. I will have to wait then for some of my other orders," he laughed.

Conner rolled his eyes and looked to Isabella. "I hope this view pleases my lady."

"It does, in fact. Quite an assembly of people. I see the great Houses aren't lacking in their customary view."

"I don't think they truly want to be this close to the events this time around," said Conner. He lit up a cigarette and pointed out over the crowd. "You see that? Those men on stage. If you look closely you can see the world changing before your eyes. The city boys and the money boys and guess who isn't in that conversation at all?" He flicked his cigarette and leaned back in his chair. "The great Houses can only look down and wonder what they are discussing."

Bruno gulped on his Scotch. "Now there's the truth of it. I think Gaventas put this whole thing together tonight. Paid for it top to bottom. Must make the houses insane with their antiquated proprieties. Ha! Serves them right! Now they must look down as spectators."

Isabella turned to Conner, "I don't suppose that you have some horse in this race, do you?"

"Well, of course, I do. This flat wasn't paid for through my lamentable inheritance. This is a new era. There is money to be made and opportunities to jump on. The quick mind with a flair for the new can roll up their sleeves and make a tidy profit on it. Doesn't take much of a betting man to know which way this wind is blowing."

"Isn't that the truth?" said Bruno.

"Are you familiar with that man with the wiry moustache talking to the Mayor?"

"Yes. Yes, indeed I am," smiled Conner. "He is the emissary of the force of history: Castilla, head man at Gaventas. A horrible man sick with ambition and little soul to hold him together; that said, he is in a way, my hero. May we make a toast? Let's toast Castilla, the man responsible for our night here." Conner raised his glass.

Isabella smiled at the bizarre irony of it and clinked the glasses. "To Castilla," she said. "May he reap what he sows."

Isabella doubled over coughing. Her stomach was a tangle of spiders. Her guts hurt her. Bruno had Conner get her some water and she sipped it, getting herself back together in the corner of the balcony. Her forehead moving from clammy to wet, she felt as though the excitement of the night was as exhilarating as it was draining on the little energy she had in the reserve tanks. Taking her mind off her fatigue, she stared over the plaza to witness the evening turn the page to the next chapter of the night.

Suddenly a series of screams came rising up from the crowd and Isabella stared down the street to see the crowd separate. Running up the road came the lion tamer being chased by his lion. He was yelling madly and the lion was fast on his heels. The crowd shrieked in terror until the lion tackled the man. They rolled around together until the lion tamer at last, fed the lion a beer. It slurped at the can and the crowd applauded in joy.

Their antics were interrupted by the appearance of a small ensemble of steel mill workers culled from the factories. They were visibly intoxicated as they teetered about on stage miming their daily routine on the job. Their aprons, leathers and faces were covered in grease, stains and oil, as they hammered away on imaginary steel beams. Their routine came with an accompanied song by the band where a singer sang low and deep into the microphone a reverberating, repeating cacophonous melody:

> I work and toil
> And the day is long
> By time to get off
> The day is gone
>
> I drink a big beer
> At end of day
> Gotta get up
> Toil at it again
>
> Tis a clumsy road
> Tis a dirty dozen game
> Tis a mired lot
> Tis a shame all the same

The men worked in an awkward choreography that bordered on an it's-so-bad-it's-good aesthetic. Reflecting the kind of overly determined sloppiness, one expects from a children's play the redeeming quality was that the men were having a grand ol' time. They were a backdrop to a song, and it was a song the raucous crowd clearly related to. The song was hypnotic as well. A low, slow bluesy mood, it seduced the crowd from the up up ups of the previous band to the somber slowness of the steel town players. Their antics weres interrupted by the sound of feedback on the microphone.

"Test test," the shrill voice of Defne Revan pushed out across the crowd and filtered into the rowdy, swaying plaza. The steelworkers hobbled off of the stage with one of them simply throwing himself into the crowd. The crowd laughed as they caught him, his hairy belly gleaming in the spotlights that shot down. Waddling onto the stage emerged Defne Revan dressed in a large pink dress with a white bow sticking out of her hair. She made her way to center stage and adjusted her reading glasses to read her notes. Her excitement to be behind the microphone could not be more evident.

"Ladies and Gentleman, boys and girls, welcome to the annual Barrenwood Festival. Please join me in thanking the Dirty Dozen for their incredible music!"

The crowds roared in approval. Defne smiled and continued to read.

"We are ever so glad to have you all at this great festivity. It has been the honor of the Mayor's Auxiliary Cultural Committee to plan this for the entire year, and we couldn't be happier with how things are going so far. And it is only the beginning, things are only going to heat up!"

"More beer!" yelled a voice in the crowd.

"Get off the stage, ya pink whale!" yelled another.

Defne looked visibly thrown off by the insults coming from the hoard of people. Her notes slipped from her hand and they went flittering about onto the stage. An assistant ran out from the wings and helped her as she gathered them up. The crowd laughed at the momentary comedy. They were in no mood for the antics of the houses and her timing could not be worse.

"Dear me," guffed Bruno. "This poor woman had better hurry up."

Defne collected her notes in her wiggly fingers, adjusted her glasses and continued. "Without much further ado, I would like to invite to the stage the benefactor of our night and the greatest addition to the family: Sir Elinore Castilla!" Defne clapped furiously while the crowd looked on with boredom.

Castilla wobbled up to the microphone. "On behalf of Gaventas Industries we want to say thank you to you the people of Barrenwood for being leaders of invention, leaders in innovation, leaders in the fight to make the world more industrious and profitable! You are the backbone of the future and we at Gaventas want this night to be a thank you to the people of this city."

A tomato flew up out of the crowd and landed to the side of Castilla as he spoke. Blood red vegetable matter exploded by his shiny Velonton shoes, the guts spreading in an array of mess and seeds.

"Gaventas is a people eater! You can't buy us off with your stupid party rich man!"

The boos and insults began to swell up from the audience in a growing cacophony of anger. What had started with jabs at Defne were turning into a more profound polis of inebriation. Castilla frowned from behind his long black moustache. He dropped the microphone onto the stage and the thud could be heard quite audibly reverberating across the plaza. He stormed off, his feet pounding down in percussion. The show took a sudden pause as no music played nor person held the microphone. The quiet in the storm.

The stage manager tried his best to cajole Defne Revan back onto the stage as planned, but she planted her feet, refusing to face the antics of the unruly hoard. Her arms were crossed and her face scrunched up tight as a squeegee. The din of the crowd quickly filled the void as the sound of laughter and yelling began to once again fill the air.

Suddenly, a shrill shriek rose up that grew in volume, overwhelming all jokes and jibes. It was a piercing laughter that put the hair on end and sent shivers across the crowd and those on stage as well. It was a squeal from another world—a primordial hysteria with amplitude and perverse conviction. Isabella knew it all too well. It was the shrill pig sound of her most demonic brother.

Chapter 29

"Up here, you imbeciles! Up up, ascend your eyes on high toward the heavens. Let us remember that you dirty rats are soil bound in oh so every way."

Isabella turned her attention to the blue tarp top of the statue where Fennel gingerly stood, his hand on a large microphone, his small body holding onto what must be the statue's hat. He was as usual in all black, the light glistening off the shine on his tie and top hat. He waved down at the crowd, the microphone sending a wailing sound of feedback. His face was all smile and wickedness.

"Oh, if I had a tomato, I would throw it back at you! A bunch of rot for you sods, I say. You deserve what you get, ya drunk bunch of munchkins." Fennel pointed down at the crowd. "Ya chased that fat pink toad off the stage, but from my vantage point, you all are sort of a fat toad, now ain't ya? All of you, Barrenwood, every last worrywart out there— tired, beat down and boring to boot. You look down at a gutter rat and spend ya days hemming and hawing, but ya just a big mass of no nothing. Dum dums every last one of ya. Looking down at this circus, I would feel sympathy if I couldn't stop laughing my little belly. You're a pie of pride and saturated fats is what ya are."

And with that, Fennel pulled a tomato out of his pocket and tossed it mockingly down below. It went splat in the center of Ellingdale Plaza.

The crowd stared up at him hypnotically. He was a peculiar sight to say the least—a tiny child reprimanding the entire populace of a city with a Cheshire smile so broad and bright, his rhythm and rhymes captivating in the extreme as they tangled up in the minds of the masses.

Isabella heard Conner gasp and she looked over to see her host turn a ghostly pale.

"Not him," she heard him whisper almost to his inner soul. The words in him stirred just the tiniest bit of water and Isabella took it in through the air. Fennel's antics did have their rewards. He stood up on high and continued in grandiloquent fashion.

"But let's not waste time on idle discourse, right, my friends? Let's dig into this soil as tonight is a night to remember and cheer."

The stage manager, standing next to Defne, tried his best to turn off the volume on Fennel's microphone but strangely to no avail. For whatever reason, the microphone seemed to be powering itself. As Fennel went on, the stage manager had to suffer through the hysterical whispers of Defne Revan.

"Get him off there! He wasn't supposed to do this! This was not the agreement!"

At what seemed long last, as it was all happening in a matter of seconds, the stage manager mustered his courage and marched onto the stage with the microphone. He did his best to out speak Fennel, his voice competing for airtime against the whiny sound of the child reprimanding from on high.

"Thanks so much, sir. And now ladies and gentlemen . . . " the stage manager said, doing his best to appear officious and in control.

But Fennel wouldn't have it and the look in his eye was of one glad to have an obstacle to untangle. Instead of competing for sound, he merely wailed into the microphone. "Gaspar Mathers. Can you hear me, Gaspar Mathers?"

The stage manager's eyes widened at the sound of his name being broadcast so absurdly loud. He did his best to ignore it but had to finally relent, "What? What is it you want, good sir?"

Fennel laughed and did a dance on the top of the statue. "Ha-ha, good sir. I like the sound of that. Now it just isn't polite to speak on top of me."

"Well, it isn't polite to speak on . . . "

"Hush hush, Gaspar, it is my turn now. My volume switch goes to eleven and yours I'm afraid only goes to ten. So be a good boy and admit defeat. Now you see I have you at an unfair disadvantage. I know you, Gaspar. Or come on, let's speak frankly shall we, I know you, Bill Upton."

Gaspar Mathers or Bill Mather's face went white as a ghost. His body froze as though he had just been placed in a freezer. Isabella sensed yet another Fennel surprise.

"Ha-ha, I thought that would get your attention. You know, when I use my little tricks I always hope it is someone like you. Someone deep deep deep in a lie so kind. I can sense you all the way up here. The good news is that all in all you are a good man, so congratulations. I mean you no ill. I truly don't. But would the truth hurt really? In the long run? It would be good for you."

Bill Upton looked up, his face confused and terrified.

"Ladies and gentleman of Barrenwood, I present to you Bill Upton who changed his name to Gaspar Mathers. Some of you might remember him as a child. Where did he go? So many people ask that, don't they? He is here! A man who has worked himself up into the ranks of the nobility, but whose birthright is with you people down in the District of Jed. His mother went mad. Poor thing. And his father remains a hardworking cobbler. He is still alive. Yes, Gaspar, he is still alive! He may be in the crowd right now! Oh, but you pretend now, don't you, boring Bill? You like to tell the likes of your new community that you are from an upper crust family out in Ipswich. And you relish telling jokes with them at the expense of the people you grew up with. Now ain't that some ugly business? What a pity. You just want to be loved now, don't you, my little popper?"

The crowd began to boo and Gaspar felt as though he might faint. Why had he gone out front? He was always meant to be behind the scenes. He shuffled off the stage as quickly as possible with the crowd laughing and booing at the same time. Fennel found the entire thing amusing and continued to dance on the small top of his statue.

"Test, test. Yes, this still works. Poor Bill. Don't be mad at him. He is just like you. I can tell. I have a knack for reading people. But not just individuals. I can read a mob, too. I can read your collective palm. Now does anyone else want to interrupt my night of glory?" Fennel looked out over the crowd and for the briefest pause in time the plaza was stone cold quiet.

"Okay, now where was I? Right, so I made a gift for you and yours. It's a lil' ditty carved out of the rough-hewn logs of the underbelly of dreams. It's that strange familiar feeling you get when you admit—admit whatever. Anger is the complacent's replacement for embarrassment. Don't be afraid to be dumb, because to do otherwise is to pretend you're something you're not. You slobber your epithets tonight and with good reason and little direction. Here and there none of you knows which way is up. But I am up. I am up here. Looking down on you in oh so many ways. I am reminding you, because alas that is my forlorn tragic job, to simply tell you who and what you are. And you, my sad sack o' the masses, are pathetic in the extreme. Ladies and gentleman, I present to you, The Toil!"

And with those final words Fennel leapt off the statue, grabbing the edge of the tarp. It unfurled off the enormous pale green stone statue as he lithely landed on the stage. The tarp fluttered in the air as a parachute slowly but surely descending toward terra firma, revealing the monstrosity that resided beneath.

The crowd went silent. On the balcony where Isabella sat, she heard the gasp of guests—their collective eyes all taking in the enormous stone statue that rose up five stories and loomed over the crowd.

It was hideous. A sad, weeping aged man, wrinkled and suffering from work, leaned onto his crutch, his eyes on a distant horizon. His tattered clothes hung off his body in rags and his cock-eyed hat rested sideways on his head. The weight of the old man's body split between his cane and his right foot that planted itself firmly on an elderly woman's head that lay beneath him, crouched as a child smiling madly. The man's face was dumb, his expression confused and eyes wistful with tears as though he were too stupid to know the difference. The woman below his foot smiled as though this was all she ever wanted. In her arms, she held a child that she gripped with all her might, and the child was crying madly as though the world was the worst place in the world. It was gruesome and mean-spirited—a joke gone sour, a flatulent houseguest made of stone now residing in the center of the city.

Isabella had to turn away. What she thought would be a moment of victory, was, in fact, a moment of horrifying brutality. She couldn't stand it. The creepiness of this statue with its enormous scale escalated their mutual antics into a realm of grandeur that she was unaccustomed to. They always longed to bring to people's attention their insufferable forgetting and denial, but upon seeing it, she hated it. She felt sympathy for the drunken mob as they eked out dreams under the gun. She knew they didn't need this thrown in their face, but in their face it was. She hated the tragedy. The pathetic paradox. She hated its hatred and its putrid disdain.

Despite her horror (or more accurately because of it), she felt the water come spilling into the air—the statue tearing off the scab of a collective wound—and the water came rolling into the night air. She could feel it entering her body, making her more vital and alive. She hated that she benefited so greatly from something she increasingly saw as insipid and sadistic. Isabella turned her eyes to the heavens. She could only admit in her heart what a terrible creature she must truly be.

Perhaps she should go back to Le Chateau de Crawler and die quietly on the couch. Let the world disappear from her and the sorrows that she brought along with her in a handbag. Now she had her brother prancing about in the limelight. She couldn't just leave that alone. Even if he was a vile beast, he was her kin. This was no corner he had crawled into. He had choreographed a sumptuous spotlight to bask in. The public eye focused on him and what he delivered was memorable in the extreme. In a split instance, he had changed all the rules of the game. Their proclivities in the shadows would never return. As much as she had hoped to escape the traps of Marty, she had never considered simply destroying the paradigm altogether—but now the Raven had.

After his descent, the crowd stood silently in awe. They stared at The Toil and many saw themselves. They saw their pain and their agony, their pathetic hopeless trauma splayed out in front of them, a victim of a carriage accident. They saw a statue that told them that this is what they deserved. It was devoid of hope and it was presented by the city—the city that had failed them, the city that had crushed them. It wasn't them. It wasn't their fault.

"What a wretched thing that is!" said Conner. "My god, they must destroy that immediately. Who on earth approved such a monstrosity?"

Someone else at the party said, "Who is that little man? What a strange creature he is."

Isabella certainly knew the truth of that. It was as though she understood exactly what was driving her mad hatter kin and simultaneously, felt in the pit of her stomach that some new, unfamiliar iteration of Fennel had ferociously emerged. Bruno looked over at Isabella and whispered, "This isn't going well."

Isabella didn't look at Bruno. A foreboding feeling rose up in her belly. She could feel the water pouring all around her. It was hypnotic. The joy of it felt incredible inside her and she could hear a beautiful siren inside herself telling her, "Let it all fall apart."

But Fennel wasn't done. From the stage, standing at the front, with a microphone held firmly in his hand, he reached out to the crowd beseeching them to listen to his every word.

"That isn't all, my friends! No, no, no! You get more than The Toil for all your hard work and suffering, I also grant you the greatest gift that you forgot to love. Look out if you can to the harbor, to the docks. We at the city have decided to return your most beloved citizens."

Fennel pointed his finger out over the crowd and toward the docks just a few blocks away. The night was dark and one could make out just past the gas lamps at the docks the careening motion of that to which he drew their attention. There, moored against the dock, stood the boat that had brought Conner and Fennel together not so long ago.

"My god," gasped Conner. "What is that doing here?"

Fennel continued, "This is for all of you, for all that you are, for everyone who forgot what mattered most."

As Fennel said those words, his eyes rose up above the crowd, shot out across the plaza and looked straight into the eyes of his sister. He caught her look which shrunk the distance between them. Zoomed in and it felt as though she could feel his chocolate breath on her cheeks. She stared back with longing and awe—the twinkle in his eye brighter than the North Star or the firecrackers now exploding in the sky. No matter what pot he stirred, she missed him terribly. She felt his tender messed up heart and wanted to hold him. To tuck him in. To play Battle Ball. To take him with her to the grave.

And with that feeling came a rushing of the water sound. It poured and grew—the brook into a river, the river into a flood. Water sound poured all over Isabella as the mayhem grew. The crowd sound rose from a mad swirl of delight to the frenetic orchestra of chaos. Out on the docks at the far end of her sight, she saw it—the Drunken Boat, the ship of the mad had returned with its torn sails, ragged gangway and cabins of mercenaries. Now it was going to unload its cargo of humans into the already combustible masses.

The lunatics descended the gangway in their flour sack robes, their mouths wide and frightful, their eyes alive with the embrace of the frantic qualities. Some couldn't make it the entire way and lay on the dock weeping. Others refused to even get off the boat. Many were hitting the streets with their bare feet and their arms held out as though to embrace the entire crowd. They rushed with tremendous vehemence onward. The mercenaries on the boat shouted at the unruly mass to get a move on.

The lunatics raced forward, a mob of perhaps two hundred all told. Their sullied frames plowed into the plaza as the drunken masses leapt to get out of the way of their manic embrace. The movement toppled people over. Children went underfoot. Beers were spilled, cotton candy dropped. Men in beards pushed and punched back. Quite quickly the appearance of the crazies elevated the masses from a crowd to a mob. They became frenzied. Fennel's assault had taken them aback, and now they were in the midst of a drunken confused rage.

As the lunatics filtered into the crowd, pushing and shoving, fights erupted as though on cue. Isabella sat and watched transfixed. Everything was happening so fast. Across the way, she could see the balconies of the great Houses evacuate. Their nervousness turned frenetic as they moved to get to the back doors where the carriages waited. Their party had become a tremendous disaster. She watched as the Barrenwood police rushed to contain the crowd. Billy clubs came slamming down on whoever was in the way. The lunatics, so out of sorts, took the brunt of the violence with hysterical obliviousness. The police attempted to use bullhorns to bring the crowd to attention, but the madness had reached too feverish a pitch in too tight a space. More than quelling the crowd, the police's violence only escalated what was a rowdy mob into a battalion. Lines of people began to emerge as the police protected the stage and the great Houses behind it. The crowds heaved and pushed, exhaling the mass into the shields and billy clubs.

Fennel stood on high looking down at his creation. It was exciting in the extreme. He gave a loud whistle and Isabella knew what that meant: he had summoned Zarathustra. Fennel's eyes seemed to twist phantasmagoric as the intoxication of the water and his own masterful choreography overwhelmed him. Up next he had hoped to send the poison dart into the forehead of Elinore Castilla: the drought-maker, the evaporator. Fennel's entire orchestration had at its heart a return of the water, and sure as shinola, he wasn't going to let the night end without the evisceration of the maker of so many clocks, asylums and burgeoning workweeks. A dullard of the most managerial kind, Elinore Castilla was bound for a most loathsome demise. But as Fennel pointed his diminutive crossbow toward the stage, he noticed, to his shock, that Elinore Castilla was nowhere to be found. He scanned his Raven eyes out across the crowd only to note his prey being escorted by a hoard of men in black into an awaiting carriage. The drought-maker would live to fight another day.

Castilla escaped at what appeared to be the right time. The city was erupting below. From celebration to riot to perhaps petite revolution, the air became illuminated by the red streak of a Molotov cocktail that came flying out from the crowd, its fiery tail spinning and dripping flame, and splattered flame and glass across the stage. The crowd cheered and the police retreated for just a millionth of a second. The rapid escalation of the event told everyone that this night was now headed into uncharted territories.

Isabella gathered herself together realizing that she felt worse than ever. Rising to her feet was no easy task and Bruno took her by her arm. Before she turned her attention to heading back into the house, she saw what she knew she would see if she stayed too long—Marty McGuinn. It was just the briefest moment, but she spotted him backstage wearing a straw hat, smoking a pipe as usual, and in his hands he held a pair of shears. She watched as he hobbled his cranky self across the far end of the stage, slowly making his way toward her dear brother Fennel. Marty moved like a dream. Not a soul seemed to touch him though pandemonium was letting loose all around his wretched stinky self.

The chaos only grew. The crowd had quickly overtaken the police as they retreated back toward the orchestra pit. The crowd began to crawl their way up onto the stage in a show of ownership. The stage became a symbolic stage to be conquered. They would make this event theirs. The crowds flew past Marty and suddenly the performers were face to face with their audience. The city officials froze suddenly terrified. Defne, the Duke of Revan and Bill Upton were trapped in a corner with nowhere to go. They now stood out like a sore thumb. Three blind mice.

A momentary pause occurred as both sides considered that something most historic was about to transpire. The next moment took place in the blink of an eye. A group of very large men ransacked the officials. The officials disappeared into the center of this hoard of angry muscular proletarians. And another contingent, one just a tad bit more organized, rushed past Defne and Gaspar, and grabbed the Duke of Revan, who appeared to be halfway to a heart attack. His face was red as a tomato as they tore the robes and jewelry from his body. They dragged him, beaten and distraught, with much of his pride gone like light, toward center stage.

It was at this point that the entire Ellindale Plaza seemed to go quiet. The crowd took a brief pause in the mayhem to witness a moment many of them thought not possible. An extremely large black man with tattoos all over his shirtless body and a line of teardrops tattooed under his left eye lifted the Duke by his hair to stare out into the crowd. The silence in the crowd was only disrupted by the occasional pop and sizzle of the fireworks still going off above. For this moment, the houses that had lorded over the morass of a broke ass city were in the angry hands of their children.

Fennel, who was just ten feet from the action, had his eyebrows knit together in confusion. As mean as he was, he hadn't planned on so calamitous an affair. The entire debacle was far outside his compositional aspirations.

The tattooed man yelled out into the crowd in a booming voice that all could hear. "Death to the King! Long live the Mortestrate!" he yelled as he pulled from his pocket a long knife. It glinted in the stage light. The two men stood on the stage next to each other, protagonists in an epic drama played out in the present that was the past and future. But the knife was real and it cut through the Duke of Revan's throat with ease. Blood spurted everywhere, transforming the staged spectacle into a new gore filled reality. The Duke's body went instantly limp gaining weight as the tattooed man let go of the Duke's hair. The man, once a king, the Duke of Revan, was now a corpse, lying in a tangled heap—dead as can be.

Cheers, as well as terrified screams, went up from the crowd. Even a mob remains predominately humane. Blood covering his enormous frame, the tattooed man leapt off the stage with a howl and the crowd caught him in their arms.

King Gerald was dead. Isabella felt Bruno pull on her arm. "My god, we should get out of here. We are all in danger," he said and the look in his eye said it was true. Isabella got up from her seat;, her feet wobbling precariously beneath her.

On the stage, Fennel remained unflappable. He squinted at the king's lifeless body and shook his head slowly as though considering this turn of events. Even if the circumstances had surpassed his own chaotic designs, he would simply have to embrace the madness in all its splendor. He marched slowly out to center stage, imagining the audience staring in wonder at the mighty genius of this social architect. Standing directly in front of the corpse, with his small head held high, he began to wave his arms gently in the air as though he was a conductor of some grand symphony—the silent music of the lunatic eve, playing metronome to a somnambulist parade. His arms gently careened in a ballet before him as the crowd continued to yell, fight, blather and squeal.

311

While the brawls continued, Fennel appeared to be the one person on the planet caught in an eddy of serenity. A maestro in his element. His hypnosis so thorough, he was oblivious to the pace of the sweating, smoking Marty who made his way slowly across stage to cut him down, his shears dragging along the wooden deck of the stage.

Isabella witnessed the scene playing out before her in her dazed hallucinatory eyes. Her stomach turned against her in bile and the impending danger to her brother called up a last gasp of adrenaline that shot up into her veins. With a flurry of energy, she flung herself off the balcony ten stories down into the crowd below. Her fall was neither gentle nor lithe, but hard and fast. She hit the cobblestone plaza with a thud and a crunch. Blood poured out of her and spilt on the beer soaked stones. She briefly saw the frantic look of Bruno, staring down from above until his gaze was blocked by a frantic crowd of people who gathered around her. She was in a panic and she was deeply hurt. Her head swam. People were fighting all around her. She wiped her nose on her sleeve and launched herself onto her feet in time to see Fennel turn to see Marty sauntering his way.

Fennel gave a visible smirk to his disgruntled Master. "Glad you could make it, Marty, my boy. I wanted this to be the last thing you ever did see before you met your extraordinarily belated demise."

Marty raised the clippers at the same time that Fennel came charging toward him. Isabella couldn't believe what she was witnessing. Her brother had lost his mind so much that he was actually considering taking on Marty. To call it a bad idea would be too generous. It was suicide. Marty caught Fennel in his grip while Fennel looked like some deranged dog trying to bite anything it could. Fennel snapped his teeth and struggled while Marty laughed in evil fashion holding Fennel further up in the air.

This would not go well. Isabella had to rescue her brother and soon. The crowd was too tight for her to move quickly and her view was impeded by the crush of bodies. She jettisoned herself up to the top of the crowd, light as a feather and ran with her failing might across the top of the crowd, her every foot landing on a shoulder, cap or tangled head of hair. It was everything she had left. She dove as hard as she could over the police barricade in front of the stage to land next to the both of them. She grabbed Fennel with one hand and tossed him as hard as she could toward the side of the stage. His body tumbled in a pile while Marty lifted his eyebrow at the appearance of what he affectionately referred to as the she-bitch. Her appearance briefly startled enough—just enough—to jar his dreamy stupor. Isabella ran over to her brother whose eyes were red jewels in a sea of yellow. He was in the midst of a deep hypnosis.

"Sister, I'm so glad you could make it. How grand is this? This divine symphony."

He stood up, dusting himself off, completely unaware of the impending arrival of Marty. He was both there and not there; lost in a dream. Rapturous at the height of his colossal experiment, he was oblivious to all that was happening around him. His soul had ascended to the heavens above where it belonged and, were his body not affixed now to that stage, he would be looking down from miles above at the play he had just directed.

"Fennel, I'm saving you! Marty is trying to kill you!"

"Ha! I got that ol' coot in my grips," he said, his eyes slightly coming to. Fennel looked back to see Marty nearly upon them. He laughed loud and put out his arms. "Let's give it another shot, you pathetic excuse for a man." Marty, who was only a few feet away, paused, leaned back and took a puff on his pipe.

"A man can't turn his head but a sec. Now look at dis mess. All spillin its beans on da city. Dees shears are heres for a clippen."

They could smell his urine-stained clothes. His teeth appeared to still have the remnants of some gumbo feast and his eyes spun around as though inebriated from a travel so messy. He pulled up the shears in front of his face and gave them a good clip to highlight their sharpness.

"Ha, ha, ha," his eyes twinkled. "Can't recon if I ever did see such a mud pit as dis. Scratch stirred up a wild hornet's nest. Sure is fun. Gotta admit. Look at all dees dum dums walkin round not a clue in da heads? Dis a real land o dummies, ain't it? Glad dey feed us when dey can. But you two ain't dat different. Look at you. Stupid as de day you was born. Haha, you don't know nuttin. Haha. Ya bout as dum as dees dummies." He stared down at them with strange wild eyes. He wasn't for sentimentality or consideration. He was vengeful, hungry, manic and mad. His voice had a snarl in it that Isabella knew all too well as the preamble to punishment.

"What does it matter, Marty?" Isabella whimpered, the strength out of her and her near resignation welling up in her. She wanted to escape, but her feet had brought her right to the mangled shoes of her lowly master. "We don't matter."

"Dat much is true. Less dan ever," snickered Marty. "You shoulda stayed down low in da brush. Now ya out in da limelight sucken da blood like a leech."

Marty puffed on his pipe and clipped the shears. "Now yous been oh such a naughty lil ricket. All mixed up inna somethin ya do not know. Now ya makin pups wit da plebs and sneakin outta da digs so deep. I gotta me a pocket full-o-ducats from dat muddy carny and I wassa lookin ta have me a fat whoop up. Now I be a handyman for da whole fat town. Time ta burn dat leech off da blood."

"I'm not going, you cruel strange man," Isabella found herself whispering. She hated him so much—the way he asserted himself over her with all the power and madness of a world so mercurial and without care. His boisterous fickle qualities hovered over her entire life without reason or care. "Never again. I will die if that is what it takes, but I'm done. I'm so done."

She began to sob, her body pulsing up and down on the stage. Her tears falling out of her, hitting the wood, and spilling into the blood of a dead man once a duke. Her frustrations welled up in her and she let her tears go. Marty would not care, but neither, it seemed, did the big universe above. She was lonely as all could be and no one it seemed could come to her rescue.

"Well, you knows me, lil water gnat. I don not take a no for da answer and I could laugh at puttin ya lil tears into a shoebox grave. Time to clip both your wings."

Marty gave a quick kick to Isabella's stomach. She bent over in pain and heard her brother leap forward.

"Keep your hands off her!" he screamed as he found himself again in Marty's clutches. The two of them wrestled feverishly as Isabella tried to get to her feet. Marty's sinuous arms strained against the peculiar vitality of her madcap brother who had no hope of winning. Her strength betrayed her. She could not get up in time. Fennel fell back onto his knees overpowered by the might of their master. She watched in agonized disbelief as Marty pulled the shears out. He raised them up high above his head as Fennel wiped the sweat from his brow in a dazed confusion. And then, quick as a hummingbird, Marty brought the shears down straight into the eye socket of her brother. He screamed in great agony. Blood spurted out and onto Marty. Fennel's face was a mess of gore as he instinctively pulled the shears out and threw them across the stage. It was all Isabella could do to stretch out, grab her brother's leg and send him flying in the direction of his waiting horse. A one-eyed boy went sailing through the air, landing most skillfully on the back of Zarathustra. Isabella stared bewildered as the pair galloped their way to who knows where.

Marty looked down at her. His rage was beyond reason. He was blind in hatred. He gave her a wild kick that sent her flying out into the crowd. She flew into the mob landing hard on the stone. Her body ached from the blow and twisted into a curl amongst the array of boots and shoes below the bodies of the mob. She willed deep into herself to find the strength to get to her feet as some stranger lifted her up.

"You okay?" a plumber from the Mortestrate asked, his face hardened from days in the gutters.

She could not answer but limped her way away from the stage. The chaos was still playing about her with the police slowly making progress. She could see the police billy clubs still swinging to keep the crowd at bay and she saw that Marty was no longer on the stage. She could feel him coming for her. She hobbled her way through the crowd, her head aching with fear and loss.

"What on earth is happening?"

She was small in this mob and she slid between the bodies still rustling about. Her stomach was beyond sick, her face pale as sun-baked pearl. She heaved between people hoping to get as far away as possible until the next face to appear was again Marty. He grinned in saturated gums and without missing a beat his foot came flying hard into her gut. Isabella went soaring back into the crowd, her head knocking against the hard wood of a carriage.

She couldn't take this. She got to her feet again, barely holding on, leaning on the carriage. Her mouth was bleeding. Vomit rose up in her as well as the end of her strength. Her head swam as she began to lose her grip on these awake moments—the voice asking her to sleep, gaining traction as fatigue made its way toward victory. She was going out this way.

In a blind series of stumbles, she found an unoccupied carriage. She dragged herself up and inside and closed the door. She lay in the backseat and felt as though she could die.

The sound outside was madness. Screams, yells, and the most haunting laughter, all rose up into her ears. It was a chorus of emotion so vivid and strong. As sick and battered as Isabella was, her body knew that she was in the midst of a flood. The water had come on strong and it was circulating through the air above the mob. She pulled herself up to the carriage window to take a glance. The water circulated through the air. A torrent of madness, desire, violence and fanatical fever that made the air electric and even gave energy to the bile in her mouth.

Isabella noticed that her arm was bent backward, making a perpendicular angle away from her body. She stared at it. It looked to be a limb of someone else attached to her. She wrestled with it trying to straighten it out, but the limb remained bent. She was broken. Cracked. All she could do was lay in the back of this carriage and wait for Marty to finish her off.

But as fate would have it, Isabella noticed Marty slowly but surely rising up, levitating slowly, to hover above the crowd itself. His body rose up out of the mob and he was sailing in the air. His eyes were wild, his

315

greasy hair blowing this way and that and his tongue hung out of his mouth like a dog. He sailed in the effluvia of the water that moved through the air, luxuriating in the bath that Fennel had unleashed. He was hedonistically basking in the water. Isabella watched mesmerized as he let the water enter into his mouth. It poured into him and he hovered above the crowd in a haze of intoxicated glory.

Isabella stared in wonder and awe. She knew all too well what he was doing. It was what she wanted to do. She just wanted to eat this moment up. Let it all come into her body and warm her aching heart. And as if on cue, the smell of gasoline filled her nose. She smelled him before she saw him. The Duke of Izmir came hurling down from above. He was hovering in the air as well. His cape flying behind him, he held onto his top hat and took the water into himself as well. He levitated across Ellindale Plaza from Marty, getting his fair share of the cascading water—the river of madness and sadness filling the void that seemed to lurk in the bodies of these two super beings. It was as though these two men were caribou stopping to drink from a stream before they headed back into the desert.

She had only a second to spare, and she knew that this was her only hope. She had to get the attention of that superhuman who had joined Marty at the riot.

"Duke of Izmir, please save me! I'm like you!" she screamed at the top of her lungs.

It wasn't the most elegant thing to say, but she had to be direct. She was panicking and time was running out. Her screams, fortunately, caught the attention of the Duke who looked down at her at the same time as Marty McGuinn. The Duke looked to see Marty staring at the same thing. He came sailing down fast as lightening. The carriage exploded into a thousand pieces. Isabella closed her eyes thinking this was the end.

When the dust cleared Isabella realized she was in the Duke's gasoline arms. His eyes looked drunk with fever. He growled audibly as he looked down on her and pressed his nose close to her flesh. He inhaled her like a beast, the hairs on his face brushing up against Isabella's fish belly skin. For the first time, someone other than Marty or Fennel was sensing her. He growled in his throat and his arms reached down and covered her in a warm embrace. She lay there and gave in. She couldn't go on. This was her last resort.

She could hear his heart beating heavily, a motor for a beast so large. She had to speak. She had to let him know. Marty would be upon them and she only had this chance to find a world so potentially beautifully beyond.

"Please help me. I am broken. A twig cracked. He is. He is trying to kill me."

The Duke looked down at her. His eyes were immense and spoke of a world she barely understood.

"Marty McGuinn won't be bothering you, little thing. You are safe now."

He petted her head and for the first time in her life she felt safe. His hands were like baked leather and hot to the touch.

"Be still now. We will take you in. You've too long been out in the cold as you are. You are like me, small child."

"Is it true then?" asked Isabella, staring crazy eyed into the heart of his inferno—his face a map of lines so deep.

"Yes, little girl. Be still."

"Are we gods, then? Can it be?"

"Yes, pretty thing. We are gods. Though being one is not the glory one might imagine."

The Duke launched into the sky.

Isabella closed her eyes as she flew with him. She felt the night wind take hold of her and the smell of gasoline blend with the gunpowder smoke of firecrackers. Her hair caught the wind and she didn't notice at all her extremely broken arm.

He was taking her away! And away was a place that she had been searching for all her life. Fennel had escaped on a horse and she was in the arms of this Duke. He rode through the sky magical and she knew, yes, she knew—she and Fennel were like him.

A god. A god divine. Even if she still hated who she was, and how much she relished the pain of others, and how much the world of Barrenwood still toiled and suffered under the grin of the god's impulsive laughter, she was not alone. She could finally be with her kin who not only looked over the world but also took capricious pleasure in its unending despair.

Nato Thompson is a writer and curator residing in Philadelphia.. He has written two books: Seeing Power Art and Activism in the 21st Century (2015) and Culture as Weapon: The Art of Influence in Everyday Life (2017), both published by Melville House. This is first work of fiction. During his day job, he works as a curator of contemporary art.

A wonderfully tragic sequal to Marshsong forthcoming...

www.ingramcontent.com/pod-product-compliance
Lightning Source LLC
Chambersburg PA
CBHW030640020726
47493CB00006B/1803